CONFLICT OF LIONS

In the hiatus following the Falklands War a group
of hardened SAS troops is sent to a quiet West
African backwater, Free Guinea, as a safeguard
against rumblings of political discontent against
the moderate elected government. It is intended to
provide the ideal location for the men to rest after
the violent burst of full-blooded warfare in the
South Atlantic. And so it does – that is, until a
tourist is found dead on the beach . . .

With CONFLICT OF LIONS Terence Strong has
written his most pulsating and powerful novel to
date. Capturing the mood of dark foreboding in a
country of deep political unrest and division, he
combines a varied cast of characters with
nerve-tingling suspense and adventure.
CONFLICT OF LIONS is further evidence of
Terence Strong's great talent for frightening
credibility.

D0293554

Also by the same author,
and available in Coronet Books:

WHISPER WHO DARES
THE FIFTH HOSTAGE

CONFLICT OF LIONS

Terence Strong

CORONET BOOKS
Hodder and Stoughton

Copyright © 1985 by Terence Strong

First published in Great Britain 1985
by Hodder and Stoughton Ltd.

Coronet edition 1985.

British Library C.I.P.

> Strong, Terence
> Conflict of lions.
> I. Title
> 823′.914[F]   PR6069.T7/
>
> ISBN 0 340 38310 0

Printed and bound in Great Britain for
Hodder and Stoughton Paperbacks, a
division of Hodder and Stoughton Ltd.,
Mill Road, Dunton Green, Sevenoaks,
Kent (Editorial Office: 47 Bedford
Square, London, WC1B 3DP) by
Cox and Wyman Ltd.,
Cardiff Road, Reading.

For 'The Bushpigs'.
In recognition of
so much done with
so little by
British charities
in The Gambia.

And for the warm
people of the world's
'most peaceful country'.

Author's Note

Amongst the honoured guests in London for the Royal Wedding celebrations during July 1981 was President Jawara of the ex-British colony of The Gambia.

Back in West Africa his absence was used by a Gambian political activist named Samba Sayang as an opportunity to seize control, aided by malcontents within the country's own security forces.

The operation, which was backed by Libya with the connivance of the Soviet Union, almost succeeded.

And it stunned the Free World. Because The Gambia was not just *any* volatile African state. A 'true democracy' with a working parliament and regular elections, it had enjoyed sixteen peaceful years of independence under a moderate and compassionate leader.

It was held as a shining example to all Third World nations as to what could be achieved by understanding, political tolerance and progressive attitudes. It was enjoying a boom in tourists from Britain and Scandinavia. Indeed the country was described in *The Guardian* as "the most peaceful country in the world".

All this and yet it still fell victim to the vicious international chessgame where nations and their peoples are merely expendable pawns.

Samba Sayang's coup failed only through the timely intervention of a four-man British team from 22 Special Air Service Regiment and the help of friendly French-trained troops from neighbouring Senegal. But it was a close-run thing.

On the surface the situation now appears to have returned to normality. But has it?

During my first research trip in April '83 I had a secret meeting with a man introduced as Samba Sayang's father. Through an interpreter I was told that his son was training in Cuba, preparing to return "quietly as shadows in the night".

Indeed I learned on my second visit, in January of this year, that two of Sayang's comrades had been arrested trying to re-enter the country. Arms are being smuggled into the country via the socialist revolutionary organisation, Movement of Justice in Africa (MOJA). It claims to have cells throughout the country and to have infiltrated the establishment. And, just as significant, the air of political discontent amongst the people had heightened noticeably.

This book is not a prediction of what *will* happen in The Gambia; it is a warning of what *could* happen in a similar country.

Whilst the setting is based largely on The Gambia there are many important differences: several geographical liberties have been taken; there is no foreign 'policing' force involved; the political leaders are fictitious, and all other characters are imaginary or amalgams of various people I have met.

However, many incidents are based on anecdotes from the '81 coup, or drawn from my own travelling experiences.

Finally, it should be remembered that the Soviet Union has just recently been deprived of its foothold in strategically-important West Africa. Since the events written in this story, the Marxist regime in the Republic of Guinea (Conakry) has fallen in a pro-Western *coup d'état*.

So there is one lion on the loose again, desperate to find a new prey . . .

TERENCE STRONG
LONDON, 1984

My thanks for assistance in research go particularly to 'Kinte', and to Alan Rake and Julie Kitchener of New African *magazine for their introductions. Others, whose help, kindness and hospitality is not forgotten, are best named only as: David (with apologies), 'Sajo', Billy, Alison, Eddie, Nana, Heather and Garth with a very special thank you to my good friend Dawda.*

Conflict of Lions

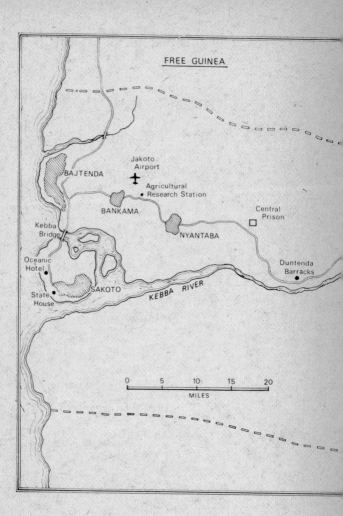

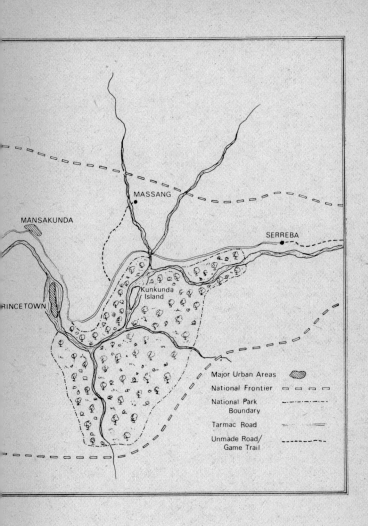

MASSANG

MANSAKUNDA

SERREBA

Kunkunda
Island

RINCETOWN

Major Urban Areas

National Frontier

National Park
Boundary

Tarmac Road

Unmade Road/
Game Trail

Prologue

The man was going to die.

And Ahmed Ashur was going to kill him.

For nearly three hours the Libyan had been waiting patiently beneath the trees until the soft, scented August evening finally surrendered to nightfall. Warm and velvet.

The fluttering shape of a bat swooped repeatedly over the track which separated him from the splendid Gothic silhouette of The Hunting Lodge Restaurant by the back gates of Windsor Great Park.

It was a perfect spot for the assassination of President Essa Jammeh of Free Guinea.

It was quiet and remote. Away from the bustling main road, reached only by the narrow, curving tarmac track. And opposite the canopied entrance to the exclusive eating-house, a dense copse of broad-leafed trees offered excellent cover, and an ideal getaway route.

Ashur smiled gently to himself.

So strange, he thought, that only that very morning he was in deep despair that he and his brother-in-arms Abdul Ghadir would be unable to complete their mission. They had sat in the upstairs room of the Libyan People's Bureau in St James's Square, drinking mint tea and poring over all the information they had on President Jammeh's ten-day unofficial visit to London.

Their source within the Embassy of Free Guinea, situated just around the corner from their own building, was impeccable. The detail they had was vast: several visits by Jammeh to a private clinic; shopping trips to Harrods, Fortnum & Mason, Gieves & Hawkes of Savile Row and Harvie & Hudson; informal meetings with politicians and civil servants; evenings at top nightspots like Annabel's and Quaglino's; nights at a suite in The Savoy.

Ashur had looked at his friend Ghadir and shaken his head. London, London, London . . . tight, confining and with no room to manoeuvre. Always private bodyguards and an armed detective from the Diplomatic Protection Group.

Nine days had gone by with never a chink in the security curtain. Both men were despondent. They did not know how their leader would react to their failure. Colonelissimo Gadaffi was unpredictable at the best of times, and they knew he dearly wanted Jammeh dead. He had not forgiven the President of the former West African colony of British Guinea for kicking out his diplomatic staff two years earlier, just prior to the Libyan's abortive coup attempt.

Then the telephone had rung. Ten o'clock. It was their source at the Embassy of Free Guinea. A change of plan. At the suggestion of his wife, the President had decided on an impulsive trip into the English countryside. A glimpse of lush green fields was a treat that only an African could truly appreciate.

They would go for a drive by the Thames at Runnymede and finish the day with a sumptuous meal at The Hunting Lodge Restaurant so beloved by the gourmet rich.

Allah, at last, was smiling upon them.

"I think, Ahmed, that they will not be long now."

It was Ghadir's soft voice behind him. Soft and attractive like the young man himself. But in the darkness Ashur could not see the moist brown eyes, the handsome honey skin, or the determined set of the chin.

"You are right, Abdul. Go to your position now. Keep to the shadows. Be bold and fear nothing. Allah will be with you."

He could not see his friend's warm smile, but he felt it. "Allah is great."

And so, thought Ashur, are you. Because he shared more than a common age of thirty-two with his friend. He shared his life and his love.

An owl hooted somewhere deep within the copse, and Ghadir was gone.

Quietly Ashur unzipped his corduroy bomber jacket and

lifted out the compact Skorpion machine-pistol. He could smell the liquorice scent of graphite oil. Carefully he checked the magazine, fitted the silencer, and cranked back the spring-loaded cocking handle.

It was his job to take out the security men and the chauffeur.

He had seen them often over the past nine days, and he was not impressed. They had been hired from a specialist firm operating from an anonymous office in Sloane Street. Citadel Security. They were not young men.

One of them even walked with a pronounced limp. He was a big, bearded man and one of his legs squeaked slightly each time he moved. A bodyguard with a tin leg. The tiny state of Free Guinea must be hard up.

The man had arrived before the main party in a nondescript grey Ford Capri. After checking over the restaurant Ashur had seen him return to his car and use the telephone on the dash. He was shaking his head vigorously; evidently he was not happy with the security aspects of the outing.

But he must have been over-ruled by the President, because an hour later the gleaming Ford Granada swung down the track.

The vehicle looked ordinary enough, but Ashur knew different. For a start it weighed 1,000 lb more than a conventional model. That was the layers of ceramic and plastic armour that had been added by Crayford Engineering of Westerham. Along with armour-plated windscreen glass and a fuel tank filled with aluminium foil to prevent it igniting.

No, President Jammeh must be cut down before he could reach his fortress car.

But that, Ashur was confident, would not be difficult. In Britain private security men could not be armed. And, tonight, away from London, the President had insisted that there be no armed protection from the Diplomatic Protection Group.

The most Ashur had to worry about was an unarmed man with a tin leg.

Dave Forbes came out first and looked over the Granada and the Capri which were parked right outside the entrance.

The sophisticated electronic warning systems had not been triggered. After an extra eyeball check beneath the vehicles he was satisfied.

He was glad to get into the fresh air after the smoky hubbub of the restaurant. The food had been good, excellent in fact. But it was difficult to relax and enjoy it when you knew it was your responsibility to ensure the safety of a Very Important Person. And they didn't come more Important than a Head of State. Even if that state was only a tinpot Commonwealth country.

Forbes had sat with his old mate from 22 Special Air Service Regiment, Jack Ducane, and the chauffeur, another Sentinel Security man, at a strategically-placed table. From it they had a clear view of the adjoining diners and all the doors. The table at which President Essa Jammeh sat with the stunning 'Lady' Precious was only feet away.

Actually, as VIPs went, they were okay. Jammeh was mild-mannered and good-humoured, and his wife was so vivacious it was easy to overlook her less agreeable pretensions.

There was no real reason for concern. All appeared calm in Free Guinea and the attempted coup two years earlier was fast fading into history. There was every excuse for Forbes to have relaxed his guard a little. But somehow he couldn't.

He felt unaccountably ill-at-ease. Perhaps the food was too spicy; he preferred simple fare. Perhaps it was the lack of booze; only Perrier water when on the job. Perhaps it was his artificial leg. Even after two years it still chafed where it joined at the knee. That had been his last mission with the SAS – snatching a British hostage of Khomeini's Iran.

Thank God his old mate Jacko had looked him up and saved him from drinking away the meagre income from his disability pension. This wasn't exactly like the old days, but at least he was amongst old comrades.

Forbes had just lit a cigarette when the chauffeur came out through the heavy oak doors. "They're making a move, Dave."

Dave Forbes scanned the road again. Its uneven surface

was brought into sharp relief by the light from the restaurant windows. Apart from that the surrounding woodland was inky black. He shifted uncomfortably.

Forbes nodded. "There could be an army out there. We'd never know. Swing the car round, will you? Put some light on the undergrowth for me."

"Sure, Dave." Pete was sympathetic; the ex-SAS sergeant was always seeing ghosts in the shadows.

As the chauffeur switched on the headlamps and steered the Granada around until the beams illuminated the ferns that grew alongside the track, Forbes moved his position slightly to get a better view. Carefully he quartered each area that offered concealment, then let his gaze return. Just in case anything had moved or changed. Old habits died hard.

Suddenly he thought of his Iranian wife, Hameda, waiting at home in their poky bedsit. Poky but cosy. Once Jammeh was on the plane tomorrow he planned to spend a few days away with her. Nothing fancy; maybe a guest house in the Cotswolds.

"*Is the car ready, Dave?*" Jack Ducane's voice buzzed in the discreet earpiece of his Pye Pocketfone radio. It was a useful bit of kit they'd used in the Regiment.

"Just a minute, Jacko. Pete's getting the Granada into position now," Forbes replied.

"*Okay. Don't hang about. I think Lady Precious has had a drop too many.*"

"That's her problem."

A pause. "*Is everything okay, Dave?*"

"Yes, Jacko." But there was a hesitation in his voice.

"*A feeling?*"

"Maybe. You too?"

That's it. He *did* sense danger; he was not alone. The famous team together again. The dynamic duo, working as one. Forbes had thought they'd lost the old magic.

The tyres of the armoured Granada crunched as it eased as close to the entrance as possible. Forbes opened the rear passenger door and extracted the heavy-duty AL22 security torch from its retaining clips.

He said: "The car's here, Jacko. Let's make it quick, eh?"

He could almost feel the adrenalin coursing through his body.

Then Jack Ducane was there at the door: a tall, athletic figure with thinning fair hair and alert blue eyes. He didn't look his thirty-six years.

"Take the left, Jacko," Forbes said. In his hand he weighed the 12-inch tubular steel torch with the bulbous head impatiently.

Immediately the ex-SAS officer complied, swinging to face out into the darkness, matching Forbes' stance on the other side, forming a human wall between the restaurant entrance and the open door of the Granada.

Then they heard Jammeh's jovial, booming voice as he thanked the head waiter profusely. The one-sided conversation seemed to last an eternity, and the two bodyguards became mildly irritated. A high-class giggle issued from Lady Precious.

The oak door was swung fully open. The rotund figure of Jammeh emerged, resplendent in his new Savile Row mohair, which served to emphasise the sylph-like frame of his wife beside him.

Forbes' eyes still stared into the darkness of the summer night, trying to penetrate it. And when he saw the shape emerge from the nearby bush, for a fraction of a second he didn't believe it. It crossed his mind that it might be a customer, but then he registered the tatty jeans and corduroy bomber jacket . . . No way!

"Jacko! Trouble!" he yelled. As he did so he recognised the ugly shape of the Skorpion machine-pistol being raised, and he knew he could never cross the twenty feet between them.

The vicious splutter of the emptying gun magazine tore the still air apart as Forbes' thumb found the button on the torch. Instantly the multi-filament head discharged the entire combined power of its batteries in a blinding flash of paralysing white light that stunned the senses.

For a vital second the shooting stopped. Forbes grabbed the opportunity to pitch himself forward, low and hard, in a rugby tackle at the vague shape a few feet before him. He was aware of bullets spraying around him again befcre his head made contact with the soft area of the gunman's groin. The two of them toppled backwards into an ornamental shrub with Forbes wielding the torch like a truncheon.

Meanwhile Ducane had swung round, grabbing President Jammeh by the sleeve. Pushing the African's head down, he unceremoniously threw him into the back of the car and onto the floor. Lady Precious was hurled in after her husband landing with a shapely but inelegant splay of long legs.

As Ducane was about to throw himself at the open door he saw the second gunman. Young and slim with good-looking Arabic features and a mop of black hair, he appeared behind the Capri.

The pistol was raised, held straight and steady in a professional two-handed grip. It was pointed not at Ducane but past him at the open door of the car.

In a flash it became clear. The first man was to have killed the bodyguards. This one was after the President. And the look in his eyes said he intended to do it.

It all happened so fast that it was later difficult to recall the exact sequence of events. Ducane saw the hammer come down, deafened by the loudness of the reports, again and again, as the Libyan approached the last few feet trying to push his way past Ducane as Pete stamped the accelerator of the Granada to the floorboards.

Ducane's left forearm came up under the gunman's revolver, pushing it skyward. Pivoting awkwardly he drove a hard knuckle-bunch with his right into the man's solar plexus.

Then it was over. The Granada was swallowed into the night, its rear passenger door still swinging wildly. Ducane found himself kneeling on the gunman's spine, pressing the Libyan's face into the tarmac. Quickly he extracted the revolver from the wrist that was jammed awkwardly behind the gunman's back beneath his knee.

He looked up to see Forbes being helped across by the stunned and shaken restaurant doorman.

"Are you all right, Dave?" Ducane called.

A thin smile broke beneath the heavy black moustache, but he was sheet white. "I think my bloke's got a broken neck. He can't move." He glanced down at his own body.

11

The lower part of his left leg protruded at a grotesque angle, the pink-coloured plastic of the prosthesis disfigured and torn with a dozen burnt bullet holes.

Ducane frowned.

Suddenly Forbes began to laugh like a drain. "Someone somewhere's got it in for my bloody leg!"

In their later report Citadel Security estimated that thirty-six rounds hit the Granada, a mixture of 7.65mm machine-pistol rounds and five from a heavy Colt .357 Magnum with a 2¾-inch barrel. Two of the latter found their way through the open door and tore away the back of the front passenger seat. If President Jammeh and his wife had not been on the floor, but seated in the rear, one or both would almost certainly have been killed.

The next morning the Foreign Office requested an urgent meeting with President Essa Jammeh before his return to Free Guinea in order to discuss various aspects of security.

PART ONE

NO PROBLEM

You can never have a revolution
in order to establish a democracy.
You must have democracy
in order to have a revolution.
Tremendous Trifles,
G. K. Chesterton

1

They came in on the last flight before the storm broke. An advance party of four.

Nothing distinguished them from the steady stream of returning Guineans, businessmen and expatriate British families who trudged down the steps from the parked Boeing 707.

Two of them travelling separately, as an engineer and a salesman, and the other pair as tourists taking advantage of an off-season bargain break, they joined the passengers making for Jakoto Airport's two-storey terminal building.

As they crossed the concrete apron the brooding tropical rain-clouds pressed down with deliberation, trapping the humid air in a vice between land and sky. Only the insect world seemed unaffected by the oppressive heat. Their incessant cacophony rose as loud as ever from the shrubs beside the pathway to the building.

The leader of the party was a tall dark-haired man in his mid-thirties. By the time he was inside he was already sweating freely. The accumulated body heat of the clustered passengers became insufferable as he joined the queue to Passport Control.

He slipped off the jacket of his lightweight business suit while he waited and positioned himself strategically below the churning overhead fan. It did little to help and he noticed that many of his fellow passengers were visibly wilting. Hardly surprising after a six-hour flight and being subjected to the inevitable movie. A combination guaranteed to produce sore eyes and a headache.

He'd avoided both by going to sleep. It was a useful trick he'd learned during his tours of duty with 22 Special Air Service Regiment. He'd lost count of the endless hours of monotonous travel by air, land and sea. Now the professional soldier's solution was first nature to him: however lousy the circumstances, make yourself as comfortable as you can and kip for as long as you can.

He certainly felt fresher for it. And at least the airless heat of Free Guinea had one consolation. He felt truly warm for the first time since returning from the Falklands. That cold had gnawed into his very bones and even the mild summer weeks back in Britain hadn't helped.

Instinctively he surveyed the gathering mass of people, first searching out the members of his team. Corporal Lionel Witcher was the easiest to spot, with his tall, slightly hunched figure and a mop of unruly fair hair that floated like an anemone amidst a sea of black faces. From the earnest conversation he was having with an obviously wealthy Guinean, who was loaded down with a massive portable stereo set, the leader guessed that his Intelligence expert had already begun taking informal soundings.

Two more tourists entered the building and joined the end of the queue. There was no mistaking Sergeant 'Brummie' Turner. Uncomfortable travelling in civvies, he had a curious notion of what the typical British tourist should be wearing. The tropical lemon jacket, evidently bought in a hurry, strained around his stocky frame. His muscled calves, more at home in baggy DPM combat trousers, were squeezed into blue-and-white striped slacks that could have been mistaken for pyjamas.

Only a straw 'kiss-me-quick' hat was missing to complete the picture as he took an unseemly interest in a group of female Swedish travel agents on a tour operator's freebee. Clearly the gruff NCO from Birmingham was determined to make the best of his role. Today only the usual unshaven chin and unkempt hair seemed familiar.

Before they'd left Brummie stated that he intended to treat this operation as a holiday after the traumas of the South Atlantic. Clearly he meant it.

At the time they had all laughed, but now their leader wasn't so sure. He recalled something the CO had said at their Hereford headquarters before he left. And the thought made him uneasy.

By contrast Brummie's companion was moderation itself. As usual Corporal Bill Mather was quietly dressed, unobtrusive, with an uncanny knack of melting into his surroundings. It was an art the 'old timer' had perfected during continuous service with 'The Family' dating back to the last year of the Borneo campaign.

But despite his retiring, placid attitude he was not the sort of man that others crossed. There was a hidden menace in the pale grey eyes, deadpan in a burnished ruddy face. Years in the sun had failed to disguise the ageing freckles or to fade the ginger moustache. Now he just observed his companion silently with watchful eyes.

"Jest luv te keep ye waitin', these woggies." The broad Gorbals accent jolted Captain Johnny Fraser from his thoughts.

"Sorry?"

The big bearded fellow Scot, with a chest like a barrel, grimaced. "Ah said these woggies, they luv te keep ye waitin'."

Fraser grinned. Ian Hammond had been seated next to him on the aircraft and, in the true tradition of the international clan of the Celts, had been only too pleased to strike up a conversation with a fellow countryman. It was a gift of birth for which Fraser had been thankful on numerous occasions during his travels over the years. But this was not one of them.

"It's a sign of importance," Fraser said, his soft Edinburgh brogue in sharp contrast to Hammond's heavy drawl. "The higher up the pecking-order you are, the longer you can keep lesser mortals waiting."

"Aye, ye dunna have te tell me tha'. One o' them buggers doon in Nigeria kept me waitin' fer three whole days. Ah jest hope these fuckas dunna have the same idea."

Fraser shook his head. "I don't think you'll find it as bad here in Free Guinea. Strong British influence and mostly they like to behave the way they think the British would. Well, in Government circles anyway."

Hammond laughed throatily. "Is tha' supposed te be reassurin'?"

The Glaswegian had already explained at monotonous

length how his efforts to bring the benefits of the World Federation of Trade Unions to the working masses of Africa had met with stiff and cunning resistance. Especially so from some of the more barbaric and totalitarian regimes. He was unsure of his reception in Free Guinea.

"The country's affiliated te our organisation, but tha' dunna mean a monkey's toss in reality. It's all doon te what the Big Man thinks," Hammond said, scowling at the passport officer who was now only feet away. "Ye know some o' the Government ministers here, d'ye? What ye say ye were, an engineer?"

"I don't know anyone who'd be of help to you," Fraser hedged. His cover-story as an engineer wouldn't stand up to too much scrutiny. He'd studied the subject at college before he earned his commission with the Royal Electrical and Mechanical Engineers, but that had been many moons ago. He knew precious little about the commercial business.

Hammond snorted. "Dunna be too sure. All these buggers know each other or are related. It's all a question o' corruption an' influence in Africa. Do me a favour, will ye? If ye make a good contact in high circles nod me the wink. These Governments are no too keen te let us hold our seminars on trade unionism so Ah can do wi' all the help Ah can get. Ah'm booked in at The Oceanic." He extended a big hairy paw.

Fraser shook it. "If there's anything useful, I'll let you know. I'm staying there myself for a day or two."

Fraser had meant what he'd said, but not with any thought of helping Hammond in his evangelical mission. The Prague-based World Federation of Trade Unions was a front for the KGB, like the International Union of Students and the World Peace Council. So if the big Glaswegian was making headway both he and Lionel Witcher would be more than interested.

A row of strong teeth showed through the mass of black beard. "Perhaps we can get together fer a dram."

They reached Passport Control and the smartly-dressed black officer took the offered passport, and adroitly flicked through it. "Mr Fraser? An engineer?"

Fraser returned the smile. "That's right."

"Business or pleasure?"

"Business."

The officer stamped the passport with a flourish. "I see you've been here before. Was that business too?"

"Alas yes," Fraser replied.

A sympathetic smile flickered on the face. "This time you must find time to enjoy yourself as well." He handed back the passport.

"I'll try," Fraser promised. He'd almost forgotten the contagious charm and warmth of the people in Free Guinea. Visitors often found the endless questions and natural inquisitiveness irritating, but it was just their way. Like the courtesy of shaking hands and making small-talk, even if you just wanted to ask the way. He smiled as he recalled how the habit had stuck for a while after his last visit. He'd received some very odd looks from the locals in The David Garrick on his return to Hereford.

With a wave at Hammond, who had already managed to lose a potential friend by upsetting the passport officer, he walked out to collect his luggage.

Lethargy had set in amongst the woolly-hatted airport porters. They had dumped all the luggage from the 707 in the outer compound and left the passengers to scramble over each other to sort out their belongings.

Johnny Fraser waited for the scrum to subside, then took his single suitcase through the open glass doors. Instinctively he took note of the lone armed guard who stood idly talking to a Guinean air stewardess. It certainly didn't look as though trouble was seriously expected.

From the grass verge opposite a big black face beamed down a dazzling white smile from the giant poster hoarding: WELCOME TO FREE GUINEA – THE FRIENDLIEST NATION IN AFRICA.

Let's hope it stays that way, Fraser thought grimly, and set his sights towards the taxi rank.

"Captain Fraser?"

He turned, surprised to see a chauffeur in a smartly-pressed tunic jogging towards him from a parked Daimler saloon. At its bonnet the Union Jack hung limply.

Immediately Fraser knew what was happening.

He was furious. He had sent specific instructions that no one from the British High Commission should meet him. It was bad enough that both he and Corporal Lionel Witcher had been known in the country two years earlier. But to telegraph their arrival to potential enemies by sending an official car was unforgivable.

"Captain Fraser?" The chauffeur grinned, gasping to catch his breath.

The SAS officer feigned puzzlement. "I'm sorry, you've got the wrong man, old lad."

The chauffeur's mouth dropped and the smile disappeared. "But, sir, you fit the description . . ."

Fraser laughed. "I'm sorry." Then, his mind starting to hum, he added quickly: "That's the man you want. That big Scotsman with the beard."

"Ah!" The chauffeur's face brightened. "The Scottish! He is the man. But he looks . . ."

"In disguise," Fraser assured, but the Guinean looked doubtful. "A word of warning, he told me he is travelling under a pseudonym."

"Ah!" The chauffeur's confidence didn't, however, match his tone. He didn't want to offend by not understanding.

"A false name. Hammond, I think. Best not call him Fraser, eh?"

With a gracious bow of thanks and an appreciative grin, the chauffeur sped off to claim his passenger. As Fraser climbed into the battered Peugeot taxi he glimpsed a delighted but bemused Ian Hammond striding alongside the chauffeur who struggled manfully with his huge case.

No doubt the Scotsman considered an official car to welcome him was an auspicious start to the uphill task that lay ahead of him.

The end of the world came during the unnerving taxi ride from Jakoto Airport to the capital Sakoto which lay twenty miles to the south by road.

First came the wind like some unseen demonic force, scattering leaves and palm fronds across the narrow pitted road. Above, the anvil-shaped stormheads nudged against

20

each other, blotting out the sun and smothering the countryside in an eerie gloom. Lightning bolted viciously at random targets somewhere beyond the trees and rows of corrugated iron shacks that made up the roadside village compounds.

Then came the rain. Sheeting down in torrents, it drummed on the taxi roof like a machine-gun. Rapidly Fraser wound up the window, closing in the pungent smell of stale sweat and marijuana.

"Hey, man," the driver laughed. "This rain the best this season. Just look! You bring it from England?" He guffawed happily at his own joke – everyone who had met tourists knew about British weather. He pressed a button on the dash and the single wiper cranked into action, scraping away a film of dead mosquitoes.

Fraser grinned. It was good to be back. There was something about Africa you could never forget. It was a call that never died, haunting, distant in the recesses of the mind, luring you back. There was a strange plaintive majesty in the land, a vastness and a timelessness. Already he could feel it beginning to spin its magic web anew. His spirits suddenly lightened.

But, perhaps, he thought, this time he had a different reason of his own to want to return.

He leaned forward, speaking in the driver's ear so as to be heard above the deep-throated thunder and gushing rain. "I thought it would be a good time! To bring the rain now from home . . . Good for the groundnuts."

The man turned back his head to speak, grinning, hardly watching the road. "Sure, we need good rain now! Just before harvest! Much drought lately. All marabou busy making ju-jus for the farmers. Still, they tell us all will be well when there are lions again in our land." Witchdoctors were still very much part of everyday life, Fraser recalled. The prediction about lions must be one of their less likely divine insights. Lions hadn't been in the country for years. However the marabou did have an uncanny knack for accuracy.

"Good ju-ju, eh?"

"Yeah, good. Very good. You English need some . . ."

"For rain . . . ?"

"For sun!" the driver boomed, laughing as he swerved to miss a woman rushing across the road to shelter beneath a wayside baobab tree.

Fraser consoled himself that the Guineans hadn't changed since his last visit. As genial and easy-going as ever. But you could never be too sure what was going on beneath the surface.

Like the coup two years earlier. No one had been expecting it, yet there must have been a fermenting discontent for years beforehand, just waiting to be triggered off. Otherwise a fanatic like Omar Pheko would never have succeeded in attracting widespread support from such a peaceful nation.

The uprising had been crushed, but there was no guarantee that the underlying grievances had died with it. Highly unlikely, in fact. Most probably the nation had resigned itself to accepting that there was nothing to be done.

But if a new leader were to emerge . . . ? That, Fraser speculated, could resurrect the whole sorry business.

It was all very well for the Foreign Office to dismiss the assassination attempt as a storm in a teacup. That in itself was a serious event. Although, if their complacency was to be accepted, it was an isolated incident that would never be tried again.

By all accounts the British High Commissioner in Free Guinea had been astounded by the news from London. The only trouble he'd heard of in the country had been the odd attack by dissident bandits on police-posts and clinics, up-country in the remoter parts of the bush. He had been adamant that there was no threat to President Jammeh. And he wasn't at all keen for a small contingent of SASmen to fly out incognito to assist the country's only military force – the glorious 400-strong Presidential Guard. It could, he insisted, only stir up hornets who would otherwise be too lethargic to be any real threat.

It was a complacency not totally shared by the hierarchy at SAS headquarters in Hereford. After all, it had been members of the regiment who had flown out when Omar

Pheko, the young black agitator, had staged his coup with the help of friends within Jammeh's own Guard.

As often the case on such occasions, the President had been out of the country at the time, but his wife and key ministers had been held hostage at a hospital in the capital. Following an urgent plea for help from Jammeh, Captain Johnny Fraser had parachuted with the four-man SAS 'Sabre' team into a stretch of the Atlantic that conveniently backed onto the grounds of the British High Commission. Coming ashore at night, the team had first been issued with white coats and then driven to the hospital.

As dawn broke the waking rebels were confronted with two white doctors demanding to see the captive wife of Jammeh who, they said, was in danger of entering a diabetic coma if she didn't receive her insulin shot.

Being new to the revolution business, the rebels allowed the two SASmen in to see the hostages. The unsuspecting guards were swiftly overcome and the President's wife, together with the other high-ranking politicians, were led quietly out down the back stairs to waiting cars.

Now free from the threat of reprisals to the hostages, the President was at liberty to invite friendly troops from a neighbouring country to come in and put down the rebellion.

They had. Swiftly and professionally, hitting hard and fast, whilst maintaining an excellence of discipline not often found in African troops. As they were later to do in a similar exercise in The Gambia, the French-trained Senegalese showed remarkable military prowess and restraint.

But restraint in warfare is a relative term. In the eight days of the rebellion around a thousand people had died, many innocently caught up in the slaughter.

The SAS contingent had been involved in directing much of the fighting and, unlike the Whitehall mandarins, the men from Hereford had seen the carnage at first hand. It was not the sort of sight that was easily forgotten.

Even now memories of the revolution flashed through Johnny Fraser's mind like scenes from an old and faded movie. Vivid, yet blurred by the passage of time. He could see the dead black child sprawled across the open sewer in the urban village compound. Its belly had swollen in the heat like a giant balloon about to burst. Its head had been hit by a stray round and the split skull was now a breeding ground for blow-fly maggots.

It may have been a military triumph in the efficient putting down of the coup, but it had been a disaster for the local inhabitants. Whichever side they'd been on.

As the taxi reached the coast road which led to the capital Sakoto, the rain suddenly stopped. At either side of the road the normally dusty tracts of red earth had been transformed into instant quagmires. At regular intervals the skeletal remains of trucks and cars, long ago cannibalised for parts, lay like stranded whales in a sea of mud.

But these became fewer as the taxi reached the salubrious residential district of Bajtenda. It was here that the bungalows of Government ministers and officials jostled for position in the mild coastal climate amongst the neatly-kept homes and gardens of the British expatriate community. Behind the high walls and hedges of bougainvillaea the Empire still lived and flourished, safe from the unseemly raw reality of Africa on the other side.

The tall white walls of the High Commission building flashed by. And the sight of its wrought-iron gates and brass plaque brought a wry grin to Fraser's face. It was a shame he wouldn't be able to see Ian Hammond's surprise meeting with Sir Nigel de Burgh.

At last the ground opened out as they approached the capital. Sakoto was virtually an island linked by an old flat iron bridge which spanned a tributary of the Kebba River and its surrounding mangrove swamps. Ideal conditions for the malaria mosquito, it didn't make the town the healthiest place in the country. And this year, according to Lionel Witcher, the Government had run out of money to give the area its customary annual dousing of insecticide.

By the time they reached the edge of Sakoto itself fingers of waning sunlight were probing inland from over the Atlantic. The underbelly of the majestic stormclouds was a wash of glowing gilt. Already the air was fresher, sweeter, scented with the musky smell of Africa as the sky began to clear.

Long shadows were throwing the white stucco frontage of the Oceanic Hotel into blessed shade as the taxi swung up alongside the cool ornamental fountain.

After a quick shower, shave and a change into grey slacks and a short-sleeved cotton denim shirt, Fraser made his way down to the bar.

As pre-arranged he found Brummie Turner and Bill Mather already there, drinks at their elbows. They were talking to the same group of Swedish travel agents they had met at the airport.

A pretty girl with a headful of gold ringlets was making moon eyes at Brummie. He grinned back at her in meaningful silence as he sucked at a pina colada lasciviously. Beside him Mather watched on dispassionately, his Scotch scarcely touched.

After ordering a local Tru-beer Fraser watched with the others as the black barman with the permanent enigmatic smile set up bar-tricks for them to ponder. Brummie bet heavily and failed to solve any of the matchstick puzzles placed before them.

Fraser engaged Mather in apparently casual conversation like two strangers meeting, as they had planned. But Brummie was singularly uninterested, becoming increasingly irritated at his failure to impress the Swedish girl with his mental dexterity. He ordered another pina colada and stared angrily at the empty wine bottle with its cork lying inside. His five-pound note on the bar said he could get it out. The expression on his face said he couldn't.

"C'mon," Fraser nudged Mather, and indicated a pair of comfortable armchairs out of earshot. As the SAS captain passed her barstool, the Swedish girl looked up. He winked at her and she smiled, watching his tall, lean frame with interest as he went by.

"What's up with Brummie?" Fraser asked, turning his chair to face into the room and settling into the deep leather upholstery. "That awful playsuit of his and drinking cocktails. Not like the Brummie we know and love. Anyone would think he really was on holiday."

Mather's eyes, cold over the rim of the glass as he sipped

his Scotch, betrayed the lightness in his voice. "That's the idea, boss, isn't it? Look like we're tourists."

"Sure, Bill." Fraser grinned. "He's doing that all right. Certainly putting your performance to shame. *You'll* never get a place in RADA."

A hint of a smile flickered on the burnished face, and the ginger moustache twitched slightly. "Play-acting or not, boss, this *is* a business trip. Just because we've won a war, doesn't mean some other cunt's not ready to start one."

The words struck like a cold blade. Fraser knew exactly what he meant. He hadn't imagined the change in Brummie's attitude; Mather had noticed it, too. Mather the iceman, the ever vigilant pro who had steadfastly remained a bachelor because he was married to the regiment. He knew that any mistress, inevitably, would lead to a conflict of loyalties one day. He also knew that The Family always demanded to come first. It was expected.

Four months ago Sergeant Brummie Turner's attitude had been the same. Another confirmed bachelor whose interest in women ranked no higher than other essential aspects of physical survival. Like food and drink. His involvements had been regular, but brief and dispassionate. To Fraser's knowledge the dour Midlander had never passed up the chance to bed a woman, pretty or otherwise. But then he'd never before gone out deliberately looking for female companionship either. There seemed to be a quiet desperation about him now as he sat at the bar, struggling to get the cork out of the wine bottle.

But four months ago the war hadn't even begun. Life lay ahead for the SAS sergeant like a long exciting journey, promising thrills and spills at every unknown bend in the road. Full of surprises. In fact it was the same road and the same fatal fascination that had held him since he'd first joined the Special Air Service fifteen years earlier.

Then in April it had all changed. Suddenly, overnight, the gloves came off. In the twinkling of an eye the endless years of training were temporarily over. To be put to the final test. The razored knife was out of its scabbard. The manacles of restraint were thrown away. Suddenly no more stupid bloody Yellow Card to wave at an IRA terrorist to give him the chance to get away. No more kowtowing to poxy foreign politicians while you spilled your blood on their land as you fought their battles for them.

No, for three glorious, heady months they were loose. Unchained. As wild and as ruthless and cunning as a pack of predatory wolves stalking the dark forbidding islands of the South Atlantic. Waging full-scale, no-holds-barred warfare at last. Flexing their muscles, testing their steel. And winning. Oh God, how they won, Fraser remembered with grim satisfaction.

Then, as quickly as it had begun, it was over. In twelve short weeks they were back on the endless Hercules flight to Ascension. A soft English July, basking in sunshine. Except for many familiar faces now missing, it was as though it had never happened.

And that was the trouble. Because they all knew it probably never would again.

Back to the odd skirmish with backward rebels, or frenzied terrorists. That was all there was in prospect. Sure, maybe Russia would try to pluck West Germany from the bosom of free Europe. But she hadn't been tempted for the past forty years, so the odds had to be that she wouldn't now. Certainly not in the time that active servicemen like Brummie Turner had left to serve. For him it was, in all probability, over. And he knew it.

Fraser said: "I guess we all need a period of adjustment."

Mather drained his Scotch in one. "Can we afford it?"

The corporal's words had a chastening effect. Fraser knew he was right. They couldn't afford deep introspective emotions, however natural.

Mather added: "I could have a word, boss. You know, discreet."

"No, Bill, let it rest. Chatting up birds and drinking three bloody cocktails hardly constitutes cause for concern."

Slowly the corporal nodded, as though weighing up some insoluble problem. "You reckon this is going to be an easy one, boss? I mean I've never been based in Africa for more than a week or so at a time. It's hard for me to judge."

"You saw the guards at the airport and at Kebba Bridge?"

27

"Sure. They didn't look like they were expecting any trouble." He added after a pause: "But perhaps they never do."

Fraser allowed himself a smile and plucked two small cigars from his shirt pocket. "You could be right there, Bill. But that trouble two years back was real enough. So was that assassination attempt. Cigar?"

Mather declined. Occasionally he rolled-his-own, but now he had other things on his mind. "I mean, boss, this place is hardly worth a scrap. It's a piddling little place. No more than a boil on the arse of Africa."

Fraser exhaled a long stream of smoke. "That could be exactly why it's strategically important to some people, Bill. That boil you talk about is the only place except The Gambia in the whole bulge of West Africa where Britain and the States have been sure of an ally for the past twenty years. And for the foreseeable future. Go south and you're into unpredictable areas like Ghana and Nigeria, or positively no-go regions like Angola."

Mather thought for a moment. "A staging post?"

Johnny Fraser shrugged. "It's the only one and it's about as far to the west of the continent as you could hope for. Free Guinea is as important for intervention in Africa as England is for the reinforcement of Europe in time of war."

"I hadn't thought of it like . . ."

Mather trailed off in mid-sentence, his eyes narrowing like a cat's. He was looking beyond Fraser to the hotel lobby.

"What is it?" The captain turned his head.

There was no mistaking the tall thin man standing in the entrance to the bar, scanning the faces of its occupants as they turned towards him. Despite the slight stoop to the shoulders, there was that air of distinction that only an English aristocrat can maintain, even if dressed in rags. Not that the slightly crumpled cream mohair suit and the well-worn Turnbull & Asser shirt suggested poverty. The sober club tie had all the hallmarks of the Court of St James.

The man irritably shifted his weight from one long leg to the other as he searched the now crowded bar. Fraser was vaguely reminded of an impatient heron looking for fish. As the faded blue eyes darted from one face to the next his head twitched so that a lank wing of silvered hair dropped across his brow. He flicked it aside with a toss.

Then his eyes fell on Fraser's face and seemed to widen, freezing into a stare. The prey had been found. The heron was ready to strike.

"Trouble, boss?"

Fraser glanced back at Mather, an amused look in his eyes. "We'll see."

He could feel the British High Commissioner's eyes boring into the back of his neck even before he swung round to the table in front of them.

"I assume you are Captain Fraser?" The thin lips, tight in suppressed anger, opened just wide enough to allow him to clip each perfect enunciated word. On his cheeks the tiny webs of blue veins were as livid as a Stilton cheese.

"Sir Nigel de Burgh?" It sounded like a pleasant surprise.

But the diplomat was in no mood for the niceties of his trade. "Just what in the blazes do you think you're playing at, may I ask? I suppose you find it amusing to make an ass of my driver. And to give me the job of explaining to some lunatic Scots trade unionist why he's been met from the airport like visiting royalty."

"Ah, sir," Fraser began apologetically, rising to his feet and offering a hand, "that little misunderstanding at the airport . . ."

Sir Nigel glared at the outstretched hand and contemplated it furiously. Finally years of training at swallowing his pride got the better of him. The long bony fingers reached out. He shook Fraser's hand brusquely, dropping it quickly as though it might be contaminated. "It was *hardly* a misunderstanding, Captain. I should say it was a deliberate act on your part at belittling official British representation here," he challenged.

"No way, sir. Avoiding rather than belittling, I would say."

Sir Nigel found himself irritated by the SAS officer's disarming smile. "Please don't bandy words with me, Captain."

29

"It's a matter of fact, sir. It was specifically requested that our arrival be as low-key as possible. The MoD issued instructions that we should arrive under our *own* steam and make contact with the High Commission in our *own* time. Otherwise there was little point in us coming in the guise of businessmen and tourists. I want to keep our presence here as secret as possible. No point in advertising the fact."

Sir Nigel helped himself to a free seat. "I suppose it didn't occur to you that I might have a very good reason for sending a car?" He didn't wait for a reply. "Your obsession for secrecy ought to be tempered with a little practical consideration. Everyone will know you're here within a few hours anyway. It's only a small country. More like a giant village really, and everyone is everyone else's cousin."

Fraser's smile didn't waver but the focus in his green-grey eyes sharpened. "I remember it *very* well, sir. I was out here during the coup. That's why I'm being cautious. I want to get sixty minutes ahead of the local gossip and keep it that way."

Sir Nigel was now convinced he didn't like this tall, lean soldier. The quietly-spoken Edinburgh accent was pleasant enough but it was getting to him. It was too reasoned and modulated. As though gently mocking behind a polite façade. "Then I suggest, Captain, you may have forgotten more than you learned. I sent the car to meet you because President Jammeh has requested you attend a welcoming reception. And whatever Jammeh wants, Jammeh gets."

The High Commissioner paused for a moment to relish the look of surprise on the officer's face. Then he added calculatingly: "So you are going to have to move a little faster if you wish to keep your sixty minutes' lead."

At that moment Brummie Turner joined them. He dumped the empty wine bottle unceremoniously on the coffee table before them. The cork was still inside. "Any of you lot any good at doing the impossible? I lose a fiver if I don't get that out."

Sir Nigel looked up at the scruffy NCO, then glanced back at Fraser. Infuriatingly Fraser's smile had returned, tiny laugh-lines now etching the sunburnt face around the amused eyes. Still they seemed to suggest some private joke.

Fraser introduced them. Immediately Brummie sensed the air of antagonism between Sir Nigel and his commanding officer. "Let me get you a drink, Your Excellency," he began politely, and the High Commissioner couldn't resist a smile of surprise. But the sting was in the tail. "Pink gin, is it?"

Sir Nigel's cheek veins glowed again. "I'm afraid there's no time for that, thank you. As I was saying, Captain Fraser, your presence is expected. And we are already embarrassingly late, thanks to your little deception at the airport."

Fraser knew he was beaten. When the Head of State who had hired you demanded an audience, there was no alternative but to accept. Only when the initial invitation had been made was there a chance to suggest an alternative. That opportunity had fallen to Sir Nigel de Burgh and he hadn't tried. Or, perhaps, even wanted to.

He said resignedly: "It'll take us a few minutes to change."

Sir Nigel glanced at the other two. "I understood there were to be four people in your advance party?"

"Yes," Fraser confirmed. "Lionel Witcher isn't here yet. He's our Intelligence chap. He said something about visiting some of his old friends. Going to a few bars he knows around Sakoto."

Brummie grinned broadly at the expression of disgust on the diplomat's face. "That's our boy. Don't believe in letting the grass grow. Keen as mustard."

"That's a curious thing to do, isn't it?" Sir Nigel said sharply. "I mean he could have done me the courtesy of receiving my official briefing first."

Fraser drained his beer. "Lionel's a bit of a law unto himself. He's got his own way of working. Very effective it is, too. Says he can find out more about a place from bar-keepers and taxi drivers than from any number of official reports." The captain gave a twist of a smile. "No offence, of course."

The diplomat didn't seem too pleased. That lank silver wing of hair had fallen over his eyes again, and he tossed it back angrily. If Captain Johnny Fraser wasn't bad enough, this Lionel Witcher promised to be a real handful. "Well I just hope he'll be discreet. If he starts asking the wrong questions in a small town like Sakoto, it could all become very embarrassing."

Brummie belched lightly and exchanged glances with Mather. Both men knew the signs. Fraser's patience wasn't as infinite as his good-humoured nature led people to believe. "High Commissioner, I would remind you that *both* Lionel and I were here during the coup, and we both know our way around."

Sir Nigel's faded blue eyes narrowed as he took stock of the mild counterattack. The SAS captain obviously had his own ideas about doing things. He wasn't the sort to be pushed around.

Taking a new line of approach, the High Commissioner said: "I was appointed *after* the coup, Captain, and I've lived here ever since. A lot can happen in two years and I assure you everything has changed. Frankly, rash action by your Intelligence man, in my opinion, can do nothing but open up old wounds."

So that's it, Fraser thought, that's what the old boy is worried about. He's on the last stretch of a distinguished career in the Diplomatic Corps. The end was in sight and he didn't want insensitive Army men with their big boots stirring up trouble.

As though in confirmation of his observation, Sir Nigel added: "You must tell your man not to expect too much of this country. Although you've been here before you must remember that, despite its many British trappings and retention of old Colonial customs, it is *still* Africa. It may be the most democratic, sedate and unvolatile country in this part of the world, but it can't adopt modern ways and thinking in a generation. Even several. Values and ideals are different here."

There was a pause, and then Mather said: "You can tell him for yourself. He's just come in."

Sir Nigel's head turned, and his mouth dropped.

It was understandable. Corporal Lionel Witcher was the complete antithesis of the popular public conception of what a member of the SAS should look like. For a start he wore spectacles, a very rare occurrence in the Regiment. In his late twenties, he was the epitome of the eternal student. He was tall and agonisingly thin, his delicate features topped by a mop of overgrown fair hair. And, despite almost constant exposure to the rigours of the outdoor life, stubbornly his complexion remained as pale as sour cream.

Yet it never ceased to amaze Fraser how the decidedly weedy-looking soldier managed to keep going when his well-built, battle-hardened colleagues began to wilt. The simple truth was, he suspected, that Lionel Witcher just didn't care. He wasn't too concerned about his appearance, his general state of health or his creature comforts. All were immaterial.

If he wanted to go somewhere, he just went, regardless of distance, obstacles or how tired he was. He would rest only when he had to, and for as short a period as possible. Luxuries like food, drink and sleep were given short shrift. He conducted his life on another plane and, just occasionally, waited for his body to catch up.

As Sergeant Brummie Turner had once told him: "Your body's just a bleedin' nuisance to you, innit? You should've been a bloody angel. An ethereal being just floatin' through life in the fourth dimension."

In Lionel's usual cheerful way, which aggravated Brummie's practised cynicism no end, he had taken the ribbing in good humour.

Rumour had it he'd spent his misbegotten youth following The Beatles' quest to India in a search for 'the meaning of life'. But he had found much more. He had discovered himself. He became deeply interested in the mystical cultures and philosophies of the Orient, and learned to share their obsession for the disciplines of the mental as well as the martial arts.

But he never took himself or his discoveries too seriously. Despite earning himself the nicknames of 'Buddha' or 'The Prof', for his abilities to solve problems, he actually enjoyed the verbal banterings with his gently mocking colleagues. Whenever a fellow trooper had a real problem, his first recourse would be to Lionel Witcher to solve it for him. And he invariably did.

When he eventually applied to 22 SAS via the Intelligence Corps, all his instructors at Hereford felt that they *ought* to fail him. But no one could find a reason that stood up. He was, simply, too good to reject.

His ready wit and fondness for unorthodox solutions found him many new friends with the SAS cerebral godfathers in 'The Kremlin', the irreverent unofficial name given for their own Intelligence unit. Three years later Witcher was a highly-trained psychological warfare expert. And the 'Psychlops' nametag had never been more appropriate . . .

"Corporal Witcher," Fraser introduced. "Lionel, this is the High Commissioner, Sir Nigel de Burgh."

Lionel Witcher grinned and extended his hand. "Pleased to meet you, Your Excellency. Found your reports most interesting."

Still recovering from his surprise, Sir Nigel wasn't quite sure how to take this first remark.

"We were just on our way to visit the President," Fraser intervened. "A summons to a reception to be precise."

Witcher's eyes lit up behind the clear, plastic-framed spectacles. "So Jammeh doesn't share our desire for discretion, eh, boss? Not surprising really."

Sir Nigel was intrigued. "How d'you mean?"

The corporal dumped his tatty holdall on the floor. "Well, for a start he's a Muslim, so he's likely to insist on re-establishing a proper personal relationship before getting down to business. To do otherwise would be discourteous. He was educated in Britain so he's a great one for protocol. And he's an African so he's a bit of a showman. He thinks our presence will worry his enemies. He'd like to let them know we're around."

"I see," Sir Nigel said, unable to keep the tetchiness from his voice. "Is there any *other* reason you might have overlooked?" Even Mather's poker face couldn't resist a wry grin.

Witcher laughed. "Only that he thinks Captain Fraser here's the greatest thing since sliced mango. They became good pals after the coup. Well, as friendly as it is seemly for Presidents and advisers to become."

"You'll be joining us?" the diplomat asked without enthusiasm.

"Sure, I wouldn't miss it for the world. Just give me a minute to change my shirt . . ."

"How were your old contacts in Sakoto?" Fraser asked.

"I could only find a couple of them," Witcher replied, helping himself to a sip of Brummie's drink. "Most have returned to their villages up-country."

"That's right," Sir Nigel said. "Many do. The tourists leave in April and the hotels close down. There's no money to be made in Sakoto this time of year. They go back to their families on the farms and help harvest the groundnut crop." He smiled ingratiatingly. "*I* could have told you that, Corporal Witcher. It would have saved you a lot of trouble and foot-slogging."

Witcher blinked. "Of course you could, sir." Then he added: "But perhaps you wouldn't have thought of it."

Before the High Commissioner had a chance to reply, Witcher picked up the wine bottle from the table and studied the encaptured cork. "What's this? A bar-trick?"

Mather sneered. "Brummie's got a fiver on it."

"'Allo, can anyone join thees party?"

Five heads turned as one. No one had noticed the Swedish travel agent cross from the bar, but when she stood in front of them she wasn't the sort of girl you could ignore. Her even white teeth were dazzling against the bottled tan.

The girl placed her hands on Brummie's shoulders and he shifted uncomfortably. "I am Ingrid. My friends ees wondering eef you want to come for a night time sweem weeth us?"

"Sorry, darling," Brummie said gruffly. "I forgot to pack me trunks."

Fraser said swiftly: "Sorry, sweetheart, but we're having a business meeting. Some other time perhaps."

Ingrid shrugged boredly. "Okee. Maybe we see you around. In thee morning maybe. I always go for early sweem." Her arms were still draped around Brummie's neck, but her eyes were fixed steadfastly on Johnny Fraser.

Nonchalantly she sauntered back to the bar, moving with a deliberate twitch of her buttocks.

Brummie's distracted gaze returned to the group. "What you doing, Lionel?" he demanded.

The corporal had just finished prodding an entire linen napkin into the wine bottle so that only one corner protruded from the neck.

"Er, just a theory," he muttered and began twisting the material around inside the bottle until the cork was caught up in it.

Even Sir Nigel momentarily forgot his agitation. All eyes were transfixed as Witcher placed the bottle between his knees and began heaving on the napkin, inching it out of the neck. Beads of sweat broke like dew on his forehead. Lean streaks of muscle began to knot along his deceptively thin forearms. The napkin, it seemed, must snap against the strain.

Then, with a loud popping sound, the napkin came free. The bottle was now completely empty, and Witcher placed it on the table. Carefully he unravelled the twisted length of napkin. The cork fell free.

Mather gave a low whistle.

Brummie's dour features lightened. "Saved my fiver from that crook of a barman, you 'ave, Lionel, you old devil."

Corporal Witcher prodded his spectacles more firmly onto the bridge of his nose. "I have indeed," he said, swiftly snatching the five-pound note from the table. "And much appreciated it is, too. Now I'd better get changed before the President falls out with our High Commissioner . . ."

Brummie Turner smouldered in furious disbelief as the corporal picked up his holdall and started towards the door.

Then Lionel Witcher slowed. After hesitating for a moment, he turned back. "Tell me, Your Excellency, there aren't any lions in Free Guinea, are there?"

Sir Nigel gave a short snort of laughter. So *this* was Fraser's Intelligence expert?

"No, Mr Witcher, a lion hasn't been seen in this country for thirty years. They were hounded out by the villagers and the old Colonial administration. Why?"

"It was just something someone said."

The High Commissioner's smile froze on his face.

*

A high wall, topped with iron spikes, marked the boundaries of State House. The mustard-coloured rendering was crumbling and pock-marked with bullet-holes. A legacy from the coup.

The High Commissioner's Daimler nosed imperiously through the gates and crunched to a halt at the foot of a shallow flight of wide steps. Sir Nigel de Burgh led the SAS team up to the entrance portico of a fine two-storey neo-colonial building.

Inside, it was sparsely furnished. The scattered wicker chairs and occasional tables with their potted plants somehow failed to fill the rooms with their high ceilings which seemed to mourn a more opulent time. There was a clean but spartan look to the faded walls, and the collection of African bric-a-brac, ancient animal heads, spears and old skin warshields that decorated them were lost in the vastness of the main reception ante-room.

Fraser thought he noticed a musty, empty, slightly desperate air about the place that he had not detected during previous visits.

It jarred his senses when the heavy mahogany doors to the reception rooms were swung open and the hubbub of excited cocktail voices swelled around him. It was like another world.

"My dear Captain Fraser!"

He stepped onto the carpet and followed Sir Nigel into the gathering of thirty or forty smartly-dressed Africans and their equally well-appointed wives.

"It's good to meet you again, Mr President," Fraser said.

"Oh, you *remember* the Captain then?" The High Commissioner looked decidedly miffed.

"Of course, but of course!" Jammeh boomed. His body quivered mountainously beneath a tent-like embroidered robe. Vigorously his big hand pumped Fraser's. "You do not forget a man like The Captain, Sir Nigel, I assure you! Especially when he has saved you and your country from falling into the hands of scheming infidels and villains! And rescued your favourite wife single-handed!"

Fraser smiled at the ebullient reception. "You exaggerate, Mr President. I had a little help."

Jammeh showed a row of big white teeth behind grinning thick lips. "It is an African's privilege to exaggerate, Captain. And a President's in particular." He tapped a well-manicured finger against the side of his thick-lensed tortoiseshell spectacles. "But tell me, I am addressing you *still* as Captain? What is happening in my beloved Britain? Doesn't our gracious lady, Her Majesty, reward her warriors anymore?"

Fraser felt slightly embarrassed. It was always difficult to explain to foreigners that promotion in the Special Air Service, if it came at all, came exceedingly slow. "In time, Mr President, I am sure it will come."

Jammeh belly-laughed. "If you'd taken my offer after the coup, you'd be a Field-Marshal here in Free Guinea by now . . !"

"And I'd be enjoying every moment of it, I'm sure," Fraser replied. "But tell me, how is the Lady Precious?"

The President pointed to the far side of the room. Fraser could just distinguish the coiffured raven hair and a glimpse of flowered printed silk amidst a gaggle of politicians and Government officials. "As usual she is surrounded by admirers. I should have them all shot, shouldn't I?"

Sir Nigel almost missed the joke and looked decidedly concerned, but Jammeh bubbled on: "She often talks of you, Captain. She often recalls the rescue." He leaned forward conspiratorially. "To tell the truth I think that was the most important and thrilling highlight of her sheltered life!"

"I'm sure not . . ." Fraser began.

"But listen to me. I haven't offered you a drink." Jammeh turned to the white-jacketed steward who had been hovering with a silver tray of iced fruit drinks. "May I recommend the lime?" He added in a whisper: "It contains a little pick-me-up."

Fraser took a tall glass and sipped at it. There would be no tell-tale smell from the liberal lacing of vodka.

"And my dear friend Corporal Witcher!" Jammeh said, noticing the NCO for the first time. He shook his hand enthusiastically. "That is right, isn't it? W-i-t-ch-er. Like our own marabou here. Witchdoctors. Makers of fine ju-ju!"

"That's right, Mr President," Witcher replied amiably. "And what an export if *only* you could export it along with the groundnuts . . !"

Sir Nigel looked on, horrified that the scruffy soldier had upset the President's sensibilities. But Jammeh just roared with laughter, drowning out nearby conversation. "That is the best suggestion I've heard this year! Many governments would enjoy such unbridled power. An excellent idea! Should I fire my export minister and hire you?"

"Tell me, Mr President," Fraser said. "This most pleasant reception isn't *just* in our honour, is it?"

Jammeh tried to look hurt, but his smile broke through. "You think I would insult an old and dear friend by not having a welcome party! I owe too much to you! Besides, my Precious insisted."

That Fraser could believe. Lady Precious, as she was known, would find any excuse for a party.

"And the matter of discretion?" the captain hinted.

"How can such matters be discreet in Free Guinea, my dear Captain? I promise I told no one except my wife and my Head of State Security. Of course, you haven't met my good colleague Colonel Kwofie. But as your men will be training the Presidential Guards, he *had* to know." Jammeh held up a finger. "But that's all I told. And yet the next day my steward asked what he should be planning for your arrival." Again the laughter rumbled with the force of a suppressed volcano. "You see, there *are* no secrets in Free Guinea! And maybe that is a good thing."

Fraser sipped at his drink. "But a little security *is*, Mr President. Even the most popular of men have enemies. And popularity and power can make others envious."

The big man shrugged. "Sure I have enemies. Mostly politicians. *Until* I offer them a Government post, and then they change their tune. Free Guinea is too small to allow the luxury of enemies."

Fraser wasn't to be deflected. "We know you have at least one, Mr President. London proved that."

"Bah! London proved nothing." He stepped back and waved his hand. "Come with me, Captain. For a moment."

Fraser followed him to a secluded corner of the room.

"All London proved," the President hissed, lowering his voice, "was that I have *an* enemy in London. We all know who that is. I kicked out the Libyans from here over two years ago. My police found them trying to train guerrillas for terrorist activities. So I closed their embassy. You know what happened." Behind the thick lenses, Jammeh's liquid brown eyes were in deadly earnest. "Within six months they'd got their agent Omar Pheko to mount a coup which you and the gallant Corporal Witcher helped to put down.

"The man fled. As always, a coward will not stay and fight. There is universal suffrage in this country, Captain. Every man and woman can vote and any candidate may stand. Only last year I was voted in for another five years. Where were my enemies then?" He paused for effect. "Perhaps they were in London. They were not here."

The background conversation seemed suddenly muted.

Jammeh added quietly: "In case anyone has doubts, it is as well that they *see* I have my famous advisers here from Britain. This is a democracy and I am proud of it. But it does mean that constitutionally I cannot have my police hound and harass political opponents. There are no death camps here. No prisoners tortured. And no jails filled with dissenters."

Slowly Jammeh looked around the room. "But I *am* able to illustrate that I am in control. That I am strong. Believe me, Captain, you will do more good being seen here tonight than the months you may spend training my Guards and improving security, as you put it."

Fraser drained his drink. The President of Free Guinea was as impressive as ever.

"Essa, you are keeping the delightful Captain Fraser all to yourself!" The gushing voice like popped champagne wouldn't have sounded amiss at a debutante's ball in Kensington. Precious Jammeh had been educated in London, and it showed.

"M'lady, it's a pleasure to renew your acquaintance," Fraser said with deliberate formality. He accepted the delicate hand and kissed the simple gold Cartier ring. "And may I say how stunning you look this evening." He meant it.

She made no attempt to retrieve her hand, stepping back in a mock swoon.

Lady Precious was tall and slender, even at the hip which set her apart from the average West African woman. And the white and beige silk print dress, which almost certainly came from a leading French fashion-house, emphasised the fact. Modestly cut with a high throat, it nevertheless touched at all the right places.

"As always, Captain Fraser, you know how to flatter," she chimed, at last withdrawing her hand. The wide, mischievous eyes, highlighted with gold shadow, were alive in the finely-boned ebony face.

It was no wonder, he thought, that Jammeh's first wife had been relegated to the obscurity of one of several presidential homes when Precious arrived on the scene. Now the woman was rarely seen in public.

"Now do tell me what you've been up to since that awful business of the coup? I suppose you've been down in the South Atlantic fighting on those little islands?" She didn't wait for a reply. "Everyone here thought it was all so exciting. Absolutely everyone in Free Guinea thought the British were marvellous. They were all supporting you and were so thrilled when you won."

Fraser could believe it. In some respects Free Guinea was more British than Britain. Since independence in the early 1960s they'd adopted the free vote, a single-tier parliamentary system, and an African version of the legal system. As a result, compared to countries like Nigeria, there was a cordial relationship between the blacks and the small white community that verged on mutual affection.

"You must understand, M'lady," Fraser said, "I'm not permitted to say where I've been." He winked. "Let's just say it's nice to be in a warm climate for a change. . . ."

Precious pealed like a bell. There was nothing more to be said. No sign of regret or expression of sorrow. No mention of those who had perished. Fraser doubted that such things even crossed her mind.

"I am sure," she said, "that Colonel Kwofie will be delighted to meet you. Like you he is a professional soldier. He, too, was trained at Sandhurst."

She linked her arm through his and steered him through the crowd. As the guests stepped respectfully aside, Fraser noticed the odd disapproving scowl. In a conventional Muslim society, where women took a back seat, he could well believe that Lady Precious wouldn't win any popularity contests. Nor would that be likely to worry her in the slightest.

The tall man turned as his name was called.

He was immaculately dressed in the ceremonial No 1 Dress of the Free Guinea Presidential Guard. The lovat material of the brass-buttoned tunic had been sharply pressed, Fraser noted with a professional eye, and the yellow piping down the side of the trousers disappeared neatly into a pair of brown leather cavalry boots. They gleamed almost as brightly as the diagonal cartridge belt across his chest which carried the gold Lion's Head emblem of the President. Essa Jammeh, Guardian Lion of Free Guinea.

"Colonel Kwofie," Precious said, "I'd like you to meet Captain Johnny Fraser of the British Army Training Team."

The light from the chandelier caught the texture of the taut skin across the African's high cheekbones as he turned to look at her. His hands remained firmly clasped behind his back.

"Don't you think the President would wish to make the formal introductions, M'lady?" There was no emotion in his voice. He didn't even look at Fraser.

The expression on Precious' face became suddenly fixed. She smiled sweet acid and those beautiful dark eyes glinted like granite. "And don't you think you should remember that you are talking to the *wife* of the President, my dear Colonel." It was such a simple sentence, yet it held all the threat of an unsheathed blade.

This was not the promising start to the working relationship with Kwofie that Fraser had hoped for. He said quickly: "Of course, Colonel, you are so right. We military men understand the importance of protocol. It nevertheless remains an honour to have met you."

Kwofie's glance stabbed in the direction of Precious, momentarily. The thin moustache over his thick upper lip quivered slightly. Sweat gleamed on his deeply receding forehead giving it a polished sheen.

For the first time he looked at the SAS captain. Kwofie's eyes were fathomless pools against the bright whites, one iris slightly disfigured by a yellow-flecked mote. It was impossible to judge his feelings, but Fraser guessed that he was deeply resentful. Understandably so. However well-intentioned, the arrival of a foreigner to make an independent assessment might unsettle the most efficient commander, even the most humble. And Colonel Kemo Kwofie, Head of State Security, Chief of Police and Officer Commanding the Presidential Guard could not be expected to be that.

When at last the African spoke, it was with slow deliberation as though he was being forced to eat glass: "It is, of course, my great pleasure to make your acquaintance, too, Captain. I am sure we will learn a lot from you."

Fraser's smile was genuine; the man was no fool. By an obvious play of humility after the rebuke by Lady Precious, he had forced the SAS officer into a position where he could only appear rude and condescending. Or offer praise. Fraser decided to oblige: "I'm sure there's very little we can teach your splendid force, Colonel."

One of Kwofie's eyebrows raised in feigned surprise. "Oh really?" But the tone said, quite distinctly: *Then why are you here to waste my time?*

The verbal struggle for supremacy was not lost on Lady Precious, but any further antagonism was saved by the arrival of the President. He had Corporal Witcher in tow.

"Ah, my friends, I'm neglecting my duty again!" Jammeh boomed. "I see, Captain, that you have met my worthy guardian of law and order." Kwofie inclined his head politely to Fraser in acknowledgement, as the President burbled on: "The Colonel was appointed just after the coup. And ever since there has not been the slightest hint of trouble, is that not so?"

With difficulty Kwofie adopted a modest expression.

"Now, Colonel," Jammeh continued, "you must meet another trusted friend of mine and colleague, Sergeant Major Witcher – " Seeing the flicker of surprise on Fraser's face, the President added quickly: " – Promoted in the field."

Evidently Jammeh had adopted a status that he felt Kwofie would respect. Witcher, judging by his unperturbed expression, had anticipated such a move and had fallen in more quickly than Fraser.

Jammeh turned to Precious. "My dear, why don't you talk to our two other guests whilst we men discuss military matters."

He indicated to where Brummie, who had resorted to a defensive scowl, and Mather were having an evidently stilted conversation with two Government ministers. With a graceful smile Lady Precious happily glided off in the direction of two potential new admirers.

Meanwhile Witcher had quickly opened up a conversation with the reluctant Kwofie: "You must be very proud at having policed this country so effectively since the coup, Colonel?"

Kwofie could see the same ploy he'd used against Fraser a few minutes earlier turned on himself. He, too, was trapped. "One can never be complacent," he replied stiffly.

Jammeh, apparently, had failed to see Witcher's line of approach. "Even the calmest sea has its rough moments, does it not, Colonel?"

Kwofie shifted uneasily. "Of course, it is only to be expected."

"Oh really?" Witcher said innocently. "What sort of rough moments?"

"A little street crime, you would call it." Kwofie shrugged. "Nothing more."

Witcher looked sympathetic. "That's unfortunate. That sort of civil violence was unheard of when I was last here."

Jammeh and Kwofie exchanged glances, before the President said slowly: "We are a poor country, Sergeant Major. And we've had droughts over the past ten years. The situation gets no better, you understand. These times are difficult. Especially for the young educated men. They become resentful. They learn of the wealth of other countries. They see the tourists flocking into our land. Suddenly a taxi-driver finds he can charge four times the fare he would charge a fellow countryman. They see them pay a day's wages for a drink. So some young men get confused. They resort to crime. . . ."

Witcher said softly: "That's sad." He peered gloomily into his glass of lime. "It's always sad when people resort to crime to get money for food."

Jammeh's smile seemed to lose some of its warmth. "I did not say that."

"No," Witcher replied mildly. "But somebody did."

Jammeh looked awkward.

"Who said this?" Kwofie's voice had grown full of unmistakable menace. Fraser was watching the exchange with keen interest; he said nothing.

Witcher shrugged. "Just someone I bumped into. In one of the bars in town. He said your Government couldn't afford to distribute the food aid it was given, so the stuff was sold off for income. Only then the people it was originally intended for had to buy it from the traders."

This was dangerous ground and they all knew it. Fraser began to feel uneasy. A wrong word now and their mission to Free Guinea could be dramatically foreshortened. But he needn't have been concerned. Witcher defused the situation as swiftly and as skilfully as he had engineered it. "Of course, the man was a drunk . . . !" he added with boyish charm and finished his lime.

At first the President's chuckle came in a stutter, a trickle of relief. Then it gathered momentum until it became a full and flowing belly-laugh. Even Kwofie smirked uncertainly.

"You know . . ." Jammeh said as he gasped for breath, ". . . if what this man said is true, I'd have been swept from power at the last election." He was keen to nail the rumour firmly in its coffin.

"Still no serious rival politicians then, Mr President?" Fraser asked.

Jammeh's mirth had subsided to a gentle bubbling. "Only one, Captain, way up-country. A man called Fofana. He was elected last year. I've offered him a post in Government, but he still refuses. He has been a trade union leader for many years, you see. A man of high principle. Still, eventually he will see sense, I am sure."

Since independence Jammeh had run the only properly-organised political party. It was drawn mainly from the majority Mandinka tribe who mostly inhabited the rural areas. Only every five years did the rival parties get their act together at the approach of an election. But they never quite had the financial resources and political skill to make much of an impression against Jammeh. In the true African tradition the villagers felt most comfortable with a trusted, respected and powerful leader.

Fraser sensed that the President was keen to steer the conversation onto safe ground. So he was not surprised when Jammeh suddenly announced: "Now, Captain, tomorrow we must discuss the deployment of your team. There are some old barracks about midway up-country at Duntenda. A charming spot near the river. Colonel Kwofie's men have been cleaning it out for your party. I am sure it will be ideal for your purposes. And tomorrow we shall both discuss everything with you at great length."

"I am grateful."

"But no more business talk tonight, I think. You must have some more refreshments . . ."

Jammeh had not appreciated the anticipation of the well-trained steward. Having noticed the empty glasses the youth had moved up behind the President.

Jammeh's beckoning hand struck the silver tray an upward glance. The steward looked horrified as the iced glasses jumped and bright liquid slopped down his starched white tunic. The musical sound of tinkling of glass brought the buzz of conversation to a shuddering halt. All heads turned to see the unfortunate youth down on his knees to pick up the pieces.

"I am most humbly sorry, Your Excellency," the steward blubbered. Tears of shame trickled down his face. They dropped into the spreading pool on the floor. Wafts of lime and orange pervaded the room.

"I am most humbly sorry," the steward bleated again as high-ranking officials scowled with disapproval.

Jammeh hid his irritation with a thin understanding smile. Taking their cue from the President the gathering began to laugh at the steward's misery.

Witcher's consoling voice was quite distinct above the mumbling mirth of the onlookers. "Never mind, young man. All will be well when the lion returns. . . ."

A smile flashed across the youth's upturned face. Then vanished.

The sudden, hushed silence was stunning in the crowded room.

2

Igor Dovzhenko was beginning to sweat.

It had been a long wait. Three days in the claustrophobic room in the shabby Tripoli hotel. Three days without air-conditioning, without a decent drink, and without word from the Colonelissimo Gadaffi.

At times like this Dovzhenko almost regretted his chosen career as a major in Russia's most secret and effective military organisation. The Glavnoye Razvedyvalelnoye Upravleniye. Better known in more informed intelligence circles as the GRU – the Second Chief Directorate of the Soviet General Staff.

But then, he reasoned, it was because he had the military man's ability to take the shit, as well as throw it, that he was here at all. As a professional he could ignore the discomfort demanded by the need for secrecy. Not to mention the humiliation of being kept waiting by the volatile Libyan leader.

If his mission was to have been easy, it stood to reason that even those political apes from the KGB could have handled it. And he wouldn't be here now to put things right.

Dovzhenko glanced at his watch. It had only been ten minutes since the old-fashioned telephone had sung angrily from his bedside. Just ten minutes since Gadaffi's officious aide had informed him that a car would be sent immediately and that he should be ready.

Of course, at such short notice, he could have been unprepared. Unshaven. Without a clean shirt. Even languishing in the ancient enamel bathtub.

But in fact, the stout middle-aged Russian had predicted

Colonelissimo Gadaffi's strategy exactly. A manoeuvre to put him at a disadvantage even before their meeting began.

It was an attempt as crude and effective as asking a rival an important question at dinner when he'd just filled his mouth with stroganoff.

Dovzhenko leaned over the washbasin and studied his baby-smooth chin and heavy jowls in the grubby, cracked mirror. His thin, wide mouth twisted in a smug little smile. The Colonelissimo would have to get up early in the day to catch the GRU major with such pranks. He had been prepared to move at a moment's notice since his arrival three days earlier.

He had laid his carefully-pressed alpaca suit from the GUM store in Moscow over the back of the chair and had waited on the bed dressed only in his vest and underpants. He had shaved twice a day in readiness, and had run a flannel of cold water over his stout, muscular body at regular intervals to keep cool.

But now, dressed with a clean shirt and blue knitted tie, he was beginning to perspire again. He knew it wasn't just the muggy atmosphere in the little room. For, although he'd rehearsed the forthcoming interview countless times in his mind, he knew the encounter with Colonelissimo would not be easy.

He still had the feeling when the driver arrived and drove him through the darkened streets of the capital. Although he knew the place quite well it was impossible to be certain of his exact destination as the vehicle weaved and threaded its way through countless deserted streets. He thought he recognised a building that was used as a conference centre as the car pulled up, but he couldn't be sure.

Armed troops appeared in the headlamp beams, menacing and ghostly in the stark light, directing the driver to the allotted parking space. As Dovzhenko stepped out into the chill night air of the desert he wished he'd worn a sweater beneath his jacket.

"This way," the driver said briskly.

The major followed the Arab into the building and out again through a back door onto a patch of waste land. They took a rough path which seemed to go on forever.

Flames glittered ahead in the gloom. As they stepped closer he could see half-a-dozen soldiers tending a log fire. In the dancing glow cast by its flames he could see snaking cables stretched across the dusty ground. A heavy diesel generator formed a throbbing base to the lively treble of crackling firewood.

The guard told him to wait and Dovzhenko peered into the blackness beyond the halo of the fire, anticipating the shape of a car. Another journey perhaps?

Dovzhenko was surprised. He had been standing just a few yards from the Colonelissimo's tent, but in the darkness he had not realised. He followed the guard's pointing finger into the dimly-lit cave of material that billowed gently in the night air.

Colonelissimo Muamar Gadaffi sat behind a white desk that was ludicrously small for a man who struck such dread into rational politicians and newspaper headline writers across all the continents.

The desktop was awash in an untidy sea of papers and documents, almost covering the single ancient telephone. Behind it the slim hunched figure with the thick mane of black hair could have been an overworked and harassed clerk. A white trench coat was draped over the slender shoulders; beneath Dovzhenko glimpsed an open-throated military shirt.

The Russian was not surprised when the Colonelissimo did not look up. Many years in the Middle East and in Africa had taught him that men of supposed stature liked to make it plain that they were busy with more important matters of state. It was all part of the opening gambit.

But Dovzhenko was an excellent player of chess and he refused to be intimidated. Instead he glanced patiently around the big tent. Like the desk it was an unspoken statement. The tent was typical Bedouin style of neatly-stitched multi-coloured squares. The desk was a symbol of Islamic modesty. A simple man obedient to the will of Allah.

In one corner stood a glowing coal brazier, supplemented by a portable electric radiator. A single low chair in cream plastic and tubular steel sat immediately in front of, and slightly lower than, the Colonelissimo's desk.

Dovzhenko's grey eyes flickered with understanding and faint amusement. Perhaps 'The Leader' was not quite as humble before his God as he would have others believe.

So the Russian was not unexpectant when, with a sudden gesture, Gadaffi dropped the paper he was signing and stood up. His dark eyes were bright and friendly. The face was younger than Dovzhenko remembered, and the blue-shadowed cheeks a little more gaunt.

"Dear Major. It is good to see you again." He reached across to shake hands. The gesture emphasised his elongated frame and long arms. "Forgive me if I do not attempt Russian, Major. I find it such a *difficult* language."

Dovzhenko accepted the intended slight against his own nationality with an understanding nod. "*Lughtkum al Arabiya al jaiyda munasib alaya. Walakin min al mumkin tafadal al Inklesia ou al Faransa,*" he replied with a deliberate and practised fluency that would have been worthy of a Bedouin chieftain. *Your fine Arab tongue suits me. Unless, of course, you would prefer English or French?*

For a moment Gadaffi's eyes sparkled. He liked a worthy adversary and he'd forgotten just how sharp this unassuming GRU major was. In fact his very presence underlined that Moscow viewed this meeting to be of considerable importance.

"You must explain to me your request for this meeting, Major," Gadaffi continued in Arabic, ignoring Dovzhenko's counter put-down.

"You have heard about recent events in London, Colonel?"

The Libyan leaned back in his chair. "Much happens in London. Most of it is of monumental insignificance to me."

"I refer to the assassination attempt on President Jammeh of Free Guinea."

Gadaffi shrugged. "I have heard something of it. The man is a Fascist, and a virtual dictator. And he is a neo-colonialist, a puppet of Britain. He gets all that he deserves. His friends in Britain really should take more care of him."

Dovzhenko nodded sagely. Dealing with the Colonelissimo was like handling an unstable tank of nitroglycerin. "I realise, of course, that you would not necessarily have had

51

prior knowledge of this act by these Guineans trained in your camps here in Libya."

"I have no knowledge of their nationality, Major." Gadaffi's voice rose only an octave as he spoke. He was well-used to fencing-off such accusations. "They were, however, revolutionaries. As such I can only say that they chose their target well. Even if they have yet to perfect their technique."

Dovzhenko's eyes glittered like white mica crystals in grey granite. He was determined not to let the Libyan leader have it all his own way. "There *is* no doubt that the men were trained here. They were trained at the top camp at Raz Hilal by Russian, Cuban and East German instructors. Would you like their names?"

Gadaffi waved aside the offer. "Names are of no significance in revolution, Major. They are as individual waves in the tidal flow for freedom . . ."

"Those men," Dovzhenko persisted, "were drawn from your Islamic Legion. Some of your best recruits from the Middle East and Africa. But they were patently not ready for the mission on which they were sent. And, more importantly, that mission was in direct contravention of our agreed policy on Free Guinea."

Gadaffi steepled his fingers together thoughtfully. "Revolutionaries are the essential free spirit of the world, Major. A fact which you, as a Russian, should be fully aware of. It has been so since the world began, and it will never change. That is why here in Libya I have divorced the revolution from political power. I am not even President here, nor Head of State. I am merely 'the Leader of the Revolution'. All I can attempt to do is influence the Revolutionary Committees of the people who control their own destiny. But I have no power."

The Russian understood Gadaffi's strange philosophies. He was considered to be an expert in the GRU. That was why he was here. His gaze didn't falter as he listened to this strange idealist who had sworn that even his own father would not be re-housed until every Libyan peasant had a home of his own.

"This way," the Colonelissimo continued, "we have done

away with government. And with politicians and the whole class structure. Only this way can all men live in freedom, happiness and peace." His dark eyes moved away from the Russian and became fixed on his steepled fingers. "Indeed just as your own revolutionaries *tried* in your motherland."

The implication of their failure could not be missed. A hush fell over the tent, disturbed only by the undulating rustle of the flaps in the breeze.

No wonder Moscow could never fathom the enigmatic Libyan leader, thought Dovzhenko. No wonder that their attempts at co-operation so often ended in acrimony. They would pour in millions of roubles of equipment and skilled terrorist instructors to train the disillusioned from around the world. Every potential rebel with or without a cause.

But the Soviet Union could never guarantee the end result of the resources put at the disposal of Gadaffi's free-wheeling international revolution. They would supply instructors for his training camps at El Beida and Maaten Biskara, but when their job was finished they had little control of their deployment. In the Colonelissimo's tradition of the free revolutionary spirit, the terrorists were usually pointed in the general direction of a target and left to get on with it. Chaos and disaster frequently followed. At best they could hope that their respective objectives coincided in some way. At worst the terrorist activity had a general destabilising effect that the Russians could work at to achieve something more positive.

Dovzhenko found himself strangely transfixed by the quiet magnetism of the man whose revolutionary philosophy amounted to total and absolute anarchy. To let the people of the world get on with it without proper government to get in the way. No wonder those thick-skulled politicos in the KGB had given up in utter frustration. To them Gadaffi's concept of world freedom was even more alien than it was to the democratic world. Freedom without absolute control was unthinkable.

The major had no time for either politicians or philosophers. He was a military man who saw the views of both only as additional weapons in the war that he constantly waged. And yet he had to admit a certain grudging admiration for the unwavering purity of the Libyan leader's fanatical idealism.

"Colonel," the Russian said solemnly, "I fully understand your desire not to deter any hot-blooded revolutionary who has set his sights on one of the enemies of freedom. I also appreciate that our countries' concepts of that freedom do not always coincide exactly. But in the case of Free Guinea we already failed once. As a result a plan has been agreed between us. That plan specifically does *not* involve the assassination of President Jammeh."

Gadaffi shrugged. It was of no consequence.

"As a result," Dovzhenko said, "the British Government has sent out an investigation team from their SAS special force."

The Colonelissimo's eyebrows raised. As a military man involved in guerrilla and revolutionary terrorist activities he had great respect for the men from Hereford. But he said nothing, deciding it was time to let the GRU major state his case. "Colonel, I understand you prefer impulsive action for change. The coup d'état. You have made it work in many instances. But it *failed* in Free Guinea.

"It would be a great shame," Dovzhenko continued, selecting his words carefully, "if the act of *uninfluenced* rebels upset our plans of co-operation at the eleventh hour. It would be a shame to repeat the tragedy of Omar Pheko."

Gadaffi's face was a mask and he had paled slightly. Omar Pheko had been a young black hothead recruited from a Stockholm university and prepared at the Patrice Lumumba University in Moscow for an eventual return to Free Guinea. He had been sent to Libya for final preparation because the population of his home country was 90 per cent Muslim. But with typical Libyan over-optimism, he had been encouraged to go back prematurely and had grabbed for power through a direct coup. That was Gadaffi's way, not Dovzhenko's. With a Russian's natural gift of infinite patience, he preferred the grass roots revolution. Mobilising the people in the time-honoured tradition of his own country. It took longer to achieve, more planning, but because it was a genuine – even if manipulated – people's revolution, it was more permanent.

Then Omar Pheko, confused by conflicting indoctrination and ideologies had committed his second error. With control of the two radio stations, he began broadcasting that he was leading a Communist revolution. Any other sort of revolution would have suited the Africans fine. In Free Guinea Communism was interpreted simply as meaning 'Godless'. All other definitions were secondary. To the devout Muslim population it would be a blasphemy to follow such a man and would be certain to invite Allah's divine retribution.

The sweeping support Omar Pheko had enjoyed in the first seven days of the coup evaporated overnight. As President Jammeh mounted a counter-coup, with help from the SAS and friendly troops from nearby Senegal, Omar Pheko's followers had melted away.

"What do you want of me, Major?" Gadaffi asked darkly.

Dovzhenko was conscious that he was perspiring. He felt the sting of sweat in his eyes. "Entrust me with *total* personal control of the Free Guinea enterprise."

Gadaffi's eyes widened in surprise and his even white teeth glistened in the lamplight. "And what do I get in return for that great privilege?" His voice was hard with sarcasm.

"You will have a successful Islamic Revolution within nine months."

Gadaffi snorted, his nostrils flaring like an angry bull's. "I find your interest in the Islamic faith very touching, Major. If I were cynical I might think that the Soviet Union had discovered a new means to an end since the fall of the Shah."

Choosing his words carefully, Dovzhenko spoke with as much sincerity as he could muster. "Jato is a good man. I imagine him being very much like yourself in your younger days."

The Colonelissimo sat slowly back in his chair. Dovzhenko could sense him trying the comparison for size. The tall, strong, lean and muscled black buck, proud and arrogant with intense, intelligent eyes. A speaker of natural passion and rhetoric who could hold men in awe and women spellbound. It was a good comparison and the Russian knew it.

And, as a slow smile broke over Gadaffi's face, he knew the Libyan leader had seen through it. He also knew he had won.

"Major, you shall have your way. You are a competent man and a militarist. I like that. You think straight, unlike those crafty political devils in your KGB. For that reason I think you can achieve what you say."

Dovzhenko began to smile.

"But there are conditions . . ."

"Such as?" the Russian asked cautiously, his smile waning.

Gadaffi stood up suddenly, seeming to tower over the ridiculously small desk. "You and *only* you may have direct contact with Jato . . ."

"And?"

The Colonelissimo strode into the centre of the tent, forcing Dovzhenko to turn his head to follow him. A large map of Africa was suspended from a tent pole.

"Mali, Nigeria, Mauritania, Cameroon, Tunisia, Egypt, Sudan, Benin . . ." Gadaffi stabbed a finger at each one in turn, ". . . Niger, Chad, SeneGambia, Free Guinea, Upper Volta, the Ivory Coast . . ."

He turned sharply. "*All* of these are our agreed targets for the activities of my liberators of the Third World. To me the most important is Chad. It is on my southern border. It has mineral wealth, and I am already committed. But you choose Free Guinea as the most important to you. Why?"

Dovzhenko climbed to his feet and walked across to the map under Gadaffi's unwavering gaze.

"You are right, Colonel, of course. I am here exactly because I am military and I do not deal in ideologies. And the crucial military factor on your continent is South Africa. As you are aware, by geographical good fortune – the luck of the devil, you may say – it contains more rare minerals than any other country on earth. That includes 90 per cent of the chromium supplied to the United States. Without it the modern technology of her war machine grinds to a halt."

"But we are talking about *West* Africa!" Gadaffi pointed out.

"Quite so," Dovzhenko replied quietly. "And that is because we are slowly isolating South Africa. With Zimbabwe gone she is now surrounded, beleaguered." He waved a finger. "With pressure from the outside, even from her traditional friends, and revolution brewing from within. Recall the chaos in the West when there was an oil shortage alone. Deprive it of all essential minerals and it will only be a matter of time before the United States has to move to protect her vital interests. But South Africa is a long way off. A staging-post will be needed. A reliable one. Free Guinea is on the north-west bulge – the nearest landfall to America. As vital to them as Grenada is to us for Latin America."

Gadaffi nodded slowly. "There are not many black African states who would help America in such circumstances. And in the face of world opinion against the fascists of South Africa. Maybe The Gambia, or Senegal, if the French agreed – but no one can trust them."

"And President Jammeh of Free Guinea?"

"Certainly," the Colonelissimo said with a nod of his head. He bit his lower lip thoughtfully. "So it is of great importance to you."

"Vital." Emphatic.

The Colonelissimo lifted his eyes to meet those of the stocky GRU major. "Then as a condition I will trade your priority of Free Guinea for mine, Chad."

Dovzhenko blinked rapidly. In his confidence at winning the chess game with the Libyan leader he had exposed his queen. "I'll need to consult with my superiors in Moscow."

Colonel Muamar Gadaffi seemed satisfied. The meeting was at an end. Dovzhenko felt suddenly weary. The days of anticipation were over, the tension of the last half-hour thankfully past. Now he could afford the luxury of soaking in the ancient discoloured bathtub back at the hotel. He looked foward to it.

"Tell me, Major," the Colonelissimo said suddenly. "If you think Jato is so much like me, how do you know he can be trusted once he is installed? We revolutionaries can be very unpredictable." There was a hint of mockery in his voice, the dark eyes sparkling mischievously.

Dovzhenko thought for a moment, then said slowly, trying to recall the exact words: "A party's aim is to achieve power under the *pretext* of carrying out its programme."

Gadaffi's eyebrows raised. He was impressed with the quotation from his own Green Book, a pale and convoluted version of Mao's famous sayings and philosophies. "So you do not really worry what policies Jato carries out, as long as he is your man?"

Dovzhenko scratched at the jowls of his cheeks. "I am a military man not a politico. I care only for objectives, not the means by which they are achieved."

Gadaffi nodded in understanding.

But Major Igor Dovzhenko knew that the Libyan leader did not understand. The man was essentially a politico despite his soldierly background.

Military men left nothing to chance.

As soon as the door closed Brummie Turner regretted it.

The girl led him across to the bed like a child eager to show a favourite uncle her latest toy.

"You sit, *toubab*," she said.

At least the covers looked clean, he thought, like the rest of the establishment. Feeling slightly foolish he sat on the bed and drew his feet up. He hadn't done anything like this for years, and he felt decidedly uncomfortable. What the hell had got into him recently?

She stood back looking at him. A slender, delicate girl with a lustre to her skin that suggested she wasn't long into her teens. Her eyes were dark and twinkling. In the darkness the bright whiteness of her smile seemed genuine. She looked confident and pleased with herself. It was not yet the sour humour of the professional whore.

Brummie cleared his throat. "What's your name, love?"

She grinned widely. "Me? I am Diamante."

He gave a snort. "That doesn't sound very African. Who gave you that name?"

Diamante reached behind her back for her zipper. "That is what the man call me. He says my eyes sparkle. Like diamond stone."

"Well, I can see his point."

The simple pink dress slipped from her chocolate brown shoulders to reveal a girlish vision with pert immature breasts and a slight flare to her hips.

He swallowed heavily and felt the unpleasant aftertaste of too many cocktails.

"You like?" she asked coyly.

Brummie grunted. He felt uncomfortably like a father contemplating incest.

She sat beside him on the bed. "We make love?" Her fingers were at his shirt, soft as butterflies. "Make you feel like king."

Her hands were cool against the skin of his stomach. "Why should you want to make me feel like a king?" He felt suddenly angry. Mostly, he realised, with himself.

She looked bewildered. "You are nice man, *toubab*. You pay."

Something snapped. He eased her firmly aside and swung his legs off the bed.

Diamante's mouth dropped with disappointment. "You don't want? You want suck?"

He rubbed his hands roughly through his hair. Why the hell was he doing this?

"I have offend you?" There was a hint of shame in her voice.

He turned to face her. When he saw the concern in the pretty black face he smiled reassuringly. "No, Diamante. You haven't offended me. I'm tired, that's all. Let's just talk, eh?"

Her face clouded. "You pay to talk?"

He shook his head in despair. It was the same the world over. "Is money so important to you?"

Suddenly she looked very serious. "When I have money I go to England, maybe. With money no problem. And maybe here I meet nice man. Like you. He takes me to England." Her face was bright with expectation for a moment.

And one day, he thought, pigs might fly. But instead he said softly: "Sure, Diamante, we'll talk and I'll pay."

Her glum expression melted into a smile and she shuffled closer across the bed on her knees.

"You nice man, *toubab*. I like you."

She reached forward and planted a kiss firmly on his lips. It tasted sweet.

Captain Johnny Fraser and Corporal Bill Mather sat at a table in the covered courtyard bar of the bordello and watched the curtain of rain drip steadily from the bamboo awning. The storm was easing now.

Mather finished his beer. "How much longer are they going to be?"

"I wouldn't be surprised if they've fallen asleep on the job," Fraser replied with a grin. He took the last small cigar from the top pocket of his shirt and unravelled the cellophane. "It's been a long day. That damned reception on top of a six-hour flight. I can hardly raise my eyelids let alone anything else."

Neither of the men had been upstairs. Fraser had only ever paid for a woman once in his life and it had been a sleazy, miserable business. He always joked that it was his natural Scots parsimony. He wasn't sure of Mather's views or how he took his pleasures. Certainly it was never when on assignment. Like most aspects of the veteran corporal's private life, it was a closed book.

It hadn't been his team's idea to visit the Green Mamba. As the reception gathering at State House had begun to disperse, one of the guests had informed them that further entertainment had been laid on. The man had introduced himself as Berno, a distant cousin of one of the ministers. An extrovert Jamaican, he had returned to Free Guinea to discover his roots and make his fortune.

He had achieved the latter, anyway, by setting up the Green Mamba in a large, tatty colonial house which he converted into a highly-priced members-only drinking club. The original rear courtyard, which overlooked a spotless white beach, was now a bar where the two SASmen sat.

In the rooms above wealthy expatriates, Government ministers, businessmen and their guests were free to enjoy their pleasures in private. With each other's wives or with the hand-picked house-girls. It was select, orderly decadence with total discretion – provided you could pay the price. Someone, no one said who, had picked up the tab for Fraser's men.

Their heads turned at the commotion at the top of the steps. A gross Lebanese businessman in a tent-like suit of grey silk plodded down. A girl clung to each arm and a third followed, giggling, behind. They could scarcely have been sixteen, although the provocative dresses and make-up added years and a look of artificial sophistication.

"I settle tomorrow," the fat man called to Berno, who sat at a bar stool totting up the night's takings.

"No problem. You are our best customer," Berno said through his permanent wide smile. And the sly eyes clocked-up another row of noughts on his bank statement.

Still the young girls giggled as they clung around the fat man like limpets and smiled up at his face which perspired from the exertion of descending the steps.

As the Lebanese went through the door and the delighted squealings of the girls melted into the night, Berno sauntered across to the SASmen.

"More drinks, my friends?"

Fraser declined and Mather ignored him.

"And you sure you don't want no girls? Like them."

"No," Fraser said. "It's stopped raining, so we'll be going soon."

"You don't like my girls?"

"They look pretty enough," Fraser replied non-committally.

"Sure," Berno said, the broad black face beaming above his flowered shirt. "My house-girls the best. That what the customers pay for. Young virgins."

Fraser's eyes narrowed. "Those three?"

Berno grinned obscenely. "Sure. They come into Sakoto to make their fortunes, see. Their brothers, too. But they soon find there ain't no way to get decent job. Not without education. Or no family connections. So they hear about my glamour pussies at the Green Mamba. Good money, good life and meet important men. Rich men." He waved his big black hands expansively. "We teach 'em social graces first. Like always smile. And always say yes." He chuckled earthily.

"How long have those three girls been at it?" Fraser asked, masking his rising disgust.

"One for a year," Berno replied, warming to his subject. "The other two, this is first night. The big man will show 'em what's what. He likes lot together. Shares 'em with his friends. That take the smiles off their pretty little faces. They'll be well and truly fucked and buggered before the sun rises . . ." Again the earthy chuckle.

"Let's go," Mather hissed.

Berno hadn't heard him. "Village girls good, see. So long they not circumcised. They used to doing what they told. No question."

"Let's go," Mather repeated, louder.

The pimp looked surprised, even hurt. "You don't like my girls here at the Green Mamba?"

Mather rose swiftly to his feet and gripped the collar of Berno's shirt at the neck. He jerked the Jamaican's face to within an inch of his own. "No, you shitbag, frankly I *don't*."

Fraser said quietly: "Leave it out, Bill."

As controlled as ever, Mather released his grip. In his effort to pull away, Berno catapulted himself backwards. He landed in a wicker chair with a resounding crash.

He scowled up at the SAS corporal, his courage returning. "Better here than some cheap fly-boy rent them to tourist. A fuck for the price of a beer, and a dose of clap free extra!" His venom formed flecks of spittle around his thick lips.

Mather's jawline jutted in suppressed anger and he glared at the ceiling. "Let's get out of here, boss."

As Fraser was about to agree, Brummie Turner and Lionel Witcher came down the steps.

"Come on," Fraser called. "We're just leaving."

Brummie shrugged. "I could use a drink . . ."

"The party's over," Fraser snapped.

The four men walked out of the bar and down to the beach. The hotel was only a couple of miles along the shore.

Berno glared after them. He spat contemptuously on the floor and straightened his shirt.

Bloody white trash, he decided savagely. The house-girls of the Green Mamba had been all right for the other two.

"Sorry, boss," Mather muttered as he trudged across the wet sand. "That was unforgivable. Must have been tiredness and the booze. Not as if I haven't seen all this before."

"They were okay, the girls," Brummie declared appreciatively. "I like a bit of chocolate."

"Don't we all," Mather said. "But those kids are used. Exploited."

"They're happy enough to get fed and clothed and earn a bit of pocket-money," Brummie replied. "Don't kid yourself otherwise." He glanced sideways at Witcher who was concentrating on the plod of his own feet. "What about yours? All right was she? Liked an intellectual screw, did she?"

They all laughed. "Bet he read her a Shakespeare sonnet first," Brummie provoked.

Witcher prodded his spectacles higher onto the bridge of his nose. "I don't expect you louts to believe it, but we just talked."

"Oh," Mather said. "Interrogated her did you? Ve aff vays of making you screw . . ."

"Then beat her with his plonker," Brummie guffawed. "Talked indeed. I reckon all the blokes from Int. are queer. Always have."

Witcher took a playful swipe at the stocky NCO, but the older man's reflexes were too quick.

"You were wise," Fraser added. "It's not going to look too clever if we all go down with the clap. This might not be a front-line assignment, but it's not supposed to be a holiday either."

"She was too young, boss," Witcher explained. "Except for the colour, she reminded me of my kid sister. I couldn't bring myself . . ."

"You don't have to," Brummie chimed. "That's what you pay for."

Witcher ignored him. "She only came down from the country a few weeks ago. And, if she's to be believed, everything in Guinea is not as cosy as everyone would have us think. If we do consider this jaunt as a holiday, I reckon we could be in for a rude awakening."

Suddenly the rumble of the white surf, incandescent in the starlight, seemed very loud. Involuntarily the group's pace slowed to catch Lionel Witcher's words. "Apparently those isolated cases of trouble aren't that isolated. Events aren't fully reported in the press. Not surprising as it toes the Government line. But the villagers get to hear. Raids on police-outposts. Knocking off medical supplies from remote clinics. Quietly but regularly."

"Sounds familiar," Fraser said. He recognised the pattern.

Witcher nodded. "Does have a certain ring to it, doesn't it? And it's consistent with other rumours I picked up earlier around Sakoto. This 'when the lions return' business."

Fraser pulled up sharply. "Yes, what the hell's that all about? Back at the State House reception I thought you'd accidentally dropped a grenade."

"When the lions return," Mather repeated thoughtfully. "I heard someone say that in the hotel. A porter, I think."

"Yes," Fraser agreed, "now you mention it, my taxi driver made a similar quip."

"And old Sir Nigel nearly had apoplexy when you asked about lions," Mather recalled. "At the time I just thought you were being a bit thick. So did he."

Witcher grinned. "Oh ye of little faith."

"This expression about lions has some connection with the terrorist activities out in the bush?" Fraser asked.

"I may be putting two and two together to make five, boss, but it would seem likely. Trouble is, no one's willing to say too much. Which is surprising for Free Guinea. Last time we were here you couldn't stop everyone giving their views about the coup." He paused. "It seems that 'When the lions return' has become a sort of catch-phrase. A slogan."

"Like 'You've never had it so good'?" Brummie suggested.

Witcher nodded. "Or maybe a secret code. A greeting between people in the know."

A thoughtful silence fell over the small group as they rounded a clump of coconut palms which hid from view the sweep of beach that flanked The Oceanic hotel. The sequined starglow had begun to melt under the strengthening pale dawn light. Beyond the crashing breakers, the sea shrugged like molten silver.

"Fishermen are out early," Mather observed.

Absently Fraser glanced ahead. Some two hundred yards away three dark figures crouched on the sand, halfway between the trees and the water's edge.

"They've got a big 'un," Brummie said, squinting into the half-light.

Fraser watched the fishermen with only vague interest as they neared. He felt thoroughly exhausted, his mind only on the air-conditioned coolness of the bedroom at The Oceanic. It took several seconds before he focused on the large shape lying on the ground in front of the fishermen. Probably a dolphin. In the increasing light of the dawn sky he could see the glint of its wet skin.

"Boss," Mather called quietly. "Something's wrong."

Even as the SAS corporal spoke one of the fishermen turned. He wore only tattered denim shorts and training shoes. In the dim light his eyes and teeth glittered brightly.

A sudden jabber of alarm carried across the rain-damp sand.

"That's a body!" Fraser gasped in instant realisation. Within a split second the years of training triggered an instinctive reaction. His tiredness and the alcoholic fuzz cleared immediately. His vision sharpened like a telephoto lens. It was as though his brain had suddenly jolted into gear.

Three men. Guineans. Young. Caught in the act. Not fishermen. No dolphin. The carcass that gleamed sea-wet was not grey. It was tanned, human.

As Fraser broke into a sprint his eyes were already searching out the tell-tale glint of weaponry.

The youths broke from their victim like a negative star-burst, black shapes against white sand. Their long legs thrashed. Two of the Guineans were already disappearing into the palms, but the third dithered.

All four SASmen were pounding into the sand, a trail of footprints speeding out behind him.

"Lionel!" Fraser yelled. "Get that bastard!"

Witcher, the youngest of the four men, had already decided to go for the third attacker who was now chasing after his companions.

With a speed that seemed impossible for such a meagre frame, he streaked across the sand like an Olympic athlete. His long legs pumped like the drive rods on an over-fired piston engine.

"Take a look at the body, you two!" Fraser snapped as he started to jog after Witcher.

Meanwhile Lionel Witcher had closed the gap. The black youth turned as he ran. His eyes were wide and sweat streamed down his back. It was a mistake. He didn't see the tree root. With a grip of iron its looped stem snapped over his foot like a trapper's snare. Yelping like a dog, his body continued forward with the momentum of his run. He crashed into the brittle vegetation with bone-shaking force.

Gasping for breath, he twisted round to see the tall thin white man break his run. His hunter had slightly stooped shoulders and a pallor to his bespectacled face. He was panting heavily as he approached warily.

Slowly a smile spread over the black youth's face. This scrawny trash was nothing to fear. He looked scarcely older than himself. Probably a student from Sweden or England on holiday. Just arrived, not yet tanned.

He reached down to touch his ankle. It was swollen and tender, but not broken. Not really even sprained.

His confidence was returning. This he could handle. As he propped himself onto one elbow, his free hand disappeared behind his back to the sheath attached to his belt.

The white tourist had slowed to a walk, the gangly frame now filling his vision, towering over him. Suddenly the black youth made his move.

Lionel Witcher danced backwards as the knife blade slashed at his shins. It gave the Guinean a chance to scurry to his feet. He hobbled back with a slight limp, and his thick lips pulled back into a dog-like snarl. He lurched forward, the knife in his right hand held wide. He was going for a sweep to the kidneys.

Humour flickered momentarily in Witcher's eyes. He stepped back, a cowering gesture, his hands raised in a plea for mercy. He read the look of triumph in his opponent's eyes.

The balled fist around the haft swept into the open target

of the white man's kidneys. The blade edge glittered. Then Witcher stepped forward, his left hand dropping onto the youth's wrist, grabbing it in a vice-like grip. He pivoted his body round until his opponent was forced to cling over his back in a bizarre piggyback posture, the joint of his elbow held straight over Witcher's shoulder.

The SAS corporal stared fascinated at the knife hand trapped in front of him by a double-handed grip. He jerked down once, and the man's elbow joint crackled, the knife sent spinning.

Then, taking a deep breath, he bowed over and heaved the hapless youth over his shoulder. The body crashed untidily into the undergrowth accompanied by a squeal of pain.

"Watch out!" It was Fraser's warning voice.

Witcher spun just in time to see the heavy branch hurtling towards him. He caught only a blurred glimpse of the second youth who was wielding it before it smashed him full in the face. He toppled backwards, falling into Fraser's arms.

"Jes-u-s!" Witcher wailed, clasping his bloodied lips.

"You okay?" Fraser demanded, steadying him.

Witcher spat out a piece of broken tooth and stooped to retrieve his glasses from the sand where they had fallen. As he put them on he saw half-a-dozen youths standing in a menacing half-circle around their injured companion. They looked wary but they were standing their ground. Each carried a knife or a cudgel.

"I'm all right," Witcher mumbled through a mouthful of blood. "You want we should give these villains a malleting?"

The gaggle of nervous youths were helping the floored man into the shadows.

Fraser stooped and picked up the youth's fallen knife and weighed it in his hand. It was a black-bladed military pattern with a bolted haft. "I think discretion might be the better part of valour."

Witcher nodded in agreement. His mouth hurt abominably and he realised the possible folly of wreaking his sense of vengeance. Any number might be lurking amongst the beach palms.

They waited until the youths had disappeared, then returned across the sand to where Brummie and Mather were tending the victim of the attack.

"How is she?" Fraser asked.

Mather shook his head. "Stone dead, boss. We tried heart massage but there wasn't even a flutter of a pulse. Hardly surprising. She'd lost a lot of blood."

The corporal twisted the slender body over and Fraser winced at the vicious slashes in the girl's lower abdomen.

"Jack the Ripper job," Brummie muttered in disgust. "Fucking butchers."

Witcher peered distastefully at the mess. "Maybe it was a sex motive . . ."

Mather shrugged. "Could be. She's topless, just wearing the bottom part. Going for an early morning swim."

"Jesus," Fraser whispered, realisation suddenly dawning.

"Yes," Brummie confirmed grimly. "It's the Swedish bird from the hotel. What's her name? Ingrid."

"Looks like they took some money too," Mather observed. He held up an empty purse. "They were going through her beach-bag when we arrived."

Witcher rubbed at his mouth painfully. "Poor cow. And to think I nearly got one of the bastards."

Brummie looked up from the corpse. "Perhaps next time you could try a bit harder," he said tersely. The fact that Ingrid had been flirting with him earlier made the whole disgusting business more personal.

Fraser intervened. "Okay, lads. This is no time for recriminations. There could be a dozen or more of them in the trees and they could be armed with more than coconuts. Let's get her body back to the hotel."

As if to underline his warning, a ripple of laughter drifted across the beach from the undergrowth. There were several voices, high-pitched and giggling nervously. The sound of frightened men who suddenly realised that they had got away with something daring.

Then the bravado began. It started quietly with one voice from the darkness. Then others joined, adding gradually like a taunting drumbeat.

"Jat-o! – Jat-o! – Jat-o!"

The chant grew louder as more voices joined in and the momentum increased to a tom-tom rhythm until it could be heard above the rush of the breakers.

"JAT-O! – JAT-O! – JAT-O!"

3

Mo Sinclair glanced at her watch for the fifth time in as many minutes. If he was much later she would never get there today.

Hands thrust into the pockets of her tight faded jeans, she strutted impatiently back and forth beneath the blossom of the giant orange tree.

Absently she kicked at the congealed mud of the parking area in front of the bungalow. For once the sun had forced its way through the persistent rainclouds and already its warmth was drying out the top layer of earth. It only served to remind her that time was moving on. Again she glanced at her watch.

"A watched kettle never boils."

She hadn't heard her father come out onto the verandah. In fact he had been standing there for several minutes, sipping at his coffee, and patiently going over the coming day's schedule of the Agricultural Research Station in the grounds of which his bungalow had been erected.

Not for the first time he wondered where Mo got her dynamism and impatience from. He had long ago learned to live with the slow natural pace of African life, learned to live with it and enjoy it. So it must be from his wife that his daughter had inherited her high spirits and the go-getting attitude that the black workers at the Station found so bewildering.

"Oh, hello, Dad," she said, her straight auburn hair swirling softly from her shoulders as she turned. "I tried to creep out without waking you."

Yes, he thought as he watched her small, almost boyish figure, hardly complimented by the masculine red-check shirt and jeans, as she bounded towards him. That's where you get all that drive and nervous energy. From your dear mother, God rest her. Like your looks. Scarcely five feet tall in your socks, but full of energy and movement that keeps your body hard and trim without a spare ounce of fat.

The face, too. That was Emily Sinclair's. Slightly too-broad cheeks, tapering to an impudent urchin chin, with dimples and eyes that defied you not to laugh with her. Even the freckles were the same, nearly hidden beneath a light veneer of suntan.

Mo was thirty now and he knew that he couldn't possibly have her here just to himself for much longer. Wistfully Ralph Sinclair thought how lucky he had been to have such a lively reminder of his wife these past ten lonely years. Not just a daughter, but a friend and companion too.

"You didn't wake me, Maureen," he said. "I wanted to make an early start today." He always used her full name, preferring it to the abbreviation that had stuck from childhood when her Wolof nanny couldn't get her tongue around the full pronunciation. "I suppose you're waiting for Sunday?"

When Mo smiled she did so with her whole face. "Aren't I always, Dad? He'll be the death of me, he really will. He took the Suzuki home last night and said he'd get it fixed by the garage before he came in this morning. I mean it was only the carburettor."

Sinclair's bushy black eyebrows raised beneath his thinning sun-white hair and he laughed. "You ought to know better than that. He's probably been taking his mates and his whole family round in it to visit his cousins. Showing it off." He eased his large body down onto the top verandah step. "Probably ended up in a party. He's a devil for oversleeping at the best of times."

"Well, he'll get a piece of my mind if he has."

Sinclair smiled. "He'll have a good excuse. He's the best storyteller in his village."

Mo's mouth pouted stubbornly. "He'll *need* to be."

"What's the hurry anyway?"

"I want to get up to Kunkunda in daylight."

Sinclair nodded in sympathy. It was a good seven-hour

drive to the island nature reserve and in the rains there was no guarantee what the roads would be like. "Take an extra day. You can always stop off with friends if you don't make it by nightfall."

She gave her father an exasperated little smile. "Dad, I *am* trying to get the practice going. My clients are always complaining that I spend too much time there as it is. Rather than here where they need me."

It was still hard for Ralph Sinclair to appreciate the demand his daughter was in since she'd qualified as a veterinary surgeon. Although she had loved animals since she could distinguish them from humans, and had a natural affinity with them, to him she was still the same tomboy in pigtails she'd been fifteen years ago. To think she was wanted to attend everything from an expatriate child's sick rabbit or a villager's lame goat to a fevered horse in the Presidential stables was difficult to grasp.

Typically she worried about her 'clients' when there was clearly no need. There were few vets in Free Guinea and none as pretty, charming and dedicated as Mo.

Of course, thought Sinclair, she could have life a lot easier if only she would concentrate on her practice and give up trying to save every injured animal waif and stray she came across. Everything from deer, monkeys, horses and, even on one occasion, a young lioness.

Invariably they would end up on the Kunkunda Island Reserve to be gently reintroduced back into the wilds or, sometimes, for the first time since being born into captivity, safe from poachers and trophy-hunters.

"I'm sorry, Maureen," Sinclair said. "I tend to forget how it must be to run a profitable practice. That's what comes of being a civil servant, you see. I'd make a hopeless businessman."

Mo put her arm around his neck and pecked his cheek. "Nonsense, Dad. You'd make a smashing businessman. You just wouldn't make any profit, that's all."

"Well, if you are going to Kunkunda, presumably you'll be taking Charlie with you. That, at least, will be a relief."

She shook her head emphatically. "He's not ready, Dad.

It'll take a few more weeks yet. He's got to trust me thoroughly before I take him to the reserve. If he runs off by himself, he won't last a couple of days in the wild."

Sinclair's face clouded. His disappointment verged on despair.

Charlie was the bane of his life.

The boisterous young chimpanzee had been brought to Mo, having been confiscated by Customs men from one of many unscrupulous wildlife traders who operated throughout West Africa. Having been injured and weakened by the appallingly small crate, which had been used so that he could be passed off as a dog in transit, poor Charlie had been in dire need of medical treatment.

Soft-hearted as ever, Mo had leapt at the opportunity of caring for him with the idea of eventually introducing him to the wild until he could fend for himself. He had repaid her kindness by creating havoc and chaos throughout the Agricultural Research Station.

Now he was advanced enough in his therapy to live by himself in the orange tree outside the bungalow. It was from one of its longer branches that he now sat and watched Mo and her father. Uncannily Charlie seemed to know when he was the topic of conversation. But then, with a record like his, it was hardly surprising that his name was so frequently taken in vain.

Intelligent brown eyes watched them steadily as he sucked idly on a leaf. He drew back his lips and grinned hugely, showing a lot of teeth and gums. He began bouncing slowly on the branch to attract attention.

"He knows you're going," Sinclair observed. "He doesn't like it. It's going to be hell. Last week he reorganised my office for me. It took two days to sort things out. You're the only one who can handle him, Maureen, and he's getting too much of a handful."

A loud shriek of agreement came across from the orange tree.

Mo hugged her father. "You're an angel, Dad. I promise you it won't be long. Charlie's learning fast. Now at least he's stopped trying to play with snakes; last week he started hitting one with a branch."

Sinclair found little consolation in the news. "He's going to give me real aggravation while you're gone. He takes it out on me." He gave a humourless laugh of exasperation.

At that moment the Suzuki jeep roared into view along the dirt track, slowing just in time for one of the workers to swing open the tall mesh gates of the Station compound.

Grinning and waving, Sunday raced into the parking area like a Grand Prix driver in a four-wheel drift, grinding to a halt just millimetres from the edge of the verandah.

Mo and her father winced involuntarily. Twice in recent months the wooden balustrade had needed repairs after one of Sunday's more extravagant manoeuvres.

By the time they'd opened their eyes the 23-year-old Wolof had leapt out of the Suzuki, full of excitement.

"I got news!" he announced.

Mo put on her disapproving face. "Never mind your news, Sunday, where in goodness have you been?"

He beamed. "Them boys at garage. They say car it not ready. They say it need new headlight."

Mo frowned. "It didn't go in for headlights. We asked them to tune the engine. It sounded like a sick hippo."

Sunday frowned thoughtfully. "It still sound like sick hippo. But it goes good, yes? You see?"

"We saw," Sinclair muttered, peering forward at the front of the Suzuki now buried in the flowerbed. "What's wrong with the headlamp?"

"Nothing!" Sunday replied indignantly. "There isn't one." The explanation was obvious.

Mo took a defiant stance with her fists planted firmly on her slim hips. "It had two perfectly good headlamps when you took it last night. Now there's only one. Did you crash it?"

"Certainly not! I am *good* driver!"

"Then what happened to it?" Mo demanded.

The boy shrugged. "Garage say they have other Suzuki with no headlights. They say we have two." The logic was undeniable. "Now each car has one. Now both see in the dark."

Sinclair shook his head in slow despair. "Sweet Jesus, bloody damn imbeciles."

Sunday frowned and nodded gravely. "That's what I tell them. Sweet Jesus, bloody damn imbeciles, I tell them."

It was with difficulty that Mo stifled her involuntary laughter. Quickly she turned her face away.

Anxious to please, Sunday added: "But garage they say they gave you new spare tyre."

"I suppose the other Suzuki had two?" Sinclair asked.

Sunday was surprised. "You know?"

Slowly Sinclair scratched his head. "If I don't know Guinean garages by now, Sunday, I never will. But that still doesn't tell us why you're so late. Slept well did you?"

The boy smiled slyly. "Sure. I sleep good. But it was that bloody damned imbecile in garage."

"Your cousin?"

Sunday looked puzzled, not knowing what that had to do with anything. "Yes, he tells me. He tells me that The Captain is here."

"The Captain?" Mo echoed. There was only one man who had that name in the area around the Agricultural Research Station.

"Captain Fraser?" Sinclair asked.

Sunday's face was alight with excitement. "Yes! My cousin's cousin is taximan. He says he brings The Captain last night from the airport. He goes to hotel. Then later with friends he goes to see the Big Man."

"President Jammeh?" Sinclair stroked his chin and glanced at Mo. Her face was ashen and she had a distant look in her eyes.

"Sure," Sunday said. "That cousin, he is good man. He does not make stories. It is The Captain he says."

"Was he in uniform?" Sinclair asked carefully.

"No. He was not dressed like a soldier. Not like before."

Sinclair turned to Mo. "You didn't tell me Johnny Fraser was coming."

"I didn't know, Dad. We haven't corresponded for over a year."

"I see," Sinclair said. He couldn't understand her evident lack of enthusiasm. They had become great friends after the coup. Fraser had helped both him and Mo in construction work at the Station, in her practice and at her camp at

Kunkunda Island. They had made a handsome couple, too. The tall, sunburnt Scots officer and his diminutive daughter, for once unaccountably concerned with her appearance and clothes. Even now he could recall their laughter together and the sudden poignant silences. The way they looked at each other.

"I hope it doesn't mean trouble," Sinclair thought aloud. "Perhaps it's to do with those troublemakers up-country."

Mo shrugged, uninterested. "They're hardly worth a police ranger. Silly boys who got big ideas during the coup."

"Still, he's almost certain to pay us a visit. He'll want to see you."

Mo's brown eyes clouded. "Well, I'm afraid The Captain's going to be out of luck. I'll be at Kunkunda Island."

"Only for two days."

She tossed her hair. "Actually, Dad, I was thinking on what you said. I do have a lot to do up there. Plenty to keep me busy for a week or two, and I do feel I need a rest."

"Oh?" He couldn't disguise his surprise. "Well, I can't pretend it isn't what you need. You've been working much too hard. But you'd better take Sunday with you."

"You can't spare him for that long."

Sinclair smiled kindly. "I'll manage, Maureen. I'd be happier for him to go with you while there's any chance of trouble up-country."

"I'm okay," Mo was adamant. "I'd prefer to go alone. Besides, Insect's there. She'll look after me."

"Insect is a mentally-retarded teenage girl, Maureen, not a bodyguard."

"Dad . . ." Imploring.

As always he gave in.

The sudden honking noise made them both jump.

Charlie, whooping with delight and gnashing his teeth, sat in the driver's seat of the Suzuki holding the wheel in both hands.

They all laughed, and as they did Ralph Sinclair realised he really had been making a lot of fuss about nothing.

The meeting went well.

Captain Fraser and his team, accompanied by Sir Nigel

de Burgh, had found President Jammeh in ebullient good-humour.

Even Colonel Kwofie was gracious and helpful without a trace of the previous evening's animosity. Although Johnny Fraser had warned his men to expect natural resentment from the Head of State Security – as they themselves might well feel if the roles had been reversed – he found himself mildly surprised by the sudden change of attitude.

After a good morning's sleep and a square meal everything looked more promising. The noonday sun had shone brightly from a clear sky into the airy office in State House. The atmosphere was cordial and iced fruit drinks were served. Only the inevitable discussion about the murdered Swedish girl served to remind Fraser of the unaccountable feeling of unease he had felt since his arrival.

"My dear Captain," Jammeh had begun. "I want you to understand that you will have my fullest support in performing your duties here. And Colonel Kwofie will afford you every assistance. Now please explain to me, how can we expect things to develop over the coming months?"

Particularly for Sir Nigel's and Kwofie's benefit, Fraser went carefully over the agreement reached in London between Whitehall and Jammeh.

That was that the British Army Training Team would be expected to advise the President on all aspects of personal and general internal security. It would involve working closely with the two State Security services, the Presidential Guard and the Gendarmerie, to establish the source of any possible threat to the President's own life, his ministers or any attempt to overthrow the legal constitutional system.

In other words, the BATT had *carte blanche* in theory – even if, in practice, it would need co-operation if its advice was to be acted on effectively.

The only specific already decided on was that the assignment would include an 'assessment' of the PGs. This was a euphemism for weeding out potential subversive or unsuitable recruits, and re-training the remainder to an efficient standard to maintain the constitution. Secondly, an idea which was reluctantly accepted by Jammeh himself, was to be the formation of a personal bodyguard for the

President, hand-picked from the best available troops or policemen.

Patiently Johnny Fraser had explained that he was 2 IC, or second-in-command of one of the 80-man SAS squadrons which had served in the Falklands. That left the squadron's major back home to continue commanding the bulk of the depleted unit. Likewise Sergeant Brummie Turner had been appointed Acting Staff-Sergeant of the Free Guinea task force, so that the squadron's Sergeant Major would be free to conduct his regular administrative duties in Hereford.

"That leaves me here as 2 IC to the Captain," Brummie explained to Kwofie. Thankfully Mather had persuaded him to abandon his 'pyjama' trousers and borrow one of his own suits. While he left the jacket buttons undone the bad fit scarcely noticed, except for an unusual expanse of white ankle between sock and trouser cuff.

"I'll be responsible initially for logistics of our team, quartering, feeding and watering the little brutes," he explained to Kwofie and the two men laughed together. "Little buggers always need mothering no matter how big an' ugly they get, eh?"

"This is true!" the Colonel agreed in the manner of a man who knew all the problems of command.

"Once that's done," Brummie went on, "my main responsibility will be in charge of our Three Team who'll be running the training programme for your crack Guards." Fraser almost smiled at Brummie's rather obvious effort not to offend the black commander. "I'll also be looking at one or two security aspects. Airports, docks, that sort of thing. You'll have that buttoned up, of course, but we might think of a new trick or two."

Kwofie straightened his fingers over his knees and nodded appreciatively.

The sergeant elaborated how the four-man Three Team was in fact drawn from a different squadron.

"We have a special Bodyguard Squad within D Squadron," Fraser added. "They're all expert in special weapons and unarmed combat. They're also qualified instructors."

"And the rest of your force?" Jammeh asked. He found all the military terminology baffling, but was making a determined effort to understand it.

"We four, this team, form Tactical Headquarters," Fraser said, "or the command unit, if you prefer. Three Team just mentioned are our training unit. Then we have two more four-man operational units, Two and Four Teams. They are drawn from our squadron's Boat Troop. They're all experts with boats. Aspiring sailors who should really have joined the Royal Navy. It seemed appropriate."

"Ah!" Jammeh grasped the point. "Because of our great Kebba River. I understand."

"Precisely."

"But what is their purpose?"

Two and Four Teams, the Captain expanded, would be part of the general intelligence operation under Lionel Witcher's control, manning river patrols and inland observation posts or OPs. It would be their job to gauge unusual activities or movements which might indicate the presence of insurgents.

"Or lack of them," Kwofie pointed out politely. "I shall see that you have experts on hand in this task from the Guards or the Gendarmerie."

"A most generous offer," Fraser said, smiling, "but unnecessary. My men are trained to act alone."

"But there will be much that they do not understand. This is a strange country to them. They may mistakenly indulge in rash action." He waved his hand expressively.

"Colonel," Fraser said firmly. "We have our methods. And, contrary to popular mythology, the main function of the SAS is merely to observe. To observe unnoticed and to observe *intelligently*."

Jammeh leaned forward over his vast mahogany desk. "I have worked with The Captain, Colonel – you must have no fears of rash action or bad decision."

Kwofie shrugged, uncertain. "If you are sure, Mr President." He turned and indicated Corporal Bill Mather who had been sitting in watchful silence. "And the fourth member of your HQ Team?"

Mather nodded, but let Fraser explain.

"Bill is our signals expert. He'll establish our independent communications set-up in Free Guinea, and direct-links with our Hereford base in England."

Jammeh pursed his lips. "Impressive."

"You will not direct communications through your High Commission?" Kwofie asked.

Sir Nigel de Burgh, who had been sitting with a slightly bemused expression on his face, suddenly seemed to wake up. "I trust communications *will* be passing through the *proper* authorised channels?"

"They will, sir," Mather confirmed. "But we need to maintain our own direct contact for logistical purposes. All official exchanges will naturally pass through the High Commission."

Fraser added that there would be a small Logistics Support Group to back up the four 'Sabre' teams that made up his force. That Group would comprise two cooks, an armourer to look after their small arsenal of weapons and equipment, a vehicle mechanic attached from REME, and a medical officer who would run the BATT's medical aid post.

"A total contingent of just twenty-one men," Kwofie observed, a faint smile on his face, which Fraser interpreted as relief. Perhaps the British soldiers did not represent a threat to his authority after all.

"You would not prefer more?" Jammeh asked.

Fraser laugher. "Soldiers always want more, Mr President. But they are sufficient for a training and advisory team for a country of this size. In truth, if you have too many they just get in each other's way and duplicate effort. Besides we would prefer to remain unobtrusive. Your forces already have a fine Officer Corps and a distinguished commander."

Graciously Colonel Kwofie inclined his head.

"Perhaps it would be possible for us to go on one of your anti-insurgent patrols, Colonel?" Lionel Witcher said. "Just to observe, you understand. You never know, we may be able to make some constructive suggestions."

Kwofie was slow to respond, but Jammeh evidently thought it was an excellent idea. "Of course, of course. It shall be arranged at the earliest opportunity."

As the meeting broke up President Jammeh beckoned Fraser to wait behind.

When the ornate mahogany double-doors were shut the Guinean leader led the SAS officer onto the balcony. Below them, beyond the flowering gardens and the walls of State House, the sweep of white beach shimmered in dazzling sunlight. It was deserted except for an off-duty PG soldier jogging alongside the unravelling surf. Out in the sea-haze, which obscured the far bank of the Kebba River estuary, formations of dolphins leapt from the water creating bright white scars in the shrugging blue swell.

"It's beautiful," Fraser said. He meant it.

Jammeh didn't answer for a moment. He rested his hands on the edge of the balcony, his eyes fixed on some imagined spot on the unseen horizon.

At last he turned. "Yes, it is truly beautiful, old friend. The whole of Africa is beautiful. It is vast and magnificent and men are humbled. Humbled by its size, its wildness and its power. That is the way it has always been, and always should be. Yet now man is tearing himself and the land apart here, driven by greed and revenge. Now he thinks he is bigger than the land that has always dominated his life."

The jovial face was unsmiling; the eyes behind the tortoiseshell glasses sad. "The words of a romantic and a philosopher? Perhaps, too, the words of a fool."

Fraser felt uncomfortable. "Mr President?"

Jammeh seated himself on the parapet, and carefully arranged his white robe. "Last night at the reception our mutual friend, Mr Lionel Witcher, said something that shocked me." Fraser went to speak, but the man held up a silencing hand. "It was not offensive, it is just that we do not speak of such things here in State House. There is an unspoken agreement that no outward acknowledgement is given of what the people call The Lions. In Mandinka language they are called the Jatos.

"Perhaps we think that if we do not talk of them, these Jatos will go away. People will lose interest. But I realise I cannot continue to hide this from you. Your man Lionel is very good. I have much respect for him. So soon he discovered the secret that we have been hiding successfully from the outside world."

Fraser felt his mouth go dry. "How big *is* the threat, Mr President?"

Jammeh shrugged. "I truly cannot say. Their influence is widespread, but whenever we have caught these people there are only one or two at the most. Always they know only one leader but each time that leader is different. And these people, they use what I think you call code-names that are not their own. It is like dealing with ghostly spirits. For a long time we thought these men are just individual gangs of political dissenters. Perhaps, we say, they flee into the bush after the coup fails."

"But they were not?"

"One or two only. Most of these men they are recruited since the coup. And we gradually begin to realise that these are small men. Part of a much bigger organisation. But how big? It is not possible to say."

Fraser had been half-anticipating Jammeh's revelation. It still came as something of a shock to hear his worst fears confirmed.

"It's a classic cell system, Mr President. Virtually impossible to break down. You see, it's like a pyramid structure of three-man cells. Each insurgent operates independently, reporting to just one boss. Often he won't even know the other man working for his boss. But that boss is himself one of two others working for another leader further up the pyramid. The bigger the organisation gets, the more difficult it is to destroy it. Or find out how it works."

Jammeh nodded sagely. He had already discovered that. "But a pyramid, it must come to a head."

"Do you know who that is?"

Jammeh again turned his head and gazed out into the sea mist. "He is just known as The Jato."

"The Lion?"

"The Lion of Freedom."

"Is he in the country?"

"No one knows. Some say he is. Some say not. One day it is said he has a camp over the border. Others say he always is moving from village to village in the remote up-country areas."

It was a pattern Fraser had come across in many parts of the world. "What sort of mischief does he get up to?"

"You must understand that few are willing to talk. Some of those that speak, later they are found dead. Sometimes their stomachs are torn open like an attack with a lion's claw. It is a crude but effective way of maintaining silence from these people. There is much sinister about them. Our people have much respect for mystery and the unexplained." Still he stared out to sea, his voice dropping to almost a whisper. "So I am sure we do not know everything that is done. Mostly there is talk. Propaganda talk in the villages. In the mosques. They appear to buy support with medical and food supplies."

"Ah," Fraser said. "The black market rice?"

Jammeh relaxed. It was as though he had unburdened himself of the strain of trying to conceal the truth. "Again your man Lionel puts his finger on another problem. It is true that we can afford to distribute little of the food aid we are sent. There is a lot on the black market and the Jatos have cornered it in their regions. They hand it out in return for co-operation. It serves to undermine all the efforts my Government makes."

"And the medical supplies?"

"Medical missions and clinics have been raided. Medicines have been taken at gunpoint. So in some areas you only receive treatment if you support the Jatos."

Fraser nodded in understanding. "Has anyone else been the target of attack? PGs or the police?"

"Thankfully no. The insurgents prefer to melt away rather than to fight." Jammeh smiled wanly. "That is at least a consolation."

The captain shook his head. "I'm afraid not. It will happen as their confidence increases. Tell me, do you have any insurgent prisoners that we could talk to?"

"No," Jammeh replied. "The few we had positive evidence about attempted to escape. It is apparently part of their training to try, however suicidal. Those who did not get away were shot dead in their attempt."

"I see," Fraser said, a hard edge to his voice. His eyes narrowed as he studied Jammeh's face for a flicker of guilt or conscience. Either the man was a brilliant actor or else he genuinely believed that the deaths in police custody were unavoidable. "And tell me, Mr President, has this man Jato said what his aims are?"

Jammeh stood up and led the way back into his office. As he walked slowly he said: "It is the usual garbled concoction, I gather. He complains of poverty and lack of basic foodstuffs, yet few die in Free Guinea of malnutrition. I am accused of neo-colonialism by allowing the British and Swedes to run the businesses they set up here. My ministers are accused of mismanagement and all officials of corruption, inter-tribal animosity and nepotism."

Fraser took his seat opposite Jammeh as the big man eased himself into the carved wooden chair that looked more like a throne. "How much grounds would *you* say he has for complaint?"

The President held him in a steady gaze. "This is Africa, my friend, so such claims can never be completely denied. But here I am aware of our shortcomings. As fast as I can I am trying to Africanise businesses. To replace Europeans with Guinean managers. But there are few educated people. I am constantly driving against corruption and people in power of granting favours to their family and friends. You have been to other African countries, Captain. You know the unbelievable chaos they create for themselves. You must know how much better it is here?"

"There is stability," Fraser conceded non-committally.

"Democracy and human rights. That is something I predict you will not hear this man Jato preach." Jammeh's eyes seemed to mist, his voice mellowed. "It is the most precious of gifts in this angry land of Africa. I know this thing. Yet the more the people are given, the more they want. Here the blackman mixes freely with the white. He is proud because it is *his* land and he can choose his leaders. He is not rich, but he does not starve. If there is corruption then the guilty are punished when they are found out. Favouritism exists, of course, but it is illegal."

Again Jammeh looked directly at Fraser. "I am but one man, my friend. I can only set an example and choose from the politicians the people elect to run our country. I cannot run the Government single-handed. You must know that, throughout the whole Third World, when a man gets a job of influence or power he sees it as the chance of his lifetime to make his fortune while he can. At the next election or coup he may be thrown out and be back in his village.

"All these efforts I make for my people and still it is not enough."

The office had taken on the hushed intensity of a confessional-box. It made the quiet trilling of the telephone buzzer sound disproportionally loud. Jammeh hesitated before reaching for the receiver. "Nowadays I dread answering this thing. It never brings good news."

He smiled and picked it up. As he listened the expression on his face told Fraser that the President had been right.

After a few moments he interrupted the caller with some short, precise questions. Then Jammeh slowly replaced the handset.

When he looked up the brown eyes behind the tortoiseshell glasses were moist. "I am afraid, my friend, that you were correct. At midday today an isolated police-post in the up-country region was attacked. Three policemen were killed."

"We've got to get out and see for ourselves, boss." Lionel Witcher was adamant.

The four SASmen were sitting together in a secluded corner of the bar at The Oceanic hotel.

"I agree," Fraser replied, "but I don't want to call on Kwofie for transport. He'll insist on providing a driver and everything will be reported straight back to him, you can be sure of that."

They had already discovered that suitable hire cars weren't available outside the tourist season. "A taxi?" Mather suggested.

Fraser lit up one of his small cigars. "No. That'll restrict us to the roads. And it's likely to grind to a halt at the slightest flooding."

"I don't fancy enlisting the High Commissioner's help," Brummie said. "I get the feeling we're not his flavour of the month."

"I think we can rely on Sir Nigel to be as obstructive as diplomatically possible," Fraser observed drily. "He's pretty desperate to keep the lid on things here until he retires next year."

"What about old Ralph Sinclair?" Witcher suggested. "He might lend us a vehicle."

Fraser glanced up. It was a sound idea. During their last tour after the coup the Sinclairs had become good friends. He was sure that Ralph would offer him every assistance if asked. Fraser's hesitation was on purely personal grounds.

He had become very close to the man's daughter. For a confirmed bachelor it was a little too close for comfort. For the first time in his life he had thought he could hear the sound of church bells in the distance. Mo Sinclair had been the only woman out of the many in his life he had ever seriously considered marrying.

As was the way of things in the Army, he had received his marching orders from Hereford on the morning of the day he had planned to propose. He only had time to send a hastily-scrawled note before he caught the return flight back to England.

Although he had written consistently afterwards Mo's chatty and flirtatious return letters had suddenly cooled after a few months. Endearments had become steadily more sparse. Eventually they disappeared.

Finally she had informed him that her veterinary work demanded so much from her that she had little time for luxuries like letter-writing. With great reluctance Fraser had at last accepted the unwritten message between the lines.

It was ironic, he thought, that whilst he was blessed with a personality that seemed to draw the opposite sex like a magnet, the one girl he had ever really wanted for keeps had lost interest.

Without enthusiasm he said: "I guess it's worth a try, Lionel. We'll take a taxi out to the Research Station first thing tomorrow."

Ralph Sinclair was just returning from his early morning inspection of the test-beds when the battered taxi pulled up outside the bungalow. He recognised the SAS captain and the bespectacled Corporal Witcher immediately.

"I knew it wouldn't be long before you came," Sinclair announced, settling himself in the deep armchair with floral covers that wouldn't have looked out of place in an English country cottage.

Fraser shook his head in disbelief. "I see the old bush telegraph is still working efficiently."

"About the only thing that is," Sinclair chuckled. "I once heard it said that the bush-telegraph moves just slightly quicker than a fast car. Amazing. But, you know, I'm afraid you've missed Maureen by a day. I'm sure she'll be sorry about that."

It seemed as though the bush-telegraph was fallible after all, Fraser thought. "That's a shame, Ralph. But we'll be around for a while so I'm sure we'll all have the chance of getting together." In truth, he was thankful she was away. It could have been embarrassing.

Sinclair's thick eyebrows knitted together. "Am I allowed to guess why you're here? This rubbish with the Lions, I suppose?"

"You know about that?"

Sinclair gave a snort of disgust. "What there is to know about that lot seems precious little. If they're anything like Omar Pheko's mob, they're bad news. It cost this country millions of pounds to put right the damage. Plunged us into debt with the IMF. It'll take a poor country like this ten years to recover fully."

"Do you know who they are?" Witcher asked.

Sinclair grimaced. "No one does for sure. Some say they're rebels who fled into the bush after the coup. Others say they've been trained in Cuba. Sunday here says he's heard they've been trained in Libya. Isn't that right?"

Sinclair's boy, Sunday, had seated himself by the

shuttered windows and had been grinning in awe at the soldiers who had impressed him so much during the coup. He nodded happily. "They say this man is new. They say he trains in Libya. He is a mighty man. Tall, big, and with the strength of a lion."

Sinclair snorted again at the description.

Taking his cue from his boss, Sunday looked deeply serious. "Bloody damn imbeciles."

The SASmen suppressed their smiles. "I suppose you don't have any names?" Witcher pressed.

"Just Jato," Sunday replied. "That is what they call the big man. But no one sees him. But they say he is mighty powerful. Everyone fears him."

"Well he won't get far if he uses the same methods as Omar Pheko," Sinclair said with feeling. "You remember when he made those radio broadcasts during the coup? All those demented rantings. Sounded like Adolf Hitler. The man was an imbecile."

"Perhaps they've learned their lesson this time," Witcher observed.

"Well, you could be right," Sinclair admitted. "This Jato fellow never talks about Communists. No one in the Guinea wants a Godless society. They like to be sure Allah's on their side." He chuckled. "They need his favours for the rains. The marabou are the link between the ordinary people and Allah. No, Jato preaches a Muslim revolution."

Fraser let out a low whistle. "That *is* interesting. Mind you, I suppose Muslim fundamentalism is the thing to sell an Islamic society."

"It's only the packaging," Witcher added. "There are few differences between Islam and Socialism. Mostly Allah. Once you've had your revolution, it's easy to blur the distinctions." He turned to Sunday. "What sort of support has Jato got?"

Sunday was pleased to be included in such an important conversation. "He is big man. Mostly up-country. Many hear him talk. Many people bring his message to the villages. The mullahs talk highly of him. And he bring food and medicines. People say this man, he good. He is honest, his words are true."

"Bloody hearts-and-minds," Brummie muttered.

"Taking our weapons," Mather agreed.

Sinclair was confused. "I don't understand."

"Our outfit has pioneered anti-insurgency techniques," Fraser explained. "And the first thing one should learn is that you can't support a dishonest regime and win in the long term. The second is that peasants around the world don't really give a toss about politics. They just want to be left alone to scratch a living. Most, though, are interfered with by Government or gun-toting militia who are thoroughly corrupt. In desperation the peasant will turn to anyone who promises him a better life. It's only natural.

"So if you're fighting insurgents you have to make sure the peasant realises you can offer *more* than the insurgents. And make *sure* he gets it."

"Hearts-and-minds?" Sinclair asked.

Fraser nodded. "First eliminate intimidation by the Government in power. Then deliver the goods you've promised. Clean water supplies, medicines, food . . . Then you can get at the insurgents because then they start to lose their grass-roots support with the people."

"Ah!" Sinclair exclaimed. "Now I see what you mean. This Jato fellow is using your weapons. He's doing what you would do to combat his influence."

Witcher said: "This is Moscow, boss. Gadaffi goes for the short-term coup. The Russians take the long-term philosophical approach. If the Libyans *are* fronting this through their Islamic Legion, then there's no doubt that either Moscow or Havana is heavily involved too."

"This is losing me . . ." Sinclair said. "I certainly didn't realise this Jato chap was that significant."

At that moment the cook brought in tea and biscuits, under a tirade of orders from Sunday.

"I haven't seen young Kali around," Fraser said, suddenly reminded of the young trainee vet who had worked with Mo. "Is he still with you?"

"No," Sinclair replied, "he left to study. He was a bright lad and we're all hoping he'll return soon, fully qualified. Maureen could certainly do with his help. It's too much for her now, trying to run her practice and working up at Kunkunda Reserve."

"That's where she is now?"

"Yes. She drove up yesterday morning."

"So you're a vehicle short?"

A smile slowly spread over Sinclair's face. "Don't tell me the Army makes you walk everywhere nowadays."

Fraser laughed. "Our vehicles come out next week with the main party. We're trying to do a little informal reconnaissance. When we were last here we made good friends at many of the up-country villages, so it seemed a good opportunity to re-establish old links."

Sinclair sipped thoughtfully at his tea. "You might not find them as friendly this time. As Sunday was saying, that's very much Jato territory nowadays."

"We're loaded down with glass beads," Brummie quipped.

Ralph Sinclair inclined his head towards the window. "You can borrow my Merc G-wagen. She's not very luxurious but she's got four-wheel drive and good ground clearance. How long would you need it?"

"Three days. We'd be back the day after tomorrow."

"No problems," Sinclair grinned. "I'm not planning to go to Sakoto until the weekend. And take Sunday with you. He's a country boy and knows his way around. Useful if you have to make cross-country detours because of the rains. And for finding you petrol. Most of the stations are nearly dry and they might not sell to *toubabs*."

"It's a bad shortage?"

"Bad enough. It's the worst yet. Silly thing is there are two tankers sitting off the coast. But they won't land the stuff until Jammeh coughs up the money."

Fraser exchanged glances with Witcher. That didn't sound good. He said: "Anyway, Ralph, we'd be most grateful if you can spare him. Is that all right by you, Sunday?"

"No problem, man, no problem." His delighted expression belied the casual agreement.

From the kitchen came a tremendous crashing of crockery and a hysterical scream from the cook. Seconds later, Charlie the chimpanzee swaggered into the room, waving a teapot over his head and whooping in excitement. He stopped and blinked at the strangers in the room, baring his teeth in a half-snarl, half-grin. The yell of the cook in hot pursuit decided the ape that it would be safer up his tree in the compound than with these newcomers.

Grabbing a handful of biscuits from the plate on the table as he went, Charlie gambolled out of the door.

Mather nudged Brummie in the ribs. "Aren't you going to introduce me to your old dad?"

4

There was no made-up road along the south bank of the Kebba River, just a dusty laterite track which often became impassable in the rains. It was the main reason why the South had remained under-developed.

But the north-bank tarmac road which ran out of Sakoto was in quite good condition once it cleared the urban shanties of Bankanra and Nyantaba.

Under a wash of clear blue sky, the G-wagen made good progress as Sunday gunned it for all it was worth. There was little traffic. Mostly colourful minibus bush-taxis, the occasional lorry over-loaded with market produce and lift-hitching locals, and sometimes an official car on government business.

Even the roadside villages warranted no more than a ferocious warning hoot as Sunday stamped on the accelerator. Emaciated goats, sheep and chickens scampered in terror. Women, old men and infants sitting under the village trees would invariably turn and wave.

"*Toubab! Toubab! Toubab!*" The delighted squeal of the children followed them as they sped by.

"Makes you feel like bleedin' royalty, doesn't it?" Brummie grinned. He'd just discovered that, after waving to heavily-laden cyclists going in the opposite direction, they would try to turn and wave – with dire consequences. It was good fun.

As they moved deeper inland, the ugly corrugated-iron shacks and fences of the wealthier coastal region were giving way to the rectangular mud-brick and thatch affairs of the poor rural areas. The occasional minaret towers of small mosques rose amid the rustic settlements, seemingly over-elaborate and quite incongruous.

Here, life had not changed for centuries. The motor vehicle was the major concession to the age of space-travel, but most were clapped-out second-hand cars and lorries owned by a few rich merchants and tradesmen. Only the major townships knew the luxury of spasmodic electricity and, occasionally, running water. What little money was available came from cash crops of groundnuts or rice, grown in swamp fields farther up-country. Others grazed cattle or sheep; in the dessicated bushlands, most villagers grew a few vegetables to supplement their meagre diet.

By midday the sun had begun to throb relentlessly until the entire landscape shimmered. And the further inland they went, the higher the temperature and humidity became. Even the slipstream passing through the open-topped G-wagen failed to keep its passengers cool.

Either side of the road the bush, that eight weeks before had been stunted scrub, was swathed in ten-foot tall savannah grass. Dotted amongst it were palms and other strange-looking trees.

Despite the heat, it was an exhilarating journey. The sights, sounds and smells of Africa kept the conversation lively, with jokes and observations. And always the questions, which Sunday took a delight in answering. This was their patch now, and the SASmen were keen to unearth its secrets. For the next few months home, to them, would be in this strangely timeless world. To survive, they would have to understand it. Know what made it tick.

After a brief stop at a wayside bar for some bottles of warm Guinness – which seemed to have gained widespread acceptance in a Muslim society for its 'medicinal' value – they pushed on again.

A hand-hauled ramp ferry took them across to the faded island settlement of Princetown. The old colonial town had gone into decline with the falling importance of river-traffic. But here the importance to Free Guinea of the mighty Kebba itself, a wide mirror of cut diamonds, was unmistakable.

It appeared to pulse with quiet energy, a vibrant main artery that brought life to an otherwise dry and unforgiving land. Lush vegetation fringed the banks which teemed with exotic birdlife. In mid-stream, the old *Kebba Queen* steamer towed a line of barges carrying produce, blots of its smoke merging with the sun-white sky.

Beyond Princetown the villages became noticeably fewer and the mud huts were no longer squared, but round in shape. Still the heat and humidity cranked up remorselessly.

Fraser had decided to visit one village in particular. It was a remote place called Massang.

The chief, or alkali, had known Jammeh since they were children and he was a loyal supporter of the President. The SAS captain had used the village as a base-camp whilst his team tracked after runaway rebels who had hidden in the vast National Park area of sub-tropical forest that bordered the Kebba River. It had taken weeks of painstaking surveillance, tracking, and night ambushes to bring back the renegades. Dead or alive.

The inhabitants of Massang had been impressed with the Captain's warrior skills, and particularly thankful for the work the SASmen had put in during their periods of rest and recreation. Irrigation schemes, well-digging and bridge-building, not to mention the running of a make-shift clinic, had hardly been relaxing, but then there had been little else to do. Besides, the soldiers had enjoyed the amazement and delight of the villagers, as the feats of primitive engineering took shape. They had become good friends. At least at Massang, Fraser reasoned, they could be fairly confident of a warm reception.

Fifteen miles beyond Princetown they turned off the main road and plunged down a narrow game trail. The tall bristled grass closed in, rustling and whispering in the light breeze, screening out the landscape apart from a ceiling strip of blue sky above their heads.

"The road it no good here," Sunday announced, struggling manfully with the wheel of the G-wagen as it rolled jerkily through the welts of red mud.

"Must be near the river, boss," Mather observed.

"You can smell it," Fraser agreed. "And there's more birdlife around."

Brummie glanced up at the western sky. "I just hope we find this place of yours before dark. Don't fancy getting stuck out here in the mud without any kit. Can't exactly call the AA, can we?"

Fraser smiled. Like most soldiers, the sergeant felt naked without weaponry or equipment in hostile terrain. When you were trained in the dangers and how to overcome them, it didn't go down well to realise you were ill-prepared. And, in a strange terrain, with known bogeys on the loose, there was a comfort in a Sterling's cold steel beneath your fingers.

"We'll get you there, Sarge," Witcher promised cheerfully. "I'd recognise the path anywhere."

Brummie gave him a withering look. "That's what worries me, sonny. With your navigation, this path could *be* anywhere."

More trees began appearing overhead, towering above the grass. First a cluster of giant mampattos with a gang of green velvet monkeys shrieking excitedly from their branches. Then some rambling fig trees and afzelias joined the frequent gingerbread plum trees at increasingly regular intervals.

Sunday pointed skyward. "Drongos. Water is near now."

Eyes followed his finger to the black, fork-tailed birds wheeling and swooping in giddy loops and circles like distant Battle of Britain pilots in their hunt for airborne insects. Above them, a fish-eagle circled patiently, a dark shape against the eggshell sky.

"Stop the car!" Fraser ordered suddenly. He had been listening for the sound of the Kebba River tributary. But now here was another sound.

Sunday obeyed in surprise.

"What is it?" Witcher asked.

"Ssh!" For a moment only the whispering grass and the muted cries of birds could be heard above the uneven thrum of the G-wagen's engine. Then they all heard it. Dull, menacing, like deep heartbeats, throbbing through the bush.

"Drums," Brummie said. His mouth was suddenly quite dry.

Mather shifted uncomfortably. "Sounds like fuckin' Apaches."

"Those, they message drums," Sunday explained lightly. He didn't understand their consternation.

"What I wouldn't do for a 'smudge' right now," Brummie muttered, imagining the reassuring grip of a sub-machine gun in his hands.

"I didn't think they used the drums nowadays," Witcher said.

Their driver shrugged. "Not much. But sometimes for special ceremony."

"D'you know what they say?" Fraser asked.

Sunday laughed. "Not me, man! Only old men can read drums." He didn't sound concerned.

"Well, do we go on or not?" Brummie asked tersely. His opinion was perfectly obvious.

Fraser glanced at the narrow track, the grass brushing both sides of the vehicle. "I don't think we've much option really."

The G-wagen lurched forward, the distant boom of the drums always with them. But as they eventually broke out of the grass and turned along the riverbank track, the noise ceased abruptly. Everyone relaxed. Everyone, that was, except Brummie. He remained unimpressed with the gurgling river, dappled gold in the fading sunlight, and the excited swooping of the yellow weaver birds and pied kingfishers.

Fifteen miles later, as they neared the wooden bridge that spanned the tributary, they began to hear music drifting through the musk-scented air. The beat of *sabaro* and *kuturiba* hide drums was joined with the sound of human laughter and the shrill pierce of musical whistles.

At last Brummie looked relieved. "This explains the drums. Sounds like someone's pleased to see us after all."

They all laughed, even Sunday. Perhaps none of them had been as unconcerned as they had appeared.

With difficulty they negotiated the lashed tree boles of the bridge which Fraser's old team had built. The sound of festivities continued radiating from the thatched huts of Massang, now outlined against a livid yellow sky in the gathering twilight. The smell of wood-smoke, cooking and perfume hung heavily in an aromatic mist around the woven compound fences. A tattered blue flag, signifying allegiance to the President, hung limply from a post.

They parked the G-wagen a hundred yards from the entrance and approached on foot, leaving Sunday to protect the vehicle from inquisitive small fingers.

"*Toubab! Toubab! Toubab!*" The inevitable cry of glee went up from the crowd of children by the gate.

The youngsters formed an excited escort as the older villagers parted timidly to let the newcomers in.

A large bloated baobab tree spread its rootlike tentacles skyward, dominating the village compound. A religious symbol of unity and strength. The place was teeming with people. Beneath the baobab sat groups of women dressed in their finest *ashobi* dresses and jewellery, squatting round bowls of rice, squeezing the contents into lumps and eating it. Eyes looked up, hands poised, mouths open. The scampering children were suddenly stilled, watching.

The music stopped.

Fraser's eyes moved across to where he remembered the headman's hut had been. He was thankful to see it still there, half-obscured by the gathering of village menfolk. Some of their faces were vaguely familiar.

They remained motionless, unsure. After the din before they had entered, the silence now was deafening in its intensity. The open fire crackled as globs of fat fell from the sizzling meat being cooked over it. The smell was tantalising.

Fraser called out: "I come to speak to the alkali!"

There was a movement from a rank of elders seated near to the musicians. Then Fraser recognised the frail doubled figure of the alkali, the once-fine robes faded and torn.

"The Captain?" His dim rheumy eyes glittered beneath the flat-topped woven linen bonnet, light catching the grizzled tufts of hair around his large ears.

Helped to his feet by sombre-faced elders, the alkali tottered forward with the aid of a gnarled stick.

"It's good to see you, old friend," Fraser greeted, shaking the bony hand.

The wrinkled head shook in disbelief. "Ah, and to see you. It is good. The English," he laughed, eyes twinkling. "The English is not so good, no? My old head forget. But you come at time that is good. Today my son he marries."

"That is good," Fraser answered, and held out a paper package of kola nuts to the alkali. "Greetings, old friend. And may your son's wife bear you many more grand-children."

The old man's eyes lit up with pleasure that his friend remembered the traditional greeting gift. Bitter nuts prized for their medicinal and aphrodisiac properties and regarded as 'holy food'.

In a sudden jerky movement of his twisted old body, he beckoned his fellow elders.

In Mandinka, he demanded reproachfully: "Do you not recognise this *toubab*? My eyes are older than yours, yet your memories are more dim. It is the soldier Captain who helps us in the troubles."

The transformation in the bizarre tableau of wary villagers was total. No one had recognised the legendary soldier without his battle fatigues. Only the old man, who had relied on his acute hearing for many years, picked up the unusual accent of the whiteman.

Now an expectant murmur rippled through the gather-ing. Glances were exchanged, old stories rapidly recounted, and excited voices rose. People began smiling, laughing.

Catching the change in mood, the musicians began to play again. The beat of the drums pulsed their rhythm into the still night air, the sound softened by the plucking of *kora* harps.

Sensing that providence and Allah were smiling on this wedding by sending back old friends of the village, the women began dancing into the centre of the compound, clapping happily to the beat and chanting, shuffling into a circle.

The handshaking went on endlessly. No one wanted to be left out. Many came back twice. Fraser was sure half of them didn't remember him or Lionel Witcher.

"The old timers look a bit miserable for a wedding," Brummie muttered to Witcher.

"They take a philosophical view about that sort of thing," the corporal replied, "being that much nearer to Allah, if you see what I mean."

As darkness fell suddenly, and the village became bright

with fireglow, they were seated now next to the alkali with the other elders. Ravenous after their long day's journey, they made short work of the *benachin*, a traditional mix of rice, an oily groundnut sauce, fish and vegetables. Strips of smoky meat were handed around, together with corn cakes and savoury boiled bananas that tasted like potato.

More food followed. Like the incessant chatter and laughter, it seemed to flow as though there would be no end to it. The steady rhythmic shuffle of dancing feet blended with the strangely haunting music to create a drugged sense of unreality. Pubescent girls gathered nearby to watch the white men. Eyes flashed with unmistakable meaning. Nubile hips passed by the men with a provocative sway, though careful not to let the elders see.

His hunger satisfied, Fraser idly watched the smoke from the fires waft up through the branches of the great baobab and into the vast dome of indigo sky. It seemed to span eternity, overspilling a billion bright stars that you could almost reach out and touch.

"Puts life into perspective, eh, boss?"

It was Lionel Witcher, grinning with a mouthful of meat. "Makes you see how insignificant we are, how small." He followed Fraser's gaze up to the heavens again. "Back home people find it hard to follow the thinking of primitive people. The importance of religion, of superstition. How life evolves round water and bread. Not the latest car or telly."

Fraser smiled. "It makes you wonder who's got it right. These people or us."

Witcher looked across the scene of uninhibited gaiety such as he had rarely seen in England. "I don't think that needs an answer." Suddenly he frowned.

"What is it?"

"Have you noticed, boss? There's a lot of small music drums here. But Massang doesn't appear to have a message-drum."

Before Fraser could answer, the alkali reached forward to grab another gourd of food from the selection before them. "You eat, Captain."

Fraser patted his stomach. "No, thanks. Too full. Too much."

The old man frowned as though seriously concerned for the captain's health. "*Domada.* It good. You like."

Thinking quickly, Fraser plucked two of the small cigars from his shirt pocket and held out one. The alkali showed his broken yellow teeth in a crooked smile, the gourd of *domada* forgotten.

His mouth puckered around the cigar end, his cheeks sucking in and out like bellows. He drew the smoke deeply into his lungs as though it were a mild cigarette, and exhaled in bliss, his eyes half-closed.

"Where is your future daughter-in-law?" Fraser asked.

The alkali had vanished behind a thick bloom of smoke. As it drifted aside, he replied: "She stay at family compound. Tomorrow she come for ceremony."

"And she has to miss all this?"

The old man nodded sagely. There was nothing unusual. It was the custom.

"Your son has chosen wisely, I expect? A beautiful bride?"

"Beauty is in the eyes of you. Other things are more important." He examined the glowing tip of the cigar. "But, yes, my son choose good girl."

"Where do they live, after the wedding?"

The alkali looked directly at him, almost angry, then shrugged. "She will stay for short times. Until the dowry is paid for her. Then she will go to house of my son for always. Two years maybe."

Fraser was surprised at the news. During the time of his last visit the alkali had been one of the wealthiest men in the area. As a direct descendant of its founder-family, he had considerable prestige as village leader. Not only was he responsible for judicial matters, like land distribution and solving petty squabbles, but he was also the local tax collector. That earned him a handsome ten per cent for his troubles.

Even the years of bad drought and the fact that this time of year, before the harvest, was not the best season to raise a dowry, hardly seemed a rational explanation.

The old man leaned sideways conspiratorially. "My son choose wise. A beautiful, educated girl. Young. She make good mother. But her father – bah! – he wants to see me bleed. You alkali, you pay. He is rich merchant. He wants he is richer. Dowry . . ." He raised his hand above his head. ". . .Today I do not collect tax. That is gone. Now the Government, they collect themselves. I am too old to farm."

"And your sons?" They could be expected to support their father.

A sad look came over the liquid brown eyes. "So many daughters. But only three sons. Not good." He shook his head sadly. "Now there is no grazing for cattles. And every year the Government it pays so little for groundnut. Each year more little. So after the coup my sons they go to Sakoto. Meet tourists and make much fortune. I do not see them. Just Dawda now. He is good son. He is a butcher. That is his trade. Good. Make his father proud. But tomorrow he has wife of his own."

Fraser couldn't place the two sons in his mind, but the image of Dawda flashed vividly in his memory. A cheerful seventeen-year-old with bright eyes and a gummy smile with big white teeth. Like so many adolescents, he had been full of the Kung Fu craze that was sweeping the country. His father had wanted him to be a butcher. The boy had wanted to be Bruce Lee – or at the very least, a village wrestler. Fraser and Lionel Witcher had taught him a few new tricks to help him realise his ambition.

"Dawda still wrestles?"

The alkali nodded proudly. "He leads our village team. No one beats us."

The compound was filling with swirls of smoke and dust beaten and dried by a hundred gently stamping feet. The smell of flower blossom mixed with perfumed body-oil and the bitter-sweetness of fresh sweat to create a heady aroma. Through licking yellow flames, there was an impression of ebony black glistening through a blur of movement. To the shuffling beat of the dancing women, was added a soft, melodious voice. The slender bodies swayed in harmony, urged gently by the steady tattoo of fingers on stretched hide.

The voice rose. A young girl's voice.

The tempo deepened and another girl, small, waif-like

and stunningly beautiful for one so young, moved forward into the firelight.

Fraser shook his head to clear the soporific effect as the staccato clapping of the dancers filled the compound.

The girl's head flung forward.

Her arms flew out and back. A bird.

On the ground her feet became a dazzling dance, a bewildering burst of movement.

The dust rose. Sweat glistened like rain on black satin.

Still the clapping rose like a wave, driven on by the drumbeats. Higher, higher . . .

In Fraser's head it was like a machine-gun, echoing, echoing, echoing. Seeming to rise to a never-ending crescendo. It must end . . .

It ended.

Slow. Infectious.

Bodies sway, slowing now,

A softer rhythm.

The melody of the young voice rose sweetly again.

Fraser felt the tension go from him. His muscles relaxed involuntarily. His mouth felt dry and the sweat stung his lips.

Brummie was staring ahead, mouth agape. He shook his head in disbelief and turned to Witcher. "Jesus, that was something else. I feel like I've just had it off."

The corporal laughed. "I think that's the idea. Most dances are about warding off evil spirits, sex or good harvests. I think that was sex. Well, this *is* a wedding, after all."

Brummie glanced up at the curious faces of the teenage girls who had edged slowly closer during the dancing. "I need a bucket of cold water."

Mather gave a lop-sided grin. "Boasting again?" The mood of the night had even penetrated his steel reserve.

The dancing had given Fraser an idea. He turned to the alkali. "My good friend, I wish to ask a very private question."

The brown eyes crinkled. "Ask, good friend."

"The dowry," Fraser said. "What is the price? And what has Dawda paid?"

The brown eyes hardened. "That is indeed private."

"Trust me, good friend."

The alkali thought for a moment, then leaned forward to whisper in Fraser's ear. The Scotsman nodded. Nearly one hundred pounds sterling. High indeed. A year's earnings for the average farmer. And there was still thirty pounds outstanding.

"I have a suggestion," Fraser said. "Tonight is a night of celebration. Let us have a wrestling match. Three of us against Dawda and two of the best boys of his team. The winning team takes the betting money."

Brummie overheard him. "I do hope you're joking, boss? I'm knackered."

"That's what I'm banking on."

The alkali worked out the captain's words, uncertain. It would be good entertainment – if only that solemn old Imam could be persuaded it did not run counter to the religious character of the ceremony.

"I must speak with the elders," he said reservedly. But the twinkle in the dim old eyes told Fraser the idea appealed to him. "Then tomorrow morning we hunt together, like the old days. To have extra food for your peoples during tomorrow."

"Bushpig?" Witcher asked with enthusiasm. The old hogs roamed the savannah. They were killed for the damage they did to crops, but weren't eaten by the Muslim villages. However spit-roasted bushpig pork had to be tasted to be believed.

The alkali gave a toothy grin as he hobbled to his feet. "Yes, there is bushpig. Near village. I know you like. Yes?"

Fraser sprang to his feet and stood before his three seated colleagues. "Right, you shower, I want two of you to do something your old recruiting sergeant told you never to do."

"What's that?" Mather asked.

"Volunteer."

The crack of the musket shot reverberated through the misty dawn air.

Fifty yards ahead, the old sow gave a brief snort of

surprise. On reflex, its fat old body bolted towards the nearby kutofingo bush. But it didn't make it. It half-slid onto its hindquarters, its snout open in a silent squeal, then slowly keeled over. Dead.

A dozen feet behind Fraser a cheer went up from the small gathering of villagers and the rest of the captain's team.

He lowered the home-made flintlock thankfully. You never could tell when those contraptions might blow up in your face.

"You give me gun with bend in barrel," he called as he retraced his footsteps. "I was aiming for the bush."

A hoot of laughter rippled across the chill landscape. The alkali, now dressed in a tatty sweater and with a woollen cap pulled low over his ears, cackled happily. "Gun for shooting round corners! You shoot good like before. Better than you wrestle, eh?"

Another howl of derision rose from the villagers.

Fraser glanced at Dawda with thinly-disguised amusement. The lad was in his element. It had certainly been his day. Within twelve hours he had not only won great honour by defeating the legendary white soldiers at wrestling, he had also taken the pot money. Just enough, with Mather acting as bookie, to pay the balance of the dowry for his bride.

He had, Fraser decided, grown into a fine young man. His skinny frame had filled out and hard work at his butchery had developed lean muscles. Most importantly, he had not lost his good-humour and ready smile. Today, he looked happier than ever.

His winning of the match the previous night had been a spectacle to delight the crowds. The sight of Fraser, Brummie and Witcher in the traditional belted loin cloths had reduced the villagers to tears of laughter. Wrestling matches were always preceded by the teams parading and strutting, enlisting supporters and taunting the opposing side. Last night had been no exception and the SASmen had camped it up for all they were worth. And the people loved it.

They loved it even more when their home team tripped

and tumbled each whiteman in turn, winning twice as many falls as their opponents. Then the music and dancing had begun again with renewed vigour.

Later, when the men were bedded down in different huts, the teenage girls had abandoned their timidity and had come, one by one, to the SASman of their choice. For every one of the team the night took on an exotic dreamlike quality. There was a strange purity in the childish and willing passion of the girls that made it impossible to resist.

The coming of the thin dawn light, and the need to leave the sleeping warmth of the tender creatures, had not been welcome. Now they were back in the cold reality of day.

As the alkali limped alongside him on the way back to the compound, Fraser asked: "What do you know of the return of The Lion?"

The old man shuffled to a dead halt, with Dawda at his side. He waited as the gap grew between them and the villagers, who were carrying the dead bushpig to the compound.

"That is why you came?"

Fraser nodded.

"It is as I think. Others, too. My son says that is the only reason The Captain comes back to Massang."

For once the smile had gone from Dawda's face.

"Who is he, old friend?" Fraser asked.

The alkali leaned against his stick and studied the ground. "I talk of this to no man. In Massang I forbid all to talk of the Jato."

"I understand," Fraser said softly.

The old eyes looked up. There was a sadness in them. "I tell them when the Jato returns to our land it will be not good time to rejoice. Because blood is spilled. The Jato wants to be king of all animals. It is his way. His nature. That is why we drive him from our villages, our country. To live safe. Now people want to welcome him." His gaze drifted away, focusing on some distant spot beyond the mist. "I tell people of Massang. If there is Jato, there will be a hunt. Because we already have a king to this land. There cannot be two. You, good friend, are the hunter."

Dawda watched his father with concern, his eyes flickering between the two men, confused. "It is true? You, soldier friend, come to kill the Jato?" He found the significance of it all awe-inspiring.

Fraser said: "Maybe to kill. Or to drive away."

"Do it!" There was an unexpected violence to the old man's voice. He almost spat the words. "Destroy the Jato before he destroys us!"

"My father will allow Massang to have nothing to do with Jato," Dawda blustered. "Always our village support President Jammeh. My father knows him from a boy. A good man. He keeps peace and order. Allah smiles on him."

I just hope, Fraser thought grimly, Allah has a strong sense of humour.

"The man you want," the alkali continued, "is like an evil spirit. He is not seen. But everywhere he is felt. Everywhere he is feared. Before he was in the land to the east, but every day he is closer."

"You've had trouble?"

"I do not talk of such things!" the old man said harshly.

"If you are in trouble, you must tell me," Fraser insisted. "We can help you. Protect you."

The old voice crackled with dry mirth. "Against an evil spirit? Your guns are no good against bad ju-ju, *toubab*. You are a friend, a good friend. But you cannot help us here. We must do things our own way."

"Where is the Jato?"

Dawda wanted to speak, but hesitated first. He glanced nervously at the old man for permission; the alkali nodded.

"They say he has now been seen," the boy said quickly. "At a secret place. I do not know where. Before no one knows him, but now he is seen by many. They now say he is a mighty one. They say Allah is with him." At this the old man spat contemptuously. "They say he is known before. From near Sakoto."

"His name?"

Dawda's ebony skin took on a sickly looking pallor, his eyes wide and bright. "I don't say. No one breathes his name. His curse will be on me. He has powerful marabou with him. His ju-ju *terrible*!"

"Tell me!" Fraser urged.

The lad shook his head. He looked down at his feet, muttering, shamefaced. He shuffled uncomfortably.

"Pheko. He is called Jato Pheko." The old man's voice was bright and defiant.

"Just a final word of warning, gentlemen. This is *not* the South Atlantic. I have it from impeccable sources that there are no Argies lurking out in the bush. So no trigger-happy target practice, and no organising game-hunt safaris for the tourists . . ."

Captain Johnny Fraser paused as the ripple of humour went through the gathering of soldiers lounging on the make-shift seats in the concrete-brick barracks hall at Duntenda.

It felt good to be back in uniform again and even better to know that the force from the Squadron's Boat Troop was now up to full strength. They had landed the night before in three Royal Air Force C130 transports which had parked discreetly in a remote corner of Jakoto Airport to unload.

He knew most of the new arrivals personally. Only the four-man Sabre team drafted in from D Squadron to train Jammeh's PGs and to create a new bodyguard were unknown quantities to him. But they seemed competent enough, and good-humoured.

"Any questions?"

He smiled as several hands went up. Although he thought he and Corporal Witcher had covered the essentials, these SAS troopers seemed an eager, inquisitive bunch. Very promising.

"This guy Pheko who's behind the Jatos. Is he related to Omar Pheko who organised the coup?"

It was one of Four Team's men, a tall thirty-year-old SAS medic and signals corporal named John Belcher. Like several of this force, including Fraser, he had been part of the Regiment's team to snatch a hostage from the mullahs of Iran back in 1980.

"Pheko's a family name," Fraser explained, "and it's a pretty big family. Like the Smiths back home. But births, deaths and marriages aren't that accurately recorded out here."

Belcher scratched at his thinning crop of short hair. "So unless we watch every bloke by the name of Pheko, it doesn't help us much?"

Fraser smiled. "We're trying to track down his family, but it's a slow process. Many people have two surnames which are freely interchangeable. That doesn't help. Anyway, we've nothing yet."

"What's this Pheko chap's complaint?" Mark Benjamin asked. A cheerful Jewish corporal with a mop of dark hair and a baby-face, he commanded Four Team.

It was Lionel Witcher's turn to reply. "The usual for Africa, Mark. Corruption of police and officials. Government incompetence. Lack of medical supplies and failure to distribute food where it's needed. And raging inflation. Then there's a touch of tribal jealousy. President Jammeh is a Mandinka and draws his support from the rural areas where the tribe predominates.

"But they're regarded as country bumpkins by the townies around Sakoto, particularly the minority Aku and Wolof tribes. Jammeh tends to pick his ministers and top officials from those better educated people. Natural enough, I suppose, but it gives fuel to Jato Pheko's charge that Jammeh has betrayed his Mandinka voters."

"And how bad's the corruption?" Mark Benjamin pressed.

"Like most of Africa, it's pretty well endemic. Ministers and managers of State concerns particularly. But at least Jammeh's trying to clear it up – even if it is like trying to ski uphill without snow. The police are the ones who are supposed to stop it, but often they're the worst offenders. Especially at the end of the month when they haven't been paid."

The next man to ask a question was 'Young Tom' Perrott. Now a fair-haired thirty-two-year-old veteran, he had left the Regiment for a couple of years in the late 'seventies. He had thought that being back with his original Parachute Regiment would allow him more time to spend with his crippled young Irish wife, whom he'd met on assignment in Ulster. But the marriage hadn't worked out and he was back at Hereford by the summer of 1980.

"Boss, I realise Two and Four Teams are to be the eyes

and ears of the President, as you put it. We'll be looking out for arms smuggling, unusual activity, secret meetings and so on. But, off the record, who's behind these Jatos? Internationally, I mean. Just the Libyans?"

A perceptive lot all right, Fraser thought.

"You're correct. This monkey didn't just climb out of a tree and decide to start a civil war all by himself. Our old friend Gadaffi is behind him, that's for sure. But it's all too careful, too planned. It's been discreet enough not to alert the outside world unduly. Except, of course, for that clumsy assassination attempt in London . . ."

Lionel Witcher interrupted. "Let's just say beware of strange men in astrakhan coats bearing gifts."

The smiles were half-hearted. Now the men knew what they were up against.

It was noon before the briefing ended.

Each man had his allotted task and was anxious to get on with it.

The dilapidated barrack buildings with their rusted corrugated iron roofs had been half-heartedly renovated and fumigated by Kwofie's men, but it left a lot to be desired. While the mechanic, armourer, chefs, and medical officer were left to fight over which building best suited their requirements, Acting-Staff Sergeant Brummie Turner ordered the ex-Guards of Three Team to fortify the compound in case the Jato insurgents paid an unexpected visit. As they got to work digging machine-gun emplacements and organising sandbags, he left for the nearby village to organise regular food supplies from the market traders.

Two and Four Teams held a plans meeting to decide on a schedule for initial patrols to familiarise themselves with the country and to select suitable sites for observation-posts. The latter would take a couple of outboard-driven Gemini inflatables up-river whilst the other team used the roads, intending to push on to Free Guinea's easternmost border. It was with Two Team that Lionel Witcher intended to travel, as the numerous riverside villages made it difficult to remain inconspicuous when moving by boat in daylight.

"I'd like to drop in on that opposition MP who refuses

to take a post in Jammeh's Government," he explained to Fraser.

"Fofana?"

"That's the one," Lionel confirmed. "I'm intrigued why he refuses to succumb to the bribery of power. Would appear to be a very incorruptible character."

"Not to mention brave," Fraser agreed, "seeing that his constituency is slap in the middle of Jato territory."

The two men began walking towards the vehicle. Kangers Webster, an Australian and 'Tiger' Jit Ratna, a Gurkha, were already aboard with the driver, a chirpy cockney called Jim Perkis.

"Keep your head down, Lionel," Fraser warned. "Don't forget we're committed to give Jammeh a full list of recommendations next week, so you're not going to be much good to me as a corpse."

"That's nice. Only want me for my body."

"You can keep it, old lad, it's your mind I want. Unfortunately the two go together."

Not for the first time, Johnny Fraser found himself bemused by the corporal's methods. Experience had taught him to let the man get on with things in his own way. But it wasn't always easy. Witcher operated on his own mental plane and often on a line of approach that was beyond his comprehension. He just hoped he was going to be right again this time.

"What's this, then?" Witcher asked, kicking the vehicle's front wheel with the toe of his boot. It wasn't a standard SAS 'Pink Panther' Land Rover.

"Lovely, innit?" Perkis crooned, stroking the steering wheel. "She's a Sandringham 6. Six wheels, see, not four. 'Andy for these rains. Hotspur lightweight armour throughout an' a range over 1,500 kilometres. Not to mention a 2,000 kg payload. Good bit of kit, eh?"

Witcher didn't share his enthusiasm. "New issue?"

Perkis wrinkled his nose. "No, worse luck. Never will be either, knowin' them miserable penny-pinching cunts at the MoD. This is a field-trials job HQ managed to wrangle. Only snag is I've got to write a bleedin' evaluation on it. Them was the conditions, see."

Witcher climbed aboard into the passenger seat along-side the pintel-mounted general-purpose machine-gun fixed between him and the driver. "I suppose the seats *are* more comfortable than the old Panthers."

Shaking his head in despair, Perkis let out the clutch and the Sandringham growled forward, splashing its way imperiously through the mud and puddles of the compound.

They'd been waiting now for two hours.

He must be an important man, Nyomi thought, to have kept them waiting for so long.

Patiently she looked around the gathering of people in the remote clearing. There were a few faces she recognised from her village, but mostly they were strangers. There were so many of them. She had never seen so many people together in one place.

It must be like this in Sakoto. Although in her fifteen years she had never been farther than the next village she had heard that in the capital thousands of people lived together. She wasn't sure what a thousand was. But she could count to a hundred and she knew that was a lot of people. And there were a lot of people here.

All these people had come to see one man. One man whom no one had seen, but whose voice had inspired them all. Inspired them to put aside petty family feuds and inter-tribal jealousies. To forget that your neighbours had raided your cattle or had cheated you on a deal in the village market. To put aside all hatred from your heart and rejoice together for the good of all mankind in Free Guinea.

Nyomi looked up at the sky. Two hours ago it had been clear and blue. But now the sky was grey and sombre. Scudding clouds raced over the landscape on a chill strong wind that forced the palms to bow and rustle their fronds way above the heads of the crowds.

From where she sat, Nyomi could see across the mass of people to the old open-topped truck where a handful of young men stood, talking earnestly. Even at that distance, their bright yellow headbands stood out sharply. They were handsome young men, Nyomi decided. Strong and straight and cheerful with ready smiles and an eye for the girls. One had smiled at her earlier and she had flushed and looked down at her feet.

But she wasn't sure about the guns they carried. They were not hunting-muskets such as her father used. They looked modern and mean. They were ugly-shaped with bits sticking out of them. They were sinister and they frightened her. But the men did not point them at anyone so probably it was all right. Obviously they had to protect the big man.

"He comes!"

The voice of one of those in yellow carried across the clearing and its effect was magical. Immediately everyone was silent, for once even the women. Everyone's eyes followed the pointing finger, but no one could see above the tall grass.

Excited chatter broke out and there was a frantic scramble as the crowd climbed to its feet, everyone jostling, peering over the person in front for a sight of the big man.

Then Nyomi heard a distant boom, low and deep, that seemed to travel through the ground on which she stood. It was like a heart-beat and she felt her own heart skip with anticipation. *Boom-boom*. It came again. It was almost as though the clearing floor itself trembled, the sound seeming to come from the very centre of the earth.

The talk of the message-drum always thrilled her and, until recently, it had been rarely heard. But nowadays its resonant tones could be often heard at twilight, like the heartbeats of the world. Somehow menacing, but somehow comforting. Now Nyomi understood why. It meant the big man was giving a message to his people.

"Jato!" someone called from the lorry. "Jato! Jato!"

"Where? Where?" she cried desperately, trying to peer over the heads of the crowd.

Then the others took up the chant: "Jat-o! Jat-o! Jat-o!"

More joined them, their voices filling the air, drowning the rustle of the trees. "JAT-O! JAT-O! JAT-O!" The sound swelled like a torrent, filling her head and numbing her senses. Everyone shouted and she joined in as loud as she could. "JAT-O! JAT-O! JAT-O!"

Someone shouted: "There he is!"

Another: "I see him! Jat-o! Jat-o!"

"I can't see! I can't see!" Nyomi cried, but no one listened to her. Even standing on tiptoes, all she could see were ranks of bobbing heads and a forest of waving arms. She jumped up and down, but could only glimpse a group of four men standing on the back of the lorry.

"Here," said a voice. "Let me help you."

She turned. Immediately she recognised the young man who had smiled at her earlier. Above the cheerful mischievous eyes, the yellow bandana was at a rakish angle, cutting a bright dash through the mat of tight black curls. The colour was most becoming, she thought.

"Why don't you let me help you into this tree? Like we were children," he said. "Then you will see over the tallest people."

Again she felt her skin flush and she looked down at her feet. She said: "That is not a nice way for a girl to behave. It is not good. My father would not allow it."

"But he is not here. Besides, I shall pretend you are my brother."

She giggled. "That is not very flattering."

He laughed. "I did not say it would be easy. Jato comes and will want you to hear his words. In the eyes of Jato and Allah we are all brothers and sisters."

That seemed reasonable, Nyomi thought. She accepted the out-stretched hand as he helped her into the fork of the tree.

High on her perch, she could see a mullah standing on the back of the truck on the other side of the clearing. He looked very serious and sober in his long robes and skull cap.

Her eyes moved on to the next man. He, too, looked serious – angry even – with dark accusing eyes. He had all the hallmarks of a marabou. And around his neck, draped over the fine blue silk of his robe, hung clusters of magical ju-ju emblems the like of which she had never seen before.

Nyomi had heard of the marabou who travelled with Jato. He was reputed to live in a cave in the remotest part and the strength of his powers was known throughout the land. Some said his ju-ju charms could stop bullets, could

113

turn them into water. Others that he could create the spirit of a living lion to destroy all those that betrayed Jato.

As she watched, the marabou raised his hands, the yellow palms facing the crowds. And at once the people were still. Expectant, waiting. Even the rhun palms dared not rustle.

And then the Jato stepped forward. Nyomi gave a little gasp, and gripped the branch more tightly with her thighs.

She had never seen such a man. He was tall, like a tree, as they had said he was. And broad, with a deeply-cleft chest as though hewn from a trunk of ebony wood. He wore a simple sleeveless waistcoat of dun-coloured hide that hung from his powerful shoulders. Nyomi could see how the sweat glistened on the muscled plane of his belly. Like tiny jewels of light against the purple-black lustre of his taut skin.

It was Jato's face that Nyomi studied last. She felt she needed courage to look upon it.

Her mouth dropped slightly at the corded muscles of his neck as he twisted his head right and left, his firm jaw jutting, his lips firm and arrogant, as he looked out over his followers. The nostrils in the strong broad nose flared for a moment and his eyes seemed to look directly at her. Eyes that were bright and fiery and seemed to smoulder with passion inside the black polished skull.

"My people!" he said. And the sound of his voice thrilled her, as it carried firmly across the clearing. "I bring you a message. The Lion has returned to Free Guinea. The Lion of Freedom is here!"

For seconds his voice hung in the air, electric. Then a chorus of voices rose to catch it. "JAT-O! JAT-O! JAT-O!"

It was some minutes before the chants and cheers subsided. Then Jato spoke again, more softly this time, but every syllable could be distinctly heard. "You people today are chosen. You are from many villages. You will be the voice of the Lion. You will return to your villages and tell them what you have seen today. You will tell them my message!

"I have not been seen before, because there are those in power who would seek to hunt the lion to his lair. And I shall not be seen again. Until I am triumphant in Sakoto!"

A ripple of awe ran through the crowd. One brave soul demanded: "How soon?"

Jato's head jerked, his smoky eyes immediately fixing on the source of the cry. "Soon, very soon! And you people will be the claws and teeth of freedom's lion! For I am but its head. Its body is the people of Free Guinea!"

Nyomi was transfixed by those heady words and she felt her heart beat faster.

"We call our land Free Guinea – but *are* we free? My friends, I tell you we are *still* slaves. As we were many years ago when the Portuguese and British took us away in chains across the great ocean. Now those countries and others run our business and industry.

"No, we are still prisoners in our own land. Prisoners of poverty! Prisoners of corruption! Prisoners of incompetence! Prisoners of disease! Independence has changed nothing; nothing is changed.

"Our land is turning into a desert, and all our wealth is being exported by imperialists!"

He paused, waiting for the murmur of agreement to ripple through his audience.

"We have had vast investments in our agriculture and in new industry. Thousands of foreign tourists visit our lands. They corrupt our young and desecrate our Muslim code with their drinking and whoring. Yet we are tolerant. Tolerant because Jammeh tells us it brings us wealth to our land." He hesitated again. "Where are these riches we are promised?"

Jato spun on his heel and pointed directly at a man in the front row. "*You!* Do you have these riches?"

Bewildered, the man shook his head. Jato turned and demanded the question of several others. None had seen the wealth.

He stood erect and defiant. "You have not seen it, my people, because it goes back to the foreign lands of the investors. And nor do we get a meagre profit. Like the cream from the milk of our goats and cattle, it is skimmed away by the corrupt politicians of our land.

"And when we elect new men, they, too, are sucked into Jammeh's web of corruption. So, as ever, you remain slaves – to poverty, to hunger, to illness, to ignorance . . . !

"I tell you, thousands of tons of rice are sent to us in aid, so that our children will not have hungry bellies. Is that rice in your store-sheds? Is it in your eating bowls? Or is it sold by a corrupt Government to the NA shops, then sold back to you at extortionate prices by greedy Mauritanian merchants? . . !"

A howl of anger rose from the crowds; they understood Jato's words so well.

"And," the great man continued, turning from side to side like a caged cat as he looked across his rapt audience, his eyes ablaze, "you toil in the hot sun on your co-operatives to sell your produce to the Marketing Board. But who runs the Board? Who fixes the measly prices? Who keeps you poor?"

"The Government!" someone cried.

"Jammeh!" cried another.

"Down with Jammeh!" yelled a big man near the front. "Down with Jammeh!"

Others took up the chorus. "Down with Jammeh! Down with Jammeh!"

Jato raised his hands and slowly the chant petered away. "Now the land of the Lion stretches halfway across Free Guinea. This land is now *truly* free. I make no rash promises like Jammeh. This harvest you shall be paid *double* for your rice and groundnuts. Yes, DOUBLE. You shall have medicines, and you shall have schools!" Already Nyomi had heard of the transformation that had come over villages that supported Jato.

He went on to talk of many other things, many of which she did not understand. But although his words were lost on her, she still found her attention riveted by his oratory. Certainly the men around her seemed to agree with every-thing he said. In fact, it did strike her that he said nothing with which it was possible to disagree.

Meanwhile, the threatening thunderheads had gathered, bulbous and weighted with rain, casting a dark shadow over the swaying sea of savannah grass around them. Flecks of rainwater touched the skin of her face.

In the blustering breeze which gathered strength by the

minute, Jato's voice became more difficult to hear. At one point, the mullah spoke, but no one was very interested. He said something about this being a *jihad* or Holy War. Everyone was pleased when Jato spoke again.

"Now I come to a sad moment," he said. "You see behind me three men who disobeyed the will of the Lion. Two weeks ago they killed a white girl in Sakoto. They killed her in my name because she was a tourist and offended Allah with her behaviour . . ."

He scanned the crowd, waiting until he was sure of their absolute attention. ". . . But it was *they* who offended Allah. God does not tolerate murder in his name. Our enemy is the Government and puppet-police and soldiers of the Jammeh regime. These murderers must learn to obey the law of the Lion." He stepped aside and Nyomi could see that three thin, sullen-faced youths stood behind him on the body of the truck. They wore just underpants, with their hands tied behind their backs. Their heads hung in shame and from their bowed necks three flax ropes had been run up into the bare branches of a kapok tree.

"Before I go, I say to you again that you shall not see me again until our victory is at hand. Comrades, your job is to educate our brothers and sisters about the truth. Only by unity can we defeat the Government and the military. They cannot kill us all!

"Today you take a risk to see me here. But there are other good men who preach the word of the Lion. Such a man is Fofana. He is a good man. He calls a rally soon. Take your friends to see him, to listen."

Jato stopped then and consulted the mullah and the marabou. They nodded in agreement and looked at the blackening sky.

"Now, my people, the Jato returns to his lair . . . until he is again king of our land, conquering over the imperialist lackey Government – corruption – and intimidation!"

"Long live the Lion of Freedom!" shouted a voice.

"LONG LIVE THE LION OF FREEDOM!" echoed the crowds, a thousand voices merging as one.

Then the marabou stepped forward, raising his hands to the forbidding blue-black heavens that had turned day into night. The thin wail of his incantations rippled across the clearing and the deep, rhythmic thud of the message-drum began again.

A spear of brightness ripped through the sky, illuminating the clearing with its brilliant radiance, as the million volts of lightning embedded itself on the horizon. Everyone gasped in fear and surprise. And then the sky was filled with a mighty roar of thunder.

Nyomi trembled, her eyes white with alarm. It was like the roar of a lion from heaven.

Hastily, she scrambled from the fork of the tree, stumbling in her terror. Clinging to the boy's arm, she looked back to where the truck had been.

She had not seen it go. All that remained were three thin bodies hanging like broken dolls from the kapok tree. Their heads lolled and their mouth slack, big raindrops now splattering their gently twisting torsos. All the men in yellow had vanished like magic.

Nyomi did not understand. She turned back to the boy. He was smiling and his yellow bandana had gone.

"What is your name?" he asked, offering her the shelter of his cloak.

"Nyomi," she replied, shyly.

"They call me Sunday."

5

They ran before the storm, racing inland at a breathless pace along the northbank road.

"At this rate, Jim, you'll never get the chance to write that evaluation of yours!" Lionel Witcher said, his voice raised against the rush of the slipstream.

Perkis flicked him a sideways glance, his grinning face fixed ahead. "Psychlops, old son, that's *some* bleedin' consolation, believe me! Anyhow, you're educated. If I tell you what I think of 'er, you could write it down in good English. Really persuade 'em it's what we need?"

"Drop off!"

Perkis had decided to drive everywhere at maximum speed. There had been reports of mines on the road and he was taking no chances. Past experience had taught him that if you travelled fast enough when you trigger an explosion, the chances were you'd be past as the thing blasted. He didn't, however, point this out to the rest of his four-man patrol in the rear compartment. He'd also jury-rigged an upright cutting pole on the front bumper in case someone had the bright idea of running a decapitation wire across the road.

"Of course," Witcher said. "If this precious monster of yours was lost to a mine, it wouldn't have to be returned!"

"That figures, smart-arse," Perkis retorted lightly, before he sensed that the Intelligence whizz-kid was stating more than the obvious. "I'll see if I can find a mine. Then I'll request a replacement." He meant it.

Witcher laughed. "Can we do it on the way back, please . . . ?" The smile froze on his face. "AHEAD! WATCH IT!"

"I've got her!" Perkis assured, slowing rapidly as they

approached the thick carpet of cattle dung spread across the road.

Before they had come to a standstill, the protective cover had come off the powerful twin GPMG 'jimpies' mounted in the rear compartment by the laconic Australian, Corporal Kangers Webster. Its ability to put down a sustained curtain of 7.26mm round at well over a thousand yards was an effective deterrent to would-be trouble-makers. And Webster knew how to use it.

Perkis slid down in his seat to shield as much of his small frame as possible from view as Witcher scrambled out carrying his short-barrelled Armalite AR-18 sub-machine gun. He crouched down by the front wheel arch, aware that Gurkha Jit Ratna was right behind him.

"Cow she shit pretty big in this country," observed the little man from Nepal. Apart from being a signals wizard, 'Tiger's' fieldcraft was applauded by everyone who had ever worked with him.

"What d'you reckon?" Witcher rasped. "I can't see anything ahead. Well, no further than that bend at a hundred metres."

"That shit not dropped by no animal," Tiger said firmly. "It been put by human. And recent, soon."

Witcher grimaced. "I'll have a look-see."

A brown hand planted firmly on his shoulder. "No, Psychlops, you stay put. Boss not thank me your head blows off."

"Fuck me," Perkis muttered, "everyone's so bleedin' worried about Psychlops' 'ead, I'm surprised Captain Fraser didn't insist on 'im wearin' a crash-'at."

"Not a bad idea with you at the wheel," Kangers Webster rejoined.

Before Witcher could reply the Gurkha was down on all-fours, snaking his way towards the dung pile. Whilst the others scanned the waving savannah bush at either side of the road, he gingerly began prodding at the muck with his bayonet.

"Got anything?" Perkis called.

A chuckle drifted back from the prone man. "The cow she eats beans in can for breakfast."

Witcher and Perkis exchanged glances and shrugged. Tiger had a sense of humour all his own.

They later realised he meant he had discovered the tin casing of a mine. It took ten nerve-chewing minutes before Tiger managed to unscrew the detonating pressure-plate and render it harmless. Grinning he held it above his head.

The crack of the rifleshot sounded insignificant. Its whine as the round tore a chunk of tarmac out of the road beside Tiger was more menacing.

"Ten o'clock!" Perkis yelled. He'd been quartering the road dead ahead.

Despite the temptation to look forward, Witcher kept scanning the right-hand side of the road and rear. He heard the rasp of the cocking-handle as Kangers swung the big GPMGs. Involuntarily he braced himself for the noise.

It came, an ear-cracking stutter as it spat out its venom in a controlled two-second burst as the firing mechanism snatched hungrily at the belt feed. The thirty-odd high-velocity rounds scythed through the copse of tabbo trees at the bend in the road. Screeching cries drifted across the intervening savannah from a gang of monkeys in the trees as their protective screen of foliage was stripped away. A giant yellow butterfly fluttered away across the bush.

"Kangers, old son," Perkis said evenly. "Most people find a net more effective."

"Too late now, mate," the Australian hissed through an uncertain fixed grin.

"Get in!" Perkis snapped and gunned the Sandringham forward, scarcely giving Witcher time to throw himself at the passenger seat.

As the vehicle went past Tiger at gathering speed Kangers reached out to haul the Gurkha aboard.

"What's up?" Kangers shouted at the driver. "Afraid of scratching your paintwork?"

But the tension passed as they cruised by the tabbo trees and no one fired. Tiger insisted he had seen someone wearing a bright yellow headband disappearing hurriedly into the bush. But no one else could confirm it.

*

With many calls to make and new terrain to explore, it was two days before they reached the easternmost township of Serreba.

On the way they had been met with increasing reserve and suspicion at each village stop. In the end, rather than the usual enthusiastic reception from the village children, mothers had been hurriedly snatching away their offspring and retreating to their compounds.

More disconcertingly, the sound of distant drums had accompanied them almost constantly after the incident with the mine.

Serreba itself was like a ghost-town. As they drove down the mainstreet of corrugated-iron compounds and occasional open-doored concrete sheds displaying foodstuffs and housewares, there was hardly a soul in sight.

Only the town madman came out to see them, a strange character with wild eyes and unkempt hair who stared at them from a safe distance. His body, naked except for a tatty loincloth, was covered in dust and grime.

He made a deep growling noise and waved his club at them as they drove past. Involuntarily Witcher shivered. It wasn't the lunatic that worried him. That was just a symptom. It was the thousand watching eyes in the darkened doorways and windows. He could feel them.

Perkis swung the Sandringham off the road into a side alley that ran uphill between two ghetto compounds. The sickly stench of raw sewage was thick in his nostrils.

As the vehicle crested the slope, the low concrete block bungalow belonging to the politician Fofana came into view.

Perkis killed the engine and Witcher climbed out. "Better leave my Armalite behind. Don't want to appear unfriendly."

Behind them the madman was plodding up the hill. Kangers grinned. "Just hope that's not Fofana. Otherwise you might be needin' it."

Cautiously Witcher climbed the shallow steps to the open door. He put one tentative foot in the welcome shade and tapped lightly on the frame. A small shower of peeling paint cascaded onto the dusty cement floor.

"C'me in!" a voice boomed from the depths.

Removing his bush hat, Witcher went in, squinting as his eyes adjusted to the gloom.

The patched leather armchair was the centrepiece of the musty-smelling room. In it sat a tall heavily-built man, his bulbous black face offset with grey frizzled hair. It was easy to pick out the grubby white of the vest he wore under a voluminous, crumpled blue suit. As the man uncrossed his legs, Witcher noticed that he wore black patent leather shoes with no socks.

"Mr Fofana?"

"Yes it is. Who are you and how are you?" The voice filled the room. It seemed to Witcher that all African politicians were big and spoke with equally big voices. Presence was everything.

"I am well, thank you. My name is Lionel Witcher, and I am a British Army soldier on secondment to the Free Guinea Government." As he spoke he was dimly aware of rows of shelves stuffed to overflowing with books, magazines and papers. A zebra skin that had seen better days covered another wall; beneath it was a sideboard topped with framed family photographs and African trinkets. Obviously a man of learning. A man to respect. Above the armchair the moth-eaten head of a lioness snarled down at him.

"This is a courtesy call, Mr Fofana," Witcher added, accepting the out- stretched hand. "I'm on a fact-finding mission and I'm sure our meeting will prove useful."

"Ye two-faced devil!" The Glaswegian accent was shattering in the dark room.

Witcher turned. He had not seen the two men seated in a dark corner alcove to one side of Fofana.

"Ian Hammond?" Witcher half-asked, and half-confirmed with his mental list of names.

"Aye, it's Hammond," the Scot replied. "And didna Ah see ye back a' The Oceanic wi' tha' man Fraser – he didna say he wus a soldier. No wonder he didna manage te pull strings fer me wi' the Government!"

Witcher smiled disarmingly. "You seem to be meeting the right people nevertheless. Besides, Captain Fraser's been pretty tied up. I know he's interested to hear how you got on."

Hammond scowled. "Ah jest *bet* he is! Na doot ye're here te put obstacles in ma path."

"Not at all. Why, did the Government refuse your request?"

The Scotsman looked uncertain. "No' exactly. Ah canna say they were over the moon wi' enthusiasm, but they've agreed fer me te hold three rallies."

"Then Captain Fraser can hardly have been putting obstacles in your path, Mr Hammond, can he?" Witcher didn't wait for a retort, but asked: "And may I ask who your friend is?"

Hammond glanced sideways at the stout grey-haired European whose clean shaven jowls and smart suit were in marked contrast with the Scotsman's scruffy appearance. "This is Mr Rubashëv from Prague. He is an organiser from the World Federation of Trade Unions . . ."

As the man stepped out of the deeper shadows, Witcher shook his hand. "Pleased to meet you."

"The honour is mine." Rubashëv spoke in a dry clipped manner. "I didn't know British soldiers were serving in Free Guinea."

"It's not generally advertised," Witcher replied curtly. "Just a small training team."

"Is that necessary? I thought the Presidential Guards were quite efficient."

Witcher could sense a leading question. "You know how it is for the military. Ours not to reason why . . ." He smiled, and turned back to Fofana who was watching the encounter with amusement. "Is Mr Hammond to speak at your rallies, sir?"

Fofana eased his bulk out of the armchair which creaked with strain. "Indeed he is, indeed he is! As a true socialist politician I welcome Mr Hammond to speak on the same platform. In fact I am already late – well, an hour – so you must forgive us if we leave. In fact in two weeks I shall hold a rally in Sakoto when Mr Hammond will address members of the Free Guinean Labour Union. If you are not doing anything, you must come along then."

"I'm free *now*, sir," Witcher said quickly. "If it's acceptable, my colleagues and I could come to your rally this afternoon."

Fofana smiled and shrugged. "Why not?"

"Is ye vehicle armed?" Hammond demanded.

Witcher nodded. "We'll be pleased to escort you."

"Escort?" Fofana asked. "For protection? What on earth for?"

"There's been some trouble with insurgents, sir, I'm sure you are aware . . ."

"Corporal Witcher," Fofana said pointedly. "This is *my* country and *my* people. I do not need escorts by soldiers."

Hammond leaned forward, the black bristles of his chin jutting belligerently. A faint smell of whisky carried on his breath. "An offer of an armed escort, Mr Witcher, *could* be interpreted as intimidation. Ah wouldna put it past Jammeh te send ye here fer tha' specific purpose."

Witcher raised his hands in mock horror. "Okay, okay! Point taken. We'll have any hardware put well out of sight and we'll keep a discreet distance. I really am interested in what Mr Fofana has to say."

The politician nodded graciously.

"Ye should do well te be interested, too, laddie." Hammond snarled. "And ye might see fit te turn ye swords inte plough shares an' throw in your lot wi' the workers of the world . . ."

Back down at the mainstreet of Serreba a number of Fofana's enthusiastic supporters had gathered in a rag-tag collection of vehicles.

As was normal for African politicians, it was the big man's battered black Austin that took the lead. Jim Perkis discreetly slid the Sandringham between two lorryloads of fervent Fofana fans, who grinned widely down at them and waved bottles of Coke in greeting.

"Some military operation, this," Kangers muttered. "I feel like we're taking part in a bleedin' carnival."

The procession gathered speed as they hurtled down the narrow dirt track towards the out-of-town rally point. Singing voices came from the truck in front, accompanied by the squeaks and groans of the vehicle's rusted suspension. Bystanders stood and waved as the convoy rushed past with growing momentum.

More supporters joined them, and a bright yellow Volkswagen with a big VOTE FOFANA streamer swung out into the head of the cavalcade. It tooted noisily to be rejoined tenfold with hooters and cheers from the rest.

Perkis glanced in his mirror. "Wish these cunts'd slow down. From what I've seen I don't suppose anyone's brakes work. And that's a bleedin' great two-tonner behind us!"

The yellow Volkswagen disappeared into a sharp wooded bend.

"Christ!"

Even from that distance they could hear the force of the smash as metal ripped into solid timber. The sprawling caterpillar of transport slewed right and left in confusion, each driver trying to miss the vehicle in front. The steady munch of metal against crumpled metal worked its way down the column towards them. Tinkling glass crackled musically above the screams of hysteria and anger.

Perkis moved faster than most, changing down and spinning the steering-wheel to take the Sandringham out of line with the concertina pile-up. Kangers glanced round to see the towering form of the two-tonner looming above him. The driver's face was a mask of horror as he covered his eyes with his hands, letting the wheel spin free.

A dull wrenching thud came from the rear passenger compartment as the truck's bumper ripped the Sandringham's smoke-dischargers from their offside mountings. But the six 16inch tyres of the SAS vehicle were biting deep into the rutted mud track, its screaming V8 hauling it free.

"Jesus," Perkis breathed as the two-tonner flashed past them and splattered its bonnet in the rear of a stationary coach. The two vehicles seemed to merge into one, indistinguishable, like the obscene mating of two giant steel reptiles. Steam clouds from a ruptured radiator engulfed the scene.

"For God's sake step on it, Jim!" Witcher snapped. "Let's get down to that bend!"

Perkis stamped on the accelerator, swinging wildly to miss the confusion of vehicles now spilled off the track, tooting in warning as he passed. By the time they reached the bend,

Kangers and Witcher had between them remounted the GPMGs and Tiger had his Armalite at the ready.

"Fuck me . . ." Perkis murmured as they rounded the wooded blind bend. Instinctively he slowed.

The yellow Volkswagen looked like a squashed insect. It had tried to bury itself nose-first into the gigantic netto tree that had fallen across the track. Scarlet patterns of blood glistened brightly on the crunched canary paintwork. A mangled black hand waved limply from the flattened bodyshell.

"Kangers, see if you can do anything for that poor sod," Witcher ordered. As the Australian grabbed his medical kit and sprinted to the scene of the carnage, Witcher walked over to where Fofana was struggling to get his bulk out of his black Austin with Hammond's help.

The vehicle had helped to pile-drive the Volkswagen under the tree and had itself been rammed in the rear. But Fofana, though shaken, looked relatively unscathed.

He dabbed a handkerchief at a cut on his forehead. "That was meant for me," he muttered to no one in particular.

Hammond scowled at the SAS corporal. "Ye dunna have to tell Mr Witcher tha'. Na doot t'was his friends who cut it doon. Ah said he wus comin' here te intimidate us."

Anger flashed in Witcher's pale eyes. "Don't talk such bullshit, Hammond. If my people had ambushed you, you'd be dead, believe me. *We* don't piss about."

Hammond opened his mouth, thought better of it, and shut it again.

"I suggest you let us take you to your rally. Obviously someone doesn't like Mr Fofana's manifesto, so it might be a wise precaution."

Hammond glanced at the politician, uncertain. The man mumbled his thanks, and stumbled on with the Scotsman's help towards the Sandringham.

Taking a last look at the wreckage around the tree where Kangers was organising a band of helpers, Witcher turned to follow the others. Tiger joined him.

"I take look at tree," the Gurkha said out of the corner of his mouth. "They saw through pretty damn quick. I see marks of chain-saw. Fresh. Few minutes maybe."

Lionel Witcher frowned. "Shouldn't think many villagers own chain-saws around here."

Tiger nodded sombrely. "That what I think."

"No," he said. "No, my friend, I just simply do not believe it."

For once Jammeh's booming voice was subdued as he sat hunched in his throne-like chair. Thoughtfully, he rested his elbows on the arm-rests and steepled his fingers at the front of his white embroidered robe. He looked withdrawn, his eyes moist and nervous behind the tortoiseshell glasses.

Lady Precious sat to one side of him, prim and defensive, her face set in a beautiful mask of determination. To one side Colonel Kemo Kwofie leaned against the wall and examined his fingernails as though the conversation had nothing to do with him.

"I'm afraid it's true, Mr President," Lionel Witcher insisted. "You may have won your election a year ago, but if there was another tomorrow it would be a close-run thing."

Precious shook her head defiantly. "How can you possibly know this? You have only been here for a fortnight." She turned to her husband. "Essa dear, this can *only* be speculation. And not very inspired speculation at that."

"Please be quiet, woman." Jammeh's voice was distant.

Captain Johnny Fraser felt it was time to add weight to his Int. man's assessment. "The problem, Mr President, is that the Jatos are well-organised and skilful. It is a far cry from Omar Pheko's bungled attempt at a coup. Jato's socialism is wrapped up in Islamic fundamentalism. And that makes a pretty irresistible package to an uneducated rural community. The one thing they've all learned is the teachings of the Koran, even if they haven't managed to read and write."

"That's not fair," Precious snorted, her nostrils flaring magnificently. "We've worked hard at our education programme since independence in the 1960s."

"That's true," Fraser conceded. "But it doesn't alter the fact that there's only twenty per cent of the population literate in Arabic, and fifteen per cent in English."

"In fact," Witcher added, "education actually works against you in two ways. The more educated your young people become, the more aware they are of injustice, corruption and opportunities they think their country has missed. They leave high school expecting a good job and find themselves reduced to hustling tourists because there's no work."

"Well, really!" Precious began.

But Jammeh silenced her with a wave of his hand. "I know what you say is true, good friend. It is the price we pay for civilisation."

Fraser said: "The trouble, Mr President, is that the Jatos are using your own efforts against you. They're using rice aid against you by redistributing black market produce in their areas. They're using captured medicines in the areas of *their* choice at the expense of villages loyal to you. They're recruiting *your* teachers for their own schools in the bush."

Jammeh chuckled mirthlessly. "You make it sound as though I just can't win."

Fraser hadn't intended the prolonged pause that followed. Lady Precious blinked at him, hard. Colonel Kwofie stopped inspecting his nails.

"Mr President," the SAS captain said. "We believe it could already be too late . . ."

"What nonsense!" hissed Precious.

Fraser shook his head. "No, hear us out. I am not a pessimistic man, but I must tell you that it will be an uphill struggle unless we act immediately and pursue our recommended course of action. *Without* reservation and *with* determination.

"And it will require the complete honesty and co-operation of *all* your ministers and officials."

Jammeh held him in a steady gaze. "I trust you implicitly, old friend. I have the greatest faith in your judgement, even if half of what you have already told me sounds absurd." His eyes flickered for a moment to Kwofie, then back to the SAS officer. "This situation has not been fully revealed to me before. So whatever you want, if it is within my power, it shall be done."

Lady Precious looked a little more comfortable. She'd

obviously, Fraser decided, had a vision of having to exchange her jewellery for a pawnbroker's ticket.

Fraser smiled. "I'm glad you said that, Mr President. Very."

From the deep shade of an ancient spreading mendiko tree in a corner of the Duntenda barracks compound, Johnny Fraser watched the trudging column of Guinean NCOs.

Absently, he peeled a mango fruit with the razored black blade of his combat knife. The men looked smart in their new striped camouflage 'tiger-suits'. And at last their movements were starting to become co-ordinated and precise. Their attitude was less sullen, their behaviour more disciplined. In short, they had started to look and act like professional soldiers.

The continual use of live ammunition had unnerved many of them at first, but it soon proved its value. The 'Small Group Tactics' of fire and manoeuvre had been difficult to master but now, house and wood clearing, as the instructors speeded up process, was becoming routine. For the more technically-minded, there were courses on vehicle maintenance and elementary military engineering.

'Brummie' Turner suspected that trouble-makers in the upper echelons of the PGs, resentful of being returned to military school, had been advocating non-co-operation and stirring discontent amongst their men. Fraser had no reason to disagree with Brummie's assessment. He may have been a dour and taciturn pessimist, but the SAS veteran was a match for the tantrums of any jumped-up officer or NCO from the Third World. He'd seen it all before.

Neither did Fraser have any qualms about Brummie's master-plan to overcome the hostility of the training batches. It was made widely-known that only those completing the training-courses to the British Army Training Team's total satisfaction would receive a smart new 'tiger-suit' and, even more important, a pair of new boots. It had worked like a dream – even if it did make for a motley-looking collection on the parade ground. Everyone wanted the new 'tiger-suit'.

Corporal Witcher had added his own dimension to the

incentive plan by designing a new shoulder patch which he had embroidered by the local village women. This featured crossed spears beneath a Lion's Head, the symbol of President Essa Jammeh, Guardian Lion of Free Guinea.

It was a most sought-after item and served to confuse the issue whenever people started talking about the Jatos. After all, who were the real Lions? An unseen ragtag army of rebels reputed to be in the bush, or these smart soldiers, whose presence was highly visible. One thing was certain. Only the Presidential Guard bore the distinctive Lion's Head emblem.

In one fell move Witcher had snatched away one of Jato Pheko's most valuable propaganda weapons – an evocative and inspiring name – and turned it against him. Or so they hoped.

Fraser finished the mango and looked up through the canopy of mendiko leaves at a clear azure sky. It hadn't rained now for five successive days, and the break heralded the start of the dry season.

It was strange to recall that it was only six weeks since that fateful and tense meeting they had held with Jammeh at State House when the bald facts of the Jatos' threat had been put before him.

The President had been as good as his word. He had listened carefully to Witcher's planned campaign of psychological warfare designed to stop Jato Pheko in his tracks.

"The trick," the corporal had explained, "is to surround Jato territory and contain it. Not just with steel and military force, but with a soft balloon of public opinion – by reshaping the perceptions of the people in the target areas."

"No direct confrontation?" Kwofie had asked incredulously.

"Only if you have hard information about base-camps. Even then, it's too easy to hit innocent villagers.

"Trying to strike at the Jatos will only make them martyrs," Witcher explained. "If you try to hunt them down you will probably fail. In accordance with the famous philosophies of Chairman Mao, guerrillas don't need to physically hold territory. You do. They can melt into thin air. Your expeditionary forces can't. They'll be wide open to ambush."

"So what do we do?" Jammeh had asked.

"We draw our line where the Jatos' advance is to be halted. This is patrolled and protected from intimidation by insurgents. Not too overtly, but by the correct use of surveillance and ambush techniques that are far more successful. It will allow you to keep the initiative. We'll show you how to do this."

Kwofie had looked impassive. He was back studying his fingernails.

"Then we pour in all possible resources to the area behind our front-line," Witcher continued. "Firstly, we feed them with our propaganda. Promises of change. Then, lo and behold, within a week or two, these promises are *seen* to be fulfilled. It might be a new well, a new school, medical assistance, a river-bridge . . . These actions will talk louder than a thousand words. As the lot of the villagers is improved, support for the Jatos will, eventually, wither and fade.

"Then we start to urge the insurgents from the surrounding areas to improve their conditions, too, by coming over to the Government side."

Kwofie smacked a mosquito that landed on his wrist, and distastefully plucked off the bits with his thumb and forefinger. "Is that what the Americans did in Vietnam?" he asked pointedly.

Lionel Witcher's eyes danced with angry light. "No, Colonel. And that's why they lost the war."

That convinced Jammeh. After the meeting he had energetically begun to marshal resources to put at Witcher's disposal. Discussions with the Gendarmerie and the PGs were held to decide on the demarcation line between villages supporting the Jatos and those still loyal to the Government. Detailed plans were prepared and officials sent to report on the priority needs of each village.

Heads of all the relief aid organisations were called in and asked to reschedule their operations to concentrate on the front-line target areas. The Government request met with a mixed reception. Some of the charities saw it as an attempt to use their good offices for political purposes; others saw it as an unwelcome interference with their own plans.

Sir Nigel de Burgh found himself in a difficult position. He was furious at the SASmen's proposed hearts-and-minds campaign. He warned that the motives of many of the charity-workers were 'suspect'. He proved particularly difficult when Fraser asked him to request additional emergency aid from the British Government. As the High Commissioner had insisted all along that there was no emergency, it meant him having to admit to his superiors in London that he'd read his tea-leaves wrong.

Not surprisingly, Sir Nigel's unenthusiastic request brought little response, and even less by way of additional resources.

Fraser tried a different tack and flew back to England for a face-to-face meeting with the CO of 22 Special Air Service Regiment at Hereford to explain the exact position.

Now, as he sat beneath the mendiko tree, he had the 'Old Man's' official response in his pocket. Whilst Whitehall couldn't approve any increase in Fraser's BATT presence, an informal appeal had gone out to the Royal Medical Corps, the Royal Veterinary Corps, and Royal Engineers to hold limited field experience exercises and special leave-of-absence over the coming months. 'The appeal has met with considerable and favourable response' the CO had written cheerily.

There's more than one way to skin a cat, Fraser mused. He just hoped Jammeh's treasury had enough readies to pay for the air fares.

He turned as one of the team's open Land Rovers roared into the compound and pulled up neatly in the shade. It was laden with provisions.

Brummie Turner turned off the ignition and climbed out. "Afternoon, boss. Just back from the Tesco run. Also had a chat with Kwofie in Sakoto."

He sat down, removed his bush-hat and wiped the sweat from his brow with the back of his hand.

"Are you still on talking terms?"

"No danger, boss." He formed a circle with his thumb and forefinger. "We're like that, me an' old Coffee. It took a bit of doing, but a few pina coladas in the Green Mamba an' he was nattering away like my old mum."

"I just hope all this comradely boozing is paying dividends in mutual co-operation." Fraser pulled out a cigar and unpeeled the wrapper. "I've a sneaking suspicion your sojourns at the Green Mamba are just an excuse to get your teeth into that little bit of chocolate of yours."

Brummie grinned sheepishly and plucked a mango from the pile beneath the tree. "Well, there *are* compensations for his company and that fucker Berno who runs the joint." He sunk his teeth into the ripe fruit, spitting out the pith. "But it *is* proving worthwhile. He's actually letting on about the various attacks on police-posts and Government officials now. Before, he was keeping it all to himself. Even Jammeh was only given half the picture. Reckon Kwofie was afraid he'd get the boot if he let out the whole truth in one go."

"And how bad is it?"

Brummie stared out across the compound, running a professional soldier's eye over the drilling troops. "Well, boss, it isn't gettin' any better. I've passed the details onto Lionel – for what good it'll do."

"How do you mean?" The tone of his voice had Fraser concerned.

The sergeant looked uncomfortable and sucked at the flesh of the mango, giving himself time to choose his words carefully before replying.

"Don't get me wrong, boss. Lionel's a pretty smart operator. I mean we pass all this gen onto him and he files it all and sticks pins into maps. And, as far as I can see, bugger all else happens. Meanwhile, that black cunt out there has full rein, doing the hell what he likes. He's got it all his own way."

Fraser exhaled a steady stream of tobacco smoke. "We've got to give the programme time to work, Brummie. It all came together in the Omani campaign."

"Yes, boss, but this *isn't* Oman. I'm not sure we've the time for all this hearts-and-minds caper. At least in Oman we made the sods keep their heads down. We had a full Squadron out there, *plus* an army *plus* local tribesmen."

"I know," Fraser replied. He understood what the sergeant was getting at. "But there's no way our strength's going to be increased. So we'll have to make do with the PGs. The training looks as though it's going well."

Brummie gave a sardonic sneer. "Sure – for a bunch of fuckin' monkeys. They mean well, y'see, an' some of them are really quite bright. Trouble is most of 'em are townies, young bucks from the back streets of Sakoto. I tell you, half of them would shit 'emselves if they saw a snake. Believe me. In fact, they found one in the barracks two nights ago. Curled up in the rafters. Jesus, you've never seen a place evacuated so quick!"

"What happened?"

"Nothing. They all charged out, locked the door and all peered in at it through the windows. Hours of brave talk about how each was going to destroy the thing. In the end, it was one of the cleaning women from the village who disposed of it, calm as you like."

Brummie replaced his hat. "And you should see 'em dismantle a machine-gun. They're dead keen, but no one wants to do it by himself. One will hold the barrel, one the butt, another the mechanism, another the bipod – and they all shout instructions at one another . . . Jesus bleedin' wept!"

"And you want to put that lot against the Jatos?" Fraser challenged.

"Hell, boss, there are *some* good ones. We could get a small team together. I reckon we'd get almost a company shaken down in a month or so. All insubordinate ones and trouble-makers I'm recommending to go to Sandhurst. Bad news for them on their return, but it'll get them out of our way during the critical period. And it *is* critical, boss, I'm sure of that. My water tells me, so help me." He thumped a balled fist into his palm in frustration. "We've got to smash the bastards. Give 'em at least one good hiding that will set 'em back a few months."

Fraser sympathised, but life wasn't that simple. "This isn't the Falklands, Brummie. The war's over. The political strait-jacket is back on."

The sergeant's eyes took on a distant look. "And don't I know it, boss. It's starting to piss me off, really it is. We got it right then. Gloves off and get stuck in. Bang, bang, thank you, ma'am. In and out. Minimum casualties and over in the twinklin' of an eye. And we were doin' what we're best at. Being hooligans."

Fraser smiled. The 'hooligans from Hereford' tag had become a catch-phrase with all the Army and Marine units. Whatever misfortunes befell the Argentinians, from lack of supplies to trenchfoot, it was all down to the ''ooligans from 'Ereford'. The troopers had relished the thoughts of imagined mischief 'the pilgrims' had been up to.

And just how close those vivid fantasies were to reality was not known to many. Even they would have been surprised to learn that Spanish-speaking SASmen had created havoc by striding authoritatively through Argentinian lines, commandeering vehicles and supplies on behalf of General Menendez. The enemy had been sent hither and thither in total confusion for days until the unnerving truth dawned. The British were in amongst them. The story had never been told outside the confines of Bradbury Lines barracks.

"You're living in cloud-cuckoo land, Brummie," Fraser said reproachfully. "We're back in the real world now."

"Yeah," the NCO replied after a pause. "And lucky to be here. I suppose."

There was something about the way he said it that chilled Fraser. Perhaps it was the underlying tone of fatalism. A hint of regret.

Perish the thought, the SAS captain scolded himself. It was just his own imagination. People like Brummie didn't change. They were hewn out of granite. Indestructible.

Out in the compound the tiger-suited training cadre was stood down and the sudden gabble of excited, happy voices drifted through the still afternoon air. A tall SAS trooper in olive green fatigues detached himself from the crowd and strode purposefully towards the mendiko tree.

He went down on his haunches beside the two men. "Delivered, batch of supertroop Action Men, one," he reported in an accent that would have sounded good on a polo field. Even white teeth grinned in a handsome sun-burnt face.

"Thanks, Alex," Fraser acknowledged, thinking that the only thing the ex-Guardsman from D Squadron lacked was a duelling scar on his cheek. But Alexander Thorpington-White, bodyguard and unarmed combat expert, would never have let an opponent get that close to him. "How are they?"

"They're all right, boss. Well, whilst we've got our eyes on them. It's really a question of how they pass their training on to their own men."

Fraser appreciated the problem, it was nothing new. "And what about Jammeh's bodyguard?"

Thorpington-White grimaced. "That *is* difficult. We thought we had the makings of a team last week. Then we were practising with me playing President when someone let off a negligent discharge. My bodyguard dived under the nearest table and left me standing there. Lovely target. I could've been shot."

Brummie chuckled. "Wish I'd been there, Chalky. I'd've bleedin' shot you. No danger." The dour NCO's paranoid dislike of the idle rich was known and cherished throughout the Regiment. And the regular appearance of the Thorpington-White family in the society gossip columns of the press made Alex a prime candidate for Brummie's scorn.

"You won't say that, Sarn't, when they save your life." The ex-Guardsman added with relish: "They're in this batch you're taking with you to Sakoto."

The sergeant snorted and turned to Fraser. "See that, boss. I've got to drive 'cause not one of the little buggers knows how. We'll have to start a course."

Thorpington-White stood up. "Shall I bring round the deuce-and-a-half?"

"Please, Chalky," Brummie returned, not looking forward to the long ride in the battered two and a half ton truck. "Just make sure the little sods aren't armed. I don't want to get shot by accident."

Thorpington-White laughed. "With the friends you've made, it wouldn't *be* an accident."

As he strode off, Fraser said: "Brummie, listen, I promise you I will consider your point of view. Hitting at the Jatos, I mean. I'll discuss it thoroughly with Lionel."

"Thanks, boss," the NCO said stiffly.

Fuck me, he thought, that's just bloody typical. Discuss it with know-it-all Corporal Witcher. A guaranteed way of making sure nothing happened.

He walked off after Thorpington-White.

But something was to happen far sooner than he expected.

Yet, he was to tell himself later, he should have been expecting it. As he manhandled the lumbering truck down the makeshift track towards the main road, he had felt a foreboding of trouble.

Many of his colleagues had that ability. In the same way that an animal will sense a predator nearby before there is any giveaway sound or smell. Different men felt it differently. A familiar itch with some; a niggling worry with others, like a headache before an approaching thunderstorm. With Brummie, it was a feeling like dyspepsia. A discomfort in his gut that made him irritable.

The reason he had ignored it this time was probably his preoccupation with the conversation he had just had with Captain Johnny Fraser.

He rated the SAS officer highly, but he was unhappy about the way he followed Lionel Witcher's recommendations so blindly.

Perhaps Fraser's attitude was just another unfortunate legacy from the South Atlantic. Maybe the Scotsman wasn't eager for another fighting war just yet. Wanting to give other methods a try.

He knew the Falklands War had shaken Fraser. Its total ferocity had mollified even the most hardened SAS veterans. They had continued as though it meant nothing to them, with the slightly patronising air of those who could walk on water. Living up to their reputations.

But Brummie knew different. He'd noticed even Johnny Fraser's quiet good humour become a little brittle. A man who had spent his life challenging death and adversity, suddenly realising that, this time, he might not get away with it.

The helicopter crash had brought it home. Suddenly twenty SASmen and seconded helpers had been snatched away. Wiped out. Vanished off the face of the earth. Into the grey, icy and unforgiving depths of the South Atlantic.

Heroes of South Georgia, Pebble Island, and even the famous battle of Mirbat back in 1972. Some had served since the early sixties. It gave victory a sour taste.

Who dares dies.

Brummie shivered.

"You okay?" Major Badji asked.

The sergeant glanced at the small Guinean next to him. He was the senior officer in the training cadre, a devout disciple of Colonel Kwofie. He was efficient and soldierly, but Brummie disliked him. Shifty eyes and a sneery smile.

"No problem," Brummie grunted. "Someone walked over my grave."

"Ah," Badji said, looking confused. It wasn't an expression he knew. "Maybe you get malaria."

"Maybe you get my boot up your arse," Brummie snapped.

Badji smarted and sulked back into his seat, staring ahead with a slightly trembling lower lip.

Ahead, a donkey-cart meandered in the middle of the road where it narrowed between two dense patches of rattan palms. Brummie tooted angrily and slowed down. Again he was aware of the feeling of discomfort in his gut. Perhaps it was the groundnut sauce he'd had at lunchtime . . .

"Sergeant!" Badji yelled.

At the same moment Brummie realised that the donkey-cart was not moving aside. The young man was leading the animal deliberately across their path.

The screech of scorching rubber wailed as Brummie braked the two and a half tonner hard, preparing to throw it into a high-speed reverse. Vaguely, he was aware of someone emerging from the back of the donkey-cart. Sunlight glinted on gunmetal. In the sudden burst of fire that followed, he felt the front tyres go, and the truck start to slew. He spun the wheel, vainly trying to compensate. Then the picture became a blur as the cab twisted around to face the side of the road. Brummie cursed. If only he'd realised! He should have driven straight through the donkey-cart.

The cab toppled over the embankment and came to

rest, its front wheels spinning freely. Below, a swollen water-course burbled around the roots of the rattan palms.

"OUT!" he shouted at Badji, grabbing for the Armalite stowed beside the seat.

The Guinean major had swiftly grasped the situation. He had already extracted the snub-nosed .38 revolver from his belt. In the back his men would be dangerously exposed. Brummie had insisted that only one man actually carry a weapon in order to avoid accidents.

Now the SAS sergeant cursed his own caution as he imagined the frantic rush in the exposed cargo-body as each man fought his way to the weapons crate.

A dull thud shook the ground. He glanced back down the road just in time to see a tall palm start to topple like a giant nine-pin. It crashed across the road, dragging smaller trees with it. As dust clouds sprang into the late afternoon air, he realised there was no going back. Someone was doing a thorough job, cutting off their line of retreat.

He'd been expecting gunfire. He was mildly surprised that it hadn't come, but that was only because time seemed to slow in moments of acute danger. Suddenly the wind-shield was blasted out of its mounting, vicious slivers of razor-sharp glass spitting into the cab. Shells tore away at the soft steel bulkhead behind his head as he scrambled out after Badji.

More shells ricochetted off metal while he dropped to his knees beside the cab. The scene in the cargo-body was complete chaos. Some of the men were standing, arms raised, trying to surrender. Others had found their weapons and were returning fire at the muzzle-flashes that blinked through the dust storm that had sprung up magically around the stricken truck.

One of the standing troopers was blown back by the force of a bullet slamming into him. Toppling over the truck side, he disappeared from view.

The sight of it seemed to stun his colleagues into action. They dived for the meagre cover offered by the cargo-body, and hunted in earnest for their weapons.

Badji raised his revolver and snapped off a couple of shots at vague targets. It was a futile gesture.

Brummie scanned the scene. Fire was streaming in from the far side of the road. Behind him the watercourse offered a tempting escape route, kept free by their attackers to give them a clear field of fire. If the Jatos had the time to prepare, or sufficient equipment, it was probably mined. But there was little choice between that and being annihilated in the vehicle.

The sergeant nudged Badji's shoulder. "Get your men off the road, Major! Pronto! I'll follow on. We'll RV beyond those trees!"

"RV?" Badji queried. Another PG fell, blood pumping out of a gaping chest wound to saturate his new tiger-suit.

"Rendezvous!" Brummie shouted. "Beyond the trees behind us. Now shift!"

As Badji wriggled forward on the road beside the truck, shouting up at his troops, Brummie opened the cab door and rummaged beneath the seat for an ammunition pouch. Finally he found what he was looking for.

He grabbed several No 83 smoke grenades, started pulling the pins, and hurled them up-wind of the lorry. Instantly, billowing green smoke tumbled out of each canister like a genie from a lamp, and began drifting in thick wafts across the rear cargo-body. Seeing the retreat covered, the tiger-suited PGs started to dismount under a tirade of abuse from Badji. With no targets offered the stutter of gunfire from the ambushers began to peter away.

As the first PG passed Brummie, the sergeant clapped him reassuringly on the shoulder. Seeing the nerveless SASman grinning unconcernedly appeared to restore his flagging courage.

"Remember, don't panic," Brummie said gruffly, pointing towards the watercourse. "We'll get out of here in the confusion. But remember what you've been taught. Move slowly and carefully using cover. The others will follow your example."

Brummie released his grip. The man nodded and smiled nervously, although the sergeant doubted he'd comprehended a word.

However he was never to find out. Because, as the man picked his way down the embankment to the watercourse, a solitary shot rang out. The guardsman gave a short gasp of surprise and pitched headlong down the slope. With a loud and untidy splash he disappeared beneath the green water. A small flurry of yellow bubbles marked his instant grave for a moment, before it drifted away on the down-stream flow.

"Shit," Brummie muttered tersely. The other PGs faltered, the idea of orderly retreat had suddenly lost its appeal.

"What is it?" Badji demanded. He was hiding his panic with anger which was directed at any of his troopers who moved, or anyone who didn't.

"They're outflanking us," Brummie replied, nodding towards the spot where the palm had been felled on the road behind them. "The people who blew the tree have moved to our rear on the high ground overlooking the watercourse."

"So. What do we do? You are the instructor."

"Form two groups, Major, like you've been trained," Brummie hissed. "One for covering fire while the others move. Then reverse the process. Now move it!"

The Guinean officer looked uncertain, then yelled at his men to follow their fallen comrades. Obviously he didn't intend to lead by example. Prompted by his anger, his men threw themselves down the slope in a disorderly scrum.

More shots rang out from the treeline and another guardsman fell, screaming at the sight of the fist-sized hole punched in his own abdomen.

Brummie Turner viewed the spectacle with dismay. Their situation looked precarious. After the rigours of the South Atlantic, he didn't intend to suffer an ignominious end like this. He weighed the Armalite in his hand and studied the treeline where he knew the outflanking snipers must be. Rapidly he let off a succession of well-aimed rounds.

Then a movement up on the road caught his eyes. A trail of red dust marked the approach of a vehicle beyond the fallen palm. He squinted hard through the drifting veil of smoke to make out a white Suzuki jeep. It had pulled in by the tree and a white youth in a sunhat, check-patterned shirt and denim jeans was standing on the seat, apparently to get a better view of the battle going on before him.

Brummie wondered if a cry to fetch help would carry the distance. Then the whipcrack of gunfire from the snipers gathered momentum and he knew it wouldn't. He glanced back to the Suzuki and saw that the figure had gone to the rear of the vehicle.

Answering fire came from the watercourse as half-a-dozen PGs, followed by Major Badji, reached cover. But their trail was littered with bodies of fallen guardsmen, some wounded and wailing pitifully, others killed or twitching in their death throes.

Christ, Brummie thought, I led these poor bastards straight into this. That mistake over the donkey-cart was bloody inexcusable. Then self-criticism became smothered by a rising anger against the unseen enemy.

Gunfire suddenly burst from a new position. He scanned back to the Suzuki and his spirits lifted. Using the fallen palm for cover, the youth was pouring a steady stream of bullets into the treeline which held the snipers who had pinned down Badji's party.

The rifle being fired was only lightweight stuff. It sounded like a .22 repeater. Just a hunting job for small game, but it was having the desired effect. Finding their own rear vulnerable, the snipers were having second thoughts about pushing home their attack. There was a sudden scurry of movement in the undergrowth. Dark, bent figures began moving rapidly in the shadows. A glimpse of bright yellow. Taking careful aim, Brummie squeezed off a succession of rounds. It was hard to tell if he'd hit anything.

Behind him, the smoke grenade had almost spent itself and Brummie clambered back onto the cargo-body of the truck. Through the shifting ribbons of smoke, he scanned the landscape for signs of the original ambush party.

Nothing. Several hundred yards away, he saw the outline of men moving, grey forms in the dust-haze. Shrinking, receding rapidly into the bush. The donkey-cart, too, he noticed, had disappeared.

Only then Brummie realised how hot he was. His entire

body was drenched in sweat, his olive bush shirt clinging like a second skin.

Cautiously, he moved onto the road, the Armalite held at port, ready. But no gunfire came. Breathing a long, slow sigh of relief, he edged towards the Suzuki.

As Brummie approached, the youth peered darkly from beneath the sunhat, the rifle held awkwardly and still smoking.

"Thanks, sonny," Brummie said. He held out his hand. "I think your timely arrival saved our bacon."

The youth's white teeth grinned through his dust-smeared face. "I don't make a habit of rescuing the military. Naturally I expect them to be looking after me."

The voice was lighter than he'd expected and the hand in his palm, cool, small and delicate. "We walked slap into an ambush party. It looks like they've scarpered now, but I'd stay around if I were you. We'll see you have an armed escort back to Sakoto – if that's where you're going?"

"Not quite that far. Just to the Agricultural Research Station near Bankama. I'm Mo Sinclair."

Brummie stared, speechless. "Mo . . ? Sinclair . . ? Jesus, I'm sorry, lady. I didn't realise . . ."

The sound of girlish laughter was like a balm after the sudden burst of chaos and carnage. "It's my fault for dressing like a tomboy. Dad's always telling me about it."

She removed the grubby white sunhat to reveal a bun of auburn hair and grinned impishly at him. A mischievous light in the hazel eyes mocked at him. "There," she said. "'Hope I don't still look like a fella."

"No way, Miss Sinclair," Brummie blustered, his eyes resting on the snug fit of the denim jeans around her slim hips. "I'm Sergeant Turner by the way. Call me Brummie."

"From Birmingham?"

His smile was more like a leer as he nodded. "Well, you certainly *don't* look like a bloke, even if you shoot like one."

She peered at the barrel of the .22 and wrinkled her nose disdainfully. "I don't expect I hit anyone. I had my eyes shut. Dad's made me do some target practice, but I've never hit anything yet. He still insists I take it with me for protection."

"A wise man."

Mo looked past Brummie at the line of PGs making their way back across the watercourse towards the lorry. "You've had some casualties."

He followed the direction of her gaze. "I'm afraid so. Would you mind running me back to Duntenda barracks? I need help."

"You take my jeep, Sergeant. I'm a veterinary surgeon, I might be able to help here."

He looked doubtful. She smiled thinly. "Men and animals are different, but injuries are the same. I've treated a lot of victims of poachers."

Before he could reply, he heard the nearing sound of a Land Rover, its engine screaming at maximum revs as it tore into view, trailing a whirlwind of dust in its wake.

"Bleedin' cavalry's late again," he muttered.

As the Panther loomed larger he recognised Fraser at the wheel with Thorpington-White beside him. In the rear compartment he could see the heads of the rest of D Squadron's training team. The vehicle was loaded down with weaponry of every description.

The vehicle fishtailed to a skidding halt as Brummie strode forward to meet it. Even before it had stopped, everyone had scrambled off and was making towards the scene of the ambush.

"We heard gunfire. What the hell's happened?" Fraser demanded.

"Ambush, boss. I'm afraid I went smack into it."

"Casualties?"

Brummie grimaced. "Heavy, boss. Six dead, a dozen wounded and about six or seven survivors."

"Christ," Fraser breathed. "What about the enemy? Are they still in position?"

"No, boss. They've scooted. Mostly to the north, but there's a sniper party to the south."

"Strength?"

"A dozen, I'd say."

Brummie indicated towards the diminutive figure of the girl waiting by the Suzuki. "That's Ralph Sinclair's daughter, boss. She turned up in the nick of time and scared

145

the daylights out of 'em. Lucky she had a shooter with her."

Surprise flickered in Fraser's eyes, but he only shifted his gaze momentarily. "I want a full Sitrep, Brummie, as soon as you're back at Duntenda and we've looked after the injured. Understand?"

"Sure, boss." Brummie blinked. "Of course."

Fraser scanned the scene again, his chin set in a firm line. "This is bloody unforgivable. Jammeh will want answers. No doubt Kwofie will have a field day." He shook his head in disbelief. "Christ, this must be thirty miles beyond the demarcation line of Jato territory."

Brummie sniffed. "You want to tell that to Lionel, boss. It's Psychlops who's got the maps. Perhaps he ought to give one to Jato."

The captain's eyes flashed. "*Lionel* wasn't driving the truck, Sergeant." The sudden use of rank was a reprimand. "And, listen, standing orders from now on . . ."

"I know, boss," Brummie interrupted. "Armed escort with all troop movements."

"Right."

"With our four vehicles that'll be a piece of piss," Brummie grated as he turned and started back towards the wrecked truck.

Fraser's face coloured, but he resisted the urge to call the sergeant back. Now wasn't the time for recriminations. Anyone of them could have driven into the ambush.

As he walked slowly towards the Suzuki, he removed his bush hat. "Hallo, Mo. It's been a long time."

Her smile was hesitant, her eyes dark and questioning. "Hallo, Johnny. Dad said you'd come back."

"I'm sorry we had to meet again under these circumstances. But, anyway, I gather thanks are in order."

"It was nothing. I've offered your sergeant help with the injured. I think some are in a bad way."

"That's kind," he said. And as he spoke he felt an old familiar tightness in his chest. She hadn't changed in the slightest since he'd last seen her. He found himself grinning foolishly. "It's lovely to see you again, Mo, really it is."

The look of uncertainty on her face fell away and she

smiled broadly. He had never forgotten the effect of those dimples in the sunburnt freckled face.

"It's nice to see you, too, Johnny." She paused, a distant look in her eyes. "About the letters, I'm sorry. I had to stop writing. I hope you've forgiven me."

"Of course. I understand." But even as he spoke the words, he knew that he didn't.

"Things alter, you know. It was nice while you were here, but when you'd gone. You know, life goes on."

"Another man?"

Her cheeks flushed, her tan deepening. "No, Johnny. It was nothing. It wasn't . . . it just wasn't that simple. It was something and it was nothing."

"And you were busy?" he said. He'd meant it to be unkind, but it just sounded like understanding.

She touched his forearm. "Thanks, Johnny. Thanks for not being angry. Time moved on, that's all." Then she stood upright to her full five feet and smiled again. "I suppose I'd better go and see what I can do."

"Sure, thanks . . ." Fraser began, his voice trailing off.

As he watched her go, a feeling of anger and frustration welled inside him. And a desperate yearning. God, she was special.

No woman had ever made him feel quite like that before.

6

Colonel Kemo Kwofie's visit had left him in a foul mood.

Instead of tackling the mountain of paperwork, which seemed to have swollen each time he glanced at his IN-tray, Johnny Fraser paced his makeshift office at Duntenda barracks, unable to concentrate.

Of course, had he been Head of State Security, he reasoned that his reaction would have been the same. No commander liked hearing that his men had been led like lambs to the slaughter. Butchered in the simplest of ambushes that should never have been allowed to happen. Kwofie had been furious and rightly so. And the fact that it was one of the men who was supposed to have been training the PGs that had got them into the situation did not help.

For an hour he had had to listen to a barrage of scarcely-veiled insults, made worse by Kwofie's natural arrogance.

Although he had made a spirited defence on Brummie Turner's behalf, Fraser realised that his string of excuses must have sounded pretty lame.

The only good news to come from the confrontation was that Kwofie had actually agreed to let Fraser go on an anti-insurgent patrol with the Presidential Guard the following week. That in itself was an achievement. The black commander had resolutely side-stepped all such requests despite Jammeh's agreement to the idea.

However, even that minor triumph did little to take the sourness from Fraser's mood. He slumped in his chair and studied the fat blow-fly trapped in a corner window pane. He shared its sense of buzzing frustration.

Not for the first time since this assignment had begun he wondered if he was up to the responsibility it demanded.

Back at Hereford the 'Old Man' had as good as told him that there was promotion in the offing.

"Course Alan Hawksby did a first rate job in the Argentine." Even now he could hear the precise, no-nonsense tone of OC22 as though it was only yesterday. "Months of secret surveillance right under their noses. Even an occasional bit of mischief. Cheek of the devil, he's got. But then, of course, you know that, Johnny. I was forgetting you were with him in Iran."

"Mine was only a small role, boss," Fraser had replied, knowing full well the Colonel had forgotten no such thing. "But I got to know Major Hawksby as well as anyone."

That famous inscrutable smile of the Old Man's. It could mean any one of a million things. "I understand, Johnny. 'The Hawk' always did play the game pretty close to his chest. His own man. Tough as the proverbial brickhouse.

"But there was a price to be paid for all those months hiding under the nose of the enemy. Major Hawksby's starting to show his age." The CO's eyes had been pale, distant. "Not my assessment. His. But whether he's right or wrong, the thing is he may return to his unit. Cavalry. There's a vacancy going. Lieutenant Colonel."

Fraser had almost smiled. The military merry-go-round. Musical chairs. All move along one. He knew what was coming next. "If he does, his Squadron here would become free. Might you be interested if you were asked?"

Major Johnny Fraser. It had a ring to it. Jesus Christ, you just bet he'd be interested! At last, his long-awaited majority. Commander of a full SAS Squadron.

It would also mean the end of his career worries because, as Hawksby was about to do, he would almost certainly return to his own unit, REME, above the rank of major. And 'major' was where everyone stayed in the British Army if God and the Chiefs of Staffs intended them to go no further. The big hurdle. Cleared!

"If it was offered, boss, I wouldn't say no." He found himself silently mouthing the same words he had uttered to the 'Old Man' then.

But, as always, there would be a catch. And now he realised it was Free Guinea.

Like all SAS initiative tests, it had a built-in 'sickener' factor. Possibly the Colonel of 22 Special Air Service Regiment had realised it would provide a tough test? Probably. It would be typical of the man.

Put Fraser on a politically impossible and militarily impractical exercise and see how he shaped up. In charge of his own mini-Squadron, with no allies.

He smiled to himself. The challenge and the reward had been unspoken. But they were blatantly obvious. Sort out Free Guinea's little problems and the majority is as good as yours. Foul up? Then just forget it.

He knew that the anger he was directing at Brummie Turner was half-aimed at himself. The sergeant had challenged his acceptance of Lionel Witcher's policy, and there was a lot to be said for the blunt criticism. There was no way of knowing which was right. But that hardly seemed the decisive attitude expected of an SAS officer about to be promoted to major.

He looked up, suddenly aware of another presence in the room.

"Sorry, boss, I'd have knocked if there was a door."

Lionel Witcher was in his usual good spirits. For once he looked quite tidy in dark green jungle fatigues, the shirt tucked neatly into his stable-belt. He had even had a haircut which emphasised his slightly jug ears and the sprout of bushy fair hair on his crown.

"What is it, Lionel? I've a stack to get through before sundown." Fraser, uncharacteristically, couldn't hide the impatience from his voice.

"I think you'll feel the interruption's worth it, boss. Sorry anyhow."

"Don't be smooth."

The blue eyes blinked behind the plastic spectacles as Witcher raised his hands in mock surrender. "Okay, okay, boss! I just thought you'd be interested to know our friend Rubashëv is back in Sakoto. You know, the Czech from the World Federation of Trades Unions. I met him on our first up-country patrol. He was meeting with that Scotsman, Ian Hammond, before one of Fofana's political rallies."

Fraser wasn't in the mood to be spoon-fed. "Yes, Lionel,

of course I remember him. You ran a check with SIS to see if he was a known KGB man."

Witcher nodded. "That's right." It had come up negative on the files of Britain's Secret Intelligence Service. "Mind you, I didn't have a photograph of him. Anyway, he left soon after I met him."

"Why's he back?"

"Supposedly to help Fofana and his rallies. Ian Hammond has got three lined up for him this month. He's addressing the three major unions. The Seamen, the Taxi-drivers and the Government workers with the Marketing Produce Board."

Fraser shook his head. "President Jammeh should put a stop to it. Temporarily at least. It'll only ferment trouble, however well intended – and *that's* doubtful."

"Jammeh won't do it, boss. Reckons it'll just allow the Jatos to say 'I told you so.' It would only play into their hands. Confirm that he was restricting political opposition."

"Obviously you agree with him," Fraser observed sourly.

"Let's say I can see his point-of-view." He tapped at the sheet of paper in his hand. "The thing is, boss, I've had a discreet watch put on Rubashëv. And, lo-and-behold, he made a visit to the Green Mamba with adjoining rooms to Boris."

Johnny Fraser's eyebrows lifted. 'Boris' was Witcher's nickname for the resident KGB agent in Free Guinea. A short, tubby man with myopic vision, he was a sort of caricature of the joke-spy. Full of furtive gestures and move-ments, he was given to turning up the collar of his jacket and wearing makeshift disguises. Dark glasses one day; a workman's overalls the next, and dressed as an American tourist in Bermuda shorts the day after. Everyone knew him and used to point to him and call out a greeting.

But, although he'd obviously been put out to grass in this African backwater, he wasn't totally ineffectual. On more than one occasion, he had been found wandering around State House or other Government offices when they were closed. Always he had some transparently untrue alibi. 'I'd called to see a minister but he forgot and went home.' 'I was taking a short-cut.' 'I thought this office didn't close until eight.'

Security, before Brummie Turner persuaded Kwofie to tighten things up, had been appalling. No one ever locked up. They either forgot, couldn't be bothered, or else the keys had been missing for years.

The cover 'Boris' used most was an import-export business which, as far as Fraser could determine, mostly imported rare luxury items in return for black-market sterling.

"Do we know," Fraser asked, "if 'Boris' actually *met* this chap Rubashëv from the Federation? That pimp Berno is bloody tight-lipped about his clients."

Witcher tapped his nose. "Trust me, boss. We have someone on the inside."

"Not Brummie's bit of skirt. I'd hoped that was all finished."

"My lips are sealed."

Fraser checked a smile. The answer was plain enough. "Did our mystery agent learn anything?"

"Only that Rubashëv was checking on various import shipments made recently through the 'Boris' trading company. Going by the Customs declarations, it's been low-grade agricultural equipment, spades etc, some medical supplies and vehicle parts, pens and paper. Big quantities though. But since when can you rely on Customs declarations?"

"It certainly looks as though 'Boris' is moving into a different league. A change from soft tissue bog rolls, hi-fi sets and fancy perfumes."

The corporal nodded. "And *all* the stuff of potential use to someone doing a hearts-and-minds job on a lot of people. Anyhow, I hope you think it was worth the interruption?"

"Of course, Lionel." Fraser stood up from the desk. "Sorry I was a bit snappy. Bloody paperwork getting me down. That and operating so much in the dark."

"Try and get out more, boss."

"I'll try." He didn't have to force the smile; he felt better. "By the way, I suppose we're no nearer to discovering the identity of Jato?"

"Ah, Mr Pheko! Brother of the late lamented Omar, or not? That's what the alkali of Massang thought."

"And there's still no sign that Omar had a brother?"

Witcher shook his head. "Omar was an only child and his mother died in childbirth. If there *is* a connection, Jato may be a half-brother, perhaps born to a second wife. Unfortunately, the father went to meet Allah five years ago. As for the official records, forget it."

"What about elders in the village? Doesn't anyone recall?"

"Trouble is, boss, they're too eager to please. Don't like saying no. So, depending on how you ask the question, you get a different answer. But always in the affirmative. Just go round in circles." He smiled. "Eager to please or else just dead crafty."

"So a complete blank?"

"I'm trying a new tack. Presumably Jato Pheko went a similar route to his alleged brother. That is you don't become a skilled rebel leader sitting under the village mango tree."

"Moscow? Cuba?"

"Or Libya. Again records are the problem. Whoever he is, he must have left the country at some point. And, if he came back recently by an *authorised* method of entry, then even Kwofie's gendarmes should have been able to trace him by now."

"So we're looking for a national who's officially listed as being out of the country?"

Witcher stared past the captain to the window. Another blow-fly was trapped in the corner pane. "But which name did he use when he left? I bet it wasn't Pheko."

Fraser, too, found himself mesmerised by the frantic buzzing of the fly. "It's like looking for a ghost."

"Perhaps," Witcher said, "we ought to call in a ju-ju man."

"Ten seems a bit late in the morning for a dawn swoop."

Bill Mather's observation was made as the three SASmen approached the ramshackle headquarters of the Presidential Guard. The two dozen dilapidated barrack huts of concrete block and corrugated iron sprawled over an uneven dusty compound adjoining State House. A sprinkling of lounging black soldiers added to the untidy look of the place. Sullen white eyes followed them as they crossed towards the administration block.

"Not many tiger-suits in evidence," Corporal Lionel Witcher added. "And I don't recognise any of these lay-abouts."

"They all look the same to me," Mather replied. "But there's not much sign of activity. Perhaps they're forming up somewhere else."

Fraser rang the bell at the glass reception window to the outer office of the Adjutant's quarters. Its ringing tone reverberated forlornly somewhere beyond the locked door. Nothing happened.

"Like raising the dead," Mather grinned. "Not even a guard on duty. Brummie would have a fit if he saw this lax security. Kwofie's promised him things would change. Pity he didn't come."

Fraser hit the bell again. "I want him to keep a low profile until the storm over the ambush has died down. What's the time?"

"0945, boss," Witcher replied. "Ah, here comes some-one."

A thin youthful trooper with darting, suspicious eyes entered the office and crossed warily to the glass window.

He shoved it open. "Yes?"

"Captain Fraser and party for Colonel Kwofie."

The man shook his head. "He not here."

He went to slide the glass shut again, but Fraser inserted his hand. "One moment, my good chap. If he's not here, *where* is he? He's expecting us. We're going on patrol with him."

"Patrol gone," the trooper said.

"Gone?" Fraser was incredulous. "We were told to meet at 1000 hours. It was arranged last week."

The trooper shrugged. "Patrol go early this morning."

"Where to?"

"I cannot say. It is security matter."

Mather turned away in disgust. "Can't say or won't."

"You come back later," the trooper said, and snapped the window closed, narrowly missing Fraser's fingertips.

"That's typical of Kwofie," Witcher said. "He's never

wanted us to go on one of his security patrols. When you put him on the spot last week, boss, he had to agree. But he can stall like this for evermore. He'll probably say he sent you a message about a change of time but it never arrived."

They stepped out into the blinding sunlight just as the familiar sight of Ralph Sinclair's G-wagen drove into the far side of the compound.

"I wonder why he's in such a hurry," Fraser thought aloud.

"Unfortunately," Mather observed, "he hasn't got that little dolly of a daughter with him. She did an ace job on the casualties after the ambush. I didn't get a chance to thank her."

"She got thanks enough," Fraser said with a smile. "Our lads were queuing up to show their appreciation."

A rare smile cracked Mather's face. "I know where to go next time I need a boil lanced."

Fraser stepped forward to meet the G-wagen. "Hello there, Ralph. What're you doing here?"

"Hi, Johnny." He scrambled out of the seat. "I'm paying a visit to Colonel Kwofie. Got something interesting to tell him."

"You're out of luck, I'm afraid. He's out on patrol."

"When's he back?"

"Later. That's the official Guinean line."

Sinclair nodded thoughtfully. "Ah, well, that could be days. No problem. Oh, by the way. I was sorry to hear about that dust-up you had with the Jatos. Maureen told me all about it. Bloody vicious thugs. Bit of a bloodbath by all accounts."

"Mo was magnificent."

Sinclair smiled the smile of a proud father. "Yes, I do believe she was. Now, why don't you and some of the lads pop round for dinner one evening. It would be nice for you and Maureen to reminisce over old times."

Fraser said quietly: "Things aren't the same between us, Ralph. I've talked to her. Sorry."

"Mmm. So am I." He took a deep breath, resigned. "Still there you go. Women and their funny ways. I suppose . . . ?"

"What is it?"

Sinclair grinned. "This information I had for Kwofie.

Well it's to do with this Jato nonsense. You might be interested. I expect the Colonel would just sit on it. Or just ignore it. Why don't you come and lunch with me? I'm on my way there now."

"Where's that?"

The Union Jack Club was the last hallowed sanctuary of the Englishman in Free Guinea. The ten acres of sandy, scrubby turf that made up its eighteen-hole golf course was the central jewel in the smart Bajtenda residential suburb.

Light Atlantic breezes kept it comfortably cool whilst white-coated stewards bustled around elderly patrons in the solemn atmosphere of the pavilion restaurant and bar.

"Never seen so many white faces," Mather said as they walked onto the terrace. "Like being at home."

"The white man's ghetto," Sinclair laughed, catching the eye of the drinks steward. "A sort of Brixton in reverse. What'll you have?"

"Judging by these accents," Witcher said, "we'd better make it G and Ts."

"Mine's a Tru-beer," Mather said pointedly. A few heads turned.

As they waited for their order to come, Fraser asked: "What was it you had for Kwofie, Ralph? You sounded excited."

Sinclair laughed. "Well, if the immediate conclusion was right, I'd be half-way to being a millionaire."

"Lucky man. How so?"

"It would appear that we've discovered a new strain of groundnut plant with double the normal yield."

"Yes?"

"Well, at the Agricultural Research Station we get yield reports from the Government Produce Marketing Agency. At this time of year their inspectors are out at the local weigh-stations buying the crops from the farmers. And so far this year the groundnut yield is nearly twenty per cent up on the same time last season."

The steward came and began distributing the drinks. Fraser said: "That's good news, Ralph. What caused it? Good rains?"

156

"No way, Johnny. It's a load of old bull, the whole business. Somehow a proportion of the crop is recirculating, I reckon. It's checked at the weigh-stations, the inspectors give the farmers their chits to cash at the local Government commissioner's office. Then somehow – God knows how – the farmer gets hold of his sold crop and takes it back to the weigh-station again. Gets paid twice. It's the only explanation. It's going to cost the Ministry of Finance a packet!"

Fraser frowned as he considered the implications. "Wouldn't the treasury people realise something was amiss?"

Sinclair chuckled bitterly. "This is Guinea, Johnny. They don't have forward computer projections for comparison and all that sort of sophisticated financial back-up. They'll suddenly realise the money's running out and *then* start asking questions. When it's too late."

"What would the Government do?" Mather asked, a froth of Tru-beer decorating his ginger moustache.

"Immediately they'd lower the payment rate for ground-nuts. They'd have to. And that would go down like a lead balloon with the peasant farmers. Especially those who *aren't* in on this racket."

"You're sure it's a racket?" Fraser asked.

"I've lived in Guinea twenty-five years, Johnny. I can smell a racket a mile off."

Lionel Witcher said: "Remember that report I made when the team went on that initial up-country recce? We came across a lorry. They said they'd shed their load of groundnuts, but we reckoned we'd just interrupted a robbery, although they wouldn't admit it to us."

Sinclair shook his head. "That's not the way it works here, Lionel. They were *helping* to have the Government robbed of a few bags. They'd then grease the palm of the official receiving the crop back at Sakoto. A few sacks here. A few sacks there. That's how they're doing it."

Mather drained his drink. "So those nicked sacks will find their way back to the farmers?"

"What a way to run a revolution," Fraser said thought-fully.

"It's a good way to pay for one," Witcher observed.

Ralph Sinclair seemed pleased to have solved the mystery himself. "All this detective work has given me an appetite, lads. I recommend the smoked salmon. It's flown in three times a week from Britain."

The three faces lit like beacons. Six weeks of living on field-kitchen food had made them desperate men.

"Hello," Mather said suddenly. "I reckon word's got round about the salmon. Isn't that Chalky? He must have smelled it."

Heads turned to see Lieutenant Thorpington-White threading his way through the tables towards them. From the look on his face it didn't seem as though the menu was the first thing on his mind.

Fraser rose to meet him. "What is it, Chalky?"

The lieutenant was breathless. "Thank goodness I found you, boss. I've been looking everywhere . . ."

"Trouble?" Fraser asked impatiently.

Thorpington-White nodded. "Mark Benjamin radio'd in at . . ." He glanced at his watch, ". . . 1215 hours. They were on river patrol, manning an OP, when they heard shooting from Massang village."

Fraser felt his blood turn to icewater. "What happened?"

"It's been turned over, boss. Pretty bad."

"Jatos?"

The lieutenant shrugged. "Looks like it. It's pretty well known the alkali there won't co-operate . . ."

"Yes. He's a stubborn old sod."

"I've got the Sandringham outside. She's fully loaded. A steward's standing guard over it."

Fraser said: "I'll take it. Our vehicle's down at the PG barracks." He turned to Sinclair. "Ralph, would you mind dropping Chalky back there?"

"No problem. But is there nothing else I can do?"

"No, Ralph. That'll be a great help. I'm afraid that salmon will have to wait for another day."

Sinclair smiled grimly. "It'll keep."

They hit the road like a tornado. With Fraser at the wheel, they kept up a punishing pace for four hours, the wheels humming over the hot tarmac as they rocketed along the deserted up-country road. Mile after weary mile flashed past; village after endless village.

Not long after Princetown the drums started.

It was a two-note beat. The first long; the second shorter. Two syllables. Boom-bah! Boom-bah!

Ja-to! Ja-to!

No chances were taken. Fraser swung the vehicle off the road onto the tortuous cross-country route. Both GPMGs were manned and cocked. The mounting tension combined with the furnace-dry heat of the interior to draw the sweat from their bodies. It evaporated instantly in the stifling air, leaving the skin caked with a film of salt.

At last the sun started to wane in the dust-filled sky, a bright silver medallion set in a grey mother-of-pearl bed. Its diffused light touched the dying razor grass so that it shimmered like rustling gold rods.

"It's misty ahead," Mather observed as they bumped along the riverside track. The torrent that had been gushing on their previous trip was sluggish now. Its level had dropped several feet since the rains had finished.

Fraser glanced towards the fairytale spirals of mist that hung in the still air and he knew Mather was wrong. He'd seen the effect back home. In the autumn when the farmers burned acres of stubble at a time.

"It's smoke," he stated simply. They said nothing. They knew it was in the direction of Massang. And, if they had any doubt, the grotesque hovering flight of the vultures soon dispelled it.

As they approached they saw that there was no ragged blue flag of allegiance to the President. Not even a post to hang it from. No woven rattan walls to the compound. No compound. No village.

Massang had gone. To all intents and purposes it had been wiped from the face of the earth. Blackened support timbers poked from the scorched remnants of burnt thatch like accusing black fingers. The mud blocks were crushed or discarded like a child's bricks.

A pitiful wailing floated on the wreaths of smoke. It was a woman's voice.

As he neared he could see that even the sacred baobab

159

tree had been ravaged by the blaze. The smell of death lingered in the air with the smoke. It was sweet and sickly.

Mark Benjamin saw him first. His green denims and bushshirt were ripped and smudged with charcoal. The bloodstains had soaked and dried into angry dark patterns.

He stood up from the wide-eyed black girl he was bandaging. She looked no more than five years old.

"Is she bad?" Fraser asked.

Benjamin's eyes looked sunken and haunted. "Phosphorous burns to the leg. Not a nice sight, boss. Some fucker was chucking grenades all over the shop. This poor little blighter was a lucky one."

Fraser smiled down at the child. She looked away.

Benjamin said: "I brought John Belcher over from the OP, boss. I hope that was okay? Slenzak and Perrott are still there. As we had a medic it seemed only sensible . . ."

Fraser put a hand on the other's shoulder. "That's fine, Mark. Good move. He's had his work cut out."

Benjamin pulled a bitter smile. "He's been working sodding miracles, boss, believe me. You should've seen the carnage."

"I can see enough," Fraser replied tightly. Above, a hooded vulture wheeled in, stiff-winged like an evil black kite, excrement dribbling from its tail as it descended on a neat row of mutilated corpses. A young lad beat it away with a stick. Reluctantly it lifted heavily into the air, ready to wait and watch for another opportunity.

"Wicked buggers them," Benjamin said. "If you leave the injured for a minute they come an' peck their eyes out."

"How're you coping?"

"It's all right now, boss. It was bloody shambolic when we first got here, but we called in the local VSO team. You know, Voluntary Service Overseas. There's a nurse called Sally, and two youngsters Kevin and Brian. They've worked like stink. And there's a useful bloke called Rod Bullock. He's worked here for years with a charity outfit called *Direct Action*. Knows the locals well. The villagers' first instinct was to charge off into the bush to hide, but he got them organised into work details."

"Sounds like a good man."

"First rate," Benjamin agreed. "Then, as luck would have it, Mo Sinclair turned up. Right little angel of mercy she's turned out to be."

"What's the extent of the casualties?"

Benjamin fished in the pocket of his bushshirt for a boiled sweet and handed it to the small girl. "Come on, I'll show you. We've accounted for twenty dead bodies and at least thirty VSI." Army jargon for Very Seriously Injured, it meant exactly that.

They passed more smouldering remains of collapsed huts until they came to a makeshift canvas shelter under which the wounded were being tended. There Fraser immediately recognised Mo dressing a murderous-looking stomach wound. A tall girl with short fair hair was helping John Belcher to sedate another villager whose leg was about to be amputated.

"That's Sally Richards," Benjamin explained. "The biggest problem is fresh water, boss. The sods who did this threw one of the dead bodies down the well."

"What about the bowser?" They had brought the small tanker trailer with them from Hereford. The idea had been to use it to help win over villages when drought threatened. This was one use they hadn't bargained on.

Benjamin nodded. "I got through to Brummie earlier and they're going to get it out here first thing tomorrow."

Just then Lionel Witcher approached, talking as he walked alongside a thick-set man in blue T-shirt and worn blue jeans.

"This is Rod Bullock," Benjamin introduced. "Captain Fraser."

Steady grey-blue eyes scrutinised the SAS officer from above a thick wad of dark beard with unkempt sun-bleached ends. "So you're the famous Captain." The cigarette between his lips twitched as he spoke from the corner of his mouth.

"Pleased to meet you, Rod," Fraser said. "I've heard about your work here; the bridges and wells, etcetera. The alkali was full of praise for what you've done for his village."

Bullock's gaze was unfaltering. Carefully he plucked the

cigarette stub from his lips and tossed it to the earth. He ground it out with the sole of his plimsoll. "And a lot of good it did the poor fuckers. Perhaps he'd've done better listenin' to a lecture from you on guns, than on how to grow onions."

There was something about Bullock's use of tense. Fraser felt his heart sink. "The alkali's dead?"

"Very much so," Bullock replied. "But not before they'd hacked his balls off and stuffed them in his mouth. It's a quaint African custom. Nothing new. A warning to others."

Fraser shook his head in slow disbelief. A harmless old man. Harmless and wise. But stubborn. That had been his downfall. Suddenly he recalled the marriage ceremony all those weeks earlier. "What about his son? Dawda? Did they get him too?"

Bullock extracted a crush-pack of Chesterfields from his shirt pocket and stuck one of its contents in his mouth. "It was his lucky day. He holed his fishing canoe yesterday and went down to the river to fix it this morning at first light. When the attack came he was able to hide," he explained wearily. "But the bastards got his new wife. I won't tell you what they did to her."

"Dead?"

"Dead." He lit the cigarette and drew deeply on it. It seemed to help. He sighed. "When you see something like this, Captain, it makes you wonder if it's all worthwhile." He gestured towards a forlorn black figure hunched over a covered body on the parched earth. It was Dawda.

"The poor little bugger's sobbing his heart out. Been doing it all day. Torn apart by grief. He was my best pupil when he was younger. Set his heart on being a butcher and wasn't afraid of hard graft. Reckoned he was going to show the Guineans how to do things for themselves . . ." His voice faltered. ". . . Now this." The big man's eyes were moist.

"We'll stop them," Fraser pledged. Brummie Turner's earlier criticism was suddenly bright and sharp in his ear, like a bugle call.

"Sure, Captain, you'll stop them," Bullock said quietly. "But at what cost? I had a feeling that the coup wouldn't be the last of it. I've seen this sort of thing happen all over the

162

Third World. Give the peasants guns and tell them to run things for themselves. And off they go, rushing, shooting and killing into the twentieth century. Why should Free Guinea be any different?" A thin smile crossed Bullock's face. "These young activists and their political leaders are all so goddam keen on catching up with the rest of the world they don't realise they're destroying their own in the process."

He stared across at the first-aid post. "Before today I even had a sneaking regard for the Jatos. They seemed to be smart operators. Set up their own education programme, advised their villages on agriculture and set up clinics – even if they did nick most of the stuff from us.

"You know we have about three hundred Guineans working for *Direct Action*. A lot of them are pretty disillusioned with Jammeh's crowd; in fact many used to work on the Government's own aid projects. They got pissed off with all the corruption and got fired when they spoke out. So they joined us because we get things done.

"So Jammeh doesn't really trust us with so many suspected 'subversives' aboard. But we're too well-known for him to do anything conspicuous about it."

"And you think some of your chaps support the Jatos?" Witcher prompted.

Bullock hesitated. "Well, I suppose some are bound to . . . That's why this is so bloody stupid. It'll turn my blokes right off. For all his faults – God's gift to Africa and all that – Jammeh wouldn't tolerate this sort of thing."

Witcher held up a tatty piece of yellow ribbon.

"What's that?" Fraser asked.

The corporal replied: "It's what passes as a uniform for the Jatos."

Rod Bullock nodded. "They'd been tied to the limbs of all the murder victims. If your lads hadn't turned up when they did, I doubt anyone would have been left alive. I'm no great lover of the military, Captain, but I was most impressed with your lot during the coup. And the civil aid your chaps gave afterwards. I hope you can do as well this time."

"Thanks," Fraser smiled. It was rare enough to hear genuine appreciation. "The name's Johnny."

Bullock tossed away his cigarette half-smoked. "The light's failing. I'll see about some fires."

As he left Fraser walked towards the first-aid post with Witcher. "Lionel, I want you to call up Two Team's OP and get Tiger down here before dawn tomorrow. He's probably the best tracker in the Regiment, so we may as well make full use of him."

Witcher nodded. "Shall do, boss."

It would be imperative for the Gurkha to arrive before sun-up because tracking spoor, particularly over dry terrain, was usually only possible at dawn and dusk when the light was at a low angle to show up the lightest of impressions and indentations. "But, boss, I don't think we should allow this incident to upset our policy. I mean, forays into the bush to try and hunt the Jatos will only end in disaster."

"Thank you, Lionel," Fraser said stiffly, "I shall bear that in mind."

He was aware that his tone had startled Witcher, but the corporal said nothing more. Fraser was thankful when he drifted off as they neared the first-aid post.

Mo Sinclair appeared from the shelter, wiping her blood-stained hands on a towel. She looked tired and hot, strands of auburn hair plastered to the perspiration on her forehead. Smudges of blood and grime discoloured her light tan.

Her smile was weary. "We must stop meeting like this, Johnny."

He felt awkward. "I seem to be spending all my time thanking you."

She glanced back at the row of makeshift beds. "I just thank God I was coming to Massang anyway. My last visit must have been two years ago. When you were last here."

"I remember," Fraser said. He would never forget that first night they had made love. On the outskirts of the village, on the banks of the great Kebba River. Under a vast sky of tropical stars. It had never been like that before. Or since.

She dabbed at her face with the towel. "It was ironic really. I'd heard there was an owl's nest nearby. Milky owls. They're beautiful creatures. But I'd been told the villagers were planning to destroy the nest and the fledgelings."

"What on earth for?"

"Bad ju-ju, I'm afraid." She shrugged. "The villagers can't understand things that fly at night. They never leave their compounds, so anything that does must be evil. Apparently they reckon they've had nothing but bad fortune since the owls roosted nearby. The marabou said there was only one solution."

"Did you save them?" he asked.

She smiled. "Yes, on my way here. They're in a cage in the back of the jeep. Covered over. If the villagers saw them they'd think this awful attack was divine retribution. That the owls really were bad ju-ju."

"Maybe they'd be right."

She looked up into his eyes. He hadn't changed. She felt drawn to their green-grey depths as she had once before. It was so long ago. Instinctively she drew back.

Fraser sensed something but he wasn't sure what. "You must be exhausted. Can you take a break?"

She laughed. It was a release. "I think I'll *have* to if I don't want to collapse over a patient. Anyway I'm a bit stuck now till more medicines arrive. Your chap John Belcher has radio'd up more supplies. He's wizard. He knows so much. And he's so good at improvising. He was making leaf poultices and all sorts. And they worked. He was saying he's not even qualified in the proper sense."

"He's had a lot of experience. And he's mad keen. His father is a famous surgeon and John failed his medical exams. The old man never forgave him when he joined the Army. And he's been fighting a battle with his conscience ever since."

"I bet," Mo said. "He reckons he wants to chat to the local marabou about cures. He may have a point. Several times they've saved my animals when I'd given up all hope. Sally, the VSO nurse, thinks it's a good idea. Wants them to run a joint study together."

"I see," Fraser said, failing to suppress a smile. "Taken a bit of a shine to him, has she?"

165

Mo linked her arm in his. "Between you and me, she thinks he's a bit of a dish. I think she's right."

Fraser grinned wickedly. "It's the uniform that does it. Never fails."

"Is that so?" Mo hadn't missed the gentle barb. He had been in combat dress the day they had met.

"Let's take a breather down by the river. It'll do you good to get away from all this."

"A good idea, Johnny. Dad keeps a bottle of brandy in his first-aid kit. I could do with some."

By the time they reached the sandy bank of the Kebba the sun had disappeared behind the inky western treeline. High above a vast formation of pink pelicans beat its way steadily south across a sky of molten gold that held the promise of more fine weather.

The river was a hundred yards wide at this point, running deep and slow. From mid-stream the loud call of a long-necked hadada floated across to them as the large brown bird flapped heavily along above the current.

The echo of its cry receded and the twilight began to fade. The silence and vastness of the landscape enveloped them with an intensity that was stunning.

Mo scrambled onto the wooden fishing jetty beside the rows of piroque canoes.

"Is this all right?" she asked. She spoke quietly, as though not wanting to disturb the absolute stillness.

"Fine," Fraser replied. He sat down next to her and placed the Armalite beside him on the jetty, as she handed him a plastic beaker. The pungent smell of brandy was tantalising.

"You think you might need the gun?" she asked.

He swigged at the beaker and felt the amber liquid burn its way down his dry throat. It had been a long, hard drive. Then the revolting sight at Massang . . . He wiped his mouth with the back of his hand. "They could still be around, Mo. This is Jato country."

"Jato?" She sounded puzzled.

"Yes. This is rebel country."

She looked into his eyes. "You don't think the Jatos did this, do you?"

A sudden stab of doubt hit him. "Of course. Everything points to it. The motive. The yellow ribbons . . ."

"No, Johnny. That's not true. It's just not true," she shook her head emphatically, her long hair tumbling around her shoulders. "*Anyone* can use yellow ribbons. I'm sure the Jatos wouldn't do that."

"What are you saying?"

"It wasn't the Jatos."

"Who then, for Christ's sake?"

Anger flashed in her eyes. "Johnny, don't you understand? It was Jammeh's men. It was the President's men who carried out the massacre."

"For goodness sake, Mo, why should they? It wouldn't make sense. The alkali was a loyal and devout President's man. I know that. Besides Mark Benjamin said they – the villagers – *told* him it was the Jatos."

Mo took a deep breath, hesitating. Then a weak smile crossed her lips. She took a sip of her brandy. It helped to clear her thoughts. "Johnny, just what do you *expect* them to tell you? As far as they are concerned you, too, *are* the President's men."

Fraser swallowed hard. Somehow there was a ring of truth about her words. He took another gulp of the brandy and then studied the beaker in his hand.

She snuggled close to his shoulder. "It's getting cold."

Her hair rubbed against his cheek. "Do you want to go back?"

"No, Johnny. I want to forget about today. Wipe it from my mind. Pretend it never even happened."

"But what you were saying . . ." Her words had troubled him.

She shifted and looked up at him. Her lips looked soft. Inviting. "Please, Johnny, let's not talk about it anymore. Especially not here. You remember?" She turned her head away, looking over the water which had turned to glittering quicksilver.

"I thought perhaps *you'd* forgotten." He squeezed her arm gently.

"No, Johnny, I never could. That night was one of the most wonderful of my life. Here with you. Beside the Kebba. You know I'd been a virgin until I was twenty-five." She glanced at him uncertainly, not used to such intimate talk. "Only one man before you. But it wasn't that. It was lovely. It was tender. Romantic. And I thought it was real."

"It was."

As she leaned against him he could sense that her eyes were closed. Her voice faded to a murmur: "It was too good to be real, Johnny. Or to last. After you had gone I realised that you'd always be married to your work. You're in love with adventure. With excitement. Danger. You don't get much of that in marriage."

Her words hurt but they still made him smile. "You make me sound like a little boy who won't grow up."

He felt the tremble of her body as she shared the joke. "Well, in a way it's true."

"You know, I seriously considered leaving the Regiment? Returning to the Engineers."

"Would you have been happy? Back to mundane duties."

It was so dark now that he could scarcely see her face, nestled against his chest. "You would have been the best compensation a man could have had."

"Exactly, Johnny. And I'm not sure I want to be thought of as a compensation."

Of course she was right, he knew that. And it wasn't a problem that could be avoided for ever. His time with the Regiment, at least in an active capacity, was fast running out. Maybe five years to go, barring injury or some recurring tropical disease. That's what finally got most SAS long-termers.

He was aware she was talking again. Her voice was a strained whisper on the nagging edge of sleep. "Besides, Johnny, there *was* another man in my life. I didn't quite tell you the truth. It's over now, but it changed things."

"I see." Her words twisted like a knife in his gut.

"I doubt if you do. I'm not sure I do myself. I suppose I found myself in love with you both. I guess I still am. The things I said to you then, I still mean them."

After a long moment, he said: "That makes me feel better. Perhaps we haven't completely lost what we had, after all?"

She didn't reply. He waited, feeling the warmth of her body against his. The smell of her in his nostrils. Alone together, cocooned in the velvet night.

Then he realised. Mo Sinclair had fallen into a deep, exhausted slumber.

7

By the time Captain Johnny Fraser reached State House his anger had subsided, but only just.

The words of the little Gurkha echoed through his mind time and again. And still he felt the same numb horror as when 'Tiger' Ratna had said: "They're not Jato, boss. No doubt about it." He had pointed to the indentation in the dried mud. It was scarcely discernible to the naked eye. "See, that's boot print. New issue, good tread."

Then the little man from Nepal had held up a brand new boot, one of those issued with the new tiger-suits to the PGs who had completed their training. "See, boss. Pattern is same. This attack not come from Jato. We got big problem, boss."

He could say that again. In fact Tiger hadn't, but the SAS armourer had.

The Ammunition Technical Officer had confirmed his worst fears. With his usual deliberation, like a man asked to volunteer to be executed, the armourer had been adamant. The calibre of the bullets so liberally sprayed around Massang weren't 7.62mm from AK47 Kalashnikovs. They were 9mm. Probably from French MAT 49 sub-machine guns. Standard issue to the Presidential Guard of Free Guinea.

On the way Fraser had forced himself to detour to The Oceanic, where he kept a single room, for a shave and change of uniform. The President would hardly be impressed by the sight of a haggard soldier, evidently overcome by anger and emotion.

He was kept waiting only half-an-hour before he entered Jammeh's office. He found the man standing at the window to the balcony, gazing at the endless rolling breakers of the

Atlantic. His long white robe danced around his legs in the light in-shore breeze.

He turned. "Ah, Captain Fraser! My good friend, I understand you need to speak to me urgently. I believe some trouble up-country. I tried to call Colonel Kwofie to attend as all security matters concern him. But he is away on patrol."

"I *know* that, Mr President." Fraser could scarcely keep the contempt from his voice. "But it's as well that he isn't here."

Carefully Jammeh lowered himself into the ornate chair behind his desk. "Oh? Why is that?"

"It's about Colonel Kwofie that I'm here."

"Oh?"

"I want his resignation. Or, to be more exact, I want him arrested."

Jammeh's large frame fell back in his seat. He recovered quickly. "I think, Captain, you had better sit down and explain exactly to me what you mean by your preposterous suggestion."

Ten minutes later President Essa Jammeh understood exactly what Fraser meant.

He stared at the file of Polaroid photographs spread out on his desk. "Who took these, Captain?"

"Corporal Witcher. It gives a fair indication of the extent of the massacre."

In a calm, modulated voice, Jammeh said: "It shows a lot of damage. And I can see some people have been hurt."

Fraser bit his lower lip. "Twenty were killed yesterday. Two more died overnight. Including your old friend the alkali. A loyal supporter."

Jammeh's eyes were cold behind the thick lenses of his tortoiseshell spectacles. "There was a time, Captain, when *every* alkali was a loyal supporter of mine."

"The alkali of Massang still is – sorry, was."

"You can be sure?"

"He told me." Firmly.

A smile flickered on the thick purple lips. "Quite so. And our good friend Corporal Witcher who took these pictures?"

"What about him?"

Jammeh carefully removed his spectacles and blew lightly at the dust on the lenses. "Is he not what you call a – ah, let me see, an expert in psychological warfare?"

"Yes . . ." Fraser began.

"And doesn't that include the manipulation of people's *perception* of things? Changing how people think? And, tell me, cannot photographs be used in this process? Like statistics, used to say anything you want them to?"

"I . . ."

"To be blunt, Captain Fraser," he replaced the spectacles. "These photographs could be anywhere. It's only because I trust you that I know they are Massang. But, I assure you, I am not going to allow them to change my *perception* of things."

"President Jammeh," Fraser persisted. "There has been a *massacre*. A deliberate slaughter of innocent men, women and children. Wanton butchery."

"And," the President interrupted, "there is a *revolution* being attempted in this land! What in the name of Allah do you expect to happen in a revolution? I'll tell you. Villagers take sides, they have to. One side or the other. They make enemies. Of the Government, rival villages, the rebels . . ."

"And evidently the President's own Guard!" Fraser snapped.

Jammeh's nostrils flared. "That, Captain, is mere *assumption*. All the evidences you offer could be pure coincidence – explained away quite easily. I shall nevertheless, as it is clearly a serious matter, ask Colonel Kwofie about Massang on his return."

"He will lie," Fraser asserted coldly.

Jammeh's eyes blazed. "*You* do not lie, Captain. I do not appoint liars. *Neither* does Colonel Kwofie lie!"

"Then I suggest you ask him what he knows about this year's miracle groundnut crop which could bankrupt your country. Or about the river-toll charged by armed Jatos to allow free passage."

The puzzlement in the President's expression told Fraser all he needed to know.

He added quietly: "Kwofie may not be a liar, but he has a habit of keeping unpleasant truths to himself."

Jammeh stood up at his desk, placing his knuckles firmly on the table. Clearly the meeting was over.

"Captain Fraser, my good friend. You mean well. But you must realise that Free Guinea is *no longer* a colony. It is run by Guineans for Guineans. And if I cannot trust Colonel Kwofie, who has *never* let me down, then I can trust nobody. Please understand that." He smiled for the first time, but it lacked enthusiasm. "I bid you good day, Captain. And you must know that, as far as I am concerned, we have never had this meeting."

Fraser closed the mahogany door behind him, and leaned back against it for a moment. He felt as though he'd just gone ten rounds against a heavyweight champ. And lost.

Just what the hell could he do next?

Deep in thought he pulled on his bush hat and started down the corridor.

The door adjoining the President's office swung open. Lady Precious stepped out, a stunning apparition in a snug-fitting trouser-suit of shot silk. A plaited rope of raven's-wing hair coiled over her shoulder.

"I was right, my dear Captain," she laughed. "I thought I could hear your voice next door."

"M'lady, you're looking splendid as usual."

She took his arm. "I do swear you've been hiding from me."

"That, M'lady, would be my very last intention," he replied. "I've been stuck up at Duntenda Barracks mostly."

She clung tightly to him. He could feel her fingertips kneading absently at the muscles of his arm. "You are looking tired, if I may say so, Captain. I insist that you relax." She stopped and turned to look up at him. "We have never played golf together. Yet you promised me on your last trip."

"Indeed we must," Fraser said politely, but unenthusiastically.

"Tomorrow?" Insistent.

He shrugged, hesitating.

"That's a date then, Captain."

Sunday sat under the enormous twisted kapok tree and silently avowed vengeance on Jato Pheko.

He might even use the brand new automatic rifle that lay in pieces on a spread of banana leaves by his feet. If, that was, he could remember how to put it back together again.

He hadn't been concentrating on his instructor's lecture. Instead he had been preoccupied with Nyomi, the girl he'd met at the Great Jato Rally.

How she has changed, thought Sunday, as he watched her strut about in smart new khaki fatigues.

She was not the shy village girl he had met two months before. It had been a mistake bringing her to the big new guerrilla camp. It had been a mistake to persuade her to join the swelling ranks of the Jatos.

But mostly it had been a mistake to introduce her personally to Jato Pheko.

He watched her as she chatted with the other women as they prepared the food for the camp. Her gestures were extravagant and her laughter free. He could guess what they were joking to her about.

Not for Nyomi, he noted, the chores of camp-life as for the other women. She would not be found pounding the rice in a wooden mortar or tossing the calabash sieve to let the wind separate the husks from the grain. Nyomi was too grand for that. She was one of the new girl warriors – a privilege that only Jato himself could bestow.

If only, Sunday seethed, that was all he had bestowed upon her! But he knew, as the whole camp knew, that Jato had taken the innocent young village girl as one of his women. And she had willingly sacrificed herself to him.

He kicked angrily at the dust.

Then he saw Jato Pheko himself emerge from a tent on the other side of the camp site. His distinguished ebony frame, and the polished black skull in the true Muslim tradition, set him apart from all the others. His height, his muscled shoulders and sinewy arms contrived to remind Sunday of the menacing presence of the ancient warrior kings from the history books. All heads turned as he walked past with the whiteman known as Rubashëv, a short but upright man with florid cheeks and a steady eye.

After a while the two men separated and Jato strode

towards Sunday, his lion's skin waistcoat trailing open to reveal his sweat-slicked chest.

"Good morning, my brother," Jato said.

"Good morning, brother." Sunday mumbled the expected greeting, finding it hard to say the words.

"I see you have problem with the Kalashnikov." He smiled. "Do not worry, my brother, you soon have much practice. The relationship with you and that gun will be as a love affair with a woman. You will spend much time together."

"When, Jato?"

"Very soon. But for now you have been here too long. Your employers they will wonder what is become of you."

Sunday knew what was coming. It was just Jato's excuse to get rid of him. To get him out of the camp so that he would be free to have Nyomi at his will.

"It is no problem. My employer thinks that I am in the National Park to find injured animals that need attention."

Jato smiled ingratiatingly. "My brother, I too know the *toubab* woman. And a *toubab* will only make so much allowance for you. And you help our cause most by being there with her. You have to do this thing. It is she who knows most about the thoughts and actions of the crackshots from Britain. The Captain trusts her and her father. And you. So that is where your duty lies for the next few vital weeks."

"But . . ." Sunday blurted.

Jato's face became as impassive and as wooden as a dance mask. "I have spoken."

Sullenly he watched as the Lion of Freedom walked away.

By all that is holy, Sunday thought savagely! To think that I looked up to this man. Was like a brother to him. Respected his wisdom and his knowledge. Loved him for his friendship and his companionship.

But that had been before he left the Agricultural Research Station to study in Moscow to become a vet.

The sixteenth on the Union Jack Club golf-course was known as an unlucky hole. Fraser had just found out why.

Lady Precious, fetchingly dressed in lightweight chequered plusfours and a feathered hat straight out of Robin Hood, could scarcely contain her amusement. Her dark eyes twinkled with mischief.

"What sort is it?" he asked.

"A rock python," she replied, not quite poker-faced. "Experts say they are harmless."

"Experts would."

He studied the deep gully of rough that cut at right-angles across the fairway. The tangled mass of fern seemed to hold a magnetic attraction for all but the best golfers, and the captain's massive handicap didn't put him in that league.

"When was it last seen?" he asked.

"Last week," Precious replied with relish. "And it appears to have grown. Someone swore it was now fifteen feet long."

Fraser did not like snakes. It was the nearest thing to a phobia that he had. He only wished someone had warned him that the gully was the home of an African rock python *before* he'd played the shot.

"To hell with it!" he said aloud and, swishing the club from side-to-side, plunged into the thigh-deep under-growth. He just hoped the thing was satisfied on its staple diet of golf-balls.

After a few minutes he found his – or someone's – and luckily dug it out with a single stroke of his sand-iron.

At least now, amazingly, he was only one stroke behind. That was the strange thing about golf: sometimes the less you played the better you got.

Precious swung and placed the ball far down the fairway. Immaculate. Fraser concentrated hard, drawing back both arms for a controlled swing.

She said suddenly: "I heard your conversation with my husband yesterday. About our dear Colonel Kwofie."

Sod it! The crafty bitch had waited until he was in mid-stroke. He watched as the ball veered and homed in on a bunker.

"Listening at keyholes, M'lady?" he demanded irritably.

She laughed brightly. "I was *only* in the next room, and

all the doors open onto the balcony. And you were *very* angry."

"I still am."

Her eyelids fluttered like black-winged butterflies. "Of course you are, dear Captain. Understandably so. And obviously the Colonel must be severely reprimanded for the actions of his men. But his men are just simple country people. Very backward. I doubt if Colonel Kwofie even knew what happened."

"It's possible," Fraser said stiffly. He didn't believe it for a moment.

When they finally met at the hole, he was three down.

Precious teed-off on the final leg, swinging her club in a perfect arc, following-through with natural elegance. She watched as the ball dropped onto the sandy grass just feet from the eighteenth.

She turned to him. "Colonel Kwofie appears to be aloof and very single-minded, Captain. He does not make friends easily. But his qualities complement those of my husband. If it were left to my husband alone, the power in this country would be wrested from him by – by the women in the marketplace even! He is a kind and gentle man. Like the country he inherited. He does not easily see evil in others.

"Once that did not matter. Free Guinea was different from the rest of Africa. But times have changed, and President Jammeh has not."

"You're saying he needs Kwofie?"

For once the expression in her eyes was serious. "Free Guinea needs Colonel Kwofie, Captain. It is time for a hard man in these difficult times. So, please, do not try and persuade my husband to get rid of him."

Fraser didn't trust himself to answer. He swung his anger at the ball. It sliced off the fairway and disappeared into the rough.

John Belcher had parked the Land Rover under the shiny dark green canopy provided by a black plum tree in the District Commissioner's compound.

He was pleased that the leggy fair-haired nurse Sally Richards had stayed behind while the other two young

VSO workers went inside to see if their pay-cheques had arrived. None of them had been paid by Jammeh's Government for two months now and they were subsidising their aid projects with their own meagre cash savings.

Kevin Shand was managing, but the shortage was causing havoc with Brian Beavis' regular drinking habits. The Geordie was in dire risk of becoming teetotal.

Sally said suddenly: "That time in Massang you promised that if there was anything I needed at the clinic . . ."

"I remember."

"So the offer still stands?"

"Of course. An officer and a gentleman never breaks his word."

"I thought you were a corporal."

Belcher laughed. "A mere technicality, Sally. Why, what's the problem?"

She looked up the path where Kevin and Brian had just emerged from the District Commissioner's administration block. "A general shortage of medical supplies, John. Money from the Government's virtually dried up and our stocks are going down rapidly. Pilfering's gone up lately, too."

"The Jatos?"

Sally nodded. "I expect that's where it's ending up. But I don't mind that in a way; from what I hear at least it will be used properly." She bit her lower lip. "The trouble is I'm using a lot more supplies recently myself."

"Why's that?"

The nurse turned to face him and he found himself drawn to her pale blue eyes. "I'm getting increasing cases of malnutrition, John. It's always been fairly rare, usually after poor harvests and never in the big towns. But last week I came across several children in Bankama. It's quite frightening."

"Just outside Sakoto?" Belcher recalled the big urban sprawl.

"I've *never* known that before. Never."

"Then let's discuss it over dinner."

Sally laughed. "I do believe that's a proposition, John!"

Belcher scratched at his thinning crop of hair. "I

178

wouldn't dare, ma'am! Just a couple of medics doing business. Perhaps I can get Captain Fraser to put some pressure on Jammeh to point some of that aid rice in the right direction."

Sally clasped his wrist. "That would be really good. Thank you, I accept."

"Fucken bas'ard!" Brian Beavis, scruffy and unshaven, was grumbling noisily as he approached with Kevin.

"What's wrong?" Sally asked. "No cheques again?"

"Fucken one month's. That's orl." The anger seemed to thicken his Geordie accent until it became almost unintelligible. "Man's got ta fucken live. An' tha' condescendin' bas'ard of a bleddy Commissioner . . ." He scowled back up the path through his thick-lensed spectacles.

"Bri's unhappy because they gave us the old song-and-dance routine," Kevin explained. "The Commissioner sent us to half-a-dozen different departments to get the right chit. Full circle until we came back to him. Calm as you like he opens his drawer. He'd had them all the time!"

"An' 'e fucken *knew* it!"

Belcher was disgusted. "Just to let you know who's boss, I suppose?"

"It's not worth worrying about, Brian," Sally said soothingly. "At least our pay's only one month behind now."

"But still no project money," Kevin reminded. "How in the hell are we supposed to run the projects and pay the trainees? They're getting browned off, too." He followed Brian into the back of the Panther. "We're both thinking about jacking it in and going to work with *Direct Action*."

"Too fucken true!"

"Don't they suffer the same?" Belcher asked.

"No," Sally answered. "Unlike the VSOs, *Direct Action* doesn't get its money from Jammeh. It's a charity outfit with its own funding and aid programme. Brian's already done work for Rod Bullock. His project's dried up. He can hardly teach engineering apprentices without tin sheet and basic tools."

"An' Bullock's lot don' fuck abou'," Brian added.

Kevin laughed. "What Bri's saying is that *Direct Action* is exactly that. They mean business." He leaned forward.

179

"So don't leave your smart Land Rover unattended, John. I tell you, it'll disappear, resprayed in DA red and it'll join Bullock's vast motor pool!"

"I'll warn the others!" Belcher rejoined and swung the vehicle out of the compound gates and onto the north bank road towards Sakoto.

From the small crowd at the bus-queue a black youth began waving and calling.

Belcher slowed. The face looked familiar. It was Mo Sinclair's assistant from the Agricultural Research Station. The boy called Sunday.

Captain Johnny Fraser and Corporal Witcher finished marking the villages on a large-scale map that was taped to the wall of the Tac HQ office at Duntenda Barracks.

"Thanks for letting me know, Rod."

Bullock, dressed as always in worn jeans with a faded T-shirt stretched across his broad chest, returned to the other side of the desk. "It's no problem, Johnny. The thing is my *Direct Action* blokes are far more likely to hear of atrocities than yourselves." He sat down in the spare chair next to Dawda and lit a cigarette.

"Your three hundred field-force is a veritable nationwide intelligence network," Fraser observed, returning to his desk. "So I really appreciate being kept informed."

"Any co-operation from *Direct Action* is most welcome," Witcher confirmed. "The Government's own security forces are – hardly surprisingly – not very forthcoming."

Rod Bullock shot Dawda an uncertain sideways glance. The youth did not look comfortable. He sat morosely with his head bowed.

"To tell the truth," the aid chief said, holding Fraser in a steady gaze, "I had to think twice about passing on this information. I don't think Dawda approves and I'm sure a lot of my blokes wouldn't."

"Why not, Rod?"

"Because, despite the evidence – yellow ribbons an' all – it seems certain that these raids have been conducted by Jammeh's guards."

"I told you that," Fraser pointed out.

Bullock nodded. "Sure you did. But that doesn't alter the fact that my blokes know you were brought in by Jammeh. To them, me blabbing to you strikes them as plain stupid. Not to mention downright dangerous."

Fraser nodded towards the alkali's son. "Is that what Dawda thinks too?"

"I guess so. That's why he told you it was the Jatos when you were at Massang. He told you what he thought you ought to hear."

The SAS captain turned his attention to the youth. "Is that right, Dawda? Do you really think I'd have anything to do with such things?"

The white eyes in the bowed head flashed uncertainly in Fraser's direction; the shoulders shrugged. But he said nothing.

Bullock spoke tersely. "The lad's confused, Johnny. Hardly surprising for a bloke who's just lost his old man and his newly-wed wife. Not to mention his village." He stubbed out his cigarette in the tin lid that served as an ashtray on Fraser's desk. "You know Massang is finished, don't you? The survivors reckon the place is jinxed. There's a curse on it. In fact, I'm taking Dawda back to Sakoto with me now. To take his mind off things with some work for *Direct Action*. Maybe see about setting up a new village somewhere else."

Fraser stood in front of Dawda and went down on his haunches. "Look, you must understand that we were all very sorry about your village. And the loss of your wife and father. You know that the alkali was my good friend, don't you?"

'Yes, *toubab*,' the lad mumbled reluctantly. He avoided Fraser's eyes as though to look at them might blind him.

"Do you believe me when I say I knew nothing of a plan to attack your village?"

A hesitation. Then: "Yes, *toubab*."

"Then why won't you trust me and tell me the truth?"

The Guinean drew away. "There is nothing to tell, *toubab*."

Still their eyes didn't meet. "*Please* tell me," Fraser persisted.

Dawda gulped, gathering courage. "It is not good for me

181

to be here. When you come to Massang before the wedding, I say to you the Jato curse will be upon us if we talk. My father does not listen. He does not fear. You remember how he talks. Then, as the marabou predicts, evil falls on us. The soldiers come . . . We are all fucked-up, man. *All fucked-up!*" He looked like a trapped and frightened animal, tears of despair starting to well in his eyes. "I do not say more. Already the curse is on me."

Bullock put his muscular forearm around the lad's shoulders and hugged him roughly. "It's okay, son. The Captain really *is* a friend."

Dark anger suddenly danced in Dawda's eyes. "Can he be a friend of mine and a friend of the President after he has seen these things at Massang?"

Bullock looked up at the SASmen. "There's your answer, Johnny." He yanked a crushed cigarette pack from the front pocket of his jeans.

Fraser offered a light. "You know, Rod, I don't believe the raid on Massang had Jammeh's approval. I don't think he even knew about it."

Bullock scowled and exhaled a stream of smoke. "That shit Kwofie, I suppose?"

"I've no evidence that Kwofie knew about it. It *could* have been a renegade PG unit."

"Crap!" Bullock snarled contemptuously. "If the guards were involved, Kwofie knew about it all right. That cunning sod knows everything that goes on in the country. And as far as the PGs are concerned, he *is* the sodding PGs. He's got himself into the position where he's Number Two in the country without the benefit of being elected. If you ask me, he's got aspirations of being Number One."

"We'd noticed," Lionel Witcher said.

"What with Kwofie and Government officials poncing around in their smart official cars while the country goes to wrack and ruin, you can start to sympathise with the Jatos. It just pisses me off sometimes." Bullock smiled grimly. "Perhaps I've seen too much. You work hard to get things changed, but nothing ever does. Perhaps I'm getting too old. Cynical. Ought to go home and start a pig farm in Wales, or something."

"Don't forget if Jato hadn't come on the scene in the first place, Kwofie wouldn't have had an excuse to flatten Massang or anywhere else," Fraser reminded. "He wouldn't have seen a need. Trouble-makers cause trouble. Action triggers reaction."

Rod Bullock studied the tip of his cigarette. "If you want the co-operation of the Free Guinea population, Johnny, you'll have to get Jammeh to ditch Kwofie," he said flatly.

"I've already had a go," Fraser replied. "But you must understand that my hands are tied. We're here at the request of the President. I'll do my damnedest, but in the end it's up to Jammeh. If he refuses to acknowledge what Kwofie's doing and we don't like it, our only choice is to leave."

"God forbid," Bullock muttered.

At that moment Corporal John Belcher's head peered in at the door.

"Sorry to interrupt, boss, but I've a visitor for you. Mo Sinclair's lad, Sunday. I picked him up at the bus stop in Mansakunda. He was on his way to see you."

"Is he there?" Fraser asked.

"Sure and he wants to talk to you pretty bad. And I think you'll want to hear what he's got to say."

"You'd better show him in."

Sunday was in buoyant mood. He sauntered in wearing smart, if worn, beige cords, a cream short-sleeved shirt and a pair of gold-rimmed sunglasses.

"Hello, Captain," he beamed and shook hands vigorously, glancing around the office. "How are you, man?"

"Afternoon, Sunday. I'm well and how are you?"

"Fine, man, fine!" As he spoke Dawda watched the new arrival solemnly from his chair.

After all the handshaking Fraser asked the reason for his visit.

Sunday hesitated before he spoke. "I know The Captain seeks the Great Jato."

Fraser's eyes narrowed and he nodded for the Guinean to go on.

"I know where you find this man," Sunday announced

triumphantly. "I have seen where this man camps. I come to this place when I am doing work for Miss Sinclair."

"Where?" Fraser demanded.

Sunday's eyes were bright. "At The Place of One Finger. In the territory they call Kunkunda."

Witcher's eyebrows raised. "The National Park."

Sunday nodded eagerly. "Yes. At The Place of One Finger."

Fraser frowned. The name meant nothing to him. "Would you be able to take us there?"

That, clearly, was not what Sunday had in mind. His skin seemed to pale and he shook his head. "I could not do that thing, Captain."

"I know where it is," interrupted Bullock. "It's deep in the forest. You'll not find it on any map. A warrior chief is reputed to have lost a finger there in battle. Hundreds of years ago. Legend has it the marabou made a new one grow. A sacred place."

"Would you be willing to take us?"

Bullock looked uncertain. He gathered the butt of his cigarette in his thumb and forefinger and drew on the last shreds of tobacco. At last, he said: "Sure, no problem. But listen, Johnny, I'll do this for you. And only because I trust you to try and sort out the mess this country's in."

"We'll try," Fraser promised.

Bullock tossed his cigarette butt in the tin ashtray. "And no bloodshed. I'll not take you there for the privilege of another massacre. Probably half the bloody Jatos are recruited from my villages."

Fraser contained his indignation. "I don't think you expect that from us, Rod. I hope not. We're anxious to locate his camp. Very anxious. We've got to find out his strength and exactly what we're up against. We don't even know Jato Pheko's full identity yet."

Sunday had been listening with interest. Suddenly he said brightly: "I know that, too, Captain."

Fraser turned. "You do?"

"Sure, no problem. Jato is Kali Pheko."

Sunday nodded enthusiastically at the SAS officer's puzzled expression. "Yes, Captain. Kali, you know? He

184

worked at the Research Station with me. He goes to Moscow to be vet." He frowned, pouting his lips with theatrical disapproval. "But he comes back an evil man. Coming back quietly in the dark like a snake."

Fraser and Lionel Witcher instinctively exchanged glances. *Kali!* The missing piece in the jigsaw. They had both known him during the coup. Handsome, broad-shouldered. Quiet and conscientious. Hard-working and, apparently, disinterested as the chaos of revolution exploded all around him.

Kali! The boy whose only interest was in animal welfare and conservation.

In all the time he'd visited Mo Sinclair during their brief affair, Fraser had never had cause to learn Kali's surname. It was unimportant. And obviously the boy himself would not have volunteered it at that time.

Certainly not while his mysterious half-brother, Omar Pheko, was ranting through his propaganda speeches broadcast from the seized radio station during the coup.

Lionel Witcher said: "When do we go?"

They moved out as the sky lightened in the east.

It seemed an eternity since they had heard the muffled splash of paddles receding into the darkness as John Belcher returned to Four Team's riverside OP in the Gemini rubber boat.

As the group had prepared at the edge of the Kebba, silence and a growing sense of isolation pressed in on them.

Rod Bullock felt it worse. He had always considered this to be his country; it held no fear for him. But now it was different. To begin with he just felt mildly foolish dressing in olive Army-issue bushshirt and denims, and smearing sticky camouflage cream over his face and forearms.

"I feel like a clown with all this make-up on," he'd complained.

"Better a clown than an Aunt Sally," Sergeant Brummie Turner had replied. The utter seriousness of his tone gave Bullock his first twinge of apprehension.

The second had been when Johnny Fraser had thrust an Armalite in his hand. "Can you handle one of these?"

He'd looked aghast. "I can handle a gun, sure. But I'm not shooting on this trip. No way."

"Take it, Rod." Fraser's order did not invite contradiction. "It's just a precaution. If we hit trouble, just shooting in the air might keep some Jato's head down. On the other hand if we get separated in hostile territory you might *need* it." His smile was full of charming reassurance. "Don't worry, we'd rather you didn't shoot. Keep it on single shot, not auto, and keep the safety on."

Now, despite the chill dawn, Rod Bullock found himself sweating nervously.

His edginess, he knew, was due in part to the shattering tiredness he felt. They had spent most of the night travelling up-stream from Duntenda, snatching only a couple of hours' catnap at the concealed riverside OP. But they had been pestered by mosquitoes and tsetse-flies so that the little sleep they had was shallow and disturbed.

As the bird world came to life with sudden spurts of excited activity he twitched uneasily. Every scurry in the undergrowth, every snap of twig had his grip tightening involuntarily on the Armalite until his palms were moist with sweat. Already he was thankful he had the weapon.

Not a word was spoken as the group moved along the overgrown game trail, the trees reaching up in cathedral columns in fierce competition for the sky. Beneath their feet the earth was a pale talcum dust, pocked and pitted with myriad tiny claw- and footprints.

Corporal Mark Benjamin walked point. After his weeks in the OP he'd become familiar with the terrain, its human and not-so-human inhabitants. For that reason he would be the most likely to notice anything out of the ordinary, and quicker to recognise false alarms.

He took the pace steadily, carrying a pump-action Remington repeater shotgun, capable of delivering a devastating short-range blast. It was well-loved for jungle warfare, its lethal outpouring having the effect of stunning a hidden enemy for vital seconds. Range was short, but the velocity and 'spread' of the shot was more important when your unseen adversary could be anywhere in the dense undergrowth.

Benjamin gently swung the snout of the shotgun with the rhythm of his walk, quartering the left-hand flank of the column. Constantly he reminded himself to raise his eyes to the trees. That was such an easy thing to forget. And fatal.

It was secondary jungle with the trees not too tightly packed, which allowed the vegetation to grow thicker on the ground. A double-edged benefit. It would shield their approach, but it also offered a haven for ambushers or look-outs.

Bullock followed immediately behind to verify the route. Behind him came Fraser, quartering the right-hand flank with an Armalite. In a fire-fight it would be his task to pick off any identified individual target.

For the first time in weeks he felt in the best of humour. Back in combat kit following the scent of a quarry. He could almost feel the adrenalin pumping through his body. After the piles of tedious paperwork and endless political manoeuvring, just the thought of positive action was as refreshing as a cold shower.

Coming up the rear, Lionel Witcher and Brummie Turner, the most experienced to play 'tail-end Charlie', reversed the order, covering both flanks with a further shotgun and Armalite respectively.

But any resemblance to a comfortable Sunday morning stroll soon ended. The ground fell away more rapidly and spindly cabbage trees grew more densely, crowding in over the path as they approached the low-lying marshy area surrounding a tributary river of the Kebba. It was a natural barrier protecting The Place of One Finger.

Underfoot the ground became soggy, giving way to rank pools of stagnant water. Mosquitoes hovered in clouds.

Benjamin turned, hand-signalling that the river was nearby. Bullock watched as the Jewish corporal offered him a small cardboard packet and grinned.

Bullock stared at the pack in his palm. Durex Fetherlite.

He looked uncertain. A *raincoata* as the Mandinkas called them.

Benjamin put a finger to his lips, shaking his head. He pointed to the barrel of the Armalite.

With a sudden grin of understanding Bullock unwrapped

the slippery contents and unfurled it over the flash-protector, the tight rubber ring forming a near-waterproof seal.

They waited for five minutes whilst Fraser made a brief radio transmission back to John Belcher's OP. Then Benjamin started forward again negotiating the slippery mangrove roots that grew in profusion around the shallow river edge.

The air smelled of damp and rotted timber. As they sank into the uneven muddy bottom, the water struck cold. It seeped fast into their boots and swirled uncomfortably around their legs, until it caused silent gasps as it reached their genitals.

In the shady light the marshy shallows of the bank could be seen clearly fifty feet away. There was a long stretch of mud, strewn with fallen branches and a rotted log.

Benjamin glanced back. Bullock's face was a grim mask of concentration. The corporal grinned reassurance but it brought no response.

The water reached chest-level before the bottom began an achingly slow incline to the far bank. Suddenly the rotted log began to move. Jerkily at first, then in a quick darting movement the crocodile slithered across the mud to the water. A beady eye glistened like a black ballbearing.

Benjamin's heart missed a beat; he felt it distinctly. Behind him he could hear Rod Bullock's gulp of fear.

With a rippling splash the fifteen foot length of armour plating disappeared into the water, its powerful tail thrashing it away upstream. Odds of four to one, it had thankfully decided, were not in its favour.

But the incident had fired the patrol's imagination and the next hour of wading through the deep stagnant waters of the mangrove swamp on the far bank became ever more nightmarish.

No one was sorry to leave the area behind and press on into another swathe of secondary jungle.

It was early in the afternoon when Mark Benjamin suddenly halted and raised a hand. They had reached a cross-track. He dropped to his haunches and examined the dust.

Peering over his shoulder, Bullock could see the indentations quite clearly.

Johnny Fraser joined them. "Footprints. Quite a few," he observed in a whisper.

Benjamin nodded. "And one or two in military boots. Not ours, though. Obsolete with flat leather soles and studs. Sort you flog off to guerrillas."

Fraser jabbed a finger at the centre of the track. "Looks like some were carrying something heavy. A pattern of four. The impression's quite deep."

"Looks like Piccadilly Circus," Benjamin mused.

A prickly caterpillar of apprehension crawled up the back of Fraser's neck. He straightened up and glanced around. There was no sign of activity except for a jabbering bunch of colobus monkeys admiring each other's acrobatic display. They seemed unperturbed.

"Careless to leave all these signs," Lionel Witcher said hoarsely. Fraser could sense his feeling of discomfort too.

"It's the right direction," Bullock said, his voice too loud.

Fraser knew from the aid chief's earlier description that The Place of One Finger was a patch of some five square miles of ill-defined territory which now lay only three miles to the east. That final approach would be vital. A well-trained look-out they might never see. If they cocked it up now they wouldn't stand a chance. Their elusive quarry would melt into the forest, or else the patrol might be jumped.

Fraser decided then to move into the undergrowth, progressing parallel with the footprints on the track.

If the patrol kept it at a hundred yards' distance, they should come up behind any waiting ambush party.

At point, Corporal Mark Benjamin had slowed his pace, deliberately relaxing so that he could become attuned to the eerie new surroundings. Behind him the patrol had closed up to only six feet between each man. He picked his way carefully through the brush, avoiding dry leaves and branches. At one point he froze. But the sudden scurrying noise a few feet ahead had just been a basking black-and-white cobra that had been disturbed by their approach.

Rod Bullock found he was now sweating freely. His shirt became sodden, clinging to his back and chest, and the perspiration on his face turned the camouflage cream to a dribbling sticky gel.

Then it happened. Through the screen of tree trunks and creepers to his right Bullock could just determine a lightening in the foliage where sunlight poured in on the open track. They were still moving parallel to it and he was thankful they hadn't lost sight of it in the wild maze of forest.

The movement at the side of that track was hardly noticeable, but it was jerky. Not the flowing sort of motion caused by a breeze. Something gleamed dully in the shadows.

His mouth dropped. "Something's there . . . !"

It was out before he could check himself. After the hours of silence his voice sounded like a bombshell in a monastery. His words seemed to echo, mockingly, bouncing around the trees.

Before he knew what had happened the corporal had fired two quick blasts from his Remington and dropped to one knee.

"Fifty yards, slightly right!" he snapped. "Edge of track!"

Someone grabbed Bullock's shoulder and threw him to the ground with a force that knocked the breath from his lungs. Simultaneously the world went mad, seemingly blowing apart around his ears. The reverberating blast of the second Remington repeater was shattering as Lionel Witcher pumped more 12 gauge ball and shot in the direction of the track.

Bullock twisted round awkwardly. Fraser's face was just a few inches from his own, the SAS man's hand still firmly on his shoulder.

"Christ, what happened?" Bullock gasped.

"We bumped into the back of a sentry post," Fraser said through clenched teeth. "Or maybe an ambush party waiting for us on the track."

"Sorry I blew it."

The distinctive *crack-thump* of incoming high-velocity rounds was heard. Leaves were scythed from the branches above their heads and floated down around them like feathers. Fraser returned fire with his Armalite.

Bullock was surprised at his own calmness. He was even thinking logically. As Fraser waited for another target to present itself, he asked: "How the hell did they know? No one could have seen us, the way we came."

"Never underestimate the enemy, lad," Brummie muttered helpfully. "Remember that."

Suddenly Bullock found himself wanting to laugh. Ridiculous. "Until today I didn't have an enemy."

More shots sang over their heads.

"You have now."

Fraser said: "That gun of yours, Rod, use it. For Christ's sake *don't* put it on auto. When you see a target fire quickly. Twice. If you miss the first time, the second might not."

As he spoke a black head appeared over a clump of ferns by the track. The bright whites of the eyes were like golf balls. Both Brummie Turner and Fraser went for it, each firing twice in rapid succession. It was impossible to tell whose Armalite hit the target, but it must have been two rounds, virtually together. The head shattered like a coconut, first jerking sideways, then seeming to blow up from within. It vanished messily.

"Like that," Brummie explained unnecessarily.

"Do you want to pull back, boss?" Benjamin asked tersely as he hastily refilled cartridges into the shotgun. A fast withdrawal, with each man in turn providing covering fire for his retreating colleague, was a standard option in ambush situations.

But this time both parties had surprised each other and Fraser evidently felt they could steal the upper hand.

He shook his head and pointed at a tall termite tower thirty yards to their left.

"Mark, come with me out on their flank. See if we can't give them something to think about. If they *don't* run for it, then the rest of you can withdraw under our covering fire. We'll meet at the emergency RV." He grinned. "If anyone can find it."

He slapped Mark Benjamin on the shoulder and immediately the corporal started worming his way through the undergrowth in a fast leopard crawl, the shotgun cradled across his forearms. As Witcher and Brummie gave supporting fire, Fraser followed close behind, his heart thudding as he strained to keep up with the younger man.

It seemed an age before they reached the cover offered by the termite tower. Like a miniature volcano of crumbling, tunnelled red earth, it rose six feet above them as they crouched at its base.

Fraser peered carefully around the edge with just one eye. They were close to the track now and could see a good hundred yards' stretch before it turned a bend. Half-a-dozen Africans were clustered around a large fallen tree trunk. If he expected to see them jabbering in bewilderment and fear, he was in for a disappointment. They wore nondescript khaki fatigues and were weighed down with ammunition and weaponry. There was no sign of panic as one spoke into a radio and two others worked to erect the tripod of a heavy machine-gun. Evidently it had been covering the track; now it was being swung to point into the forest.

"I don't like this," Fraser murmured. He hadn't really expected the Jatos to have radio communications and certainly not a bloody great half-inch machine-gun.

"Fire at will," Fraser ordered quietly.

"Poor old Will . . ." Benjamin's stock quip was cut short as his Remington boomed into action, punctuated by the sharp report of the captain's Armalite.

Caught by surprise at an attack from their flank, the Jatos' professional air deserted them. Two bodies were tossed away like rag dolls with their stuffing spewing over their comrades. Showered in a spray of red gore, the other four flew in different directions, colliding with each other in their panic.

Fraser squeezed the trigger of the Armalite. Twice. Another man fell.

Now realising the direction of the attack, the remaining three turned and raced down the track as fast as their legs would carry them. Fraser hit one more before they rounded the bend.

Benjamin let out a long slow breath of deep relief. His

heart was thumping against his ribcage. "That was easier than I thought!"

Fraser gave a wry smile. "It was, wasn't it? Let's get back to the others before they lose themselves . . ."

The hairs on the back of his neck anticipated the grating metallic noise of the cocking handle on the Kalashnikov a split second before he heard it.

"Turn around *real* slow, man!"

It was suddenly clear: the surprising confidence of the Jatos before Fraser's counter-attack. Whilst he and Mark Benjamin had been making their outflanking movement, a party of Jatos had been doing the same in the opposite direction. Only they had made a wider circle. By chance they were in an ideal position when the counter-attack came.

"Drop the guns, man!" the voice behind them demanded.

Fraser exchanged a glance with Benjamin. He shrugged. For once it looked as though their luck had run out.

An Armalite and a Remington shotgun hit the red African dust.

PART TWO

PROBLEM

Rise like lions after slumber
In unvanquishable number,
Shake your chains to earth like dew
Which in sleep had fallen on you
Ye are many – they are few.

The Mask of Anarchy,
Percy Bysshe Shelley

8

"So we meet again, Captain."

The voice came to him quite clearly, cutting through the confused nightmare.

The sunlight touched the back of his mind and he winced. Patches of colour took form in his vision, the fog dissolving to reveal shapes. Distinctive, colourful shapes.

Above him the sky was white-bright, veined with the branches of the kapok tree. He was on his back. He shifted, turning onto one elbow. The pain shot up his arm and exploded in the back of his head.

He gasped, shut his eyes again, breathing heavily as he tried to assemble his thoughts into some sort of order.

He squinted out at the world. Across the dusty compound a woman beat at a wooden mortar of rice. Thump, thump, thump. In rhythm to his heart-beat and the throb in his head.

"I am pleased you recover, Captain." Again that voice.

Fraser shifted his gaze, looking back over his shoulder.

Kali Pheko was bigger than he remembered. He towered above him, a glistening mountain of lean black muscle. The head was noble, carved in burnished wood, set imperiously in a powerful neck. The dark eyes seemed to smoulder like charcoal embers in his skull.

"Hello, Kali," Fraser said. His throat was parched and it was an effort. He struggled to sit up. His hands were bound behind his back. The hide cut into his wrists.

"Do not struggle, man. Give yourself time." Was there a hint of compassion in the voice? Just a hint?

"You okay, boss?" It was Benjamin.

Fraser managed to sit upright. The Jewish corporal was

seated cross-legged directly behind him. Alongside, Sergeant Turner lay unconscious with Corporal Witcher and Rod Bullock looking over him. Both were ashen-faced.

"I'll survive," Fraser replied. "How's Brummie?"

"They gave him a thrashing," Witcher answered. "But he's coming round slowly."

Pheko said: "He gives our men much trouble. They are not pleased at seeing their brothers slaughtered. They are free with the butt ends of their rifles."

It was coming back to him now. Fraser recalled how they had hoped the others would escape, but the forest had been alive with Jatos. Brummie had taken his surrender with bad grace. That was when the beating had started.

"I am sorry that we meet again in such circumstances," Pheko said.

"We were friends once, Kali."

"Things are different. Now circumstances force us to be enemies."

"Is that what they taught you in Moscow?"

Any humour there had been in Pheko's eyes disappeared. "Do not sneer, Captain. I went to Moscow to become a vet. I went only because Britain does not offer facilities to a poor village boy without money."

"Is this what you call being a vet? Others might call it terrorising."

Pheko's cheeks became pinched and purpled with anger. "Do not talk to *me* of terrorism!" he spat out the words. "The real *terrorists* are those neo-imperialists you keep in power! It is President Jammeh's men who butcher my brother and sister, man! You see Massang, but there are many more villages who suffer in the same way. I can show you."

"I don't think . . ." Fraser began lamely, but the pain in his head was clogging his thought process.

Pheko cut in. "Do you know who betrayed you?"

"Betrayed?" Fraser was puzzled.

A grim smile of satisfaction creased the Jato's face. "Yes, man. We know you are coming. You jump an ambush party that waits for you. Very clever. But not clever enough."

He stepped back and pointed to a shy-looking youth leaning dolefully against the trunk of the kapok.

"Dawda?" Fraser breathed. He would *never* have believed it. The son of his old friend the alkali of Massang.

The stupidity of it! The boy had been sitting there in his office as Sunday had revealed to them the location of the Jato camp. True he hadn't known what Mo's assistant was about to reveal, but he should at least have kept Dawda at Duntenda. He had just not conceived that betrayal would have been in the boy's character. It had been a fatal and unforgivable error of judgement.

"Yes!" Pheko said with triumph in his voice. "That boy had his family and village destroyed by the imperialist puppet Jammeh that you, Captain, have helped keep in power! The alkali, he wants nothing to do with Jatos. So I say, okay, man, that is your problem. We will help our brothers and sisters who have need of us.

"But that is not good enough for Jammeh. Because Massang is the territory of my control, he decides to punish the alkali. Do not co-operate with the Jatos. A truly strong man does not hesitate to punish an old friend as an example to others."

The pain in Fraser's head had subsided to a steady pulsating ache. "What happened was wrong, Kali, we both know that. But I don't think the President knows what is being done in his name."

Pheko laughed bitterly. "C'mon, man! All Free Guinea knows what is happening, so don't tell me Jammeh doesn't know."

At that point the sound of a high-revving engine drifted into the camp compound from the treeline. All heads turned and curious Jatos, some in khaki fatigues and others just wearing the yellow headband insignia of the movement, shuffled expectantly out from the shade of huts and trees. Fraser estimated two or three hundred men and women, and several dozen children.

A jeep covered in a dull layer of dust bounced into view, tooting ferociously. It jerked to a standstill a few yards from where Pheko stood. There was only one passenger. A stockily-built man with a florid face who climbed from the vehicle with a sharp economy of movement.

He glanced at the SASmen sprawled beneath the kapok tree as he brushed the dust from his civilian safari suit. Then he turned to Jato Pheko. "Who are these people?" he demanded. There was no mistaking the guttural east European accent.

"These are the crackshots from Britain," Pheko could not keep the pride from his voice. "We capture them an hour ago."

Witcher called out: "Good afternoon, Mr Rubashëv! I see the trade union movement has an encouraging following out here in the bush!"

Fraser shot the corporal a puzzled glance. Witcher nodded. "The guy from Prague whom I met at Fofana's place along with that Scotsman Hammond," he explained.

"The one who's been importing goods through our KGB friend Boris?"

"The very same. Does a nice line in Kalashnikovs, I believe."

Rubashëv turned back to Pheko. "This is stupid. Do you realise what you do? These men are dangerous."

Pheko was offended at the man's tone. "No longer. These men they are my prisoners. They will stay that way. An example to Jammeh that he cannot win."

Rubashëv's heavy jowls set firmly. "Do not be naïve. These soldiers are more dangerous than wild animals. From the British SAS. They are some of the best and cleverest soldiers in the world."

Pheko smirked. "They are not so clever an hour ago."

"You were *very* lucky. Do not count on that luck lasting. Immediately you must take two steps. First dispose of them. Then we move to the reserve camp. Not tomorrow, but tonight."

"Dispose of them?"

"Kill them," Rubashëv explained impatiently. "That is the only way you will be safe."

Pheko shook his head. "I am no murderer."

"Freedom has its price," Rubashëv hissed, "and legal niceties are a small cost for that precious commodity."

The Jato leader hesitated.

Witcher called out suddenly: "Listen, Kali, one of our

party is a civilian. He came reluctantly as a guide. You may have an excuse to kill us, but in Allah's eyes there is no way to justify murdering a volunteer aid worker."

Rubashëv looked furious. "You see what I mean? They are clever, devious and dangerous. Dispose of them."

But Lionel having brought God into the equation seemed to tilt the balance. Pheko looked uncertain.

"I give you my word," Fraser said. "We will cause you no trouble."

It was to be a week before Fraser learned that Mark Benjamin had escaped the following night.

Jato Pheko had reached a compromise with Rubashëv. The prisoners would not be killed, but they would be held in captivity in accordance with the Russian's direct instructions. For the captain now had little doubt of Rubashëv's nationality.

On his insistence the prisoners were blindfolded and bound securely by hand-and-foot at all times. He also ordered the camp to be abandoned in case of a rescue attempt by other SASmen in the country. An emergency camp had already been prepared and it was there that the Jatos were to regroup. For the journey the prisoners were separated and escorted by different patrols travelling only at night over different routes.

It was a harrowing experience. Forced to go barefoot to deter an escape attempt, Fraser was marched roughly from twilight to sun-up. The route changed and twisted frequently, so it was impossible to tell in which direction they were travelling. In daylight, even blindfolded, the warmth of the sun on the skin would have provided a clue. At night that was impossible. Feeling treetrunks for moss growth on the colder northern side of the trunk was confounded because they spent so much time in swampy territory.

For five consecutive nights they pressed on. On two occasions they crossed a large river which could have been the Kebba. Although Fraser repeatedly asked his guards for confirmation, they refused to be drawn. Evidently they didn't trust him at all. At each day-camp they kept their distance while they prepared a meagre meal of rice and a watery soup of boiled vegetable leaves. They talked in low whispers. There was no doubt that they had taken Rubashëv's dire warnings very much to heart.

Mile after mile was spent struggling through mangroves, often waist deep in stinking water. It was painful and thoroughly unnerving, and Fraser had to draw on every ounce of his reserves to keep going. And for the first time in his service career he really appreciated the survival training courses run by the Regiment.

How Rod Bullock was coping he dreaded to think . . .

It was the bay of a scavenging dog in the early hours of the sixth day that alerted Johnny Fraser that they were approaching the new camp.

As he stumbled on, still bound and blindfolded, the Jatos' quickening pace and excited conversation confirmed it. Shortly after, the acrid wafts from a smouldering rubbish fire reached him, then calls and jeers from the waiting guerrillas.

The dull dawn light stabbed in his eyes as the ragged mask was removed from his head. He vaguely registered a sea of laughing black faces and a circle of round mud huts before he was bundled through the low door of one of them.

"Welcome to our new home, boss!"

"Lionel?" Fraser's eyes adjusted to the dim illumination of sunlight that filtered through the thatch roof. The corporal sat in the centre of the hut with his hands bound behind his back. He looked tired and emaciated, his clothing hanging in tatters on his bony frame. Behind him lay the sleeping bulk of Brummie Turner.

"Dead to the world," Witcher explained. "He arrived two hours ago and crashed out. He's not too well. Some sort of fever."

The sheer elation at being reunited temporarily pushed back the nagging pull of exhaustion. "What about the others?"

"I don't know about Rod Bullock, but Mark did a bunk."

"What! When was that?"

Witcher grinned weakly. "The first night apparently.

I overheard a couple of Jatos talking about it. I reckon he used his handcuff ruse. Not bad eh?"

Fraser couldn't believe it. In fact, none of them had ever believed it would work, ever since the Jewish corporal had bought a pair of authentic-looking magician's handcuffs from a street market in the Portobello Road two years previously.

He always kept them packed in his belt-order when he was on a mission, together with two keys. His theory had been that, if he was ever captured, his guards would inevitably go through his kit. His contention was that no enemy could resist the irony of securing a prisoner with his own handcuffs.

It appeared, after all, to have worked. The good news went a small way to compensate for the crushing humiliation they had suffered.

"I just hope he got away," Fraser said. "With no boots and no rations he'd have had his work cut out."

"At least he knew roughly where he was then. That's more than we can say now. Bloody Timbuctoo, for all I know."

"I reckon we must be over the border. Even five nights' march along river lines must take us over the border. But which one? I reckon north, but I can't be sure."

"I got the same feeling. Doesn't look too clever, does it? Talking of which, you don't look too bright yourself, boss."

Fraser gave a snort of disgust. "I've had raging dysentery for two days and my feet are cut to ribbons. What about you?"

"Sure, I'm the same." The corporal smiled faintly. "But I can ignore it. It's a mind-over-matter thing. It was taught to me by one of those guys who walks on hot coals in northern India."

"Leave it out," Fraser scolded. Some things never changed.

At that moment, there was a noise outside and the rough wooden door swung inwards. The shaft of sunlight was dazzling as Rod Bullock stooped into the opening. An armed Jato followed behind.

"Hallo, Johnny, I'm glad to see you. I wasn't sure you'd all make it." He sounded surprisingly cheerful, but perhaps it was just relief that they were all together. "How are you?"

"Grim," Fraser replied. "But you look in good fettle. No chains or ties for you?"

"No, thank God," Bullock said with feeling. "And they let me keep my shoes. I was blindfolded, but it wasn't too bad. That plea for my life back at the first camp really did the trick. I reckon Pheko's easing his bloody conscience on the way he's treating you by giving me an easy time. He seems to approve of *Direct Action*."

"That's nice," Fraser said acidly.

The Jato prodded Bullock with the muzzle of his Kalashnikov. "You keep to the business," he snapped. "You give medicines."

"Don't get excited," Bullock warned. "There's no medicines to spare for us. But I've been told to give you first-aid. Jato seems to trust me."

"We need a square meal," Fraser said with feeling.

Bullock laughed bitterly. "Forget it, mate. There's no women at this camp like the other one. And domestic science doesn't seem to be the forte of young Jatos."

"Then, can you get some charcoal embers from a fire? We've all got some type of dysentery."

Bullock frowned. "Charcoal?"

"A handful will do. And some boiled water."

"What you going to do with it?"

Fraser suddenly felt irrationally impatient. "Eat it for Chrissakes. If this gets any worse, we'll be drinking boiled tree bark tar. And that we can all do without!"

Johnny Fraser awoke with a start. He was suddenly aware of someone entering the hut. Instinctively, he tried to reach for where he thought his Armalite should be. But his bound arms caused him to topple heavily into the dust.

"Okay, steady, boss." It was Lionel Witcher's voice.

Fraser struggled into a sitting position and looked up at the figure of a young Guinean girl standing in the opening. The baggy khaki fatigues and forage hat detracted from her pretty, plump face. The Kalashnikov did nothing for her at all.

"It's okay," Witcher added. "She's just bringing some grub."

Fraser was relieved. "Jesus, Lionel, don't you ever sleep?"

He was surprised to see the sprinkling of stars outside. He must have been asleep for some fifteen hours. But at least his gut felt more settled now, and empty.

"Biscuits, *toubab*," she said, proffering a basket nervously.

"It's all right, we won't bite." Fraser indicated his bound hands. "How do we eat?"

Suddenly she laughed, seeing the funny side. She shrugged. "I feed you."

"That's what I call service." Fraser smiled. "Tell me, what's your name?"

She thought for a moment; evidently her knowledge of English was patchy. "I am Nyomi."

He took a mouthful of the corncake she offered. Giggling, she caught the crumbs that fell down his chin.

"Mmm, that's good, Nyomi. Good. My name is Johnny. They call me The Captain."

She nodded. "Yes. I know that, Captain – Johnny. Jato tells about you. He says you fine and dangerous warrior. But you are on wrong side. But we must all learn to fight like you." Nyomi stuffed some more corncake into his mouth.

"You smooth old charmer," Witcher muttered in mock disgust. "You should be in psych-ops with patter like that."

"I'll see if I can't use it then. Tell me, is Brummie any better?"

Witcher glanced at the sleeping shape in the corner. "The delirium's passed, but he's still got a high fever. It could be tick typhus."

Fraser agreed. "I don't think it's malaria. But then it could be one of any number of weird and wonderful things. If it is tick typhus, he could be in a daze for weeks without treatment."

"Pity old Belcher isn't with us."

"I think there's quite enough of us here already," Fraser

chided. He turned to the girl. "Can you please tell Jato we have a sick man. Does he have proper medicines?"

Nyomi looked over Fraser's shoulder at Brummie. Concern clouded her face and she nodded solemnly. "I will speak with the Jato."

It was an hour before Nyomi returned. She looked pleased with herself, her eyes sparkling as though she had won some personal triumph.

"Jato, he say you come now. He will speak with you." She stepped aside to allow the armed guerrillas to enter and pull the prisoners to their feet. After untying their ankles, the men pushed their charges out into the compound, leaving Brummie's semi-conscious body still slumped in a dark corner, mumbling incoherently.

It was a crisp, clear night that emphasised the enormity of the star-clustered sky. The air was fresh after the confines of the hut and laced with a sweet aroma of woodsmoke from the large fire towards which they were led. There were few people to be seen, a marked contrast from the first camp. Most were seated either side of Jato Pheko, listening in awe as he spoke to them. There could be no doubt that the policies and philosophies he was propounding were meeting with approval.

The clapping and laughter subsided as the SASmen were brought into the dancing light of the fire.

Jato stood and dismissed his followers, who obediently scurried away. He turned to Fraser: "Come and warm yourselves at the fire. Forgive my inhospitality, but I have had much to do since we move our camp." He gestured Fraser, Witcher and Rod Bullock to a large log at the fireside.

"I understand one of your men is sick with fever. He shall be attended to. No problem. But it will be by marabou medicine. All modern medicines are at the clinics of our peoples. But we have the finest marabou with us in all Guinea. Your friend will recover."

"I'm grateful," Fraser acknowledged reluctantly. "Some good food would help him, too."

Pheko looked angry. "There is little of that, Captain. But

you have brought that upon yourself. Your own actions have forced us to move our camp. Here, we are less well-prepared. There is little to go around and my Jatos are on active duty. You are not. You will understand you cannot have the best. It is good for us if you are a little weak. That, too, you will understand." He smiled ingratiatingly. "Do not worry, man. You shall not starve. Also, I am afraid I cannot release your bonds. I have promised Mr Rubashëv this thing. It is a small discomfort in return for your lives."

"A fellow vet, is he, this Rubashëv?" Lionel Witcher sneered.

The light of the fire accentuated the purple-black lustre of Jato Pheko's skin. "Mr Rubashëv is a brilliant military strategist. This man, he helps us to win the war against that imperialist puppet Jammeh."

Fraser said coldly: "That's the same tired old rhetoric your brother used, Kali."

The firelight seemed to illuminate the recesses in Pheko's skull where his eyes burned with a dark intensity. "And you, Captain, are using the same putrid arguments you use against my brother during the coup." His nostrils flared. "I will not forget the times I listen to you then. I did not understand. There, in a whiteman's house, I hear only your side of the affairs. I feel shame to be my brother's brother. Shame! I told no one he was of my family. Amongst my friends, I even denied it. Like your own Peter who denied his Christ. Only now I am ashamed of how I behaved *then*. I do not find it easy to forgive you for that."

"I don't want your forgiveness, Kali," Fraser retorted, meeting the Jato's gaze and holding it. "Your brother was a dangerous fanatic. He led innocent men, women and children into a useless slaughter. Over a thousand dead. Have you seen the graveyard by the coast? That is what you inherit from your brother. An acre of corpses. Don't repeat his mistake."

Jato stood suddenly, turning his back to the fire to look down on his prisoners. "My brother Omar's mistake was to forget Allah. At the start, the peoples they were with him. It was *our* revolution, Captain, but it was crushed by out-siders. People like you, and the foreign soldiers who came rushing to the aid of their puppet. They deny us our sovereign right to determine our own country's destiny.

"In history, all great nations have been allowed to fight amongst themselves to establish a new order. You had your Civil War in England. America fought for its independence. Revolutions took their course in France and Russia. But you deny *us* the right to decide for *ourselves!*"

Fraser felt his anger rising. In his mind's eye, he could see the political lecturer tapping the blackboard at Patrice Lumumba University. Pounding home the clever arguments and logic like the skilled patter of the insurance salesman. A smart answer to every question. Every line of reasoning turning in a circle. All roads lead to Moscow. Heads, we win, tails, you lose.

"Your people, Kali, had already chosen through the ballot box," Fraser snapped. "Guinea may be poor, but it's probably the most democratic country in Africa. And it's reasonable enough to respond when an elected President wants his people protected from armed bully boys like your brother. I'll remind you that he wasn't interested in being elected properly by his people."

Pheko snorted. "Not through rigged elections. No he wasn't! Imperialists like you still rule your colonies through puppets like Jammeh. You see he stays in power!"

Fraser shook his head. It was hopeless. "That's rubbish, Kali. Jammeh's a good politician, that's all. The reason he stays in power with a virtual one-party state is because politicians here prefer the power and money of joining the Government than forming an effective opposition. It's nothing to do with rigged elections."

Pheko laughed harshly. "C'mon, man. That is the same difference! It makes a mockery of your so-called western democracy. Revolution is the birthright of mankind. It is a free spirit that is above politics. That is what was explained to us in Libya. Man, that place is the central heart of the free revolutionary spirit of the world's peoples! They took the scales from my eyes, so that I can see. It is the fundamental principle of the Islamic Legion the Colonelissimo Gadaffi is sending out to free the world in the name of Allah! As my brother knew, it is the only way for the people to get the Government they deserve. By seizing power for themselves.''

A small crowd of Jatos had gathered to watch behind them. Fraser jumped as they suddenly burst into spontaneous and rapturous applause.

Pheko looked pleased. He drew himself up to his full height.

Lionel Witcher said quietly: "It's easier to die for principles than to live up to them. Remember that, Kali.''

Jato Pheko glowered.

At that moment there was a sudden commotion at the far side of the compound. A panting Jato came rushing towards the glow of the fire, his face glistening with sweat.

Scarcely able to catch his breath, he gave a defiant clenched-fist salute. "Great Jato, I bring news! It has fallen. Princetown is yours!"

A cry of victory went up from the gathered tribesmen.

Fraser and Witcher exchanged glances. Now it was obvious why there were so few guerrillas in the camp.

They had been busy taking Guinea's provincial capital which marked the half-way point of the country.

Jato was on the march again.

"JAT-O! JAT-O! JAT-O!" The rising chorus of elated voices drowned out the fitful crackle of the fire.

Life at the Jato camp fell into a mind-numbing routine.

The prisoners were roused in the pre-dawn light, before the rest of the inhabitants were about, and taken for half-an-hour's exercise. Although he was allowed much more freedom, Rod Bullock made a point of joining Captain Fraser and Corporal Witcher each morning. When not dogged by ill-health, they tried hard to jog, much to the annoyance of their accompanying guards.

Being a heavy smoker, Bullock found the going difficult, but he seemed to share their enthusiasm for annoying the Jatos who had strict orders to stay with them.

On return from the exercise their breakfast normally comprised one corncake and a thin soup of vegetable leaves. When there were no women troops in the camp it usually meant that even the luxury of a corncake was off the menu.

During the rest of the day the SASmen were confined to the mud hut. Interest was kept alive by listening to the events that made up the daily routine of the camp-life.

The village appeared to be a headquarters and political indoctrination centre for those newly won over to the Jato cause. Throughout most mornings the trudge of drilling feet could be heard as young recruits tried to follow the tirade of contradictory orders.

In the noonday heat everyone settled in the shade for political and religious instruction. Wrestling matches were organised in the cool of the late afternoon. This was followed by community singing around the fire as supper was prepared.

It was then that the prisoners received their second and last meal of the day. Invariably this was *nyankatano*. A dry mix of rice, beans and spices, it was the staple diet of poorer Guinean villages and was just about the full extent of the Jato warriors' culinary expertise.

It was on the evening of the seventh day that they were summoned to another fireside audience with Kali Pheko. He was in fine form, evidently pleased with the way his campaign was going and he rose to greet the prisoners expansively.

"I am pleased to see that your friend here is making recovery," he said imperiously.

Brummie Turner glared.

It was the first time he'd met the black leader and, as far as he was concerned, the man was just another terrorist.

And the world lately seemed to be full of men like Pheko. Men who covered their vicious and selfish actions with a veneer of smooth rhetoric. Men educated beyond their intelligence. Disguising their personal greed and ambition under the name of some cause or other. It didn't matter which. Nationalism, Communism, Islamic Fundamentalism. It was all the same for whoever sat on top of the dung heap.

Brummie recalled the quotation by Erich Fromm. How did it go? '*The successful revolutionary is a statesman; the unsuccessful one a criminal.*' That just about summed it up.

You could see the leaders of the world's civilised powers kowtowing to them and sucking-up for favours. State visits, guards-of-honour, dinners in Washington, Paris or Buck House.

It all made Brummie spit. He had no doubt that Pheko would be another of them. Given half a chance.

He said: "I wouldn't treat a dog the way you've treated us."

The smile fell from Pheko's face.

"Cool it," Fraser hissed.

Brummie shook off the restraining hand. "If this is an example of how the Great Bloody Jato shows his compassion, then may Allah help the poor sods in Guinea if he ever gets to power."

"Shut it!" Fraser hissed.

Pheko rounded on the NCO. "Listen, man, this isn't England. This is not the green and pleasant land. You do not like the medicines you get, huh? Well you get more than the Guinean villager who cannot even afford the marabou. We have no National Health. No dole. Here, if you fall ill or you have no work, you send your children out to beg, because you are too proud! That is all you have left. Your self-respect."

The SAS sergeant wasn't deterred. "The food you've been givin' us is shit. It's swill."

"It is all we have. Perhaps you now start to understand why we fight. While our President runs around the world playing statesman, the life expectancy of his peoples is thirty-five years! Like you, he does not understand poverty and suffering. He makes sure he never *sees* it!"

Brummie Turner tottered. The waves of nausea and dizziness from the fever still lingered. He breathed deeply, determined to stand his ground. But his knees started to give and the others had to help him to a seat on the log.

Lionel Witcher turned to Pheko. "He has a point, Kali. I know you're doing your best. But Sergeant Turner is still far from well. Thank God he's a tough bastard or he might be dead by now."

The contrast of the corporal's tone caught Pheko off-balance. He hesitated for a moment, but his anger still burned. His jaw set in a firm line. "We have no medicines to spare. And food is scarce."

211

"Or are you doing this because your Russian friend Rubashëv tells you to?"

The muscles in Pheko's chest swelled. "I command the Jatos. No one else. That man Rubashëv wants you dead, man, you remember that. Your life was spared because you were once my friends."

"That's touching," Witcher said. "But if that was the only reason, you'd take more care of us. My guess would be that you're hoping to flout our capture to the outside world if you get to power."

A ghost of a smile crossed Pheko's face. "That is an idea, isn't it, man? Proof that Britain still props up its imperialist puppets by sending its crackshots to bolster corrupt regimes . . ."

Brummie was disgusted. "Dis am de fault o' de British Guddermint!" he mimicked. "God, it makes me sick. You conveniently forget about the aid British taxpayers have given this Goddamn country. A lot of sodding thanks they get for their trouble!"

Pheko was unimpressed. "To give aid to Jammeh's Government is to pour water on a desert. He can soak up as much as you can give, man. No problem. It just serves to feed the political control of our economy. It goes on grand and wasteful projects that do not benefit native Guineans. And it gives Jammeh capital so he can borrow money on the international market to keep this tottering economy going." Pheko watched his audience to see how impressed they were with his knowledge of Third World economics. He added quietly: "Do you know that since 1978 the national debt in this tiny country of ours has trebled?"

Witcher nodded. "To eighty-five million dollars."

This time it was Pheko's turn to be impressed. "You do good homework. So you can see that my country is destined to be a country of poor villagers for the foreseeable future." He turned to Rod Bullock. "It is only the charity aid of my friend here and men like him that makes contribution to the welfare of my peoples. To teach my peoples how to do things for *themselves*!"

A silence fell over the group. The sense that the great Jato leader had spoken was undeniable.

After a moment Fraser asked softly: "And what has Rubashëv promised you, Kali? Apart from guns and explosives?"

"I cannot begin to tell you, Captain. He is a military man, so his first objectives they are for us to complete our take-over. He is not interested in politics."

"I bet!" Brummie muttered.

Pheko glared. "But he helps me plan for economic recovery with all the care and strategy of a military man. He knows my brother who is now in Cuba. Between them they are planning help for after the revolution. Field workers like Mr Bullock here. But not dozens, hundreds. To teach the children, to build schools and clinics, to help in agriculture and with livestock and fishing."

"And there will be no strings? No price to pay, I suppose?"

Pheko laughed aloud. "Always the imperialists think there is a price! The capitalist way!"

Wearily Fraser climbed to his feet. "I'm going to hit the sack, Kali. But it was good to talk. Perhaps our Government should talk more with people like you. To understand your views and aspirations." He paused for a moment. "But I tell you one thing. There is always a price to pay in this world. I know the Cubans do much good work, but they don't do it just because of a love of humanity. The price will be an insidious take-over of control. In the end the repayment you make will be heavy. That I promise."

For the first time doubt flashed in Pheko's eyes. "I am sorry you cannot see more good in your fellow man."

Fraser shrugged. "Anyone else coming?"

Brummie stumbled to his feet. "Sure. I can't stand any more of this."

Lionel Witcher looked up. "No, boss, I'll stay for a while and chat with Kali. If he doesn't mind?"

For once the Jato's smile seemed warm. "Sure, man. No problem. I shall make a revolutionary of you yet!"

Sir Nigel de Burgh fought hard to control his anger as he stalked up and down his office like a heron looking for a fish to spike.

213

Corporal Bill Mather sat emotionless in a leather visitor's chair. Only his pale grey eyes followed the pacing of the High Commissioner. His sun-bleached ginger moustache gave an almost imperceptible twitch, the only outward sign that his own anger was being sorely tested.

Sir Nigel turned suddenly on the heel of his hand-made shoes. "Well, Corporal, it frankly is just not good enough. You say Captain Fraser disappeared five days ago, and yet you have only just had the courtesy to let me know!" The lank wing of silver hair fell over his accusing eyes. Irritably he tossed it back into place. "Well? I am waiting for an explanation."

Mather glanced sideways at the haggard-looking face of Corporal Benjamin. The soldier gave a tired smile. "It was only when Mark here showed up, that we could be certain of what had happened, Sir. There was no point in panicking. It's not unusual to have a communications breakdown due to atmospheric conditions in a place like Guinea. And foot patrols can be punishing on radio equipment. It only needs a set to be dropped or submerged in water . . ."

"But, for God's sake, man," Sir Nigel interrupted, "why on earth did it take Corporal Benjamin here, what is it, three or four days to get back? This country's not exactly big."

Mather's eyes froze over. He had not mentioned that he had run a sweep through The Place of One Finger the very next day after Fraser's transmissions had stopped. They had not found Benjamin then, only a recently deserted camp. "Apart from the small fact that he was wounded in his escape, had no shoes or food – and had to hide-up to escape the Jato's search parties – there *was* no reason, Sir. It was unforgivable."

Benjamin couldn't keep the smirk from his face. And the High Commissioner couldn't fail to notice it.

"Well, I just hope that'll be a lesson that you and your self-opinionated comrades from Hereford will remember. You are not infallible and would do well to listen to the wisdom of those of us paid to understand these matters."

He sat down heavily behind the empty desk and wrung

his hands uncomfortably. "First I hear that your commander has made a direct request to the President to dismiss his Head of State Security. Unthinkable! And, if that wasn't bad enough, he takes an armed patrol into rebel territory . . ." He looked up ". . . with a *civilian* from a non-political charity organisation."

Mather said: "It was only a training exercise, Sir. We wouldn't put civilians at risk, Sir. You know that."

"Do I?" Sir Nigel said with a pent-up fury of a thunderclap. "Next you'll be telling me it was a navigational error, I suppose? Isn't that the standard excuse you people use?"

"As you said," Mather murmured, "we're only human."

"Balderdash!"

Mather leaned back in his chair and eyed the High Commissioner calmly. "Well, if you know all the answers there is not much point in continuing this conversation, is there?" He smiled frostily. "Sir."

Sir Nigel de Burgh's planned retirement at the end of the year suddenly seemed a long way off. "I really do not know why they had to send you out here in the first place. I knew it was a mistake."

"The only mistake," Mather replied, "is that we're doing too little too late. The information Corporal Benjamin gleaned during his capture tallies with our up-country reconnaissance patrol. They observed small parties of Jatos moving across country. They were moving independently but all in the same direction. Towards Princetown. That ties in with reports from our other OP of increased traffic of lorries and vehicles moving west. Not carrying groundnuts or rice, but people. Mostly young men."

Sir Nigel shook his head. "No, Corporal Mather, there is no way that Princetown will fall. There's a major police-post there."

"Sir," Mather said, "armed police are no match in a fighting war. Even the few that have been through our training programme won't hold up without experienced leadership. That's why we *must* have more troops from Britain."

"I gather President Jammeh has already turned that idea down," the High Commissioner reminded scathingly.

Mather was losing patience. "Of course he has, Sir. Kwofie's got his ear and naturally *he's* not going to admit that he's losing control. But if you recommend to the British Government that they are needed, then pressure from Whitehall might make Jammeh change his mind."

"What are you trying to do, Corporal, turn this into another Vietnam? It's exactly because the British Government *doesn't* want further involvement that you were sent here as a safety-measure. A few politically-inspired bandits does not constitute a full-scale revolution. There isn't a rebel within two hundred miles of Sakoto. Do you really want me to make a complete fool of myself with London?"

The telephone shrieked, interrupting the High Commissioner in full flow. He snatched up the handset irritably. "Yes?" he demanded.

For a moment he listened, his gaze flicking from the desk to the two SASmen in front of him, then down at the receiver in his hand. "Thank you."

Slowly he replaced the handset on its cradle. "That was State House. At first light this morning the police-post at Princetown was surrounded by Jatos. They gave the occupants the choice of fighting or joining the rebel cause . . ." His voice faded.

Mather's moustache twitched in one corner. "And they went over?"

Sir Nigel looked like a man coming round from an anaesthetic. He shook his head quickly and blinked. "Er, it's assumed so. The radio-telephone link has gone dead. And, er, there have been broadcasts made by the Jato from the Government transmitter there."

Mather stood up. "If you'll excuse me, Sir, we've things to attend to. We've a lot of civilian and Army aid teams in villages beyond Princetown. All part of the psychological warfare effort. They could be in danger now."

"Yes, of course." Still stunned.

Mark Benjamin followed Mather to the door where the veteran corporal paused. "About that request to Whitehall . . . ?"

Sir Nigel de Burgh hesitated. "Very well. I'll make

your request known. But frankly I still don't hold much hope."

As he closed the door behind him, Mather said: "I don't trust that old sod, Mark. Give him ten minutes and he'll convince himself that the loss of Princetown is unimportant."

9

It was to be two more weeks before Captain Johnny Fraser's plan for a breakout was ready to put into operation.

Health had been the most limiting factor, and Brummie Turner's condition had been the biggest problem. It seemed that the fever would never fully leave him. Just when a recovery appeared to be complete, he would be struck down by a mild relapse.

As the moment of the escape grew closer, the SASmen's attention had focused on a crazy one-eyed chicken that spent its life attacking the camp goats. After weeks of prison diet the very thoughts of those skinny legs, spit-roasted over charcoal, were enough to set the saliva glands working with a vengeance. It fell upon Bullock, as the only one with relative freedom of movement, to commit the dastardly act.

"That is bloody *fantastic!*" Brummie enthused as Rod Bullock laid out the dismembered chicken in the centre of the hut and began wrapping individual segments in banana leaves. "You're a soddin' genius."

Bullock grinned. "I am, aren't I? And the little bugger put up one hell of a fight. Nearly woke the entire camp."

"What about the mangoes?" Fraser asked.

"In my shirt. I could only get seven. And they're a bit bruised."

"No problem, Rod. That and the chicken should keep us going for a day or two. We're bound to find civilisation by then. Or at least a village where we can steal some grub."

Bullock nodded, then lifted out the fruit he'd secreted around his waist. Something heavy thudded onto the earth.

"What's that?" Witcher asked.

"A piece of flint. It's razor sharp."

"No knives?" Fraser couldn't disguise his disappointment.

"I'm sorry, Johnny. These guys guard their military hardware like they were the crown jewels. They've never had anything as grand as a combat knife before. I did try, I promise."

"And the keys?" Since the police-post at Princetown had been taken their hide bonds had been replaced with steel handcuffs – real ones.

Bullock shrugged helplessly. "I imagine they're in Pheko's hut. I can't think they'd entrust them to Nyomi." He hesitated. "Talking of whom. Look, Johnny, she's a sweet kid. I mean she's done a lot to make life a bit more pleasant for us. You're not going to – to, well, kill her?"

Fraser's tight smile gave little in the way of reassurance. "Not if I can help it. But there are no promises, Rod. We're in a tight corner and the odds aren't exactly stacked on our side. If things go wrong, then Nyomi's still the enemy. Get me?"

"Jesus!" Bullock still wasn't happy. "Can't we leave her out of this?"

Fraser shook his head. "Sorry, Rod. She's our only chance of getting a weapon. And she's wearing one of our belt-orders. And, unless she's given away the contents, that'll be invaluable. Even when it's shared between all four of us."

Witcher's voice came from the entrance where he had been keeping watch. "Time's up, boss! Here she comes."

"Okay, everyone," Fraser snapped. "Brummie, down you go."

Quickly the bulky NCO dropped to the floor and curled himself into a ball of mock agony, clasping at his stomach and making small whimpering sounds. Bullock dragged open the ill-fitting door as the others stepped back into the shadows.

"Nyomi! Come quick. Man in big trouble. Bad pain!"

The girl frowned as she approached, breaking into a run and unshouldering the Kalashnikov rifle as she went. It was almost as big as she was and she had to put it out in front of her to get it through the entrance.

219

"Aaargh!" Brummie groaned aloud. He was making the most of it.

"He is real sick," Bullock said with his palms upturned in a gesture of helplessness.

Nyomi was alarmed. This was too big a problem for her. She turned. "I go get help."

Bullock's expression froze. That wasn't what he had intended. "No! You look first. See him."

She looked down at the man, sideways, as though to set eyes on him might pass on the dreadful affliction to herself. She backed away. "I do not know . . ." she stuttered. "I go get . . ."

She became aware that Bullock was trying to get behind her. The barrel of her Kalashnikov came up defensively. It occurred to her that the other prisoners were hidden by shadow. Usually they would be in the centre, ready to chat and laugh with her.

She glanced nervously back towards the entrance. As the Kalashnikov rose and pointed at his chest, Bullock's heart sank. In their rehearsal it was to have been so easy to strike her from behind when she bent to examine the sick man.

With the speed of a striking snake, Brummie Turner's feet thrust out from the curled position, engaging the girl's ankles in a vice-like grip. He wrenched hard. The barrel jerked upward and the girl toppled.

Seizing his chance Fraser closed up behind her and grabbed her throat between his handcuffed hands. His thumbs sought out the nerve trigger-centres in her neck and put on a hard, steady pressure until he felt her starting to pass out. As her body went limp, he let her slide slowly out of his grip.

"For God's sake!" Bullock protested. "You'll bloody kill her."

Witcher knelt and checked her pulse. "No, Rod, she's okay. Not dead, just sleepeth."

"Sorry, sweetheart," Fraser murmured. "Bloody lucky that gun didn't go off."

Brummie was checking the weapon. "Not really, boss. Soppy tart hadn't cocked it." He grinned.

But Fraser wasn't in the mood to see the lighter side of events. Anxiously, he unclasped the belt-order she wore around her waist and opened up the kidney pouches. Black plastic respirator cases and customised packs marked it as Mark Benjamin's kit. The contents were spilled out onto the soft earth.

All the food had gone, which was hardly surprising. The ration packs, spam spread, apricot tablets and even the emergency glucose tablet rations were missing. More amazing still, the tub of waterproof matches and the screwdrivers had disappeared. No doubt they were now the prized possessions of some would-be Jato engineer.

"Any luck, boss?" Brummie was anxious.

Fraser didn't answer. He tipped out the next pouch. There was a gentle tinkle of steel. "Thank God for small mercies," he breathed, and picked up the four thin lock-probes from the standard entry kit and handed them to the sergeant. "Get going with these, Brummie, I never could get the hang of them. If that fails, there's also a hacksaw chain."

As Brummie went to work on Witcher's handcuffs, Fraser completed his search.

He gave the compass to Rod Bullock who, if he became separated from Brummie's care in the escape attempt, would need it. The others would have to use the sun or stars for navigation. Fraser also handed over the water bottle, which the girl had kept filled, the primitive fishing tackle and small animal snare to Bullock. Again the SAS team would have to rely on their training in improvisation.

The real surprise came when, on tipping out the last pouch, he discovered the flint-and-magnesium firestarter. Obviously the gadget had been a mystery to the Jatos. Perhaps they thought it was a cigarette lighter that didn't work.

Brummie Turner started work on Fraser's handcuffs while Witcher mixed some water with the dirt of the hut floor to make a mud paste to use as camouflage cream.

As the manacles fell away, Fraser worked the circulation back into his hands and massaged his chafed wrists. It was an incredible feeling to be free after three weeks. His hands felt light and weightless as though they didn't belong to him.

From the back of the hut Brummie dug up some tatty sweaters that Bullock had stolen from the washing-line of the camp laundry, and some lengths of string. Carefully, he cut the material into sections with the sharpened flint and handed them around. Following the sergeant's example, each man slid his feet into a length of armpieces, then stuffed the underside full with the remaining strips of wool. The denim fatigue shirt of the girl, who had been left gagged and trussed topless, was used to form an outer layer. A lattice of string was finally criss-crossed over the weird footwear to hold it all in place.

"If you get the chance, reinforce the sole with something strong," Brummie advised. "Wool is no protection in thick bush. Bark will help. An old tyre is ideal."

Bullock looked dubious. "There's a lot of them in the bush."

It then took Fraser and Brummie a few seconds to prise apart a dozen Kalashnikov bullets and collect the cordite in a banana leaf, which was then folded carefully into a small packet.

At last, Fraser picked up Nyomi's weapon and quickly checked it over. The cool metal felt good and reassuring. He looked up expectantly.

"All set, lads?"

They nodded grimly.

Brummie said: "Let's get the sodding thing going, boss."

Fraser grinned a little stiffly. He was glad to get moving but he was aware there was much to go wrong. They were desperately ill-equipped for the escape without proper clothing or equipment and with their general state of health only precariously improved. Added to this was the fact that Rod Bullock, tough and resourceful though he was, lacked any military or survival training.

But the SAS officer made a determined effort to keep his tone cheerful. "Good luck, lads. See you at Sakoto."

"And you, boss," Witcher returned. "I'll have a beer waiting at the Green Mamba."

Fraser crossed to the rear of the hut and eased away a

large mud brick near the ground. They had been working at it during the past week with improvised tools; now it gave without protest. A gurgle and a heave was all it took before he was through. The night air struck cool and sweet after the confines of their prison which had become increasingly foul-smelling as the days dragged by. Carefully, he replaced the brick, then, worming his way around the perimeter of the hut, he paused to study the activity in the compound.

It was much fuller than it had been when they had first arrived. Recruits to the Jato cause were swelling by the day. In the bright glow of the fire he could estimate the silhouetted figures in their hundreds as they joined in the rebel songs and stamped their feet to the sound of the *sabaro* drums.

He began the tortuous route around the inner square of huts and new makeshift shelters of rattan weave that had been hastily constructed to house the growing ranks. It was a leopard crawl, hard and fast, between each dwelling in the direction of the perimeter guards, out there somewhere at the edge of the clearing. Another check towards the central fire. All clear, and on again.

It was twenty minutes before he reached the opposite side of the compound, their prison hut just visible through the smoky heat-haze of the fire. He was behind a recently-constructed corrugated-iron hut that Rod Bullock thought was the camp's arsenal. Normally it was well guarded, but the two Jatos on duty had their attention on their dancing comrades. Security was evidently the last thing on their minds.

From the shadow of the arsenal, he gave one last glance back across the compound to the prison hut where he knew his companions would be anxiously watching.

His heart suddenly thudded against his breastbone. Even through the flickering flames he could see an armed Jato strolling nonchalantly towards the entrance. Obviously the man was curious as to why Nyomi had been gone so long.

Fraser swiftly lifted himself from the ground into a crouch, and rested the Kalashnikov on his knee. Ready.

Please, dear God, he groaned inwardly. The Jato pushed open the door. Nothing happened.

The captain's finger tightened on the trigger.

Stooping, the Jato entered the darkened hut. The sound of Fraser's own heart seemed to deafen him. A thick waft of woodsmoke blotted out his view. When it cleared the door to the hut was shut again.

He breathed a long, slow sigh and wiped the thick gunge of mud and sweat from his forehead. He had no doubt now that the guerrilla was dead.

It was a harsh reminder that time was not on his side. Hurriedly, he began to crawl across the final stretch to his destination.

The donkey watched him with idle curiosity. It was tethered beneath the pontoon storage hut which provided shade during the heat of the day.

"Okay, lad," Fraser whispered. "It's all right then."

The animal took a step back, unsure. Its nostrils flared as it watched nervously while Fraser veered past until he reached the unguarded ladder. He climbed rapidly to the narrow edge of the platform on which the hut was built.

He fell thankfully into the shadow, breathing heavily. It was disconcerting how unfit he felt, despite the daily effort at exercise he had maintained during their captivity. It didn't bode well for a dash through the forest at night. But at least it confirmed in his own mind that it was better to try now than wait while their strength ebbed remorselessly away.

Reaching up, he released the catch to the door and let it swing open under its own weight. Then he rolled into the dusty interior of the grain store. There was just enough filtered light for him to make out the humped shape of some twenty jute sacks ranked around him.

He tied a length of rag around his nose and mouth. Then, extracting the flintstone from his pocket, he began ripping open the sacks. He shook the contents of each one out until the air was thick with grain dust, obliterating everything.

When he could finally see no more, he fumbled his way to

the door and scrambled out. Thankfully, he ripped aside his mask and gulped in the fresh night air. He blinked hard to clear the dust from his eyes, then extracted the flint-and-magnesium firestarter and the package of cordite.

Quickly, he ran a trail of the powder from under the door to the edge of the platform, finishing in a small pile. He added some magnesium scrapings to it, then scraped the flint.

Immediately, the powder trail caught, fizzing fast towards the door and into the confined, dust-laden air inside the hut. Fraser dived for the edge of the platform and launched himself at a patch of soft earth below.

The blast hit him in mid-flight.

His ears filled with a rushing roar as the dust ignited. It was as though a giant invisible hand had plucked him from the air and tossed him contemptuously aside. A debris of torn crinting and timber splinters lashed at his face as he somersaulted through space. All sense of direction was lost, like a toppled surfer beneath the waves.

Instinctively, he rolled his head forwards, covering it with his forearms.

Then the hard ground slammed into his back like a mallet. The vibration jolted the air out through his teeth. His ears still rang.

Groggily, he turned over and pulled himself onto all-fours. Looking over his shoulder, he could scarcely believe the bedlam that had been created.

Atop its pontoon struts, some of which miraculously still held, the store platform raged like a funeral pyre, its blinding brightness dulling the camp fire by comparison. The donkey, its coat smouldering, was dancing in wild panic through the flaming thatch and sacking. Its rear legs kicked in terror at the guerrillas who rushed to its aid.

Through the dust and smoke it was impossible to see the prison-hut. But if all was going to plan, as the diversionary fire blazed, his companions were making their long-awaited bid for freedom.

Fraser looked around for the Kalashnikov. It was nowhere to be seen. Sod! He had no time to look. Crouching low, he sped towards the dense covering of undergrowth. In seconds, he was swallowed up by the shadows. As the noise of the camp receded, the noise of the explosion still sang in his ears.

Dawn was a mixed blessing. It brought welcome light and warmth to the dankness of the forest. But no doubt it would also bring the unleashing of the hounds. The Jatos would be out in full cry.

Under normal circumstances Johnny Fraser would have rested up in the day and travelled at night. But, ill-equipped as he was, with the improvised shoes rapidly disintegrating, he decided that at least he might find a clear game trail if he could only see where he was going.

Indeed he had only been walking for a short time before he did stumble across a forest track. A few minutes earlier, before the shafts of sunlight had penetrated the translucent green canopy, he would have passed it unknowingly.

He decided to take a chance. At least it was heading west – the only direction he knew had to be the right one, as it must eventually reach the Atlantic Ocean. Exercising the greatest caution he made good progress for three hours. There was no sign of another human being, and the peace and tranquillity became quite unnerving.

He slaked his thirst by slicing into tree creepers with the flintstone to release the pure water within. It was sufficient to keep him going until mid-afternoon when he suddenly began to feel exhausted. Rather than risk going on with his concentration slipping, he left the track and found a small clearing. Feeling better, he opened the pack of chicken bits and ate half of it. Five minutes later he was asleep.

He awoke with a start. It was pitch black and it took a second or two for him to realise where he was. He made his way back to the track. Little of the bright starglow managed to penetrate the leaves, but it was just enough to faintly define the route, and he moved along it with a growing sense of well-being until it plunged steeply into a closely-wooded valley.

It was well-known that night travel in hostile territory could give a false sense of security. On numerous occasions they had been warned about it on training exercises, and more than once Fraser had experienced it for himself.

But that didn't lessen the shock when he suddenly realised he was walking straight towards an armed Jato.

His muscles froze. He felt the sweat break out on his body as he stood motionless on the track. Just twenty yards ahead, the black guerrilla stood on a rough-hewn footbridge that spanned a small river. Starlight glittered on the gunmetal of the man's raised Kalashnikov. The whites of his eyes and his teeth seemed to have a luminous quality. He appeared to be looking straight at Fraser.

Then the Jato turned, stamping his feet. He laid the rifle down and pulled the woollen hat he wore down over his ears.

Fraser slowly lowered himself to his knees. Inch by inch he edged crabwise into the trackside shadows. Once hidden he let out his breath in a long silent sigh of relief. It had been close.

Quickly he considered the options open to him. Despite his weak state he could probably overpower the Jato. But there could be others nearby. He had no way of knowing. Worse still, a dead or missing guard would alert Jato Pheko to the direction he ought to point his search.

No, he decided, discretion was the better part of valour. Move quietly upstream and cross out of sight of the bridge, and then rejoin the track.

He wormed forward through the brush to get a better view of the footbridge. The Jato had picked up his rifle again and stood staring into the water. Fraser's eyes followed the same direction. Then he saw them. Half-a-dozen fishing canoes drawn up on a sandy strip of embankment.

A slow smile crossed his face. Perfect. Ease one into the water and let it drift downstream. From his knowledge of the geography, all tributaries should eventually flow into the Kebba. He frowned. But the canoe would have to pass under the bridge. The Jato could not fail to see.

There was no way around the problem. The guard would have to go. Even if he was missed, by dawn a canoe would have taken Fraser miles away. Then, anyway, he could land the thing wherever he chose and strike off in a new direction.

He fished in his pocket, his hand closing around the flintstone. Silently he crept forward, edging from shadow to shadow until he was hidden in the undergrowth a mere six feet from the shivering Jato.

Fraser braced himself, his leg muscles tensing like a coiled spring. The Jato turned away. Fraser leapt onto the slippery wooden boles of the bridge, his left forearm snapping tight around the man's mouth, stifling his scream. The sharp point of the flintstone jabbed in hard just below the guerrilla's ear. It met resistance. Fraser squeezed harder, sweat running into his eyes. The flesh gave with a slow sucking noise and half of the flintstone disappeared into the jugular vein.

Fraser caught the deadweight in his arms. His right hand was wet and sticky with warm blood as he lowered the Jato onto the bridge.

There was no mistake. The click of a weapon. Deep in the shadows at the far end of the bridge. He had hardly heard the crack of the shots before he was reeling under a stunning pain in his thigh. He tried to stay upright but red lights were bursting in his vision and he toppled clumsily onto his victim.

He gasped for breath, forcing the oxygen into his lungs to clear his vision. His attacker, who had probably been asleep on the far side of the bridge, was a big man. He stepped forward with the smoking AK47 still in his hand, a fixed grin of fear and triumph on his face.

Pain ebbed through Fraser's body, bursting in tiny explosions inside his head. Through a veil of returning red cloud he could see the Jato suddenly turn at a new sound behind him.

In a weird slow-motion he saw the bulky figure pounce on the black-man, bringing him down with a force that shook the bridge. He saw the dark shape raise an arm and bring it down with shuddering force into the neck of the fallen Jato.

The shape moved towards him, hunched, and Fraser could see the white flesh glistening behind the streaks of mud that plastered his face.

Brummie Turner's voice in his ears was as sweet to hear as an angel singing.

Fraser shook his head. "Think I've stopped one in the leg. But, for Christ's sake, Brummie, what are you doing here?"

"Don't ask fucking stupid questions. That I could do without." He glanced about him. "Let's get out of here. Those canoes. I was waiting my chance when you bumbled onto the scene and queered my pitch. Didn't you learn fuckin' anything in the Falklands?"

An involuntary smile wrenched itself free. "Don't tell me, we officers are bloody useless without an NCO to look after us."

"You said it, boss." He pointed to Fraser's leg. "We'll get going, then I'd best have a dekko at that."

The pirogue had been hollowed out of a tree-trunk. It was heavy and difficult for the two men to manoeuvre the slimy hull into the black water.

Once under way Fraser had a chance to question Brummie about what had happened to the others.

"Rod Bullock and I got separated," the sergeant explained. "After you blew that grain-hut we got out. No problem. Then we ran slap into a bloody perimeter guard before we could separate. Psychlops got caught."

"Lionel? Was he wounded?"

"No, just twisted an ankle, I think. I thought it best to press on and get Rod Bullock to safety."

"So what went wrong?"

Brummie scratched at the rough beard on his face. "Good question that. Fuck knows. It was pitch black in the forest and bloody Jatos everywhere with lighted torches. I looked around and Bullock had done a bleedin' vanishing act. I went back, but no joy."

Fraser felt depressed. "So what's the good news?"

In fact the good news was that the wound to Fraser's leg was only a deep bullet crease. No doubt the result of the hellish kick-back on the AK47 which easily threw a novice's aim. It was just as well as its high-velocity round would have torn his leg apart. As it was the muscle was torn which caused him to limp, but it could have been far worse. Provided it didn't fester, he would survive.

"We're veering again," Brummie warned. "Can you pull up harder, boss?"

Fraser tried. "I don't seem to have any strength. That better?"

"Not much. Let's pull over and take a breather."

They steered into the bank and Brummie grabbed an overhanging branch to pull them in.

"Shit!" He let go again, beating at the army of red ants that swarmed down his arm.

Fraser paddled again, edging them into a shallow bank between two monstrous mangrove roots. The sergeant leapt out and dragged the bow of the pirogue canoe onto the mud.

After the constant splashing of the paddles the gentle lapping of the inky black water was almost tranquil. Fraser slapped at his neck. He examined his palm. It was stained with squashed mosquitoes. Half-a-dozen of them.

"Little fuckers," Brummie muttered in disgust. "You can hear them. Millions of the little sods."

"I don't give a toss, Brummie. I've got to crash out."

The sergeant nodded. "You do that, boss. I'll do stag. No problem. I couldn't sleep, anyway, knowin' I was being bled to death."

Brummie Turner woke the captain as the new day broke.

Fraser came to with a jolt. It had been a desperately uncomfortable, tormented night. All the time the ferocious hum of mosquitoes had stayed with them, so loud and constant that it sounded like an engine running. Millions of the insects had crawled all over their bodies and worked down inside their clothes. Despite Fraser's efforts to shield his face they had found their way through, stinging his nose and eyelids, and even creeping up his nostrils and into his mouth. There had been no end to it, and he had woken several times, his clothing saturated with sweat.

Now he ran an exploratory tongue around his mouth. Both were burning with hard lumps. "Christ, Brummie, I don't want to go through that again."

The NCO curled his lip into a cynical smile. His own eyes were swollen like a boxer who had gone the distance.

"Little fuckers have gone now, boss. Surprised they can lift their arses off the deck after the feast they've had."

Fraser sat up. "God, do I look as bad as you?"

"Worse."

"Do you want to get your head down? I'm all right for a stag."

Brummie sniffed and shook his head. "If it's all the same to you, I'd rather push on. The thoughts of another night like that . . . I'd like to clear the area."

"You look bushed."

Again the sardonic smile. "I'll get by. How's the leg?"

Fraser shrugged. "Throbbing. I'll get by too."

"When it stops throbbing, that's the time to worry."

After a breakfast that saw off the remains of the chicken they set out under a strengthening sun. Following the horror of the night, it was an almost unbelievable change. The black mirror of water broke fitfully under the urging bow of the pirogue as they paddled strongly, hugging the bank. On either side of the snaking river the forest glowed with a hundred shades of incandescent green as the sunlight played over fronds and feathered leaves. Monkeys called from the shore and hornbills swooped overhead.

At midday a solitary canoe was spotted on the turn of a distant bend. Expertly the two SASmen swung their pirogue into a sheltered cove hidden by trailing creepers.

Two men were paddling the nearing canoe. A third sat in the blunt bow, a rifle resting across his knee as he scanned the bank. His yellow headband fluttered in the gentle slipstream.

As the canoe disappeared from view, Fraser said: "That's it, Brummie. We're asking for trouble if we keep going in daylight. Besides, I'd rather keep moving at night. The mosquitoes will be less trouble in mid-stream."

"You're probably right. But this river can be a pig at night. Submerged logs and sandbanks. Still, they don't shoot, do they?"

Fraser arched his back to relieve his aching muscles. "This forest has got to give way soon. It's travelling more or

231

less westward. And north. I reckon it has to join up with the Kebba eventually."

"You reckon that camp was over the border?"

"Probably. Or near it at any rate."

Brummie scratched at his stubbled chin. "I don't know. This whole op has turned out to be a right fuckin' mess, hasn't it?" He suddenly looked at Fraser. "No offence, boss. It's none of your doing."

Fraser was amused at the NCO's philosophical attitude. To Brummie's mind his commander's action was blameless, mostly because the reconnaissance mission had been the sort of positive action he believed was needed. But the captain doubted that it would be seen in the same generous light back at Hereford. His chance of a majority now seemed remote indeed – assuming that he even got back in one piece to be able to accept it.

He said: "It was my decision. If it had worked, there'd have been no problem. But it didn't and we've got the proverbial egg on our faces."

Brummie shook his head. "The Old Man won't see it that way, boss. He'll stick by your decision. The man-on-the-spot and all that. It's the fuckin' politicians and bleedin' chinless wonders in Whitehall who might cause trouble."

"Unfortunately, they're the ones that matter."

Brummie stared out through the screen of hanging vegetation and watched a giant swallowtail butterfly probe at a bright yellow climbing flower. "Yeah. And it pisses me off. Really, it does."

"It's part of the job."

"Fuck that."

"I didn't think you gave a damn about politicians."

Brummie snorted in disgust. "I don't. And I doubt if you do, either. You might be an officer, but you're not a bleedin' fool."

Fraser smiled. "Thank you."

But Brummie was serious. "If we're not doing all this for our political leaders, then why the hell are we doing it? I mean, look at the two of us now. Not exactly going the right way about collecting our pensions, are we? We must be fucking barmy. Getting shot at and kissing the arses of some foreign king or prime minister because it suits some politician's master-plan."

"What is it, Brummie?" Fraser asked quietly. "What's changed?"

"Huh?"

"Your attitude." He smiled. "You've always been a miserable sod. Part of your charm. But never bitter. Ever since we've been here you've seemed different. Not your old self."

"What's this? Fuckin' psycho-analysis?" Brummie snarled.

"Maybe."

That seemed to surprise him. "Not the time or the place, boss. Still, you may as well know. I've had it up to my tits. I'm thinkin' of getting out." He studied his fingernails. "Maybe I'll get a gong up after the Falklands. That might help with getting a job."

"What sort of job?"

"How the fuck should I know?" Angry. "Sell insurance. Be a gardener. Open a shop. Maybe be a bloody politician."

Fraser thought for a moment. "Is it anything to do with Scottie?"

And as soon as he spoke, he knew he had hit the target. The expression in Brummie's eyes said it all. The anger and sadness seemed to burn out of the drawn, emaciated face.

He turned his head. "Maybe that made me see things I haven't wanted to see, boss. I should have been on that fuckin' chopper. Only I got a nick on the Pebble Island malleting and was sent to the Sick Bay. McDermid made bloody sure I didn't get out while he went in my place. Bloody . . . lovely . . . Scots git . . ." His voice quavered.

Fraser said nothing. So that's what had been gnawing at Brummie ever since that fateful day on the 18th May when a Sea King helicopter had sucked an albatross into its air-intake during the cross-decking to the flagship HMS *Hermes*. An albatross. The legendary bird of ill-omen to sailors. Sadly appropriate. Those who perished had been mostly veteran NCOs of the Special Air Service. What hadn't been realised by the world at large was that they had been on their way to an O-Group to receive orders for the coming invasion of San Carlos. Each one the senior member of a four-man Sabre team. In one fell swoop virtually an entire Squadron had lost its most experienced men. Every team had lost its leader and was brutally cut down to three men in one vicious act of fate. It had been a devastating loss.

Brummie Turner sniffed heavily. "What bugged me after was the thanks we got from those sodding Kelpers. Not just our mob, but all the lads. Fuck me, it just wasn't worth it. So, if that's what we get for helping our own, what's the point of propping up people like Jammeh. In a year or two it could as well be that shitbag Jato Pheko we're asked to look after."

Fraser said: "You're going soft."

But he understood.

It was just another symptom. Another legacy from the war. It scarred different men in different ways.

Back at Hereford, before he had left, the CO had warned him of the difficulties he might find. Many of those who served had realised that they would probably never fight another war like that. Nothing else would ever quite equal the challenge. And the Regiment was a magnet to men who saw life as one long series of challenges to be met – preferably each one harder than the last.

The talk of 'getting out' had been widespread and earnest after the conflict. Speculation as to what a medal would mean in 'Civvy Street' was rife. Perfectionists to a man, some had been sickened by the military bungling and ineptitude of lesser mortals. It was made worse by the knowledge that the failings of the hierarchy would be swept under the carpet. Along with the bodies.

Brummie yawned. "You're right, boss. I am getting soft. But when your best oppo gets it, it makes you think. The risks you run. Why the hell are you doing it? For what, for who? Politicians and civil service farts." He paused. "I suppose, when you boil it down, we're doing it for ourselves. And our oppos. The glory of the fuckin' Regiment. You know. To tell the truth, I didn't know anyone had noticed I was getting pissed off."

"Mather did. He was concerned about you."

He grinned. "I really ought to marry that fucker."

"On the bank," Fraser hissed. "At two o'clock."

They'd been paddling along the silky black river for several hours now. They were tired. Getting careless.

"I've got him, boss," Brummie returned, shipping his paddle.

Instinctively, each man leaned forward with his head to his knees, presenting the minimum silhouette. With any luck, the pirogue would appear to be a drifting log.

Again the flashlight danced and played across the current, probing the trailing strands of mist that floated lazily over the surface. Peering over the edge of the dugout, it seemed to Fraser that the craft had gathered momentum. In seconds the bright beam was playing over them. Both men held their breath. It seemed an age.

The blunted bow nudged something hard in the water. Probably driftwood. The stern, caught in a sudden chattering rush of water, edged out, turning slowly to overtake the bow. Whatever was holding them, it gave. Branches rustled along the side of the dugout.

"Current's fuckin' strong here," Brummie rasped, his head still down.

"Just what I was thinking," Fraser answered. "What's that?"

"What?"

"That noise?"

Brummie turned his head slightly to one side. A distant murmur rose above the bright rippling of the water. The bank was passing swiftly now; the man with the flashlight had melted away into the blanket of damp mist.

"Oh, fuck me!" Brummie grunted.

There was no mistaking the pull on the pirogue, the gurgling protest of the water growing louder as the craft began to spin.

"For Chrissake, paddle!" Fraser called, fumbling to follow his own advice.

But the dull murmur had risen to a low roar and already they could feel the mist of spray from the rapids against their skin. The heavy dugout waddled uncomfortably, broadside-on to the current, but it stubbornly refused to turn, despite the strong paddling of the two men.

Frantically, Fraser squinted through the curtain of mist in search of the bank he knew must be there. But until they could gain some steerage on the awkward craft, they stood no chance of reaching it, however close.

"Harder, boss!" Brummie bawled.

Fraser's muscles screamed as he crouched forward for maximum leverage, each stroke digging deep, hard and fast into the bubbling water with the paddle blade.

Reluctantly, the craft began to respond, its snout snuffling round as though sniffing out the right direction. The mist burst over them like a parting curtain, dark ominous shapes looming past on both sides. The bottom scraped on shingle. Resistance. They slowed. Then suddenly, with a surge, they were free again, travelling faster than ever. Around them the water began to boil, filling the air with spray.

Brummie called out something but it was lost in the sound of gushing water and the crack of timber against stone. As they hurtled on, the creaming water rose like a wall around them, foaming over the sides of the dugout as it was sucked into a narrow channel between grotesque dark rocks. Through the streaming torrent, Fraser could see the sergeant wave the paddle handle with despair and rage. The blade had snapped.

The channel flared out suddenly and the momentum slowed. With more room, the dugout began to gyrate again. Desperately, Fraser held water with his paddle, attempting to straighten up before the next cataract he could hear approaching. The pirogue would have none of it.

Horrified, he peered into the confusing murk as they slid sideways towards another narrow channel.

Twin markers of gnarled rock appeared like gargoyles, ugly sirens drawing them on. The pirogue bridged the channel, the bow and stern jamming with bone-shattering force against the channel mouth. Behind them the water built up, swirling in an angry cauldron at being denied passage. The dugout quaked and shuddered, rocking violently.

Suddenly, it tilted towards the channel, still stuck fast. Fraser grabbed for the craft's side. His fingers slipped over the mossy timber. The moon, a vague blur behind a hazy veil, suddenly shifted. His balance went. His hand slipped.

Behind them, the avalanche of water broke through, tossing the pirogue contemptuously skywards.

The pain and the dull impact of the water hit Fraser simultaneously as he disappeared beneath the creaming vortex like a sled on a downhill run. For a moment he was aware of spinning in an underwater void, then crashing from side to side. His lungs were bursting. Bursting . . .

There was no sign of Brummie Turner.

Painfully, Fraser crawled out of the rockpool and sat, breathing heavily, on the natural parapet beside the burbling cataract. In daylight, it looked harmless enough. A beautiful running cascade of glittering, swirling water through a scattering of coloured rocks. An ideal snapshot for a tourist's camera.

He shut his eyes, steeling himself against the throbbing ache in his head. Slowly, he ran his hand over his temple. His fingers came away, wet and sticky with blood. No wonder he'd been unconscious for so long.

Looking down he saw that the wound in his thigh had opened again, too, the flesh hanging in a red and sodden fringe. He waved away a fly. At least he was alive.

Something caught his eye. Under the water in the rockpool, its angular shape distorted by the reflective surface. Stiffly, he reached forward and pulled it out. Metal. The magazine of a Kalashnikov.

Then he remembered how he had grabbed the weapon as the pirogue was turning turtle. The professional's training even unto death. Keep your weapon with you. He must have grabbed the magazine, the gun itself being ripped away.

He tossed it aside and peered again down the length of rapids. Down there, somewhere, the sergeant might be. Dead probably. Or perhaps he had been lucky like himself and was caught in a rockpool beside the main flow. Or hooked on a branch. The unasked-for hand of God.

He looked beyond to where the river flattened out and disappeared in a wide sweep. There again, perhaps Brummie had clung on doggedly to the pirogue. Perhaps he'd survived the battering and had been swept to safety. On to the mighty Kebba that must surely lie out there. Somewhere.

It would take him all day to search. He'd better start. He straightened his bruised back and felt the ripple of pain like a chain of tiny explosions.

Then something made him turn. He squinted against the hot white sky where it met the crest of the cataract. Three figures, dark and menacing looked down. There was some movement, vague at half-a-mile distant, but the muzzle flashes confirmed his worst fears. The whine of ricochetting bullets on the nearby rocks was followed by the distant report of the rifles.

Sorry, Brummie, old lad, he muttered under his breath. You'll have to wait.

He limped across the pool, aware of other shots dancing into the water around him. Luckily, they were at maximum range and the Jatos would have to have a marabou's blessing to hit an elephant.

For an hour he struggled on against the snatching fingers of thorn in the forest undergrowth. At any moment he expected to hear the cry of the Jatos in hot pursuit. But it didn't come. By some miracle, he had thrown them off the scent.

The terrain had changed too. Almost imperceptibly. The distance between the trees was lengthening. Above him, the greenery gave way to an increasing amount of burning sky. For the first time since the doomed expedition had begun, he was feeling the effects of the sun, pounding relentlessly like a hammer against an anvil. Harder and harder until his head was throbbing with the beat of his heart.

Suddenly Fraser realised he was making little headway. The forest had finally surrendered to the dusty savannah which offered scant shade. He was beginning to meander aimlessly from one clump of shrivelled grass to the next. His upper leg around the wound felt numb and he was aware only of a dull throb. His knees felt watery and his muscles sapped of energy. He gritted his teeth and pushed on.

It was nearly nightfall when he collapsed beside a kutofingo bush in a state of near exhaustion. It had been sheer willpower that had kept him going; for over twenty-four hours he had had neither food nor drink and he knew he was dehydrating fast. The powdery white coating on his skin was evidence of the salt that had been squeezed from his system, and his throat was parched and swollen.

Twisting around, he inspected the bush behind him and found a few black kutofingo berries that hadn't been finished off by the birds. He plucked them and stuffed them into his mouth, taking down the sweet liquid pulp in hard greedy sucks. He felt the membrane of his throat soften. It was a blessed relief.

It was as though he was coming round from a drugged zombie-like state of semi-consciousness. He became aware of the glimmering landscape as a pale lemon sun descended slowly into a fiery western skyline.

The sound of his own brittle laugh seemed to echo. It was frighteningly like the sound of a madman to his ears. And then he realised he was listening to the mocking caw of three drifting black shapes overhead. Vultures. Evil black gliders, stiff-winged as they circled patiently on the thermals.

A smirk crossed his lips. He resisted the urge to shout at them, forcing his mind to consider how he might be able to trap one to eat . . .

It was a distraction that cost him dear. Otherwise he might have been aware of the rancid smell that suddenly pervaded the air. Or heard the stealthy pad of the stalking menace. He began to turn, then froze. So did the hyena. They had surprised each other as they came face to face, a bare fifteen feet of dusty red earth between them.

But the reactions of the animal were faster. Realising his prey was alerted, it leapt in reflex action, its muscled rear legs contracting like power-pistons and releasing with tremendous force.

Fraser's brain hardly had time to recognise what it was. Just a blurred image of a hunched, powerful dog-like monstrosity. A mangy mottled hide of black and brown fur. And a snarl of foam-flecked lips drawn back across gnashing yellow teeth.

Instinctively, he raised his hands against the full weight of the brute as it crashed into him with a force that sent him reeling. The snapping jaws caught on his left wrist. Pain lanced through him as his flesh punctured under the razor-sharp incisors. As he hit the ground the breath was forced out of his lungs, but he was hardly aware of it. Sheer panic cleared his mind of everything but the need to destroy this horrific beast with its mad, burning eyes before it literally managed to eat him alive.

He staggered to his knees, forcing against the bulk of the hyena as it leaned back on its grip, stretching every sinew in its effort. Doggedly it shook Fraser's wrist, flecks of blood and saliva blowing in all directions. He raised his right hand and smashed his balled fist into the animal's muzzle. Again and again. His knuckles made contact with the soft pulp of the creature's eye. The snarling rose to a gurgling crescendo of anger as it pulled harder on his arm, edging out of reach of the rain of blows.

He fell forward, dragged through the cloud of dust by the vice-like grip on his arm. With his free hand, he dived into the pocket of his fatigues, scrabbling desperately for the flintstone. Nothing. He tried again, his body jarring on the hard ground as the crazed hyena continued its tussle.

At last his fingers closed around the cold angular form of the flintstone. Summoning a huge effort on his tortured muscles, he staggered to his feet, and tried to drag in his left arm. He felt the flesh rip as the hyena fought back. Inch by agonising inch the snarling jaws came nearer. Face to face with the monster, it was even more horrific than he could imagine. An insane anger glowed in the creature's eyes, and blood pumped over its snout. His blood.

No closer. Even in his frenzy, Fraser recalled how the hyena could take off a man's face with one snap of those huge muscled jaws.

He judged his aim. And struck. The point of the flint-stone thudded into the blood-sodden fur of the creature's neck. It let out a whimpering howl of anguish.

Fraser stabbed again, twisting the point as he tried to locate the jugular.

Momentarily, the grip of the yellow fangs relaxed. He tried to pull away from the jaws. A sudden blur and frantic gnashing and then he felt a new burning sensation as the hyena sank its teeth into his right arm.

Fraser seized his chance, more in panic than as a planned attack, and brought up his foot into the animal's groin.

The hyena whelped and fell back in a gurgling snarl of rage. It shook its head in a spray of vermilion and foaming spittle. Its eyes looked glazed for a moment, then refocused.

Breathless, Fraser backed off. The animal leapt again, its teeth tearing at his ankle. This time he heard his own bones crackle under the force.

Almost detached from the scene of horror at his feet, Fraser took a deep lungful of air. He gripped the flintstone in both hands, and lifted it high above his head. One. Two. And then he fell on the creature with every ounce of strength his screaming muscles could gather.

The honed edge of the stone drove into its skull with bone-shattering force.

Simultaneously, the creature blew out its breath through its teeth. A curious dazed expression came into its eyes and a low, pitiful wail trailed from its blood-soaked mouth.

Suddenly the animal was still. It didn't move, but its grip remained as tight as ever as the warm blood pulsed from the star-shaped indentation in its cranium. Its eyes glazed over in a hate-filled death mask.

Fraser began to tremble uncontrollably. Gingerly, he reached out for the snout, having to prise open the jaws. Painfully he extracted his lacerated ankle.

Then he noticed the small blackened hole in the animal's hind quarters. Prodding with his fingers he found the misshapen dark lump of a musket ball just below the surface.

So that was it. The animal had been injured and had been abandoned by the rest of the pack. Like himself, it had been in pain and desperate for food. In fact, now he could see its thinness, the hollows between the bones of its ribcage indented under the tatty pelt. It had been desperate enough to attack a human with a last maniacal surge of its energy reserves.

We make strange soulmates, Fraser thought grimly.

Uncertainly he staggered to his feet, his head swimming with the effort. In the few minutes that they had been locked in combat to the death, the dim twilight had settled over the flat countryside.

Somewhere out there a sound rose. A chilling sound. It was probably miles away, but in the still air it seemed very close. The wail of a hyena.

Fraser felt a spontaneous wave of nausea break over him. It was the rest of the pack.

He stumbled on into the gathering gloom.

10

Something prodded at his face.

He awoke in a cold sweat of fear. Immediately his muscles froze.

Where am I? I'm lying. Face down.

The hyena? Dead.

The pack? Christ! Don't move. Whatever you do. Don't move.

He could feel the warmth of the sun on his back. Millimetre by millimetre he cranked open one eye. Through the veil of his eyelashes he could see his own forearm and bloodied wrist. Beyond he could see splashes of green. Mottled. Leaves.

Something scrabbled in his hair, nervously. Small probing feet.

An unfamiliar sucking sound. A few inches in front of his face. He doesn't look. He must.

"Charlie-e-e!" A distant cry.

He must be dreaming. A soft feminine voice calling from afar. A voice that had haunted his dreams many times.

Suddenly the vigorous movement in his hair stopped. The nearby sucking sound gave way to an excited whooping sound of alarm.

"Charlie-e-e!" That voice again. Closer. An uncertain pause. "Is that you, Charlie? For goodness' sake come here!"

A sudden scampering of feet and a loud, nervous laugh.

Fraser opened his eyes against the sun, focusing slowly on the blurred image of a chimpanzee. It sat thirty feet away, by the edge of a fast-flowing stream. It was jumping up and down, flailing its arms around and making pouting noises in the direction of the voice.

Christ, Fraser thought, I don't believe it.

Memories of his nightmare journey flooded back to him. The cataract, the hyena, and his pain-blinded stumble through the thorn-ridden savannah pursued by the ever-nearing wail of the hyena pack.

This couldn't be true, he told himself. A warm, gentle morning filled with birdsong. A gabbling stream that twinkled like cut sapphires in the sun. And the voice of Mo Sinclair.

He shifted his aching bones until he was propped on one elbow. Ahead of him the chimp was beside himself, screaming and shrieking and running around in small circles to contain his excitement.

Then, through the dusty screen of mushito grass, she came. Her hair tied back beneath a scarf, her drill shirt clinging damply to her slender body as she struggled up the embankment beneath the burning sun.

"Charlie!" she admonished as the chimp bounded across to the prone figure he had found. She stumbled to a halt, her mouth dropping in disbelief. "What have . . . ? Oh, my GOD!"

"You shouldn't eat too much in one go," Mo said.

Fraser laughed. It seemed that he had done nothing else since the chimpanzee had found him earlier. The sheer elation at being in civilisation and still alive was like being intoxicated with laughing gas.

He hugged Charlie, who had taken a motherly concern in him and was carefully plucking off fleas and ticks from his hair with grave concentration.

"I don't really care, Mo," he replied. "I just know I'll never eat monkey again. And that's a promise."

The black girl kneeling beside him with a gourd of *benachin* looked concerned. "*Toubab* have more?"

Mo frowned. "I don't think he should, Tombo."

"Sure I will," Fraser countered mischievously, holding out the wooden bowl.

Insect grinned hugely and dolloped out another generous helping of rice and meat.

With a cruelly-apt name so beloved of Free Guineans,

the retarded teenager with the squint had mothered him as fiercely as the chimp. She had met few whitemen and treated them all with great awe and subservience. No doubt that had led to the half-caste child she carried everywhere on her back.

"I still can't believe this is Kunkunda, Mo," Fraser said through another mouthful of the spicy mush. "We all thought we were miles farther north, over the border."

She smiled. The dimples in the freckled cheeks emphasised her urchin look. "I'm thankful for small mercies, Johnny. Without proper medical attention I'm not sure you'd have survived today."

"I expect I'd have got by."

"You haven't changed, have you?" she laughed. "Still the same dashing knight on a white charger."

He grinned. "Who swept you off your feet once?"

She tried to look serious. "We've been over that, Johnny." But her frown refused to stay, and she grinned impishly. "Don't tell me you went through all this just to impress me?"

"Ah, lady, that's something you'll never know," he replied lightly and downed the last of the *benachin*. "That's great!" He winked at Insect whose tan deepened perceptively as she fluttered her eyelashes.

"You'd better get some sleep, Johnny," Mo said, introducing a reproving tone. "And don't go exciting Insect. She's got more of a weakness for dashing Scotsmen than I have."

"The bairn?"

For a moment Mo studied the fast-flowing river which ran by the campsite. "It was some randy voluntary aid worker who had more than a gospel and rice to spread about."

"Okay, Mo, I agree I need some sleep, but I can't rest up here. We're deep in Jato-held territory and you and Insect could be in grave danger."

She placed her hands on her hips: a solid five foot nothing wall of determination. "You're to rest, Captain Fraser. Here it's me who's 'the boss', or whatever they call you. You're as bad as my Dad. He'd have a fit if he knew I was up here."

Fraser climbed unsteadily to his feet. "So he should have, Mo. Coming here's a reckless thing to do."

"I've never had any trouble. I've never even *seen* one of them." She smiled disarmingly and wrinkled her nose. "I reckon they must approve of me and my work."

He said more sharply than he meant to: "Mines don't approve or disapprove, Mo. They just blow up. And the main road has been mined."

Anger flashed suddenly in her eyes. "Well they're not stupid enough to go and let their own people get blown up, are they? So maybe they'd warn me, too, if I entered a mined stretch. It's strange that no VSOs or Peace Corps helpers have been hurt, either. So perhaps it's just your chaps and Government troops they're after?"

"Very likely," Fraser murmured.

He thought about telling her of Jato's true identity. That the awesome rebel leader was Kali. Her mild-mannered veterinary assistant who had always helped her out with the more mundane tasks. But he thought better of it. Instead he said: "I think we should leave right away. At least get as far as a radio-telephone station."

She looked at him mockingly. "Ah, that *would* be difficult. Cable & Wireless have closed down their stations at Serreba and at Princetown, and no doubt the Jatos have taken them over."

Fraser wasn't going to be deterred. "Then we'll take it in turns to drive all the way to Sakoto if necessary. We may bump into some of my men."

Mo gave a snort of ridicule. "You can't drive – you can hardly stand." She prodded him in the chest. Unable to resist, he collapsed back onto the soft earth. Charlie whooped with glee and started running in circles. "Now, for God's sake, Johnny, get this clear. You're in no state to travel until I've looked after those wounds. And your feet are a horrendous mess. Besides, I came here and defied Dad to close up the camp and collect some animals. So I'm certainly *not* going back *before* that's done."

Fraser studied her with a growing feeling of admiration. There was some indefinable quality of zest and determination that set her apart from any other woman he had known.

"I can see I'll have to carry you off screaming," he said.

Her eyes narrowed. "Just you try."

He laughed. "I don't think I dare." He glanced around the neat camp of makeshift timber huts, pens, cages and store sheds that he had helped to construct two years earlier. Nearby the stream babbled and the air was filled with birdsong. Insect sat on a bench, gently bouncing her baby on her knee. "It seems quiet enough here, Mo, but it might not last. And we've no weapons."

"I've got my .22 rifle."

Fraser grinned at her navety. "That's better than a spear. Just."

Her eyes moved across to where Insect played with her child. Thoughtfully she said: "Some people did go by on the far side of the stream last night. Only Jatos move around after dark."

"That's exactly what I mean."

"They gave us no trouble, yet they must know we're here."

Fraser shook his head doubtfully. "Guerrillas are always unpredictable, Mo."

She turned her head back to him. "All right, Johnny, we'll compromise. I'll get finished here by tomorrow morning. Just in case you're right. But I'm thinking of Insect's baby. I'd never forgive myself if . . ."

He grinned. "You drive a hard bargain, Mo. You've got a deal."

In truth Fraser was thankful for the chance to rest. After the days of exhausted travel, the sudden input of food had caused a soporific effect. Whilst Mo, with help from a rapt Insect, had dressed his wounds he could hardly keep his eyes open. Afterwards he fell swiftly into the welcoming deep sleep of the dead.

By sundown Mo Sinclair had completed her packing. With an extra passenger in the Suzuki she had lost a good part of the available cargo space. A lot of basic stores would have to be left behind, she reluctantly decided, and concentrated on packing the more valuable items of equipment. Thankfully Charlie had been easily persuaded into the trailer cage with the promise of a helping of bananas. That was her biggest regret; it seemed now that the chimp would never get rehabilitated into the wilds.

She stared out over the river, a flow of molten gold in the reflection of the sunset. God knew when she'd be able to return to the desolate beauty of Kunkunda.

Slowly she trudged up the embankment to pack the last bag of equipment. In the doorway of one of the huts Insect was giving the baby its last feed. She paused to watch and felt a sudden deep pang of envy that almost physically hurt. It was followed by a rising anger which was worse because there was no one to direct it against. Except perhaps herself.

Helplessly she felt two fat tears detach themselves from her moist eyes and crawl wetly down her cheeks. Sniffing heavily and blinking, she forced herself to stride towards the Suzuki and secure the last bag in the rear compartment. Then she made for her hut. The sooner she got to sleep, the earlier the start they would be able to make.

At the doorway she hesitated. The simple box-shaped structure had been roughly divided into two by hanging a length of material on a piece of rope across from two nails. Through the fine gauze of the mosquito-net she could see Johnny Fraser's body, dressed only in torn green fatigue trousers, lying in exhausted slumber, his bandaged left arm carelessly reaching over as if for some invisible lover.

Again she felt a knot of apprehension and uncertainty in her stomach. She wished so much that he hadn't come back to Free Guinea at all. Or so she told herself. But over the past weeks she couldn't fool herself that her frequent visits to Duntenda Barracks for news of him showed anything less than the intense concern of a lovesick woman. And ever since that morning she had found it hard to contain her elation that he was still alive and well.

Looking down at him, his tortured muscled body glittering with sweat and dappled like a gold carving in a shaft of dying sunlight, she knew she was desperately pleased to have him back in her life. Despite her misgivings.

Gently she brushed aside the net and knelt by his head. The craggy unshaven face looked remarkably at peace. As though sweet dreams were ebbing and flowing, cleansing away the horrors of his ordeal. That familiar smile she found so irresistible. That made her feel as though she was the only woman in the world. Perhaps it was a trick of the light, but she could swear he was smiling now.

Impulsively she stooped to kiss the unkempt head of curling dark brown hair, and stopped.

It came back to her. How he had warned her once never to do that. Never to do anything to wake him suddenly from sleep. It was something to do with the effect of training. Woken with live rounds flying over their heads. He hadn't been specific. Just don't do it, he'd warned kindly. It could be dangerous. And then he'd laughed it off.

She backed away slowly and drew herself up. Other memories flooded back to her. Little idiosyncrasies of his that she had grown to know during their affair. How he looked at everyone when entering a room or bar. Like a policeman. How he always insisted on sitting with his back to the wall, facing out. His habit of checking who was within earshot whenever he spoke. The ugly sub-machine gun always within reach.

Then she gave a small gasp as she realised that his outstretched hand wasn't clutching an invisible lover. It was her .22 rifle.

Feeling suddenly sickened she stepped back behind the rough partition. Deep in thought she lit the small oil-lamp, then rolled down her thin cotton sleeping bag and strung out the mosquito net.

With thoughts tumbling through her head in wild profusion, she stood and stared at the orange glow of the lamp as she plucked open the buttons of her drill shirt, slowly, one at a time.

Her mind was suddenly filled with vivid memories and images of the coup. The utter savagery of it all: the stutter of gunfire all around the delapidated buildings and shanty towns of Sakoto. The mindless horror and total confusion. Not knowing who was shooting at whom. The happy faces of all those cheerful Guineans she had known since childhood suddenly wide-eyed with fear. Some turning from genial villagers into savage killers as someone thrust a gun into their hands. Old scores settled in blood. The pitiful crying of a child as it sat beside the bullet-ridden body of its mother who lay face down in the open sewer.

Mo shivered, staring blindly at a moth battering itself against the lamp. It was just like the people during the coup, overcome by some inexplicable deathwish.

Thoughtfully she tugged the shirt tails free from her jeans. And then, suddenly, The Captain had been there. Cool, commanding and in control. As though such carnage and bedlam was routine. Calmly restoring order and discipline, directing friendly troops and offering words of comfort like a country priest.

For a long time no one had known who he was, or where he and his colleagues had come from. But the word had quickly spread. The Captain had become a legend.

She smiled to herself. It had been so easy to fall in love with him then.

But what now? Was it all going to start all over again? In her heart she knew it was. And this time the legendary Captain was heading straight for a fall. She knew that too.

"Mo? Is that you? I thought I heard someone."

She started at the sound of the soft Scottish burr.

"It's okay, Mo," Fraser said. He was standing, barechested, with the .22 rifle held in a loose grip. "I didn't mean to frighten you. Something disturbed me. I thought I'd better check."

Mo's cheeks flushed, perspiration glistening on her freckled skin. "It was only me. I'm sorry."

The light from the oil-lamp danced in his eyes as he smiled. "That's all right. But you'd best put that light out."

"Oh? Yes, yes, of course." She felt awkward. Aware suddenly of the nearness of him, she gathered the opened shirt together with her fist.

He reached out and placed his hand over hers. She shook her head gently in silent protest as she looked into his eyes. Uncertain. Her lips parted as if to speak, but no words came out.

There was a hardness in his eyes that she didn't remember. A determination, a passion. Suddenly the pale greengrey iris seemed unfathomable. Mesmeric.

His hand on hers seemed immense. It was warm and dry.

She tightened the grip on her shirt. The look in his eyes seemed to soften. Involuntarily she relaxed her fingers and, still looking closely into his face, she slowly dropped her hand to her side. Compliant.

"No, Johnny . . ." the words were tight-throated. Scarcely audible.

She turned her head away and closed her eyes. His breath was warm against her cheek, and she felt his hand on the collar of her shirt. As he peeled it from her shoulders she felt the heat of him burn into her naked breasts.

Again she said: "No, Johnny." But this time the words were totally silent.

Her head was spinning, but she was vaguely aware of him propping the rifle against the wall of the hut. His free hand cupped her chin and tilted it up towards him. She was powerless to resist as his lips crushed down on hers.

His arms felt like iron as they closed around her small body. She tremored as a forgotten ache of longing burned in her loins. Slowly her hands came up from her sides and touched his lean flanks, resting lightly on the rise of his hip bone. The smell of him filled her nostrils and, like a wild animal set suddenly free, she felt the crazed passion ebb through her.

"It's been so long, so long . . ." She heard her own mumbled words as she nuzzled against him. Her right hand slid over his hip, dropping to his groin, seeking out his urgent hardness.

Then before she knew it he was leading her down to the sleeping bag. Oblivious to the uncomfortable feel of the ground through the thin material, she embraced him with an abandoned fervour as he released the last of her clothes.

Eagerly she arched her back, raising her knees in anticipation as he pressed into her. With a slight gasp she felt herself warm and yielding, opening like a flower under the gentle pressure. Trembling she ran her tongue over her upper lip. It was salty with sweat.

Her eyes were closed, and she was unaware as he reached out and doused the lamp.

The rusty hulk of the roll-on roll-off merchantman nuzzled the quay in the gentle swell.

An hour before, the quayside had been alive with revving engines as the Lada cars had been driven up her cargo decks and secured by swarms of black seamen as they prepared for the big ship's departure.

Now, in the stark glare of her own arc lamps, she was like a ghost ship. Only the lone figure of Major Igor Dovzhenko stood on the flying-bridge. Waiting.

It had been his decision to check the loading personally. In West Africa you could never be sure of something unless you did it yourself. Even in Conakry in the Republic of Guinea, the Soviet Union's major stronghold in the area, you could not be sure that everything would go according to plan. Especially with Cubans and Libyans involved. Latins and Arabs. Both unpredictable and volatile. And, to make matters worse, all the preliminary arrangements had to be made through the resident KGB buffoon in Sakoto – old 'Boris' as he was known to far too many people.

But, to give him his due, there were no complaints yet. There had just been one minor hiccup. The Russian-built Lada cars, ideal for military use, with their high ground clearance and simplicity of maintenance, had been stored at the dockside vehicle park for six months. During that time some enterprising character had been siphoning-off the petrol from their tanks.

With the benefit of experience, Dovzhenko had checked before the vehicles were loaded. If he hadn't, he'd have had two hundred quasi-military vehicles roll ashore during the forthcoming Free Guinea revolution – and grind to an immediate halt. A disaster.

So, he reconciled himself, his visit on that basis alone had been justified.

Of course it was unusual for new cars to be imported with full tanks of petrol and ignition-keys in place. But there was a precedent. Dovzhenko had organised exactly the same thing in The Gambia in 1981. A boatful of vehicles had just *happened* to arrive at the time of that coup. Unfortunately, the coup had been routed before they could be unloaded. But otherwise it would have worked.

Below him, through the forest of masts and derricks he could see the approaching headlamps of two trucks working their way along the quayside. He smiled to himself with satisfaction. The last hurdle to be cleared. Briskly he left the flying-bridge and made his way down the succession of ladders.

The sullen-looking Cuban officer met him at the bottom of the gangway. He was a swarthy, scruffy-looking individual. Dovzhenko wouldn't have expected a salute as he wasn't in uniform, but the fellow didn't even show a semblance of respect.

"You are Rubashëv?" the Latin asked off-handedly.

The Russian nodded, his heavy jowls firm-set. "Yes."

"This consignment is for you." He thrust forward a chewed pen and tatty piece of official-looking paper. "You sign."

With deliberation, Dovzhenko plucked the paper from the man's hand. He left the pen. "I'll sign *if* I am satisfied that everything is here."

The Cuban shrugged and returned to his truck. Leaning against the wing, he proceeded to light a cheroot.

While he did, the GRU major expertly scanned the inventory:

Kalashnikov AK47 assault rifles, 2000; modernised AKMs, 50; Dragunov Sniper Rifles, 100; obsolete Simonov SKS carbines, 250; RP-46 machine-guns, 150; Makarov pistols, 50.

Nothing else.

"You!"

The Cuban looked up and shambled across. Dumb insolence. "What is the problem, comrade?"

Dovzhenko fixed him with a steady glare. "Anti-tank rockets and mortars. That is the problem, comrade."

"Are they on the list?"

"No."

"Then I don't have them."

"Then you will get them."

The Cuban officer hesitated. Resentfully he looked at this Russian civilian in a new light. He could imagine the stout figure in much gold braid and bedecked with ribbons. For all he knew, the man could be a Field Marshal. He certainly spoke with the authority of one.

He crushed out his half-smoked cheroot underfoot. "I will see what I can do, comrade."

Dovzhenko smiled and inclined his head politely. "Yes, you will. Twenty RPG-7 anti-tank launchers with two hundred rounds and ten 50mm mortars with five hundred assorted rounds." He paused. "We sail at dawn."

The Cuban's eyes widened. "At dawn? Impossible, comrade!"

"Either they are here before dawn, my friend. Or you will not be. Do I make myself clear? Comrade."

"We shall see."

"I would hate your superiors to think that twenty rocket-launchers and ten mortars had been lost whilst in your charge."

"No, comrade."

Everyone in Mo Sinclair's Suzuki felt a profound sense of relief when they reached the Government's new defensive perimeter. It was marked by an armed PG checkpoint and a long tailback of queuing traffic.

The only disappointment was that the new battle-lines had been drawn much nearer the capital than Fraser would have hoped. Duntenda Barracks were only a few miles down the road. That meant that some three-quarters of the country had already been surrendered to Jato control.

He had seen all the signs of that control on the road. No work appeared to be going on in the groundnut plantations or in the villages. At each one they passed there was a little gathering of people in the shade of the central tree. There were crowds at the mosques and an unmistakable air of expectancy everywhere. It was as intense and brooding as the atmosphere before a flashstorm. Just one spark was all that was needed.

At one village, without warning, a young boy of about twelve had rushed into their path and hurled a large stone. It had bounced harmlessly off the trailer cage and left Charlie shaking at his bars in fear and rage.

It was both something and nothing. But such an incident had never happened before. Only then had Fraser realised what had been missing in all the settlements through which they had passed. Not one flew the traditional blue pennant of the President's party.

Despite all the warning signs, he had not been prepared for the transformation that had taken place at Duntenda. The nearby village was deserted and the barrack buildings were now totally obscured by sheets of corrugated-iron that had been fixed to the perimeter fence. As they got closer, he could see the reinforced machine-gun positions, the makeshift observation tower and a battery of search-lights peering over the barricades. It was a beleaguered fortress in frontier territory. All the trees and vegetation had now been cleared on the approaches. It spoke for itself.

As the steel mesh gates swung open, Mo drove in and pulled to a halt in front of the tall figure of a very sunburnt Bill Mather.

The corporal came alongside, his grin broad beneath the bleached ginger moustache. "Well, well, what kept you, boss? Get lost, did we?" He nodded at Mo and winked. "Or shouldn't I ask?"

Fraser climbed stiffly out of his seat. It was good to be back, and he smiled. "Don't tell me I'm the last one home?"

The humour in Mather's pale grey eyes faded. "Afraid not, boss. Mark Benjamin got in about three weeks ago – more or less in one piece. Brummie got picked up yesterday. Made it to a friendly village. He's in Sick Bay nursing a badly bruised arm. Some nonsense about shooting the rapids."

Fraser nodded. "That's all the good news, I take it?"

"Afraid so. No sign of Lionel or that *Direct Action* guy, Rod Bullock."

The SAS captain cursed under his breath, then indicated the reinforced fences. "No point in asking what that lot's for?"

Mather's moustache gave its familiar twitch. "We started getting trouble soon after the fall of Princetown. There was a surprise mortar attack in the middle of the night. Killed a couple of PGs on the training cadre and put two more on the VSIL. So we took precautions. There was another attack a couple of nights back. Hit and run, nothing serious. But it's not looking too brilliant."

255

Fraser looked grimly around the compound at the patrols of PGs preparing to leave. The smart new tiger-suits were dirty and worn; the smiling boyish faces suddenly older with the tell-tale hunted look in their eyes of those who have experienced their first real combat.

Mather said: "I'm afraid they've had their baptism of fire. We had to advance Lionel's plans. They're due out on night patrol. Ambush parties to protect friendly villages."

"Any success?"

The corporal couldn't resist a smile. "Not bad, boss. They're bright lads. At least they try hard. They're not exactly seasoned troops, but thankfully the Jatos tend to run at the first sign of opposition. But then I think they're saving their best ones for the big push."

"I believe it," Fraser acknowledged grimly.

"The biggest problem frankly, boss, is the villagers themselves. They seem to appreciate our civil aid programme all right, but they still can't be trusted. No, that's not strictly true. The fact is they've all got the Jato bug. They all know the big showdown is imminent; they're just waiting. It's like being the warm-up act before the big cabaret star."

"You think it's all too late?"

Mather shrugged. "It's a personal view. But I know Harper thinks the same."

Fraser's eyes widened. "Harper? Not 'Boyo' Harper?"

The corporal slapped his forehead. "Idiot! Of course, you don't know! Hereford flew him out not long after you went missing. To take over Lionel's role and help me with the admin."

Immediately, Fraser felt as though some great weight had been lifted from his shoulders. Bill Harper, the stocky Welsh major was one of the most respected godfathers of 22 SAS's own irreverently-named 'Kremlin' intelligence unit. Now nudging forty-four, no one could remember when he didn't have some connection with 'The Family'. His lightning mind and persuasive charm had won him more friends than even his incessant, irritating chuckle had lost. His mere presence meant that things couldn't possibly be as bad as they seemed. Or that someone, somewhere, was determined that they would not get worse.

"I'd better pay my respects," Fraser said.

Major Bill Harper waited until the newly-fixed door of the office had been firmly closed before he extracted a bottle of Scotch from the desk drawer.

"I expect you could do with a snort of this, Johnny?"

Fraser laughed. "Lovely thought, Bill, but I'm not sure the stomach can take it."

Harper splashed in an extra measure of water. "Just take it slow. After all, we do have something to celebrate."

"You could have fooled me."

The Welshman's voice gurgled with mirth. "Ah, well, that's where you are wrong, see? I have instructions from Hereford that you now enjoy the rank of Acting-Major. You can expect the promotion confirmed on your return."

Fraser opened his mouth. Then shut it again. He was flabbergasted.

Harper watched with amusement. "I know what you're thinking, Johnny. You think 'Here I am floundering about like a drowning man, the situation deteriorating around my ears, and those silly buggers in Hereford go and promote me.'"

"Something like that, Bill."

Harper laughed boisterously. "Don't you believe it! We've been watching events keenly from 'The Kremlin', Johnny. You've had to deal with an impossible situation. Our High Commissioner is dead opposed to your presence, the President has got his arse in the air like the proverbial ostrich, and half the people were well and truly convinced by this Jato chap long before you even put a foot in the place. Added to which, you've been denied the military back-up that's required. Well that, I'm afraid, is the Government now trying to play down its military muscle after the Falklands."

"International politics?"

"Isn't it always? It's all right thumping a trouble-maker once in the lifetime of a Government, but they don't want to give an impression they're trying to rebuild the Empire.

Believe me, we've an entire Squadron on standby at Bradbury Lines and they're all learning Mandinka like crazy . . ."

Fraser's eyes widened.

His elation was short-lived. "Forget it, Johnny. We have to be prepared, but there's no way it will be sanctioned. You have my oath on it." He smiled sympathetically. "The fact is, you've held out with remarkable resolve in trying political circumstances. I know the Colonel has been impressed. Many a time he's suffered under similar restrictions." He paused to sample his own glass of Scotch, and licked his lips thoughtfully. "Of course, from my point-of-view, the ideal answer would be to win over Jato to our side of the great divide. Get him to ditch the Russians."

Fraser put down his drink; already it was making him feel slightly dizzy. "Back both sides?"

Harper smiled. "It's an optional course. We did it once before. In Nigeria during the civil war, although no one ever knew about it."

"The difference here, Bill, is that Jato's winning and he knows it. He's not going to compromise himself by accepting help from us, when he doesn't think he needs it."

Harper stood up and walked towards the window. "Tell me, Johnny, what's the single most important thing you can think of doing that would help Jammeh?"

Fraser didn't hesitate. "Get rid of Colonel Kwofie."

The Welshman turned. "That's what I gathered from Lionel's reports. And I understand from them that Lady Precious is keen on him, too? Encourages her husband to act on his advice?"

"That's true enough."

Major Bill Harper sat down at the desk and began to fan himself with a sheaf of papers. "Then I think perhaps you should have another go at getting friend Kwofie dismissed . . ."

Fraser was almost pleased to leave Mo, together with Insect and her offspring, at the Agricultural Research Station. Desperately, he wanted to preserve the magic of their night of abandoned lovemaking at Kunkunda Island.

258

It was a relief to be alone again with his thoughts as he drove the remaining distance to Sakoto. He had never really believed that he would have a second chance with Mo and he was determined that this time things would work out. But he would take it slowly, give them time. That was what they both needed.

By the time the gates of State House came into view he was beginning to feel the effects of his recent injuries. Earlier that morning, he had ignored the advice of the SAS Medical Officer and continued on his journey, although he'd reluctantly allowed the first of a painful series of anti-rabies jabs into the wall of his stomach. There would be time later for nursing the other wounds.

His first impression was that the PGs on the gate were more businesslike than usual as they checked his pass. But then he detected an air of controlled hysteria about them, although he could make little of the quickly-garbled replies to his questions.

However, as he parked his Land Rover at the foot of the steps it became all too clear. Two white-coated medics were carrying a stretcher down towards a waiting ambulance. The face was covered and the protruding feet had the tell-tale limpness of a corpse.

As they passed, Fraser motioned the men to stop. They were impassive as he lifted the edge of the blanket. There was something familiar about the young black features. But it was difficult to be sure because the eyes had rolled up to the whites and no one had bothered to close the lids. Slowly he lowered the blanket.

"Who is he?"

One of the medics shrugged. "They say he was the drinks steward."

Suddenly Fraser recalled the unfortunate youngster at the reception for their arrival. A dejected individual on all-fours amid the broken glasses.

"What happened?"

"He tried to kill the President, man. That's what happened."

He should have expected that something of the sort might occur one day, but the news still came as a shock.

He acknowledged his thanks to the medics and took the remaining steps three at a time.

Under the entrance portico he found Sir Nigel de Burgh in earnest conversation with a man Fraser recognised as the US Ambassador.

This time Sir Nigel's hunched stance and nervous darting eyes reminded him less of a heron and more of a conspiring vulture. By contrast, the American looked more like a sparrow. He was thin and short with a swarthy complexion that was mostly hidden by a pair of enormous black-rimmed glasses. The neat dark suit was topped with a large polka-dot bow tie which looked as though it ought to be revolving.

Sir Nigel's mouth dropped with surprise as he saw Fraser. "Good grief, Captain Fraser, this *is* a surprise!" He didn't really make it sound as though it was a nice one. "I thought you'd been lost up-country."

The SAS officer smiled graciously. "Not lost, just mislaid, Your Excellency."

The High Commissioner evidently did not want to explore the situation further in front of his American opposite number. "Well, glad you're back with us in the land of the living." He turned to his fellow diplomat. "I believe you've met the US Ambassador to Free Guinea? Eddie Brunswick."

"Your Excellency," Fraser said as the American stepped forward and offered his hand in a series of decisive but jerking movements. "Captain John Fraser. British Army Training Team. Pleased to meet you again, Sir."

"Pleasure's all mine, Cap'n," Brunswick replied. His voice had a high-pitched nasal twang that suggested one of the Southern states. "And I can see the work you boys been doin' out here sure's hell's been payin' off."

"It has?" Fraser tried to hide his incredulity.

Brunswick beamed. A little too friendly. "Sure has. Or maybe you haven't heard?"

Sir Nigel interjected: "There's been an attempt on Jammeh's life."

"I just learned a minute ago. I've been on the road from Duntenda all morning."

"An' one of the guys you trained saved the old guy," Brunswick added.

"Our bodyguard team?"

"Yep. One of the PGs you trained. I gather he threw himself in front of the President and took the blast. Hole in his thigh, but nuthin' too serious."

"And Jammeh?" Fraser inquired. "I'm on my way to see him."

Sir Nigel said frostily: "The President's a bit shaken. I've just seen him and I don't think he'll want visitors. Besides, perhaps you ought to talk to me about your expedition before you see the President, Captain. Everything's a bit delicate."

"I've been summoned," Fraser lied. "And it is a *military* matter that won't wait, Your Excellency."

The American detected the rancour between the two men. "Well, I'm sure Jammeh will make an exception, Sir Nigel. I intend to see him myself and I don't intend to be deterred. Perhaps we should put on a united front, huh?" He put his hand on Fraser's arm and steered him towards the entrance. "Don't worry, High Commissioner, I'll keep an ambassadorial eye on the Captain here."

They disappeared into the coolness of the lobby, leaving Sir Nigel simmering beneath the portico. Again, the patches of blue veins on his cheeks were darkening.

On the way up to the President's office, Eddie Brunswick probed for more details of Fraser's up-country mission. The questions were heavily overlaid with good humour and polite conversation, but the drift was unmistakable. It was like a red rag to a bull and the SAS Captain's instinct, from years of training, was to clam up tight.

Brunswick smiled as they reached the double mahogany doors. "Your sense of security does you proud, Captain. I jest wonder if you'd deny it was daytime if I asked you?"

Fraser's eyes glittered mischievously. "If that's another question, Mr Ambassador, it's night."

To the American's obvious annoyance, the President's aide indicated for Fraser to have the first audience. As the doors closed behind him, he immediately sensed the air of desperation. A large map of Free Guinea had been spread out over the coffee table and left amid a sea of unwashed cups and ashtrays overflowing with cigarette butts.

The President's desk, normally clear and gleaming with polish, was littered with a pile of state papers. Behind it, Jammeh himself sat like a dead man, his hands grasped in front of him as he stared at some indefinable point beyond the wall. He didn't seem to notice Fraser for a few seconds, until the soldier gave a light cough.

The President looked up. Immediately, the SAS officer could see that he had lost weight. The black skin hung in folds around his neck, and his cheeks had hollowed. The moist brown eyes were bloodshot behind the thick spectacles.

"Why did they do it, Captain Fraser?" The rich boom had gone from his voice. It was scratchy like a record-player needing a new stylus. "Why did he try to kill me?"

Fraser indicated the splashes of vermilion on the front of Jammeh's white robe. "Are you sure you are unhurt, Mr President?"

"It is not my blood. It is from the bodyguard. But it is still Free Guinean blood . . ."

"You should see a doctor."

"I am all right. It is this country that is sick."

Fraser tried again. "Let me send my Medical Officer down from Duntenda. He's well-used to cases of shock."

Jammeh gave a snort of laughter. "And what will he recommend? A holiday? A few weeks away from Sakoto is just what my enemies would want."

"I'm sure he can give you something."

A smile crossed the fat lips for the first time. "White man's medicine, eh, Captain? I shall see what he can offer that a good marabou cannot. After all, your people are good men. I have to admit that it was the training that you give my bodyguard that saved my life. I thank you for that."

"I'm pleased we've been of service."

The smile still lingered on Jammeh's face, but only just. "And I am pleased you have returned safely from Jato country, Captain. But you should take your own advice. You do not look well."

"I look worse than I feel."

"And what did you discover on your expedition?"

Fraser took a deep breath. "That the Jato is, in fact, the half-brother of Omar Pheko. His name is actually Kali.

After he left school, he worked for the Sinclair family at the Agricultural Research Station. You may know him, he used to help Maureen Sinclair out with her veterinary work?"

A troubled frown creased the deep forehead. "I have visited Ralph Sinclair many times, Captain, and his daughter, of course. I am not sure I recall . . ."

"Kali left their employ two years ago. To study to be a vet."

Jammeh's thick lower lip suddenly dropped in stunned surprise. "Now I remember! Ah, it comes back to me. A handsome youth, quiet." He gave a bitter laugh. "At the time I thought he was in awe of his President! We spoke about him over dinner. Ralph said how one of his boys wanted to go to London to study but he could not get a grant. I suggested to try Moscow."

It was Fraser's turn to look surprised. "*You* suggested it, Mr President?"

Jammeh shrugged. "Countries like mine, Captain, must take the best offer going. We cannot afford to look at gift horses. Whether they are Greek or Russian."

Fraser smiled at the mixed metaphor and, not for the first time in his life, found himself wondering how life managed to throw up so many unbelievable coincidences. He said: "Of course, no one realised Kali's relationship to Omar Pheko. At the time he kept it quiet. He was ashamed of his half-brother until the Russian brainwashers got at him. The Sinclairs still don't know."

Jammeh nodded sagely. "They would be upset. Besides, it is better that few people know as possible." He removed his spectacles and began polishing the lenses with the wide sleeve of his robe. "Tell me, who is it who organises things on the ground here?"

"There is one man. He calls himself Rubashëv. He came in as a delegate of the World Federation of Trade Unions."

Jammeh's eyes widened. "Then he has been working alongside Fofana? That villainous old goat! No wonder I could not persuade him to join my party." He paused to replace his spectacles. "But I understood an attempt had been made on his life by the Jatos? Perhaps it was just faked for my benefit. As a – I think you call it – a red herring."

Fraser shook his head. "No, it was genuine. If it had gone to plan then Fofana would be dead now. My men were there."

"Then who . . . ?"

Fraser's eyes narrowed. "Mr President, I have reason to believe that it was organised by Colonel Kwofie."

"I don't believe it! He knows that it is directly contrary to my instructions to interfere with Fofana. Certainly not with violence. My main strength has been political freedom. If I am seen to interfere with this democratic process, then I am finished."

"The Colonel has his own ideas about dealing with an insurgency situation," Fraser said evenly. "His method is to crush any resistance ruthlessly and indiscriminately. To rule by fear. It's nothing new."

"He knows I would not tolerate it."

"That's why he doesn't tell you. No doubt he thinks that it is best for your cause, but in reality it just drives your supporters into the hands of your enemies. I am convinced that the village of Massang was destroyed on his direct orders. The alkali was put to death on his instructions. And I now have evidence that it was a far from isolated incident. While we were held prisoner at the Jato camp we heard many testimonies to what has been happening."

Jammeh suddenly leaned forward, an expression of shock on his face. "You were actually held prisoner? I do not believe it! The great Captain held prisoner by the Jato!"

Fraser shrugged. "Unfortunately, Mr President, I am not infallible. But it may interest you to know that the main reason we were caught was a direct result of Colonel Kwofie's private scorched-earth campaign. Of all people, we were betrayed by the alkali's son. After the massacre at Massang, he was driven from being a loyal supporter of your party to go over to the Jato."

The President's eyes narrowed. "I know the boy. My friend's eldest son. Dawda? He betrayed you?"

"That, Mr President, is the way that Colonel Kwofie has repaid the trust you have put in him. Perhaps he believes he is acting for the best. Intimidation has long been a weapon of those who want to keep themselves in power. But it will

264

not work if the people have an alternative. And Kali is offering that alternative."

Jammeh climbed unsteadily to his feet. He seemed like an old man. "Tell me, Captain, you've met the Jatos and their leader at close hand. What is your view? What do they think of him?"

The SAS captain hesitated, choosing his words carefully. He felt that at last he might be getting through. "They idolise him, Mr President. They respect him and believe his optimistic view of the future. The young men, especially those who've worked in Sakoto, are anxious for change. They're aware of their poverty, especially those who've come in contact with the tourists. They want to get into the modern age and the promise of trade unions has fired them. They've carried the message back to the elders in the villages. The ideals are supported by the local mullahs. They're led to believe that wealth will happen overnight if you go, and Jato does nothing to disillusion them. He is popular. But, I am afraid Mr President, I must tell you that you are not. Thanks especially to the efforts of your Head of State Security."

Jammeh shuffled towards the window and stared out at the Atlantic rollers crashing beyond the high wall. "A week ago, Captain, I would have said that you exaggerate. I would have accepted Colonel Kwofie's soft words that everything will be all right. That we are holding our own." He turned to face the SAS officer, a look of misery and helplessness on his face. "But when your own steward, who has served under you for years, turns a gun on you, then you know that something must be deeply wrong. I shall think on what you say."

The desperation in Jammeh's voice touched Fraser, and he remembered the words that Lady Precious had spoken on the golf course. "*He is a kind and gentle man. Like the country he inherited. Free Guinea was different from the rest of Africa. But times have changed, and he has not.*"

Fraser tried to reassure the African leader with a smile. "Mr President, you once offered me command of your Guards. If that offer were to be made again, my answer would be different. An immediate secondment would be possible, although only for a temporary period."

Jammeh studied him closely for a long moment. "It seems that I am forever thanking you, Captain Fraser. But please go now. I am tired and I have yet to see the American Ambassador."

Johnny Fraser left the President's office feeling decidedly more optimistic than when he had arrived. But he was aware that he was still up against the combined influence of Kwofie and Lady Precious.

A feeling of exhaustion returned and he decided he would make use of the room the team kept reserved at The Oceanic. But first he paid a visit to the First-Aid room in State House to congratulate the young wounded PG who had saved the President's life.

As Fraser left the First-Aid room he met Eddie Brunswick coming down the stairs. The dapper little ambassador had a face like thunder and he directed a malevolent glare at the SAS officer.

"Captain Fraser, could I have a word with you?" It was pitched as an order; there was no mistake about that.

Together they descended the steps into the bright sunlight.

"What's the problem, Your Excellency?"

The American waited until they were out of earshot of the PGs on the door. "*You*, Captain. You seem to be the problem."

Alarm signals began ringing in Fraser's head. Quietly, he said, "Let's stroll around the grounds."

"I gather," Brunswick said, "that you've been trying to persuade Jammeh to get rid of Colonel Kwofie? He was asking my opinion."

Fraser sucked in a lungful of salty Atlantic air. "The man's a positive liability with his strong-arm tactics. Jammeh doesn't know half of what's going on. His intimidation has driven dozens of villages straight into the hands of the Jatos."

An expression of exasperation came over the American's pinched face. As he spoke his voice rose to a high-pitched squeak. "Listen, Captain, you've just seen Jammeh. The guy's all washed-up. We both know he's finished. He's

266

let things slide with his woolly liberal thinking. It's been happening here for years. If he'd been runnin' some poxy Central African state, he'd have been toppled years ago. He's been livin' on borrowed time. Now those Commie bastards have seen their chance and Jammeh won't stop 'em unless he gets off his fanny. And, frankly, I don't think there's much chance of that."

Fraser stopped in the shade of a blossoming hedge of bougainvillea and lit one of his cigars. "Am I reading you correctly? You see Kwofie as the new President of Free Guinea?"

A sly grin crossed Brunswick's face and the effect, with the bow tie, made him look more than ever like a smutty music-hall comedian. "The President is a sick man. The Guardian Lion of Free Guinea is now a toothless old tom-cat. He'll either go of his own accord or someone will oust him. That will be either the Jatos or Kwofie – an' we sure as hell don't intend letting that Commie shit get in."

Fraser carefully exhaled a stream of smoke so that the stiff offshore breeze carried it into the American's face. It didn't look deliberate. "I imagine the US can offer a fine selection of psychiatric clinics specialising in the mental problems of deposed Heads of State?"

Brunswick recovered from the cloud of smoke. "Sure, we have offered. We want to preserve democracy in this country, Captain, and it needs a strongman to keep it democratic and out of Commie hands."

"A man like Kwofie?"

"Hole in one. He has the support of the military here and we're prepared to back him up."

Jesus Christ, Fraser thought, don't they *ever* learn. The American anti-Communist paranoia had led them into more intractable political situations than he could recall. Support any unscrupulous bastard as long as it stopped the insidious spread of influence from the Kremlin.

And then they wondered why the desperate mass of the people turned to guerrilla insurgents backed by the Kremlin, which was never slow to miss an opportunity. A crushed and intimidated people would do anything to get rid of the devil they knew. Even if it meant befriending the devil they didn't.

Fraser asked softly: "What sort of support for Kwofie did you have in mind?"

The American hesitated, unsure how much to tell the gently-spoken British soldier. He could sense the antagonism and didn't feel inclined to give too much away. Then he shrugged. "Hell, your High Commissioner knows, so no doubt he'll tell you. Our new Rapid Deployment Force is ready to intervene in the Mid East. If Sakoto was under threat from the Jatos, I'm sure the 82nd Airborne would welcome the chance to put a little theory into practice."

Fraser nodded and studied the tip of the cigar. "I'm sure that if Sakoto is under threat, Jammeh will want all the help he can get. But that won't get Kwofie into power."

Eddie Brunswick cast his eye appreciatively over the well-kept gardens and thrust his hands in his jacket pockets. "Any help he gets from us will have a condition. His resignation in return for US support. It'll be the sort of offer he can't refuse."

Fraser didn't trust himself to speak. He dropped the half-finished cigar on the paved walkway and took out his seething anger by grinding the butt to a pulp with his boots.

11

During the short drive back along the coast to The Oceanic, Fraser's mind crowded with images of the prospect of Free Guinea under Colonel Kwofie's jackboot.

The problems seemed to be multiplying by the hour and there seemed little he could do about it. Fatigue was gnawing at his mind and he reasoned that, after a rest and a square meal, he might be able to make sense of the deteriorating situation.

He swung the Land Rover past the cluster of children touting to guide the newly-arrived hotel guests, and parked in the shade of the trees. As usual, the ever-turning sprinklers were keeping the lawns bright green for holiday-makers with scarce fresh water.

He entered the plush lobby, noticing that the Guinean security men were being more zealous than usual. Of course, it was their job to protect the guests from the persistent hustlers who offered to supply everything from black market goods to marijuana and cocaine, and boys or girls to play with. For the right price, virtually everything was available. But today they were giving every Guinean a hard time.

He made his way through to the open-air pool area where the tourist season was in full swing, the place packed with blistered torsos overdoing the African sun. White breasts and pink nipples assailed him from all directions with scant regard for the host country's strict Moslem sensibilities.

He found a vacant chair under a thatch umbrella and watched the antics of the lizards on the patio while the waiter brought him an iced Tru-beer.

It was strange, sitting amid the shrieks of skylarking

swimmers, to remind himself what was happening just a few miles outside the 'tourist compounds' as Witcher had disparagingly called the hotel areas. The holiday-makers had come here to escape the English and Swedish winters and, cosseted and cocooned against the stark African experience, kept to themselves behind the high walls and gates, guarded by the hotel security men. Tour companies did not encourage their charges to explore far. That was a shame, thought Fraser, but from the Guineans' point-of-view, it was probably just as well.

He was asleep before he'd emptied his glass.

"Captain Fraser?"

It seemed only moments before he awoke with a jolt. The waiter jumped back and spilled his tray of drinks.

"I am sorry. Captain Fraser?"

The SAS officer shielded his eyes against the sun. "Yes. What is it?"

"There is much trouble at Reception. A young lady say she knows you, but they will not let her in."

Fraser was puzzled. "She asked for me? By name?"

The waiter shook his head, a sneer of disdain on his face. "No, Captain. She ask for someone called Broomie Turner. She say he is with British Army, and I see this man with you."

Fraser climbed to his feet. "Why on earth didn't you bring her in to speak to me?"

"The men on the door not like her. She is no-good woman, you know? They do not like woman like her in hotel."

Fraser followed the man through to Reception and instantly recognised the girl who was struggling with the two burly security men on the door. Shrieks of protest filled the lobby as she flailed at them with her arms while they tried to push her out, together with her bulging suitcase.

"It's all right, gentlemen," Fraser said. "I know the lady."

They stepped back, unsure, touching their caps. "I am sorry, sir," said one. "We cannot be too careful."

"So I should think!" the girl spat. "This is *my* country. Why can't I come to this hotel! It is not right!"

Angrily, she smoothed down her dress. Fraser thought how she had changed since he had first seen her at the Green Mamba. Perhaps it was his imagination, but her stance was more self-assured, her manner more adult and defiant. How much, he wondered, had been due to Brummie Turner's influence?

"Hallo, Diamante."

She smiled bewitchingly and gracefully offered her hand. He wasn't sure whether it was to be shaken or kissed. It was a gesture he had seen before at State House. Lady Precious had it to perfection.

To irritate the security men he decided to kiss it. "I'm afraid Brummie's not here today. Perhaps I can help?"

Her eyes were wide and appealing. "He is well? He has not gone home?"

"No. He's up-country at Duntenda."

Her shoulders dropped in relief. "He has not come to me for *weeks*. I think he goes home, maybe."

"He's been away on business, but he's back now."

"That is good. I think he wants to see me no more."

One glance at that charming smile and Fraser was convinced that wasn't true. He looked down at the tattered suitcase. "Now, what's the problem, Diamante? Come and have a drink with me. Tell me all about it."

Her dark eyes flashed around the unfamiliar surroundings of the luxury hotel as they walked through towards the swimming pool.

"I never come to this place before." There was a tone of wonderment in her voice. "Only one or two older girls come here."

Fraser had seen them. Well-heeled whores who came in on the arms of rich black businessmen or Government officials.

He sat her down and ordered drinks while Diamante looked around her, evidently shocked at the sight of so many scantily-covered thighs.

"Why have you brought a suitcase?" Fraser asked as the waiter served her a disgusting-coloured strawberry champagne cocktail.

"I leave the Green Mamba," she stated firmly, sucking

noisily at the straw. "That man Berno has closed up. He leaves the country and wants to sell me to that fat man from the Lebanon. Berno say it would be good business for me."

Fraser wondered if he was hearing correctly. "He wanted to *sell* you?"

She nodded, still sucking hard. She made the idea sound as though it was the most natural thing in the world. "Yes. He say I make good price and he will give me some of the money. And the fat man he will treat me good. Make me a lady."

"I see," Fraser murmured, although he wasn't sure that he did. "And you obviously didn't like the idea?"

She wrinkled her nose in disgust. "No. He is fat. I do not like that man. And the things he make me do. I like Broomie. He treats me good. He say I am princess. Daughter of a proud chief. I tell Berno, I will get good price from Broomie, thank you."

Fraser nearly choked on his beer. "You think Broo-Brummie will buy you?"

She grinned widely and her eyes twinkled. "Sure, why not? But I must see him quick. If Berno gets me I am in big trouble. He does not know I go. He will be angry. He does big business with the fat man and Berno want the money before he goes."

A sudden thought occurred to him. "Berno is actually leaving Free Guinea?"

She nodded and gurgled away at the last of her drink. "He gets plane tomorrow. He say big trouble come. He closes house and sells many girls. He takes his money from the bank. Much money!"

Fraser lit himself a cigar. "Why does he think there will be big trouble, Diamante?"

She frowned and puckered her lips as she thought. "I think he hears from Lady Jammeh when she come."

He was incredulous. "To the Green Mamba?"

"Sure."

"The President's wife comes to the Green Mamba? What for?"

Diamante shrugged, then her face clouded with concern. "I should not say that. Berno tells me not to tell no one. She

272

comes in a car with dark windows. Always at night. You do not tell no one what I say?"

Fraser shook his head absently, his mind trying to work out the implications of Lady Precious' secret nocturnal visits to the high-class cathouse. Jammeh was not a young man, so perhaps her trips were merely to satisfy her physical needs. The one thing the Green Mamba seemed to offer was discretion. News of it would undoubtedly break Jammeh's heart – he was undeniably infatuated with his beautiful second wife – but that alone need not have sinister overtones.

"Look," Fraser said suddenly, "your secret is safe. No one will know that you told me. Now, first, if you think you may be in danger from Berno, we must find you somewhere safe to stay. The barracks where Brummie stays could be dangerous." – He grinned at her – "Besides I think you could prove to be a distraction to the soldiers. But I have friends who will look after you. I'd like you to wait here while I make a couple of telephone calls to arrange things. Okay?"

The girl grinned enthusiastically as she looked around happily at her new luxurious surroundings. "No problem. I wait."

Wondering just what Mo and her father would make of Diamante, he ordered her another drink and left to use the hotel manager's private telephone. After five attempts and an infuriating delay, he got through. As he anticipated, Mo instantly agreed, with some amusement, to give Diamante a bed for the night, provided she didn't try to ply her trade with the Research Station workers.

Then, following further even longer delays, he got through on the landline to Major Bill Harper at Duntenda. He relayed the information that Lady Precious was a regular visitor to the Green Mamba and that she had made it pretty clear that she considered that Jammeh's time had virtually run out.

The Welsh intelligence expert's reaction stunned him. "She's more right than she knew, boyo. Things started humming just after you left this morning. The first signs of trouble were in Sakoto as soon as the banks opened.

Merchants and Government ministers started the run, then everyone joined in. By midday the banks had run out of money and the gendarmes had to go in to prevent a riot."

"What triggered it off?"

"Just rumours, boyo. Rumours that the Jato would be in Sakoto within days. And that he'd nationalise all private business and confiscate private property."

Fraser studied the mouthpiece of the telephone. "Did you hear about the assassination attempt this morning?"

"Yes," Bill Harper replied. "I should think the entire country knows by now. In fact, there are reports of queues building up at the frontiers. It looks like the start of a mass exodus. Our neighbours are nervous and are taking their time in processing documents. It's all connected with the rumours. I've sent Brummie Turner down to Sakoto to review what additional security measures should be taken. He should arrive at The Oceanic any time."

"Good move," Fraser agreed. "I also think Mather ought to come down and set up a command-post here at the hotel. I'm sure the manager will agree if I bribe him with the offer of armed protection. It'll be less obvious than at the State House barracks or the High Commissioner's office. And less prone to interference from Sir Nigel or friend Kwofie."

The irrepressible Welsh laugh crackled on the line. "Great minds, boyo! Mather's with Brummie, plus a couple of spare bods. Both signallers."

"Good. No other signs of trouble up-country?"

"No, boyo. It's quiet. Too quiet if anything. Gives me a feeling in the water."

"I hope you're wrong. If there's a problem you can reach me here or at State House for the rest of the day. Cheers!"

As he hung up, the door opened. It was Arthur Murdoch, The Oceanic's British manager.

"Friends o' yours, Johnny. It's beginning to look like a military takeover . . ."

He stepped aside as the dust-caked figures of Brummie Turner and Bill Mather stepped in. The sports bags they carried looked ominously heavy.

Fraser thanked Murdoch and motioned to Brummie.

"There's a friend of yours here. A young lady who goes by the rather glamorous title of Diamante."

The sergeant had the good grace to blush. "Here, boss?"

Mather stroked his ginger moustache. "Don't reckon she's a *friend* of Brummie's. Hadn't you noticed, boss, he's been on orange juice lately?"

Fraser wasn't certain if the veteran corporal was joking. He hadn't noticed the sure sign that a man was on a treatment course for venereal disease – besides that was strictly a private matter between the victim and the MO.

"Well, Brummie, friend or not, she seems to be under the impression you're about to whisk her off to your castle in England. Or whatever yarn you've been spinning."

"Nice one, Brummie," Mather interjected.

"Piss off," the NCO growled out of the side of his mouth. "What's happened then, boss?"

"It seems like her pimp had plans to sell her off to a wealthy Arab. She had other ideas. Anyway, you'll find her at the poolside. Go and sort it out pronto."

"Sure thing," Brummie agreed sheepishly, and edged towards the door.

"And Brummie?"

"Yes, boss?"

"No rash promises, eh? I'll have her stay at the Sinclairs for a few days, but let that be an end to it. I've enough troubles."

"No problem, boss." The door shut.

Rapidly, Fraser explained to Mather about the special communications centre he wanted organised with direct radio contact with State House and the PG barracks, with the forward base at Duntenda, the High Commission, their up-country OP patrols, and with Hereford itself.

Afterwards, Mather rubbed his chin thoughtfully. His pale eyes were hard and distant. "I get the distinct feeling that some cunt is going to start a war after all."

Fraser recalled the corporal's prophetic words when they had first arrived. When was it? Back in August? It was now January. It seemed a lifetime ago.

"If he does, Bill, Duntenda will be untenable."

Mather gave a lop-sided grin. "Was that a pun, boss?"

Before the Captain could answer, the door burst open. In his haste, Brummie knocked Arthur Murdoch flying.

"Sorry, mate!" the sergeant said breathlessly.

"What the hell is it?" Fraser demanded.

"The girl's gone. Diamante. The waiter reckoned three black blokes came into the pool area and took her away. He says she wasn't struggling, but she didn't look too happy, either."

"Have you tried the security men on the door?" Mather suggested. "They may have seen which way they went."

Brummie nodded angrily. "Course I bloody have. They all know Berno, but if they saw anything, they're not saying."

"Berno?" Arthur Murdoch asked suddenly. "From the Green Mamba? If the security men haven't seen him, then he's probably gone up to his suite. He rents one of the penthouse jobs on the top floor. I dread to think what for. D'you want a key?"

Fraser shook his head. "If he means to harm the girl, that could be dodgy. I'd prefer to go in through the window. The key to next door would be better . . ."

Murdoch hesitated. "I can't do that. Someone innocent might get hurt. You can go straight onto the roof, though, and drop straight down onto the balcony. It's the – let me see – third along from the right, facing the sea."

"Gotcha!" Brummie said, moving towards the door.

"Hey, be careful," Murdoch warned. "I've heard Berno's a nasty piece of work when he's riled."

Mather picked up his sports bag. "Then I'd better take my racket with me."

He followed Brummie and Fraser through the door.

Once on the roof, Fraser and the corporal made their way across to the small parapet that overlooked the sea and the hotel balconies. Mather grasped the captain's wrist in a tight fisherman's grip while he lowered himself down the flowering trellis of creepers to the adjoining balcony. A basking lizard blinked and scurried away.

Fraser landed softly, gritting his teeth at the painful pressure on his injured feet, and then reached up to catch the small 'Hockler' – the SAS nickname for the 5.56mm

Heckler & Koch HK33 sub-machine gun – that his companion threw down. Deftly, he swung over the low partition wall, and he waited for Mather to join him.

He slid down the wall beside the large plate-glass window and peered in from the lower corner. No one expected a face to appear at feet-level, and it never ceased to amaze Fraser how people could stare for minutes in your direction without registering a peering eye around the corner on the floor.

Inside the suite it was comparatively dark, but there was enough daylight to determine the bulky striding figure of Berno. He was wearing a big straw Stetson and was pacing angrily up and down in front of the bed. His usual plastic smile had been replaced by a snarl that reminded Fraser of his encounter with the hyena.

He tried to work out what was going on beyond, but the Jamaican blocked his view. Only snatches of angry words reached his ears to give him a clue.

"You give me big trouble, woman . . . I lose much money . . . While I try to find you the bank runs out of cash . . . *No one* does this to me . . . !"

At last Berno moved aside and Fraser could see that the girl was being pinned back on the bed by two ugly-looking blacks. Her dress was torn and had been peeled from her shoulders to gather around her waist. As she struggled, her breasts shifted from side to side.

Sunlight caught on something in Berno's hand. At first, he thought it was reflecting on one of the large gold finger rings the man habitually wore. Then he saw the switchblade.

Fraser cursed to himself. The plate-glass window was on rollers. It was open, but the gap was slight. To reach it, he would have to cross the whole width of the glass in full view of the occupants.

Silently, Mather arrived beside him and immediately realised the problem. Fraser shrugged. The corporal looked sympathetic. There was no alternative.

A sudden high-pitched squeal came from inside the suite. Fraser looked in again in time to see Berno step back from the bed. Diamante's flat stomach was heaving as she strained against her captors, her body now wet with the sweat of fear. A thin line of dark blood began to weep across her left breast where Berno had split the skin like a ripe fruit.

Fraser nudged Mather, hard. They went in.

The corporal got to the window first, using both hands to shove open the heavy glass door on its rollers, as Fraser dashed into the widening gap.

"*Freeze!*" he bellowed, aiming the Hockler straight at Berno's heart.

But the man had been given a vital two-and-a-half seconds' warning as the SASmen had crossed in front of the window. Not long. But it had been just enough for him to haul the screaming girl from the bed, his forearm locked around her throat.

The other two men were slower. Now they stood hunched, legs apart, unsure what to do with their hands. One of them lifted the ancient Service revolver, and swung it clumsily towards the captain.

Mather came in behind Fraser's crouched figure, and side-stepped smartly, bringing the muzzle of his own weapon up under the gunman's chin. The man dropped his revolver as though it had scalded him.

"*Leave the girl!*" Fraser demanded. His aim didn't waver, but he knew he was in grave danger of killing Diamante if he fired.

"Just you shoot, man! Just you shoot!" Berno's voice was verging on the hysterical as he dragged the girl backwards towards the door, his free hand pressing the switchblade to the taut skin of her heaving belly. A small pinprick of blood appeared where the point touched.

"Lower your gun, Bill," Fraser hissed. "Don't drop it."

Mather got the drift. They'd reduced their threat, but it still gave the pimp something to think about. Something to occupy his mind as he fumbled for the bolt of the door.

The two others went to move until Mather growled: "One more inch and you're dead men." And the snout of the Hockler still by his side tilted upwards, out of Berno's line-of-sight.

As the Jamaican backed awkwardly into the hotel corridor, he was suddenly aware of warm breath on the skin at the back of his neck. Next, only blinding pain as Brummie's vice-like grip caught his knife hand and wrenched it up behind his back. All the way. A scream of agony echoed down the corridor, drowning out the gentler sound of tearing ligaments. In his anguish, Berno threw Diamante roughly aside and fell to his knees, unable to move the hand that was jammed helplessly into the small of his own back.

"You okay, sweetheart?" Brummie demanded brusquely. She grasped her aching throat, unable to speak. But the eager nod and the look of relief in her big dark eyes said it all. Brummie grinned and winked. Then his eyes fell on the welling bloodline across her slashed breast. His gaze moved to the big Jamaican still struggling on his knees in the doorway.

Brummie's booted foot made contact with the back of the curly black head and Berno jack-knifed forward in surprise. His head hit the floor with a resounding crack.

The sergeant grabbed him unceremoniously by the neck of his smart linen jacket and hauled him to the bed where his two accomplices already sat with their hands on their heads.

"Shut the door, Brummie," Fraser snapped.

"Hey, man!" Berno protested, tears of pain welling in his eyes. "What you goin' to do?"

"That depends," Fraser replied, his usually friendly eyes disturbingly cold and emotionless.

Brummie put one hand comfortingly around the girl's shoulder. In the other he weighed the switchblade. "If you ask me, boss, we ought to cut the big bastard's balls off."

Fraser moved his face to a few inches from Berno's and studied the frightened brown eyes closely. "That what you think, eh, Brummie? Suitable punishment for a pimp that cuts up little girls."

The Jamaican's Adam's apple bounced. His eyes were fixed on Fraser's. Mesmerised with terror. "And what do you say, Bill?"

"Let's not piss about." There was something in the corporal's quiet drawling phrase that hit a chord of sheer finality in Berno's mind. There was no threat mentioned and yet the man knew that he was as good as dead.

"Hey, c'mon!" Berno blubbered. "I didn't mean nuthin'! For Jesus God's sake! I'm sorry! Honest, man! That Diamante, she lost me big business! I got mad! PLEASE!!"

Mather picked up a black leather attache case from the top of a pile of expensive-looking luggage. Someone was ready to leave in a hurry.

He released the catch and a cloud of Sterling notes fluttered gently down to form a pile on the floor. There must have been tens of thousands of pounds.

"I don't know," Mather observed, "looks like you were doing well enough without the extra business." Then he lifted the case higher and sniffed at the lining. His ginger moustache twitched. Without a word he reached for the fighting knife at his belt and slid open the lining. Three polythene packages fell out.

Fraser's eyes left Berno's for a second. "Let me guess. It could be diamonds, but that wouldn't be your style, would it – man? Heroin or cocaine is it?"

The black woolly head shook violently. "You got me all wrong, man!"

"Corporal!" Fraser called suddenly.

"Yes, boss?" Mather replied.

"Five miles out of town on the up-country road there's a creek through a mangrove swamp."

"I know it, boss. There's a family of crocs down there. Locals won't go near it. No trace. No problem."

"HEY MAN!" Berno screamed, his spittle spraying Fraser's face.

The SAS officer ignored it and said softly: "Listen, you little snot, you've a choice, plain and simple. Pay a visit to the local wildlife. Or – " He paused for effect – "Or tell me about the visits of Lady Precious to the Green Mamba."

The Adam's apple was bobbing again, his eyes widening so much that Fraser half-expected his eyeballs to drop out. "There ain't nuthin' to tell," he muttered.

"Try again! Because when those crocs have finished with you, there really WON'T be anything to tell."

Berno's eyes flickered towards Mather. He didn't like what he saw. "If I talk, man, no crocodiles. A deal?"

Fraser didn't answer immediately. He waited until the man thought he'd lost the bargain. Then he said: "Okay."

A sly grin cracked Berno's face. "I'll tell you, man. No problem. But no charges with the police. Nuthin' on the drugs or the currency, right?"

The SAS captain's expression softened. "All right, Berno, you win. But you'd better talk sense."

"Sure, no problem!" He must have been holding his breath in a spasm of mortal fear, because he began breathing heavily. The plastic smile was back, despite the pain in his trapped arm, and he rubbed his throat with his free hand. "The Lady Precious comes to the Green Mamba to meet with Colonel Kwofie, you know. In private."

Fraser frowned. "An affair?"

Berno shrugged. "I dunno, man. I guess so. She's a lady with some appetite. I don't ask too many questions."

"She's taking a risk," Mather commented. He sounded sceptical. "Just for a bit on the side."

The Jamaican laughed; he was back on form. "You crazy, man. That chick don't do nuthin' without good reason. She can have any man she wants. But she ain't in love with Kwofie. She's in love with herself." The sly look returned. "Power, man, that's what she wants. And everything that it gets her."

Fraser climbed to his feet and looked down at the prisoner. "And how does having an affair with Kwofie help that?" he asked. But he already knew the answer.

Berno snorted. "Because Jammeh's finished, man! Everyone knows it. He's been too soft for too long. He's always been long on promises and short on delivery. The Government's bankrupt and incompetent. Everyone knows this Jato business will bring things to a head."

"Jato might seize power," Fraser prompted. "Where would Lady Precious be then?"

The laugh was loud and genuine. "You think the Yanks will allow that! Man, you're jokin'! Them peasants up-country might think he's goin' to be the new President, but they don't know. The Yanks won't stand for it. They'll crush Jato and install Colonel Kwofie." He leered. "No problem."

Fraser turned to Mather. "This man and his friends are under arrest, Bill. Get one of your chaps to take him along to the local police-post. I want him held for drugs and black market money, pimping and causing grievous bodily harm – we'll sort out the details later . . ."

"Hey, man!" Berno protested. "You said we had a deal!"

Fraser smiled gently. "I lied."

The merchantman nudged along the coast, her rusted hull clearly visible from the balcony of State House. The oily belch of smoke tumbling from her stack changed direction as she turned towards the gaping mouth of the Kebba River and the berth that waited for her in Sakoto's port area.

She flew the Liberian flag of convenience and her papers indeed stated that she had left that country's waters just six days earlier. What was not entered was her twelve-hour call at Conakry en route.

President Essa Jammeh watched from the balcony window until her shape became blurred and lost in the golden aurora of the setting sun.

"I am afraid a decision must be made, Mr President."

As always, the voice of the British soldier was warm and understanding. The voice of a friend. But this time it had the hard edge of authority. The distinct tone of a commanding officer. The voice of a man who knew what had to be done.

He wished to Allah that he did, too.

Slowly, he turned back into the office where the tall Scotsman stood beside Lady Precious. A joint deputation. As always, the President's wife was dressed straight from the pages of *Vogue*, today in a cool emerald green shift.

No matter what happened, he thought, he would still have her.

"I was wrong, my dearest Essa," she breathed. For once her smooth black brow was distorted with a frown of concern. Her beautiful eyes were clouded and without humour. "When Captain Fraser told me an hour ago, I was heart-broken that such a good friend had betrayed us. That Colonel Kwofie was indeed doing everything that those wicked rumours said. Committing massacres and murder in your name. Setting the people against you so that he could seize power when the moment was ripe."

Beside her, Fraser stood impassively. Lady Precious made it sound almost convincing. How different it was to when he had first approached her an hour earlier and confronted her with the evidence from Berno. That she was in conspiracy with the Head of State Security . . . The SAS captain had not been specific and had not needed to be.

At first his accusation had brought forth a stunned silence, which was followed by derisory laughter. But it petered out as he held his ground, to be replaced by anger and indignation. It was a posture hard to maintain when you realised that your accuser knew you'd been on your back with your legs wide open.

Finally she had smiled bashfully at him and gently picked up his hand and placed it on her breast. He didn't resist, but he didn't attempt to fondle her either. Suddenly Precious felt stupid and cheap.

"You know, M'lady, this isn't necessary," he had said softly. "The truth about your liaison with Colonel Kwofie is known only to me. So far. But it is pointless to deny it, as we have witnessed evidence from both Berno and one of his girls. No doubt there are others, if we ask."

Gently he had removed her hand.

She gulped. Her eyes looked like those of a frightened animal. Perspiration glistened above the beautifully-moulded and aristocratic lips. "You must know, Captain, that I have never betrayed my husband. Not politically. Nor have I conspired against him."

"But . . . ?" Fraser prompted.

Precious turned her head away and the shadows deepened beneath her cheekbones. "Before you, you see a woman who has been received by Heads of State. Who has dined with kings and presidents. Danced with them. A woman who has fine clothes and enjoys them." Her voice had faded to a whisper. Then, in a surge of defiance, she turned back to face him, her dark eyes boring into his. "Yet, Captain, until I was twelve, I was just the daughter of a village chief. I was not even educated, because it was unseemly for girls to be taught. I had no shoes. I ate rice in the village compound and peed behind a bush . . ." Her gold-tinted eyelids fluttered closed momentarily as if it was painful to remember. "If my husband is ousted, then it will be my fate to go back to that life. Can you imagine?"

There was a hard edge to Fraser's voice. "Not you, M'lady. Another perhaps, but not you." He paused. "Unless, of course, the President knew of your indiscretions with Kwofie. Then perhaps you would be lucky if you were *able* to return to your village."

Involuntarily, she had taken a step back. "You mean you will not tell him?"

"Not for your sake, M'lady. For his. He worships the ground you tread. You have unshakeable influence when it comes to protecting Kwofie and you've used that to help build up his power-base. To protect him from criticism." Fraser's eyes narrowed. "Because you saw the President's grip slipping and wanted to be well-in with his successor. You, along with the Americans, saw that man as Kwofie."

The proud, defiant face seemed to crumple as he watched. Her head bowed and he noticed the slight tremble of her breasts beneath the thin material of her dress as she had begun to sob in shame.

It was a far cry from her defiant posture now as she tried to persuade her husband to take the SAS captain's advice and rid himself of Colonel Kwofie once and for all.

Jammeh took a deep breath, his mouth gaping slightly, as his nose was congested with the effort of stifling tears. "You know, my good friend, that the US Ambassador has suggested that I have medical treatment in America?"

Fraser nodded. "I hope you won't agree?"

The President nodded soberly. "I am not a fool." A faint smile flickered on his thick lips. "The Americans are supposed to be good poker-players. Yet Ambassador Brunswick would be out-smarted in Sakoto market by any stall woman. I know they want Colonel Kwofie to succeed me."

Fraser felt genuine sympathy. "As soon as you had left the country."

Removing his glasses, Jammeh dabbed at his eyes with a handkerchief. "I do not think I would like that to happen . . ."

"As far as I am concerned," Fraser said, "it will not."

Jammeh sniffed heavily. "Then I must put my trust in you and in Allah. There is no one else to turn to." He shuffled around his desk to his seat and lowered himself into it. He looked more composed now. "In view of the evidence, Captain, I should like you to arrest Colonel Kwofie on a charge of treason. I shall have the Attorney General draw up the necessary papers immediately. Also, from this moment, I should like you to consider yourself seconded to the State Security Force of Free Guinea. I shall communicate through the official channels to your Government, of course. Meanwhile, I should like you to assume command from Colonel Kwofie."

Fraser nodded. The words were a melody to his ears. If only he had heard them three months earlier.

"Mr President, where is Kwofie now? At the Guard's barracks?"

"No. He left this morning for Serreba. To arrest the politician Fofana."

Fraser frowned. "Your only democratic opponent? For God's sake, why? That is just fuel for the Jatos."

Jammeh shrugged. "For incitement. It was Colonel Kwofie's own recommendation. I agreed with some reluctance."

There was nothing Fraser could do. Although there was no doubt in his mind that Fofana, a dedicated trade unionist, was acting as the unofficial political front of the Jatos, there was no evidence that could convict him. He was a popular and respected man. His arrest – or worse – would merely serve to alienate Jammeh still further from his people.

Fraser said: "I cannot risk sending a party after him. Besides, they'd arrive too late. As soon as Kwofie returns, I'll have him arrested. I just hope he has Fofana with him in one piece."

Jammeh nodded his understanding.

An urgent knock came from behind the carved mahogany doors, and a tiger-suited PG officer entered. He was agitated and overlooked the protocol of a salute in his haste.

"What is it?" Jammeh demanded.

"There is a priority message for Captain Fraser, Mr President," the soldier blurted. "The British Army Training Team at Duntenda is under concentrated attack. Major Harper is on the radio now."

Fraser turned to Jammeh. "Will you excuse me, Mr President?"

"Of course, of course. We both have much important business to attend to." He reached up for Precious who stood beside him and squeezed her slender hand. It gave him much comfort.

The radio room in State House was on the same floor and it took only moments for Fraser to reach it. The operator had a headphone-and-mike set waiting as he entered.

"Sunray speaking. Send. Over."

The earphones buzzed and crackled with static. Despite that, the strong sing-song Welsh accent was unmistakable: "*Six Zero. A heavy mortar attack began about half-an-hour ago. There's no sign of a let-up yet. Our land-line's been cut. Ten casualties. All local villagers from down the road where the Jatos have taken over. Everyone's under cover now. Just a bit tedious dodging all the stuff coming in. Over.*"

It was some consolation to hear Bill Harper's typically calm reaction. In the background, he could hear the muffled noise of mortar bombs and small arms fire. "How long can you hold out? Over."

"*Food, ammo and medicines will be all right for three days without relief. We're holding a lot of local refugees. They came in just before the attack. So that's putting a big strain on resources. Over.*"

"What are your immediate tactics? Over."

Harper's distinctive chuckle crackled the airwaves. "*Apart from keeping the old arse down, Six One wants to send out some fighting patrols tonight. We've got fifty PGs and police with us. All we're missing are you four and Six Two on river patrol. The Jatos are easily spooked at night. Over.*"

Fraser thought for a moment and stared up at the large map of Free Guinea pinned to the wall above the array of radio sets.

"Sunray. Negative on your last. I'll try and organise an evacuation for you by river. We might not be able to hold the roads, but we can preserve the Kebba River as a safe route. Over."

"*Six Zero. Roger to that. We have several aid teams still out in the bush. Our lads can look after themselves and make their way back here, but the volunteer workers might hit trouble. Over.*"

Fraser drummed a tattoo on the table with his forefinger. "Roger, Six Zero. Immediate recall to your location. Evacuate two nights from tonight. I may need that time to find a suitable vessel. I'll come back with more details. Over."

"*Six Zero Roger. Out.*"

Fraser removed the headset and turned to the senior PG officer. "I'd like you to locate the exact whereabouts of the *Kebba Queen*. I want to know her next port-of-call and when she is expected there."

The soldier saluted smartly, clicking his heels with a flourish. "Sah!"

Nurse Sally Richards was exhausted.

She shook out her short fair hair, letting the cool night air get to her scalp. Looking down at the sleeping woman, she decided that it would be safe to snatch a few hours' catnap. The worst of the fever had passed and the patient showed no sign yet of going into labour. Thank God. When that happened, Sally Richards would need every iota of experience she had gleaned in her work as a VSO nurse in Africa. And not a little good luck. Not only was the mother suffering from pre-eclampsia, but she had also been wracked with fever for days. Probably tick typhus. Fever and high blood-pressure – a bad way to take on the agonies of the forthcoming birth.

She smiled at the pudgy hands grasping the good-luck ju-ju charm the woman wore around her neck. She would need it.

Slowly, Sally stood up and spoke to her black trainee nurse who sat on the other side of the canvas cot.

"I'm going to get some sleep, Kadi. You must call me the moment our patient wakes or seems in any difficulty. Do you understand?"

The plump little Wolof girl beamed up at her. "I understand, Miss Sally. I will call."

As she walked through the corrugated-iron structure of the clinic to her own spartan quarters, Sally thought again how lucky she was to have Kadi. Although just out of her teens, the girl had a wisdom and maturity beyond her years. Not only was she bright, but she had the ability to influence the older women in the surrounding villages, whose opposition to Western medicine could make running a clinic a thankless task. Kadi used remarkable diplomacy in trying to work her new remedies alongside the traditional ju-ju cures.

She had been successful in persuading the chauvinistic husbands that it was best to trust wives to take the contraceptive pills rather than themselves. It really did work better that way. Wonders would never cease. Dear Kadi . . .

Sally paused at the doorway that opened onto the narrow highway running through the large shanty town of Mansakunda. Feeble illumination from the few bars, which had access to the restricted electricity supply, cast pools of light at intervals along the rows of concrete brick and corrugated-iron structures of the urban compounds. Usually at this time of night the place would be deserted. But tonight men hung around in groups chattering, smoking and laughing nervously. Expectancy was like electricity in the air. Somewhere a dog bayed. And far out in the darkness she could hear the distant beat of the message drum. It was unnerving.

For a moment she hesitated before extracting the pack of cigarettes from the pocket of her cream alpaca skirt. Her fifth today? She shrugged and lit one of the crumpled contents, exhaling a long stream of smoke out through the doorway.

Crazy, she thought. She'd kicked the habit a year earlier, but since the massacre at Massang, the need for the comfort of nicotine had returned with a vengeance.

Out of the gloom a truck emerged, steering by the light of one headlamp. It rattled past, tooting loudly. In the cargo-body the outline shapes of waving men were silhouetted for a fleeting moment. An involuntary cheer went up from the groups of bystanders, before the vehicle was swallowed up by the night. No doubt they were Jatos. There had been a lot of traffic on the road all day. Something was brewing. Sally Richards shivered.

What she wouldn't have given for the company of the British Army medic she had helped in the bloody aftermath of Massang. John Belcher had been so kind and understanding. Not just with the mutilated victims and hysterical children, but with her. Gentle words of encouragement that kept her going, when she just wanted to break down and weep.

It was only afterwards that Rod Bullock had explained to her that he was a seasoned veteran of the legendary Special Air Service Regiment. A hard, highly-trained killer. She had found it difficult to believe.

Thoughtfully, she ground out the cigarette butt under her foot. She had met him twice socially since then, but it hadn't made the reconciliation any easier. The interest he had in her work somehow didn't seem in keeping with the image of his unit. Nor did the generous donations of medical supplies that had arrived regularly at her clinic since.

But whether it was her work or herself that he was really interested in, she couldn't be sure. She hoped it was both.

Shutting out the disturbing street scene, she bolted the tin door and went through to the bare bedroom and erected her mosquito net. Then she stripped naked and put on a white cotton dressing gown.

She stepped out of the rear door to the outside shower cubicle and opened it. For a moment she flashed her torch at the plastic footbath to drive away the gheckos who habitually shared the water supply.

"Psst!"

She jumped and dropped the soap.

She gulped. The voice came from the far side of the yard fence. "Who is it?"

"Kev," came the bright reply. "Bri's with me. Can we come in?"

"God, you gave me a turn!"

A youthful chuckle came over the fence. "Sorry, Sal. But can you let us in? Won't look if you're in the nuddy."

She smiled gently to herself as she unbolted the high gate. "It's all right. I'm decent."

"Shame, that."

Kevin Shand, tall, thin, with a mop of shaggy fair hair, stood there, wearing his usual jeans, T-shirt and perpetual smile.

In marked contrast, Brian Beavis was dressed like the last of the great white hunters. Baggy safari trousers were tucked into canvas boots and a heavy machete was strapped across the chest of a worn sleeveless drill shirt.

"Hi, bonnie lass," he greeted, his eyes mischievous behind the thick pebble spectacles. "Sorry to disturb y' bathtime. Summat serious came up."

Sally stepped aside to let them in. It had taken her months to understand Brian's thick Geordie accent. The natives, to whom he taught rudimentary metalwork, stood no chance. And his Mandinka accent was indescribable. Somehow, though, he managed to communicate effectively with a primitive mixture of telepathy and sign language.

Both, she noted, were laden down with rucksacks of provisions. There came the unmistakable clink of beer bottles from Brian's as he placed it on the floor.

"Thought it best to come round the back, Sal," Kevin explained. Everyone he knew suffered the most excruciating shortening of their names.

The conspiratorial attitude of the two young VSO workers, both in their early twenties, alarmed her. "What on earth are you two up to?"

"There's trouble a't'mill," Kevin quipped. "A messenger arrived at Bri's bungalow half-an-hour ago. Said he'd been sent by those British Army chaps down at that mysterious barracks at Duntenda. You know, where your new boyfriend hangs out, damn his eyes."

Brian laughed. "You never were in with a chance there, lad."

"Anyway," Kevin continued, undeterred, "they're calling in all the VSOs, Peace Corps and other volunteers for a mass evacuation. By river, I think. They seem to think a major uprising is imminent, or something. Bloody Jatos."

"Fucken' monkeys!" Brian growled. "They'll wonder wha's bloody hit 'em when our SAS lads are let off t' fucken' leash!"

"They advise us to travel by night if possible, avoiding main towns," Kevin added. "We've got our bicycles outside and Bri's rigged up a trailer. Bit primitive . . ."

"Lap of bloody luxury," Brian interjected. "Just t' thing for the girl I'm gonna marry."

Sally had got used to ignoring the endless innuendoes, proposals of marriage and more basic invitations. She hardly noticed the remark. "We're a clinic. No one's going to hurt us here."

"Don't be naïve, Sal." A note of seriousness crept into Kevin's voice. "I heard what happened in the coup. When some of those city boys are given a gun and get high on marijuana or booze, there's no knowing what they'll get up to."

"But . . ." Sally protested.

"But nothing, gorgeous." It was Brian's turn. "You're coming if I have t' wrestle with you – Please! . . . We've got a little food and plenty of beer."

Sally shook her head. "Look, boys, I can't. I've got a sick woman next door about to go into labour. If she's left, she'll die for sure. And her child."

"Sal," Kevin said angrily.

"No, boys, I can't. I just can't." Final.

Brian slumped against the wall and scratched at the stubble on his chin. Behind the spectacles, the magnified eyes blinked. "Then we'll have t' hide up somewhere. Fucken' somewhere away from here. The Jatos'll come lookin' fur medical supplies. That's a fucken' cert."

"One of the villages?" Kevin suggested. "Out of the way."

Brian shook his head. "No way, mun. Y'can't trust anyun now'days, ev'n old friends. Jato's got fucken' spees everywhere. Even Abdouli's on his payroll. The local Commissioner, would y' believe!"

Sally shook her head sadly. She had been so involved in her work that she had been almost totally unaware of the massive change in public opinion that had been taking place under her nose.

"I've got it," Kevin said suddenly. "What about Kendo's?"

Brian blinked and a big grin broke across his face. "Now tha's a thought."

Kendo's was the latest nightspot in the bush. Situated a few miles out of Mansakunda, it had become the favourite watering-hole of the VSO and passing expatriates who used it like a motorway cafe on the long road to Sakoto.

In truth, it was just a large concrete brick shed, its inside walls daubed with garish primitive murals which were illuminated by a single ultraviolet light. But the beer was the best in the country. Expensive but deliciously cool.

"Kolley has boarded the place up," Kevin said, "but I expect we can find a way in. And it's got its own generator." The entrepreneurial Guinean had saved a modest nest egg while working in Britain and had returned to his home town to make his fortune. Three days ago he had realised that the Jatos and their Islamic fundamentalism would hardly be conducive to the profits he had in mind.

"Tha's great," Brian agreed, his eyes lighting up at the prospect. "An' if bullets start flyin', t'concrete walls will be fucken' good protection . . ."

"Oh, don't!" Sally gasped in dismay.

Kevin grinned. "I know what you're thinking, Bri. Forget it! Kolley took all his booze supplies with him."

The VSO engineer's face dropped. Then he winked at Sally Richards. "What sacrifices a man will make fur t'woman he loves."

Dawda didn't like the way the girl kept looking at him. It made him feel uncomfortable.

During the two days since Jato had ordered the two of them to guard Fofana's bungalow, he kept intercepting her furtive glances. Once or twice, she had allowed her gaze to linger just a second too long. And a faint pout of a smile would pass over her full lips.

What made things worse for Dawda was the expert way she handled the giant Kalashnikov she carried, whilst he fumbled with his like a child with a handful of thumbs.

It was getting hot now. The early morning chill had faded and another hot, throbbing day had begun. A haze was starting to build on the dusty road that dropped down before him to the sprawling compounds of Serreba town. There were few men left there now. Only the elderly and the very young, lingering near their waiting, anxious mothers. The only sound was the distant beat of rice being pounded in the kitchen yards.

"Listen," Nyomi said suddenly, lifting her Kalashnikov to the port position.

Dawda shifted, cocking his head to one side. "I hear nothing. Just the women preparing food."

The girl shook her head. "No. Listen."

Then he heard it, too. Deeper, like a background echo to the rice-pounding. Menacing, growing louder in the still musky air. The heartbeat of the gods.

Dawda felt his mouth go dry. "The drums."

"Someone is entering Jato country," Nyomi said.

Another drumbeat joined the first. More distinct, nearer.

Sweat gathered at the back of Dawda's neck. He knew that, at night, the sound of the message drum could be heard over thirty miles away. In daytime, the distance was reduced to only eighteen miles. By road, the intruders could be less than half-an-hour away from the bungalow.

Behind him, threaded bamboo curtains parted and the massive frame of Fofana waddled out, his frizzled hair seeming whiter than ever in the bright sunlight.

His bulbous face screwed up as he squinted across the roofs of the town to the distant savannah. His wide nostrils flared like a baboon alerted to danger.

"Good morning, sir," Dawda said politely. "I hope you are well today?"

The politician nodded vaguely. "I am well, young man. And I hope you are, too?" But he was preoccupied with the distant drums.

"Do not worry about the intruders, sir," Dawda said boldly. "We shall see that you are well protected."

A gruff voice, in a strange accent that the youth could not follow, added, "Ah jest hope y'right, lad. But Ah doot if y'an' y'girlfriend'll be much use te us if tha's a Government patrol out there."

Nyomi looked at the bearded Scotsman and scowled. She did not like him.

293

Fofana didn't appear concerned. "Do not worry, Mr Hammond. Jato has brothers in high places, including the Guards of the President and the police. We are in no danger. A patrol this far up-country will have the blessing of those brothers."

Ian Hammond sniffed contemptuously. "Well, whoever it is, Ah intend hitchin' a lift back to Sakoto. This place is gettin' a wee bit too isolated for my likin'."

Hammond was angry. His boss Rubashëv from the World Federation of Trade Unions had kept him in the dark. More than that, he was sure he had been deliberately misled. He had understood that his mission was to spread the gospel of free trade unionism to the poor sodding blacks in what was left of the British Empire. It was a mission which his old man – God rest his soul – would have fully approved. As a miner and long-time member of the British Communist Party, he had understood the subtle means by which the British aristocracy maintained its control of the world's peasant peoples, gentle but firm pressure and manipulation aimed at keeping their backs to the wall and their noses to the grindstone . . .

What Hammond hadn't expected was to be used by some mysterious guerrilla organisation which he felt sure was being run by Libya or some faceless outfit in the Kremlin. Organising trade union rallies for Fofana was one thing. Giving a respectable front to a terrorist like Jato was quite another.

He had tried to get out of Serreba three days earlier, but Fofana's car had developed a terminal fault. Although he'd tried, he had found that all other transport had mysteriously disappeared. No doubt commandeered by the Jatos.

He just hoped Rubashëv didn't turn up before he managed to leave the place. The man was a hard bastard, and not one to cross lightly.

"You have done well here, my friend," Fofana said. "Without your help it would not have been possible to reach so many of my brothers and sisters. But now your job is done. Now you will want to return to your beloved Scotland. I have heard of its beauty."

Hammond stared moodily down the track at the village

madman who was rummaging in the tip where the rubbish from the bungalow was thrown. Dressed in his tatty loincloth, he sat happily stuffing cold rice and meat scraps into his mouth.

"Too bleddy true," he said. Even his poky flat in the Gorbals tenement was paradise by comparison with Serreba. He turned on his heel and went back to the thankful shade of the bungalow and the last bottle of his hoard of Grant's.

It was twenty minutes before Dawda burst in. Fofana had fallen asleep, his head slumped over his massive belly. Hammond looked up from the grubby tumbler of Scotch.

"They come, sir!"

The politician awoke with a jolt.

"They are President's men! Guards!" Dawda jabbered. He looked like a scared rabbit. "You must go out back door! Quick before they come."

Hammond nearly choked on his drink. The only way Fofana would move quickly was with a bayonet up his fat arse.

But the old man seemed unperturbed. He just sat like an enormous black buddha, his body spilling over the armchair. "And tell me, my young protector, do these Presidential Guards wear the yellow of the Jato?"

Dawda looked perplexed.

The girl Nyomi had just entered. She, too, looked confused. "I do not understand. These men who come. They are soldiers. But they fly the flag of the yellow. What do we do, Dawda?"

Hammond felt suddenly alarmed. His guardians were young, naïve and armed. The approaching convoy could be friend or foe. In all probability, the soldiers would be equally stupid, but most definitely carrying a lot of weapons.

"Look, y'two," he snapped, "keep in doors, will y'. An' keep those firearms out'e sight. Let's no provoke a shootin' match. Ah'll do the talkin'."

Both Dawda and Nyomi were used to taking orders, and they agreed readily.

Fofana smiled widely, his hands resting across his belly. "Have no fear. I shall wait."

The convoy of Government jeeps was lumbering up the track as Hammond stepped out into the dazzling sunlight. Quickly, he counted six vehicles and estimated twenty men on board. It was difficult to determine whether they were PGs, gendarmes or guerrillas. They had discarded parts of their uniforms. Many wore woolly hats and additional jumpers and coats for what had evidently been a long, cold night ride from the coast.

There was no mistaking the yellow bandanas they all wore, or the Jato pennants fluttering from the jeeps. But, to Hammond's cynical eye, there was no mistaking the military bearing of the men as they debussed and fanned out to approach the bungalow, with their French MAT 49 sub-machine guns at the ready. They looked a professional, mean bunch.

At the trackside, the madman had stopped eating. He sat on his haunches, gazing curiously with his head to one side, a string of cattle-fat hanging from his lips.

A squat soldier, with darting eyes set in a toady black face, detached himself from the ring of armed men. He wore the uniform of a PG officer, Hammond noted, his eyes falling on the crowns on the epaulettes.

"An' what canna do fer y', my friend?" Hammond growled. He stood his ground with his arms folded. He had no intention of showing fear in the face of such a display of strength.

The dark eyes narrowed in recognition and a sneer of a smile cracked the perspiring face. "You must be the man Hammond?"

The Scotsman's face remained impassive. "Y' have the advantage, friend. Ah dunn ken y'name? Or what y'doin' here?"

Behind the closing ring of troops, the madman was gingerly shuffling towards the vehicles, his hand stretched out in awe to touch such wonders.

"Major Badji," the officer snapped. "Commander of the 2nd Jato Freedom Fighters' Undercover Group."

Hammond didn't take his eyes from the major's face. Slowly, he smiled and said: "Late of Jammeh's Presidential Guard, I see?"

For a moment, Badji's eyes flickered with menace. Then he seemed to relax and the sardonic smile took on a little more warmth. "That, Mr Hammond, is the purpose of an *undercover* group. To deceive the enemy."

"What d'ye want here then, Major? We are already amongst friends. Two of your Jatos have already been posted to guard us."

The major glanced at the shadows of the bungalow's windows. "So I see. But we come on orders from the leader to speak with Fofana."

Hammond didn't like it. "He's been a great help to your cause, Major. A staunch political ally of all that the Jatos stand for."

There was a shuffling movement behind him, and the Scotsman turned to see Dawda stepping out cautiously, his Kalashnikov pointing at the ground.

He stepped forward, looking curiously at the major as though trying to place where he had seen the face before.

"Well?" Badji demanded.

Dawda swallowed hard. "Sir, Mr Fofana welcomes you as a brother in the Jato movement. He bids you come inside." The words came in a rush, apprehension raising his voice by several octaves.

The major nodded brusquely and stepped past Hammond. It was a cue for the detail of troops to spread out to form a ring around the building.

As Badji disappeared inside, Ian Hammond found himself outside the ring of soldiers. On a sudden impulse, he made a decision. He sauntered slowly and casually across the track to where a deep shadow reached out from a narrow alley between two compound fences.

Inside the bungalow, Dawda took his place alongside Nyomi on one side of the great Fofana, who greeted his guests seated like a king on his throne. A meeting between two such great men, the boy thought, must be a very historical and important moment in the revolution of Free Guinea. Something he could tell his grandchildren.

"Welcome, Major Badji," Fofana's voice boomed like a true statesman. "It is a long time since we meet. But Jato tells me you have been doing great things in the secret war for our freedom. Do you bring news of the fall of Sakoto?"

A lieutenant and a captain stood on either side of Major Badji as he nodded graciously. He seemed to be enjoying the moment. "Soon, brother, soon. These things take a little time. But within the week Sakoto will be ours."

Fofana chuckled deeply, his huge belly quivering on his lap. "That is good, Major. I cannot wait to work alongside our Jato. For so long I preach the merits of trade unions, I can hardly believe our peoples shall be truly free by statute to demand the rate for the work they do . . . !" He sounded ecstatic at the thought. A lifetime's uphill struggle rewarded at last.

Major Badji smiled. "Alas, there is a slight problem."

"How so?"

"There is no room for subversive elements in the new regime. Your task, Fofana, is indeed finished."

The next two seconds were a blur in Dawda's mind – it all happened so quickly, yet in such grotesque slow motion. Suddenly he saw the glint of gunmetal in Badji's right hand. At the same moment, he realised that the lieutenant was pointing a gun at his own head. Next to him, the captain, smiling, had quietly snatched Nyomi's gun from her grasp.

A bright flash simultaneously lit the dingy room. A deafening crack reverberated around the concrete walls. Instantly, the air was filled with the stink of blue powder smoke.

Fofana exploded like a balloon. As the three single shots punctured the enormous belly, it was as though the skin could no longer contain the guts within. It seemed to rupture, and a bright red dribble of blood began bubbling from the blackened holes in the politician's suit. The stuff dripped between his legs, starting to form a pool on the floor.

For a moment, the great man sat with a look of utter astonishment on his face, the thick lips slack with surprise as he tried to stem the red liquid. But there was too much of it, and it began flooding through his fingers, spilling over the massive hands.

Fofana's head lolled suddenly backwards onto the head-rest of the huge armchair. Dawda stared open-mouthed.

Slowly, Major Badji returned the snub-nosed revolver to its holster on his belt. To no one in particular, he said: "Idealists like Fofana are a danger to the state. Besides, the man was a Godless Communist, that is quite clear."

The captain and lieutenant looked at each other and grinned.

Dawda glanced sideways at Nyomi. Her eyes were glazed in disbelief as she stared, her mouth agape, at the welling red pulp that had been Fofana. Two bright tears rolled down her plump cheeks.

"You two," Badji snapped. "You are now seconded to the 2nd Jato Freedom Fighters. You will travel with us back to Sakoto. Understand?"

Dawda nodded numbly.

Major Badji turned to the captain. "We will rest here for the remainder of the day. I prefer to travel at night. There will be food here and plenty to keep us occupied. As Fofana's home town, I am sure we will find it riddled with his subversive supporters."

The lieutenant laughed showing large white teeth and pink gums.

Badji continued: "Then we proceed west to break open the prison. It will keep Jammeh's forces busy when that mob of ruffians and lunatics are on the rampage."

Behind him, Dawda blinked. The words Major Badji spoke did not make sense. He had heard Jato Pheko speak many times in lectures and briefings. One thing he always said was that the Central Prison should never be touched. Looting and mayhem was all that prisoners were interested in. It just petrified the civilian population for no political purpose.

Dawda went to speak, but something made him stop.

"What about the whites. The infidels?" asked the gummy lieutenant. "There are the missions. Corrupting the Faith. And British imperialists on the route back to Sakoto. And the clinic at Mansakunda. Intent on destroying our culture . . . !" The man had a fanatical gleam to his eye.

"In good time, in good time," Badji agreed, somewhat patronisingly.

Dawda could hardly believe his ears. The clinic at Mansakunda. He knew it well. It had been the nearest clinic to Massang village. Often the fair-haired English nurse had come. As she had after the massacre. So pretty. And gentle.

"First," Badji was saying, "we must put the man Hammond under close arrest. Until we can hand him over to Rubashëv. He must not be free to blab his mouth."

The captain was staring out of the door into the oblong of brightness. "He is gone, Major."

Badji was unconcerned. "He cannot have gone far. We will find him when we sweep the town."

A high-pitched wailing warcry drifted in from the track outside.

"What is that hideous noise?" Badji demanded, striding to the captain's side.

Beside the track, the madman was standing, his skinny dusty body hunched in a defensive crouch. His eyes were as wild as the matted bush of hair on his head, as he swung his club menacingly back and forth.

Four troopers, trying to usher him from their vehicle, stood around him in a circle. They were unsure how to handle this strange creature.

Badji pushed his way forward. "If we cannot deal with a simple lunatic," he muttered in disgust, "how can we be expected to defeat Jammeh?"

Reaching the group, he flipped open his leather holster and extracted the revolver. He aimed at the madman's feet and squeezed the trigger.

The creature screamed in terror and leapt into the air, throwing his club aside. Badji fired again into the dust. And again.

Slowly the troopers began to laugh as the madman's terrified gyrations began to resemble a kind of war dance. Then one of them lowered his rifle and fired too. Others joined in, laughing loudly at the madman's misery as he whelped and jumped in the dust.

It went on for several moments. Then another shot

barked from Badji's revolver. There was a sound of finality about it.

Serreba's madman jolted and stiffened. As a patch of bright red spread across his dust-white belly, he pitched backwards onto the track. His right leg twitched, and went on twitching for a full thirty seconds.

The group of troops watched, fascinated, until the leg stopped. Then a sudden spontaneous whoop of cheering and laughter went up.

From the window of the bungalow Dawda watched as the squat figure of Major Badji moved down the track with an air of self-assurance. A conqueror.

There was something about the walk that made it click into place. It wasn't the face that Dawda had thought he knew. It was the mannerisms; that walk.

The last time he had seen it was when the masked PG commander had walked through the burning village of Massang. Just before he had put the bullet in the head of his father.

12

"Come away from the window!"

Immediately Mo obeyed Ralph Sinclair's order, stepping back out of the sun's rays.

"It's no good, Dad, they know we're here."

"Not necessarily. Besides, there's not much they can want from us. An Agricultural Research Station offers pretty boring spoils."

Mo looked across the room to where her father was opening the depleted gun-cabinet. He'd always been more interested in preserving wildlife than destroying it. But for once he wished he had more than a .22 rifle and an ornate but ancient Holland & Holland shotgun. "I'm not sure you're right, Dad. The villagers are bound to tell them we're here. They always know what's going on."

Ralph Sinclair didn't appear to be listening. "I've had the vehicles parked around the back and hidden under tarpaulins. Those buggers'll be more like magpies than ever. And the compound gates are locked."

"Wire mesh gates won't deter them, Dad."

Sinclair brought across the .22 and handed it to his daughter, keeping the Holland & Holland for himself. "What are they doing now?"

Mo moved forward.

"And don't let them see you, Maureen!"

His voice made Sunday jump. The youth was seated on the settee with the cook. They were both looking nervous and the old man's teeth were actually rattling. The noise even put the imperturbable Sinclair on edge, but he wanted to have his house staff where he could keep an eye on them.

"They're just standing by the gates. Talking. There appears to be quite a debate going on. Lots of arm-waving."

"Recognise any of them?"

"I can see a couple of young chaps from the village, I think. Hard to tell from this distance."

Sinclair weighed the half-dozen shotgun slugs in his large palm. Not much of an arsenal. But it might act as a deterrent.

At least the regular radio broadcasts didn't sound too alarmist. There was a new voice. A Brit. That was good news. Sinclair thought he recognised the voice. A quiet SASman who had been to the bungalow once with Fraser. A ginger moustache and cold, cold grey eyes. He couldn't remember the name.

The voice had been firm but reassuring. President Jammeh had declared an official 'State of Emergency'. A Major J. Fraser had been appointed as Special Military Adjutant to the President and as such had absolute jurisdiction over the security forces of Free Guinea and all military and police affairs. The seaport, airport and border crossings were now closed, and there was a dusk-to-dawn curfew.

All holidaymakers and expatriates were advised to stay put in their hotels and homes. Under no circumstances should marauders be provoked. Firearms should only be used as a very last resort in self-defence. Security patrols would check their safety and special needs within the next few days in Sakoto and the surrounding areas. Those in isolated up-country locations should stay calm, offer no physical resistance to armed mobs and do nothing to provoke or antagonise. They should stay at their usual places of residence and wait to receive instructions by any available means. Nothing more specific than that.

The situation must be bad for Fraser to have been appointed to such a post, Sinclair reasoned, but at least now things might get done. Not before blessed time.

"Dad, they're climbing over the gate," Mo announced suddenly.

"Oh, God! Oh, God!" Sunday wailed. "Silly bloody imbeciles!" Already he had visions of his execution when

303

Kali Pheko discovered this wretched Jato traitor. His teeth, too, began to chatter.

"At least they didn't blast the gates out," Mo murmured. "They look more unsure than aggressive."

"Are they armed?" Sinclair demanded.

"One has a gun. A rifle thing. Automatic. The other's got a machete."

A sharp knock came from the door.

Sinclair handed the Holland & Holland to his daughter. "Stay well back, Maureen. If anything happens to me give 'em both barrels. It's got a good spread."

Mo grinned nervously. "Okay, sheriff."

"This isn't a laughing matter, Maureen!" Curt.

"I know, Dad. Don't worry. It'll be all right."

The knock was repeated, louder. Sinclair squared his shoulders and marched to the door. He threw it open.

Outside stood two Guineans in their twenties.

He thought he recognised the one in the khaki uniform as a local village boy. The rebel waved the barrel of his gun carelessly, trying to peer past Sinclair into the dim interior.

"Yes?" Sinclair demanded with a confidence he did not feel.

"We are Jato. You have cars, please."

Sinclair hesitated, not sure that it was sensible to lie.

The man thrust out his hand. "You have keys, mis'er. Please."

"All right." He reached into his pocket. "There are two. A Suzuki and a G-wagen."

"Please," the man repeated, and snatched the keys from Sinclair's hand. "Now you go inside. No trouble. No problem."

Sinclair closed the door and breathed again, the sweat bursting out suddenly on the skin of his back.

"Well done, Dad," Mo congratulated.

He grunted. "Let's just hope that's an end to it."

For the next half-hour they watched from the window whilst the Jatos practised driving jerkily around the compound in the two vehicles.

A resounding crash suddenly echoed through from the front of the bungalow.

Sunday rushed into the room. He looked furious. "Them silly bloody imbeciles, they crash the cars into the gate!"

Sinclair and Mo exchanged glances, then went quickly to the window.

"They break my car!" Sunday fumed.

Sinclair smiled to himself, but the humour vanished as a loud knock came to the door.

Nervously he opened it. The young Jato held out the keys, grinning apologetically. "I am sorry, mis'er. None of these bas'ards drive proper. You keep them. We don't want to smash nice cars."

Until he had closed the door again the words hadn't sunk in. He turned slowly to Mo who looked equally flabbergasted.

"What do we do now, Dad?"

He put his arm around her slender shoulders. "Do what our friend on the radio advised. Sit tight. And hope it isn't too long before your boyfriend pays us a call. Hopefully armed to the teeth."

She smiled up at him. "He will, Dad. He will."

"Now look here, Fraser. Now you've got what you wanted – running the whole damn show – I want to know what you intend to do about it?" Sir Nigel de Burgh's chin jutted defiantly. He was a poor loser.

All around them, the scene in the hotel manager's office was as chaotic as the Stock Exchange on the day of the Wall Street crash. The half-a-dozen telephones that Corporal Bill Mather had arranged to be patched into the temporary Tac HQ at The Oceanic all seemed to be singing together. No sooner had one been answered than another started to shrill.

Most of the calls came from expatriates in out-of-town residential areas like Bajtenda who, with typical British phlegm, had stocked up with gin and barbecue steaks, and bolted the doors, ready to sit out the trouble until it passed over. Their information was useful in monitoring the Jato advance and in judging the mood of the guerrillas. So far, this seemed to be one of jubilation and good-humour – but then they hadn't yet met with any significant resistance.

These reports were supplemented by radio contact with a number of covert observation posts that Fraser had established with PGs at key points along the Jato's axis of advance.

Johnny Fraser glanced at a sheaf of messages in his hand. "I appreciate your concern, Your Excellency. But, as you can see, we're slightly undermanned."

The dark patches deepened on Sir Nigel's cheeks. "There's no need for that, Fraser. I've acknowledged the situation here to Whitehall. I can't do more than that. It's out of my hands."

One buck neatly passed, Fraser thought acidly. It had taken the High Commissioner long enough to admit, indirectly, that he'd been wrong. Just how long it would take the Foreign Office to admit the same to the MoD was anyone's guess.

Sir Nigel said: "Well, Whitehall was none too pleased to learn of the change of circumstances, and weren't at all happy that you'd taken virtual command of the Guinean Armed Forces. The Americans are hopping mad about it. I've been avoiding Eddie Brunswick for the past three days. I've been in so many conferences, it's not true . . ."

"That's why they give you a highly-paid secretary," Fraser replied, without sympathy.

Sir Nigel ignored the barb. "Ambassador Brunswick is livid at what you've arranged. When the world at large learns of your position here, some quarters will have a field day. Imperialist Britain back running its old colonies."

Brummie Turner glanced up from the radio messages he was studying. He had been listening with faint amusement. Now he could sense his commander's anger reaching boiling point.

He heard Fraser say in a low voice: "Sir Nigel, if you mean the Americans are worried about what mileage the Russians make out of this, I don't give a toss! For God's sake, Moscow is behind this whole sorry business. And the Yanks needn't cry any crocodile tears for their protégé Colonel Kwofie. He's not dead, he's not even in prison – where he ought to be!"

"Then where is he?"

"I've no idea – unfortunately. Our first report was that he'd left with a convoy for Serreba to arrest Fofana. But I've learned since that he didn't go with it. That was left in the hands of Major Badji."

With a flick of his head, Sir Nigel threw back his wing of hair. "Perhaps he's fled the country."

Fraser smiled thinly. "We should be so lucky. More likely he's hiding up somewhere with a hundred of the PGs who have also gone missing. No doubt he's waiting for his chance to topple Jammeh. That'll please Ambassador Brunswick, I'm sure."

Again, Sir Nigel smarted visibly. "Brunswick has his priorities, Fraser, I have mine. Whitehall's concerned about our nationals. Especially the people besieged at Duntenda Barracks. I have to tell them what is being done."

Brummie Turner interrupted: "Something of relevance, boss. I've a message here from John Belcher aboard the *Kebba Queen*. She's in position and ready to move in to evacuate Duntenda Barracks tonight."

"That's the first bit of good news I've heard today," Fraser acknowledged. He turned to Sir Nigel. "You'll be able to tell that to Whitehall. But only *after* the operation's under way, if you don't mind. I don't want any leaks to the BBC." He hadn't forgotten the careless forewarning given to the Argentinians before the assault on Goose Green during the Falklands War.

The High Commissioner took the embargo with surprising good grace. "As you wish. Just make sure it doesn't go wrong."

Fraser was about to deliver a cutting reply when Corporal Bill Mather called over from the bank of radio sets in the corner. His pale grey eyes were ringed with tiredness. "And it's about the only good news you're likely to hear, boss. I can't raise the Central Prison by radio or telephone, and the radio station at Mansakunda has started putting out statements."

"Jesus!"

"Old Jato himself has just made an announcement in Mandinka and in English. Want to hear it?"

Fraser nodded and watched impatiently as the signals

expert fed in a cassette recording of the transmission. Most of the men in the room stopped working, glad of the excuse of a few moments' respite.

"*My brothers and sisters of Free Guinea.*" There was no mistaking the strident oration of Kali Pheko. "*This is Jato speaking with you. Long live the revolution! Long live our struggle! Victory, honour and glory to the oppressed peoples of our country!*

"*On your behalf, I call upon that toothless lion Jammeh to recall his soldiers to their barracks. He cannot be king forever. Our peoples are tired of him and his bourgeois clique. No longer do they want his brand of political iniquity and the legalised corruption of his regime.*

"*Ever since independence, the Jammeh administration upholds nepotism, favouritism, tribalism, corruption and a legion of devised social classes. The chaotic condition of the Free Guinea economy is all that the self-confessed Guardian Lion has guarded. Rocketing prices, massive self-indulgence and excesses by his family and ministers, bankrupt commerce, chronic shortages, mismanaged agriculture is all he stands for. The result is social unrest and abject poverty; the only thanks for those who vote for him because there is no alternative. It is blasphemy in the eyes of Allah.*

"*But listen, brothers and sisters of the Islamic Revolution. The alternative is here! Now! Jato speaks to you as the first Chairman of the New Islamic Revolutionary Council, which now sits!*

"*All will now change. Our peoples will leave the ghetto shanties and evil fleshpots of Sakoto and Bankama, and return to the land which they have neglected for the mistaken hope of riches in the towns. They will rebuild new villages and work the land. We will irrigate our dry land with devices that are simple but effective. We do not have money but we have our labour. Our desert areas will bloom again . . .*"

Johnny Fraser frowned. That sounded like an oblique reference to the Israeli Negev Desert experiments which Islamic countries steadfastly ignored because they had been achieved by Zionists.

"*Jammeh has allowed our industries to be run by foreigners and neo-colonialists,*" Jato accused. "*And all profits return abroad. From light engineering and tourism, all we Guineans receive is a pittance. The only Guineans to benefit are the corrupt members of the Government with their secreted accounts in overseas banks.*

"*All shall change! All such business shall be nationalised or compulsorily sold to Guinean businessmen. We shall revitalise our great mother river The Kebba and use it properly. Including new fish industries."*

Sir Nigel was staring at the revolving eyes of the cassette as though it was a living thing. He snorted in disgust. "The man's a fool and an idealist! Guineans couldn't run a proverbial piss-up in a brewery . . . !"

Fraser waved him to silence and Jato's words continued, with increasing fluency as he warmed to his subject:

"And finally I come to the insidiousness of corruption deep in Jammeh's wicked regime, but also all Africa. From now on, all members of the Revolutionary Committee will have only executive powers. All financial affairs will be directed through a new National Financial Institute under my own control and regulated by an unbiased administrator from the world of international banks. On my instruction, he shall see that Free Guinea's earnings go where they are supposed to – not to the back pockets of Government members. The civil service and police shall be paid properly again. Fair prices will return to farmers."

Suddenly Fraser had an uneasy feeling. These didn't sound like the words of a Communist dictator. Beneath the rhetoric, there was some new and ambitious thinking. The ideas sounded vaguely familiar.

"Every year Jammeh has absorbed millions of pounds in aid. Into the bottomless pit that is his ruling clique. And there is little to show for it.

"By contrast, there are charity aid-workers, white and black, known to all in our land who work on a fraction of these sums. Yet they achieve much more. They supervise the digging of wells and new agriculture, they run clinics and schools and build bridges.

"They are the unsung heroes of our land. They understand our peoples and their simple ways. They teach us to help ourselves. There are a mere three hundred such men and women in our land – often frustrated because dedicated funds from Jammeh's Government go missing – yet their organisation is such that they could handle a hundredfold more money and projects.

"They will now have that opportunity. Their views and guidance will take priority in our first Five Year Plan . . ."

The cassette whirred suddenly. "Sorry, folks," Mather said. "End of the tape. I'll change it."

It took a moment for the thoughtful silence in the crowded office to return to normal. "Later, Bill, I'd like to listen to the full broadcast in private, if you don't mind."

"Sure, boss."

"Have I been hearing things?" Brummie Turner asked no one in particular.

Sir Nigel de Burgh was pale and drawn; a man recovering from shock. "It'll never work," he muttered, half to himself. "It's crazy."

"It's never been tried," Fraser replied brusquely. "The whole bloody Third World is in a mess because its leaders are trying to ape so-called Western civilisation. There haven't been many attempts to make the Third World work in its own right."

"It's still crazy," Sir Nigel repeated. "It won't work. For God's sake, this *is* Africa."

Before Fraser could reply, a PG officer brought across a fresh message. He was glad of the interruption, but not at the contents of the communication.

It seemed that Jato supporters were appearing in force on the streets of the great urban sprawl of Nyantaba. All day, the major town had been at virtual standstill whilst the men gathered and talked and many less dedicated Muslims drank palm wine from old beer bottles. The cordial liquid drawn from the trees that morning was fermenting fast into heady firewater. As evening approached, the effect of the stuff on a revolutionary mob made it as unstable and explosive as nitroglycerine. Already, some shooting and looting had been reported.

Fraser didn't have to glance at the wall-map to know that Ralph Sinclair's Agricultural Research Station was only a few miles down the road.

Quietly, he leaned back in his chair and whispered to Sergeant Turner. "Brummie, will you send a couple of spare PGs down to the Sinclairs' place with a jeep and get everyone brought back here?"

"I don't have any spare PGs, boss."

"Diamante's with them, too," Fraser reminded.

Brummie grunted. "I'll see what I can do."

The night was hot, sticky and oppressive.

All day long the temperature had been rising steadily

310

under the relentless pounding of a white sun from a clear sky. With the coming of the blood-red sunset, shimmering through a haze of dust, a coolness often fell over the land, bringing welcome relief. But not tonight.

It did little for Major Bill Harper's nerves as he waited at Duntenda Barracks for the evacuation. The awesome responsibility of getting two hundred souls from the comparative safety of the military compound across half-a-mile of Jato-infested scrub to the Kebba River weighed heavily on his mind. Out there, God willing, the darkened hull of the *Kebba Queen* would be ready to chug the last few hundred yards to the wooden landing-stage.

His charges were a mixed bunch. There were some British servicemen, whom Fraser had seconded for Witcher's 'hearts-and-minds' operations, a few dozen VSOs and Peace Corps workers and some expatriate managers. But the bulk of the refugees waiting outside in the compound were local villagers who had helped run the barracks by providing catering, cleaning and laundry services. As such, they were at risk of reprisals from the encircling Jatos. Inevitably, the refugees had brought with them their families and relatives, and all their worldly possessions, including scrawny sheep, goats and even a few head of cattle.

Something made Harper turn. It was purely a soldier's instinct because the Welshman had not heard the stealthy approach of Mark Benjamin and John Belcher.

"Sorry, Bill. Didn't mean to startle you." Only the whites of Benjamin's eyes showed in the darkness. Both men were fully blacked-up with camo cream and every reflective item of equipment had been carefully dulled. Mere shadows in the night.

But Harper wasn't given to bad nerves and, tonight, he had his mind on other things. "Ready?"

"As we'll ever be." The Jewish corporal sounded cheerful, but then he always did. "We've got two Bergens packed with fireworks. Been working on them all day."

"They'll make a lovely blaze," Belcher added enthusiastically. "Should last all of the half-an-hour you want."

In the darkness Harper smiled thinly. How had he ever

311

imagined that thirty minutes would be sufficient to move two hundred men, women, children and their livestock half-a-mile? But he kept his fears to himself. Whilst the two SASmen would have been willing to keep up the gunfire and explosives all night, they were limited by the munitions stocks held at Duntenda.

The face of Harper's watch glowed faintly on his wrist. "2200 hours. Time you were going. We start at 2300."

Benjamin nodded and hitched the explosives-laden Bergen rucksack higher onto his back. Belcher hesitated.

"What is it, then?"

The bush-doctor looked uncomfortable. "Still no sign of Sally Richards? The nurse from Mansakunda?"

"No." Harper smiled reassuringly. Even in the darkness, Belcher sensed it wasn't convincing. The Welshman realised it, too. "Don't fret, John. The chances are she came out of her own accord, probably by road. You know the state of things. Our list of who is and isn't accounted for is a complete shambles. It'll be days before we know."

"She was seen at the clinic yesterday evening," Belcher persisted, "and everything on the road's been through our vehicle check-points since then."

"I understand your concern, John," Harper replied firmly. "But I've checked with everyone who's passed through Mansakunda today. Apparently the clinic was deserted."

Mark Benjamin was getting impatient. "C'mon, John, she'll be okay. She's a capable bird. She's well-loved by the locals and she speaks the lingo. No problem."

Uncharacteristically, Belcher turned on his companion. "Don't be so bloody patronising, Mark, for Chrissake! Bleating out platitudes that *Oh, she'll be all right* is a load of bullshit and you know it. Half the country's crawling with psyched-up terrorists high on palm-wine and pot. If they get a blood-lust, anything could happen. She's an unarmed white girl who needs some sort of protection!" He suddenly realised he was shouting. He stopped short and muttered an apology.

"What do you suggest, John?" Harper asked quietly.

Belcher didn't need to consider. "As soon as the evacuation is over, I'd like to take a Gemini up-river and find her."

"Through Jato lines?"

Benjamin chuckled, the idea appealing to him. "What Jato lines, boss? By the time we've finished with our fire-work display, they'll be scattered to the four winds. I'd be happy to keep the old brain-surgeon here company on the jaunt."

Harper couldn't resist a smile. To an SASman, the chance of flirting with danger was irresistible, however lame the excuse. Throw a pretty woman into the equation and it would take more than an opposing army to stop them.

Harper said: "Between you, you'll get me court-martialled."

At precisely eleven o'clock an early dawn came. A brilliant aurora of orange light lit up the northern sky beyond the ragged treeline around Duntenda. Pounds of plastic explosive detonated in a long chain that wound through the bush. Simultaneously, small arms fire seemed to come from all directions at once, and dazzling flares descended through the sky. In a twinkling, the safe curtain of night around the besieging Jatos melted away. They stood exposed, seemingly naked and defenceless.

To the unsophisticated and basically unmilitary minds, someone, somewhere had some pretty powerful ju-ju. And it was being directed against them.

Ignoring pleas and threats from their commanders, the Jatos left their hiding places in droves and fled eastwards.

The effect on the refugees was little different. When the barrack gates were swung open, they needed no second bidding to rush towards the safety of the waiting steamer. All hopes Harper had of a silent, orderly evacuation were dashed. It was bedlam.

A trail of abandoned belongings stretched behind the refugees as they streamed out into the night.

When he reached the landing-stage, Major Bill Harper glanced at his watch, and smiled. The whole evacuation had taken barely twenty minutes.

The baby was dead.

It had been born dead during the night. A boy. Like a

black and skinny doll. For a moment Brian had held it in his arms, still warm from the womb. He had peered at it through the dirty lenses of his thick spectacles. He had never witnessed anything quite like this before. A miracle. Such tiny features, all perfectly formed: fingers, toes, genitals.

He swallowed hard. A miracle that had gone wrong. Just one of hundreds every day in the African bush. So much for the lavish aid poured from the Government of one country to the Government of another. There was no proper equipment in Mansakunda. The little bugger didn't stand a chance.

Even as he stood holding the tiny corpse, the warmth was already leaving its flesh. The little head lolled, the eyes still tightly closed.

Gingerly, he had laid it in an empty beer crate in the corner of Kendo's deserted bar. In the morning, he had planned to bury it outside. An anonymous grave beneath a small orange tree.

But dawn had brought new terrors and a change of plan.

He had woken first from the makeshift bed on the dusty concrete floor. Almost immediately, Kevin's mop of fair hair had stirred as he came alive, instantly bright and alert. To Brian, who suffered a perpetual hangover, it was sickening.

Bars of morning sunlight streamed in through the tatty gauze mosquito blinds. The gentle light was like a balm. In the corner, Sally Richards was curled in a ball, sleeping heavily after the hours of nursing by torchlight. On the portable canvas cot, the mother of the dead child was also asleep at last, whimpering gently. The nightmare was past.

Brian cleaned his glasses roughly with his shirt-tail and shoved them into position on his nose. Then, outside, he heard voices. Perhaps the nightmare wasn't quite over.

Kevin was on his feet. "What's going on out there?"

"Careful!" Brian hissed as he joined his companion by the window.

"Looks like the Jatos are here," Kevin observed calmly. But his face was pale and tight with tension.

"Fucken' hell," Brian mumbled under his breath.

314

The single-storey concrete structure of Kendo's stood at the side of the main road on the outskirts of Mansakunda. Across the dusty tarmac strip, a convoy of commandeered groundnut trucks and a couple of PG jeeps had pulled over at the first compound of the town's shanty ghettos. A motley collection of young men climbed off the vehicles, chatting loudly and laughing as they brandished a curious collection of weapons, from sophisticated sub-machine guns to improvised clubs, axes and machetes. Items of PG uniform were much in evidence; the only item common to all was the ubiquitous yellow bandana. More yellow streamers hung in festoons from the vehicles.

"Looks like a bloody carnival, Bri," Kevin commented.

"Shut up. They might look like a fucken' joke, but I wouldn' wanta get on t'wrong side t'fucken' bastards. Keep ye gob shut, canny lad!"

Kevin shrugged. He felt sure Brian was exaggerating the danger.

The Jatos had gathered around the wayside 'chop shop' opposite where an old man was cooking tripe and gobs of sheep fat on an open fire. He smiled a happy toothless smile. He wasn't used to so many customers dropping in for breakfast. It seemed like his lucky day.

In a low voice, Kevin said: "Perhaps they'll go soon. After they've eaten."

Brian didn't reply, but he wasn't so sure.

And he was right. By the time the Jatos had finished eating, it seemed that the entire population of Mansakunda had gathered around the small convoy. There was much laughing and joking. The freedom fighters were treated like national heroes, although it was doubtful if any had yet fired a shot in anger. There was much shaking of hands and back-slapping as the Jatos discovered their family connections in the town. They began drifting away in twos and threes to celebrate the revolution as guests of the locals.

The man in charge was a tall, angular PG lieutenant who had a gummy sneer of a smile, and wild-looking eyes.

For a while, he seemed to resist temptation, then he, too, wandered off with the last of his men and some flirtatious village girls. The convoy was left unattended in the blazing heat of the sun.

"Thank God for that," Brian breathed at last. "Silly fuckers left t'vehicles unguarded. I'd like t'hole their fucken' tyres."

"Then they'll never leave."

Brian shrugged. "Might not anyhow. Might be billeted here. In which case, we're likely t'fucken' starve."

Kevin grinned. "Typical of you. Bring a stack of bloody booze and forget about grub."

"'S' what did ye bring, wise-guy?"

At that moment, Sally Richards began to stir. For once, her usual smartly pressed drill-shirt and skirt were crumpled and stained, and her pale hair was lank with grime and dust as she shook it. She smiled across at the two men.

They waved back but, as Kevin began watching the road outside again, Brian's eyes followed her as she tottered across the hall, not yet fully awake. He thought how tired she looked. At the best of times, she had a narrow, classical English face, accentuated by aristocratic high cheek bones. But now, the dark rims beneath her eyes made her look positively gaunt. For months now, she had been working too hard, frequently on the road and often 'trekking' the rough bush paths in her jeep to attend the steeply increasing cases of malnutrition in the remote villages.

That's when he really missed her. Brian sniffed heavily. Unrequited love. Bitter-sweet. She was a veteran at the age of, what was it? Twenty-nine last birthday. She ran an efficient clinic and her hut was an oasis of civilisation. Always clean, spick and span. Always smelling gently of Lily-of-the-Valley. Fresh and floral. Soft. Like Sal.

Ruefully, Brian picked a bottle of Tru-beer from his stock on the floor, and flicked off the top on the window ledge.

He heard water running from the bar area and guessed she was using the last of the water tank to freshen-up.

A sudden vision came back to him. A memory. A minor incident, but one that had become etched indelibly on his mind. When was it? A year ago? He'd passed Sally's window and, for a fleeting second, he'd seen her in the shower, water shimmering over her body. She looked so long and sleek and surprisingly white, the tan of her legs, arms and face quite distinct against the alabaster whiteness of her torso.

Her face looked so serene, upturned to meet the jet of water. Not exactly pretty or beautiful. Just fucken' lovely.

He gulped down a mouthful of warm beer.

"So early in the day, Bri?" Kevin chided.

"Man's gotta've some fucken' breakfast. Tha's fucken' orl else 'air."

Sally came in from the bar, dabbing her hair dry with a towel. "What's going on outside, boys?"

"Fucken' Jato's've come," Brian replied.

Sally draped the towel around her neck and peered into the bright daylight. "Where are they all?" She seemed very calm.

"Gone to get fucken' pissed in t'ghettos. Celebrate t' taken' of fucken' Mansakunda. Great bleddy heroes."

She smiled. "Then, with any luck, they'll be too drunk to worry about us."

Kevin looked serious. "I just hope they go soon. God, I couldn't stand another day without food. I'm famished already."

Brian grinned mischievously. "It'll hav' t'be a bleddy liquid lunch then, canny lad, won't it?"

Dawda watched with growing apprehension.

The tall PG lieutenant was squatting awkwardly in the corner of the overcrowded mud-brick room, about to start on his umpteenth palm-wine. It was old stuff, too. Probably three or four days old, fermenting and well on its way to self-destruction, burning its way down to a sediment.

Ever since they had arrived at Mansakunda, Dawda had watched the transformation come over the PG officer. He hadn't seemed too bad in the first place back at Serreba when Major Badji had murdered the politician Fofana. But since he had been ordered to command his own convoy, it had gone to his head. He became aloof and boorish, frequently quoting from the Koran. During the party, his fanatical Islamic rantings had grown with each palm-wine he downed. It seemed that he conveniently subscribed to the belief that Allah couldn't see a man drink under his own roof – or, to stretch a point, even that of a relative.

Clutching yet another bottle, the lieutenant swaggered to the bed which filled half the room. There, two of his soldiers were fondling a couple of young village girls whilst their mother, a big woman, looked on with sullen disapproval. Another soldier was grabbing drunkenly at her big breasts, and she pushed him away half-heartedly.

"Get off the bed!" the lieutenant ordered his two soldiers, and he flicked the scum from the top of the new bottle with a practised hand. "Leave those two young women to an officer! A chosen warrior of Islam. I'll show you how it's done. I shall impale them both with my weapon . . . Hic!"

The soldiers went to obey, but the girls restrained them. Clearly, they were frightened by the officer's loud and uncouth behaviour.

Laughing at his own boast, the lieutenant suddenly lost interest, his legs wavered, and he slid slowly to the floor beside the bed.

His head lolled as he muttered inanely about Allah, and Jato and the Revolution, and about his mother. He cursed her, suddenly blaming her venomously for all his imagined troubles. His eyes rolled, showing the whites.

Then they opened, quickly. They fixed on Dawda, who sat just a few feet distant.

"You, soldier!"

"Sir?" Dawda replied apprehensively.

"You look at me!" he challenged angrily.

"No, sir."

"Yes, sir!" The snarling smile came to his mouth and he poured some palm-wine into it. A trickle escaped his slack lower lip. "Maybe you think we should get on with the Revolution? Long live the Jato! Long live the Islamic Revolt!"

The lieutenant staggered to his feet again, belching lightly, and cast aside the bottle of wine. The glass shattered on the hard earth floor and voices stopped suddenly. All eyes turned. Roughly, he grabbed an old man who claimed to be his relative. "Brother, it is time for the Revolution of the Jato to move on! Where are the *toubabs* in this town? The infidels who spit upon Islam! That we might take Allah's vengeance in our hands and be his instruments of punishment!"

The old man, although drunk, was surprised at this Jato's choice of words. The only *toubabs* in the town had been the nurse, an agriculturist who studied their tribal customs with keen interest, and the metalworker teacher, a wild and funny young man who spoke in a strange accent and had become a great friend.

"My brother, they have gone. There is no one at the clinic. Or at the workshops since yesterday."

A ripple of laughter and an animal's squeal of terror rose from the next room. The lieutenant pushed the old man aside and swaggered through.

The cause of the hilarity had been the slaughter of a goat by his men. They were laughing drunkenly in a circle beneath the low corrugated-iron roof, which dripped blood that had jetted from the animal's severed jugular. He could scarcely distinguish the details through the haze of hash smoke.

"A feast to celebrate the Revolution!" one cried.

"A kill for the Jato," another yelled, spurts of vermilion smeared across his perspiring black face.

The lieutenant laughed loudly. "Get the women to prepare the feast! Cook the sacrificed goat! You have tasted blood, my brothers, but you have seen nothing yet! Let's go and find the *toubabs*!"

The blood-smeared Jato gave a whoop of joy; he had never felt so strong, so tall, so powerful. "The *TOUBABS*!" he screamed and the others cheered and followed the lieutenant out of the door.

Horrified, Dawda watched as the rabble tumbled into the dark alleys of Mansakunda. This is wrong! This is wrong! The words screamed in his brain.

Shouting and jeering, the drunken mob advanced on the clinic. By the time he caught up with them, they were gathered around the deserted clinic building while looting Jatos came out with boxes of medical supplies.

The smell of burning reached him. The first licks of flame were creeping up the prickly palm-wood framework of the building.

"The *toubabs* have fled!" one Jato protested loudly, and collapsed insensible.

Suddenly someone shrieked and pointed a finger at a black woman who was trying to slip past the mob unnoticed. Immediately, Dawda recognised the girl as Kadi, the plump little Wolof who was nursing assistant to Sally Richards.

Before he could shout out a warning, angry hands grabbed her from the shadows. Her arms were twisted up her back, forcing her face up into the hateful eyes of the lieutenant. In the flickering torchlight, Dawda could see the terrified white marble of her eyes. The skin of her face was wet with perspiration.

The lieutenant's own eyes widened, and he turned his face sideways to hers, showing his fleshy gums in his mimicry of her torment.

A sound escaped his thick lips, a high-pitched giggle like a girl. Dawda knew it was the effect of palm-wine and hash. And maybe something else.

"You *toubab*-lover, woman, tell us where they are?" And Dawda knew then from somewhere deep in his heart, that this lieutenant had also been at Massang with the major called Badji.

Instinctively, his hand clutched at the ju-ju around his throat and held it tightly. For strength, for safety.

"I do not know, mighty Jato warrior," the girl pleaded, her words chosen to pacify the tall figure stooping over her.

"Do you lie to me Wolof woman? Do you try to make a fool of me before the Jatos? I am deeply empowered by the marabou. I have great knowledge and can see things. If you stab me, then I will not bleed. The knife blade will buckle. Because I am chosen. In the eyes of Allah!" His words hissed out like snake's venom.

Kadi opened her mouth and blabbered incomprehensively.

Suddenly the man reached to his side. There was a menacing rasp of steel on steel. Then the firelight danced along the blade of the bayonet. Slowly, he pressed its razored tip against her cheekbone. A pinprick of blood appeared. One red drop amid the clear dew of fear.

Kadi gasped.

The lieutenant sneered. The smell of her fear was in his nostrils. "And if my blade penetrates your eyeball, you will have nothing to fear because you tell the truth to me!"

"You . . . you blind me?"

"Only if you lie," the man cackled. "Otherwise Allah will protect!"

A silence fell on the crowd. Powerful ju-ju would put the proof of Allah to the test.

"One flick," he breathed.

The silence seemed endless; the crackle of the burning clinic accentuating the time.

Suddenly she spoke. "Kendo's. Oh, Allah help me, the *toubabs* are at Kendo's!"

"The liquor house!" someone shouted. "The evil place that spits in the face of Islam!"

The lieutenant's eyes seemed to grow in their brightness, mesmerising young Kadi. He stiffened. Then the blade dropped from her face and she shut her eyes in blessed relief and thankfulness . . .

Then, as the pain thrust deep into her belly, her eyes opened again, staring blankly in disbelief. Beneath her long skirt, her entrails dripped into the dust like writhing bright red serpents.

A howl of approval rose from the mob. Dawda felt the vomit start crawling up his throat from deep inside his gut.

"JAT-O! JAT-O! JAT-O!"

He stood, mouth agape, with tears trickling down his cheek, as the frenzied crowd jostled past him on its way to Kendo's.

Using the barrel of his Kalashnikov, he prised a passage through the excited mob of drunken Jatos and curious townsfolk.

A distance of some ten feet separated the lieutenant and Brian. From his stance, it was clear the young VSO metal-work teacher meant business. The sweep of shimmering steel machete said it all, as he weighed it threateningly in his right hand.

Behind him, stood Sally Richards, her face ashen,

supported by Kevin Shand. In a corner, a black woman had propped herself onto one elbow to peer, frightened and confused, out of her canvas hospital cot.

"I'm fucken' tellin' ye!" Brian repeated, his anger thickening his Geordie accent so much that it was doubtful whether the lieutenant could understand his words.

But the message was clear without speech. The ex-PG officer nodded sharply to one of his men and the Jato stepped forward with a sub-machine gun raised.

A smile crawled over the lieutenant's lips.

"Don't provoke them," Sally warned.

"Reason with them," Kevin urged.

Brian was angry and confused. "You're fucken' jokin'!"

"They've got *guns*," Sally insisted. "Drop that bloody knife thing. You'll just put ideas into their heads."

Brian hesitated. It made sense. But he was sure it would be a mistake to capitulate, to show them that they had the upper hand. With as much dignity as he could muster, he slowly resheathed the machete instead of dropping it.

But as he did so, the lieutenant nodded to the armed Jatos nearest to him. Their military training was evident, despite the effect of the palm-wine. One sprang forward, wrenching Brian's arms up behind his back. As he did so, four others moved in on Sally and Kevin, separating them roughly. The audience gave a gasp of appreciation.

Slowly, the lieutenant stepped forward. He ignored the two young men. It was the woman, restrained by the Jato, who fascinated him. Her clear white skin. Her eyes, a beautiful pale blue and defiant. The arrogant tilt of her jaw.

Dawda, too, saw it in the man's eyes. His heart began to thump against his breastbone, his breathing became erratic and his hands trembled. Dawda knew what he had to do, and he was scared witless.

Awkwardly, he raised his Kalashnikov and pushed his way to the fore of the mob, stepping between the lieutenant and Sally Richards.

"*Atcha!* You cannot do this! This woman, she is a good woman. She serves my village well! She is good and Allah smiles on her!"

The look of amazement on the lieutenant's face transformed into a sneering mask of contempt and then a violent anger.

"You dare to stop me!" As he spoke, another Jato stepped forward, using his rifle like a quarterstaff to come in hard and low at Dawda's solar plexus. The youngster tried to parry the blow, but moved too late. With the power of a spearthrust, the muzzle of the Jato's gun caught him just above the groin with muscle-wrenching force. His knees folded under him and his Kalashnikov skidded across the floor. Someone snatched it up; the Jatos had won a new recruit.

The lieutenant's gaze moved back to Sally's face. It was rigid like that of a mannequin dummy, the cords of muscle in her neck tensed like thin rope. The terror in her darting eyes was undisguised. Like the nurse Kadi before, he could smell the odour of fear on her. It excited him.

The lieutenant never stopped to think when his curious mixture of loathing and lusting of white women had begun. If he had, he might have recalled the time when he had finished his elementary schooling. With no work on offer, he had spent his youth as a hustler and a gigolo, chasing after the holidaying girls during the country's early days of mass tourism. They had been easy picking, especially those from Sweden who had come looking for the thrill and excitement of *svarte pick*. Black cock.

And the things that those girls had shown him still amazed and haunted him to this very day, leaving secrets lurking deep in the dark recesses of his mind.

He might have recalled the last of those Swedish *toubab* women. A heavily made-up middle-aged crab, who had taken one look at his puny erect penis and laughed hysterically. She was drunk, no doubt, but that did not change the effect of her words on the impressionable youth.

She was an old hand in Sakoto and had dismissed him in fluent Mandinka. "*Kambano*, little boy. *Kambano!*" Fuck off! The ultimate insult.

He had never had a white woman since.

The other thought that did not occur to him, and never had, was that the madness they found in his father and grandfather might be hereditary.

Slowly, he reached a hand towards the nurse in front of him now. Instinctively, she wanted to flinch. To draw back. She forced herself to stay still; not to betray her feelings as his bony hand cupped her rigid chin. His fingertips, still moist with spilled blood, stroked the fine hairs of her skin.

"So soft, *toubab* woman. Fair and soft." He spoke hoarsely, his eyes feasting on her mouth as she unwittingly ran her tongue over her fear-parched lips.

Saliva glistened in the corner of his own mouth.

"Enough of this," she said stiffly, her voice cracked.

"You speak?" The pink gums showed around the big white teeth.

"This is foolish," she said quickly. "It is not the way for a Guinean to behave. It is not dignified. It is shameful in the eyes of Allah."

Something triggered in the smiling black face. Words of his mother; distant words of the Swede who had dismissed him from her service. His nostrils flared and his eyes rolled.

Sally found herself staring at two blank, white eye sockets. The lids closed suddenly, and the big purple mouth began to babble, as though in a trance. "What, *toubab*, do you know of Allah?! Only I speak with Him. You are an infidel, a slut and a whore. You desecrate our land with your ways! Your liquor and dress that is a flagrancy of your womanhood! And your medicines insult our culture and our holy marabou!"

Fear went through Sally like an electric shock. The man was a religious fanatic, mixing Islam fervour and ju-ju beliefs in a crazed and confused amalgam. He was angry beyond reason. She could feel the heat of the anger from his body. The hot smell of him filled her head.

His hand suddenly relaxed its vice-like grip on her chin. Slowly, the sharp nail of his forefinger traced a line across her cheek, then slowly down her neck, along the hardened line of her muscles. It reached the soft hollow of her neck above her chestbone.

She was hypnotised by the burning malevolence in those fathomless eyes.

A tremor reverberated through her rigid body as she realised that his hand was on her breast. His breathing quickened. She felt the cruel kneading motion like a claw. She saw that he was shaking.

The saliva of her spit hit him directly in his left eye.

He did not recoil. His hand dropped from her breast as he snapped a stream of orders in Mandinka to his Jato comrades.

Brian Beavis stared in disbelief, unable to find the words of anger and loathing as two guerrillas twisted the girl around. Placing his foot between her ankles, one of the Jatos spread her legs apart, whilst another squeezed her neck until she bent over one of the drink tables, her face crushed into its wooden top.

"What the fucken' . . . ?" Brian began, only to be brutally silenced with a rabbit-punch in the kidneys, dealt by the Jato restraining him.

The lieutenant was oblivious to the protest. Neither did he hear the muffled pleadings of the girl offered before him, her skirt torn aside to reveal slender, lightly-tanned legs and neat rounded buttocks sheathed in a pair of simple white cotton pants.

As the girl wriggled in protest against the cruel restraining hands, the view excited him. His hands trembled. He had decided to bugger her. He remembered it from his youth spent with the Swedish whores along the coast. The memory burned darkly in his brain. There, in front of his Jatos and the townsfolk of Mansakunda. It would be a fitting punishment for an infidel. Especially as he was sure his men would want to ape his example.

But, as he stepped forward, the memory of her face as she had spat at him switched off something in his mind. Had it been the way she had looked at him? A determined pride? An utter contempt for him?

Suddenly he realised he was physically incapable of doing what he most wanted. Her eyes. The eyes of a witch. She had cast a spell over him. Even as the crazy thoughts tumbled through his mind, he felt his member shrivel to nothing. To hang uselessly between his legs beneath the smart tiger-suit trousers.

He began to tremble in frustrated rage. His eyes rolled and he cursed his mother. There would have to be another way.

The Jatos gasped as they heard the metallic grind as he unsheathed the bayonet at his belt.

It was hot now in the clubhouse. Hot with the humid heat of the crowd, the air fetid with the smell of excited bodies crushed together. Airless. Sweat began to roll heavily down his forehead. It stung his eyes as he tried to focus on the damp vee of her clenched buttocks.

He swung back his hand, his fingers tight on the haft above the blade.

With a sickening thud, the heavy metal of the butcher's cleaver fell without warning. It sunk easily through the thick bone and gristle of the lieutenant's wrist.

As the debauched scene had been taking shape before their eyes, no one had noticed Dawda regain his strength. Only lightly held by a Jato, who had never seen a half-naked *toubab* woman before, it had been easy to wrench himself free. Springing to his feet, he had unbuckled the chopping knife he always carried.

For a moment, the crowd was paralysed with shock as the lieutenant's severed fist thudded dully onto the floor, still grasping the bayonet.

The man's eyes bulged in disbelief at his remaining stump, as the main artery squirted an obscene fountain of crimson blood over the prostrate woman.

Dawda had landed at the man's feet and now found himself showered in the warm spray. The first Jato to recover leapt forward, flailing a machete above his head. Dawda raised a protective arm as the steel blade swept down. Onlookers shrieked in horror.

The machete jolted to a standstill in mid-flow as the short burst from the Armalite blew a fist-sized hole in the Jato's abdomen. He staggered backward under the force of the shot, and collapsed in an untidy heap.

John Belcher appeared from behind the bar, where he had broken through the rear window.

"*Abanta!*" Finish, he warned, waving the barrel of his sub-machine gun. A coil of blue smoke escaped its tip.

The crowd at the door began to stir, drawing aside as Corporal Mark Benjamin came through the main entrance.

Sally Richards was on the floor, oblivious to the pool of

blood in which she sat. The two Jatos who had restrained her raised their hands.

Roughly, Brian pulled himself free of his captor. Kevin did likewise, and rushed over to comfort Sally. Her cries had become hysterical.

"Christ," Benjamin breathed as his eyes fell on the girl's naked, blood-soaked legs. "What the hell's been going on here?"

"Don't ask," Belcher grated. He had seen the last moments. "Let's just say we didn't get here a second too soon."

"Too fucken' right," Brian replied, snatching up one of the fallen weapons.

Belcher shook his head. "Forget it, Brian. Just give me a hand. My Mandinka is piss-awful. Tell the Jatos to get to one side, will you? Leaving their guns behind."

As the disarmed Jatos began lining up against the wall, a curious sanity seemed to return. Half-a-dozen elder townsmen approached and began gabbling away at the two SASmen.

"What do they want?" Belcher asked Kevin.

"They're ashamed at what happened. They want to punish the Jatos for you."

Benjamin scowled. "Pity they didn't do something at the time."

"They're confused," Kevin explained. "And scared."

"So am I," Belcher returned. "I tell you, I'm sorely tempted, but it would only start a blood feud. I expect they're all related to each other."

"Taking prisoners, are we?" Benjamin sneered in disgust. "We can't get this lot back in the Gemini."

Brian interjected: "They've got lorries outside."

A slow smile crossed John Belcher's face. "Good. Split them up. Some in each. And let them keep their bloody ribbons. We'll use them as hostages for our safe journey back to Sakoto.

"Let's get things organised. It'll be better to travel at night. Africans tend to like their sleep." He turned to Brian. "By the way, who was our hero? The guy with the meat-chopper. I've seen him before somewhere."

"A boy called Dawda. He comes from Massang. The son of the late alkali."

"Ah, yes, I remember," Belcher said. "But what's his game? According to Fraser that was the bloke who betrayed his recce mission. Can't be two of them. He was at the Jato camp."

"Perhaps he's changed sides," Brian said absently, scratching at his beard. It was reaching the itchy stage. "There's a lot of divided loyalties."

That didn't cut much ice with Belcher. "Well, I'd like a talk with the little bugger. Hero of the hour, or not."

Benjamin shook his head. "Looks like he's done a bunk. He probably guessed we'd suss who he was, so he fucked off."

"As well for him," Belcher snarled. "If Lionel Witcher and Rod Bullock are dead, then it's down to him." He put the thought from his mind. "Come on. No use crying over spilt milk."

The prisoners were taken outside to the trucks and Sally Richard's patient was made comfortable in one of the cabs. Belcher returned to the near-deserted building. He found the VSO nurse leaning against a wall, still trembling, despite the tattered greatcoat a Guinean had given her. She stared blankly at the lieutenant who sat curled in a corner. He was mumbling incoherently as he tried to staunch the bloodflow from his stump with a rag someone had given him.

"I don't know what they were going to do." Her voice was a whisper. Her eyes flickered to the SASman's face. "I couldn't see. Do you understand? I couldn't see what was happening behind me."

He pressed his lips against her cheek. Her skin was cold. She didn't seem to notice. "Forget it, Sally. This is the sort of thing that happens when the world goes mad. Forget it."

"I've never hurt these people." Empty.

"This sort of evil is contagious, Sally. Let's go outside now. It's all over. We're driving back to Sakoto."

He noticed Brian Beavis lingering and beckoned him over.

"Take Sally out, Brian."

The young VSO nodded and put his arm around the girl. "What about him? Is he coming, too?"

He indicated the pathetic hunched figure of the lieutenant who sat hugging his long angular legs. Like a broken clotheshorse.

"No," Belcher said quietly. "We are the last three. Go now."

Brian understood. Outside the air was cool and fragrant. It was just three minutes before John Belcher joined them at the waiting trucks.

13

Dawn found Tac HQ at The Oceanic looking like a battle-field itself.

Rows of dirty coffee cups lined the spare table like ranks of a white china army. The occasional casualty was lying on its side, contents spilled. Cigarette stubs were littered in between, spent ammunition. The air was thick with stale smoke and the acrid smell of unwashed bodies. Their exhausted owners, black and white soldiers alike, were curled in any available corner, snatching a few hours' sleep before the new day brought a fresh flood of reports.

On cue, a telephone burst into its shrill song and the dead began to wake.

In the adjoining outer office, normally inhabited by the hotel manager's well-manicured secretary, some semblance of orderly life remained.

Acting-Major Johnny Fraser was clean-shaven and wearing freshly-cleaned battle fatigues – fitting dress for an audience with Sir Nigel de Burgh and US Ambassador Brunswick. Only the dark rings around the SAS officer's sunken, blood-shot eyes were an indication of nights without sleep.

Even Sergeant Brummie Turner, sitting casually on the table beneath the large wall-map of Free Guinea, had made the effort to smarten up.

"The situation appears very fluid," Fraser was saying, his soft Edinburgh brogue disguising the weariness in his voice. "Main elements of Jatos have reached as far as Nyantaba, just a few miles from Jakoto Airport. But I've no doubt that advance parties have got much closer to Sakoto itself. Last night there were Jato rabble-rousers in the urban area of Bankama. They held a big torchlight rally in the bus park there in defiance of the curfew. It was nearly over by the time we could muster up enough police to break it up."

Sir Nigel ran a thoughtful hand over his wing of silver hair. "The Jatos got good support?"

"Yes. Very enthusiastic."

"So what's stopping them?"

"Arms. Pure and simple. It's not easy to provide enough arms for the entire revolutionary population. Followers can run around with pitchforks and machetes, but to be effective against a Government, you need a nucleus of modern firepower. So, as each piece of up-country territory is consolidated and resistance crushed, the armed elements can move on."

Brummie added: "The only break to that pattern is when they get additional arms from surrendered PGs or policemen. That's why we've got our own men in the PG Armoury in Sakoto. There's no way that must fall into Jato hands."

Eddie Brunswick fiddled with his bow-tie. "You know why they've so many goddam weapons in the PG Armoury? It was a gift to the President from the Russians nine months ago. Jammeh was delighted at the time. The guy just didn't see what they were up to. I ask you, enough rifles to arm the PGs twice over."

"At least we haven't had too many PG defectors," Sir Nigel reflected. He was desperate to find some glimmer of hope.

"It's still too many," Fraser replied. "And they seem to be causing the worst problems so far. I gather it was Major Badji's mob who killed Fofana and then later busted open the Central Prison. Then more of his followers caused the trouble at Mansakunda last night."

"But what's Jato's main objective?" Brunswick asked. He tried to sound authoritative; it just raised the squeak of his voice a couple of octaves. "The Airport?"

Fraser jabbed a finger at the map. "It's not much use to him. But it is vulnerable, and impossible to defend completely with our scant resources. He's got to be more interested in taking Sakoto. It's got the two things he wants most. State House and the PG Armoury."

A slow, sickly smile crossed Brunswick's face. "Then we've got him. Sakoto is an island and the only access is by the Kebba Bridge." His dark beady eyes turned on Brummie Turner.

"It's mined," the NCO confirmed.

Eddie Brunswick was fidgeting in a discreet ambassadorial manner with his hands intertwined behind his back like two grappling white spiders. "So Jato holds the mainland – with an airport that's useless to him; we hold the capital."

"We?" Fraser asked.

Brunswick didn't choose to hear, and Sir Nigel said: "There are a lot of British nationals on the mainland. And Swedes. They're at those holiday hotels along the coast and the expatriate communities around Bajtenda. They could be in danger."

Johnny Fraser pulled a cigar from his shirt pocket and lit it.

"They could be, but it's probably safer if they stay put. Most of the hotels are away from the built-up areas and off the main axis of the rebels' advance. The main threat will come from the hustlers and muggers who hang around the areas normally. That's why we've put a couple of handpicked PGs at each hotel."

Sir Nigel was unsure. Massacred British tourists were the last thing he needed to crown his distinguished career. "I just hope you're right."

"A few more British soldiers," Fraser retorted acidly, "and you could bloody *guarantee* I was right."

"That is a matter for our Governments."

"*Our?*"

Sir Nigel held his accusing gaze. "Yes, Major, *our*. The British and American Governments."

Fraser's eyes narrowed. "Is this the same *we* who hold Sakoto, whilst Jato Pheko has the mainland? I mean, where do the Guineans fit into all this?"

"Meaning?"

"Meaning that, as Jammeh's authorised chief of security, I have requested British troops on his behalf as a matter of utmost urgency."

Sir Nigel pursed his lips and looked uncomfortable. "The request's been passed on to London. It's under consideration, I believe."

Fraser looked at the two men. "What's the delay? Won't Jammeh agree to stand down?"

The High Commissioner glanced sideways at Eddie Brunswick who had conveniently developed a hearing problem. Without support, Sir Nigel felt cornered. "That remark, Major, was out of order. I shall forget that it even entered your mind, let alone passed your lips!"

With a snort of disgust, Fraser screwed up his half-smoked cigar with force in the overflowing ashtray. He looked up. "There's just one flaw in your scheme, gentlemen, or hadn't you realised? Colonel Kwofie has disappeared. Gone to ground. Unless, of course, he's been given asylum at the US Embassy."

"Major! I've warned you!"

Ambassador Brunswick remembered everything he'd been taught. "Sir Nigel, I guess it's time we had some breakfast. Care to join me at my residence?"

Seconds later, the door shut and Fraser slumped in the typist's swivel chair, his hands outstretched over her typewriter. Angrily, he studied his fingernails.

Brummie Turner stared grumpily at the grinding motion of the overhead fan.

Gingerly, the door opened and the hubbub of activity from the operations room broke the silence. Corporal Bill Mather peered in. "Who's died?"

Fraser looked up.

"You, if you've any more wisecracks," Brummie warned.

The corporal sensed the problem was serious. "If it'll cheer you up, Mark Benjamin and John Belcher have just crossed the Kebba Bridge. They've got two lorryloads of Jato prisoners and the three missing VSOs."

Fraser sat up. "Including Sally Richards?"

Mather grinned. "Yep. They pulled it off. And the *Kebba Queen* should be docking in Sakoto any time."

"That's tremendous news, Bill!"

But the corporal's face didn't stay cheerful. "There could be another problem, boss. They passed through the area by the Agricultural Research Station. Apparently, it was thick with Jatos. They went through like a dose of salts, and it was dark, of course. Someone popped a few shots at them, but nothing serious."

Fraser sensed that the corporal was holding something back. "And?"

Mather's ginger moustache twitched. "They came across a PG jeep. The occupants had been, well, mutilated. I think it could have been the two we sent to the Station yesterday . . ."

"Jesus!" Fraser was on his feet. "You mean they hadn't radio'd in?"

Mather shrugged. "I'm sorry, boss. I didn't realise. There was a lot going on yesterday. I've just been through everything we received yesterday. There doesn't appear to have been any communication from them."

It took considerable effort for Fraser to contain his anger. Brummie didn't try.

"F'Chrissakes, Bill, what'y fuckin' playin' at?!"

"There were more important things going on yesterday . . ."

Fraser waved the protest aside. "Just get me a vehicle around the front of the hotel. Pronto."

"You can't go alone," Mather protested.

"We've no one else to spare."

Brummie was on his feet. "I'll get tooled up."

"Certainly not you!" Fraser snapped. "You're second-in-command."

"My girl's there, too . . ."

The minibus 'bush taxi' ground up the road towards Mansakunda on three cylinders.

With his bulky frame crushed between two plump village women, it had been an uncomfortable ride for Ian Hammond as the grossly-overloaded vehicle struggled on its way towards the coast. But, frankly, he was just thankful to have escaped from Serreba at last. He had been trying for two days, since he had slipped away from the house of the politician Fofana.

It hadn't been easy to find transport. Most vehicles had

been commandeered by the Jatos, and those that hadn't were without fuel.

Eventually, he had found a resourceful 'bush taxi' owner who had driven up from Sakoto and got caught up in the rebellion. Now the man was desperate to get back to his business interests in the capital before his brothers and uncles squandered his hard-earned wealth.

He had few takers for the exorbitant fare he was charging to cover the cost of the black market petrol.

Finally, he settled with Hammond on a fare ten times higher than any other passenger was able to afford.

It went against Hammond's parsimonious nature; more to the point, it cleaned him out. He was penniless. But he was just pleased to be alive. For a day, he'd lain low, sleeping rough in the bush until he knew Badji's men had gone. He'd anticipated trouble but the news of Fofana's murder had still been a shattering blow.

That there was a connection between Fofana and the Jato organisation, Hammond had soon realised. The politician was the political front; the acceptable face of terrorism. Like the Sinn Fein and the IRA. At first, he had little idea of Rubashëv's role in events but, as the Jato campaign gathered momentum, he had gradually been more forthcoming. One night, over a shared bottle of Hammond's Scotch, the man had more or less outlined the entire plan. On the eve of victory, he had felt safe and not a little self-congratulatory. Even then, he had glossed over the finer details.

The murder of Fofana had been one of those finer details.

Still Ian Hammond couldn't work out why. But what he did know was that anyone who could have a man like Fofana murdered in cold blood didn't deserve to run a country. Even a poxy little West African state like Free Guinea.

As the sprawling urban township of Mansakunda came into view, Hammond wondered if he wasn't already too late to stop events. He knew roughly what the masterplan was, but not the correct timetable. He wondered whether to try and reach the British High Commissioner, but decided against it. He never did get on with the jumped-up figures of the British Establishment. Public school and all that. No, he decided, he'd give his information to the SASman. The officer called Fraser. He might be military, but at least he was Scottish, so he couldn't be all bad.

The minibus squeaked to a halt by a petrol station, where the driver began haggling for a top-up of fuel. After fifteen minutes, a jerry-can was produced, its contents siphoned clumsily into the tank. The driver got a dousing down his trouser legs.

A Guinean in his twenties began talking to the minibus driver earnestly. A fare was discussed. Someone was driving a hard bargain. Pointless really, as there was no room for any more passengers.

Hammond was wrong. Incredibly, everyone squeezed up still further and the man climbed aboard. The driver followed, and the stench of petrol with him.

As the minibus got under way, Hammond's eyes met those of the new arrival. His heart froze. It was the Jato guard who had protected Fofana before the arrival of Major Badji.

The boy they called Dawda.

Bankama was a time-bomb.

It was the second largest township in Free Guinea with sixteen thousand inhabitants huddling in a vast decaying sprawl of corrugated-iron ghettos that straddled the main road to Sakoto. It had grown with as much order as iron filings drawn to a magnet, around the new light industrial estate to the north. It attracted those who could get no work in the capital or find anywhere to live in its overcrowded slums. The promise of work in the factories was irresistible.

But the reality turned out to be somewhat different. There were few enough jobs to go around and they were, naturally enough, creamed-off by the fortunate Guineans who had completed their basic education. Others set up shop in the vast market place to serve the needs of the mushrooming community. In typical fashion, every man tried for a slice of the business action to pay to feed his wife and family. As a result, every deal had a dozen wheeler-dealer middle-men doing 'business', and taking a cut along the line. It was left to the business-wise Lebanese and Mauritians to clean up, whilst the most successful Guinean still eked out his existence, living by his wits.

Meanwhile, the police made a thorough nuisance of themselves in order to earn their bribe money, especially at the end of the month when their pay packets failed to arrive. Every food price increase and new tax seemed to be directed at the inhabitants of Bankama.

The place was a hotbed of discontented, unemployed young Guineans educated enough to know there was supposed to be a better life. Somewhere. So it was hardly surprising that the seeds of the Revolution found fertile ground. And, when the inmates from the Central Prison, freed by the advancing Jatos arrived, there was a cause for great celebration. Not all were real criminals. Many were old friends and relatives who had been picked up by the police on some trumped-up charges because they wouldn't – or couldn't – pay the bribe money. All night, the wild parties had continued in the ghettos. In the misty early morning air, the scent from the palm-wine and the sweet smell of marijuana still lingered with the flower blossom. No one had slept; no one had wanted to. Expectation was like caffeine in the blood. By ten o'clock, the narrow streets were filled to brimming with people. But shops weren't serving; people weren't buying. Everyone just stood around, waiting. It seemed that the entire population of the town was out. Waiting for something.

At ten-thirty, Bankama exploded.

Johnny Fraser hit the hooter and drove around the corner in a four-wheel drift. Women in their brightly-coloured dresses scattered as the white Dormobile fish-tailed, regained its traction and tore off down the mainstreet.

"Jesus, boss," Brummie Turner grumbled. "I just shit myself then. Steady on."

Fraser peered through the fly-spattered windscreen. "Didn't you see them? Jatos. On the corner. I didn't want to give them time to ask questions."

"You didn't."

Fraser grunted. It was a thin disguise. A white Dormobile and white jackets borrowed from the waiters of The Oceanic. Hardly enough to stand up as an ambulance under scrutiny. The only equipment they had on board wasn't medical: just a pair of small Hocklers and a handful of L2 fragmentation grenades. Fraser had his weapon stashed below the seat. Brummie had his in the sports bag on his lap. Just in case.

"Like a fuckin' football crowd," he observed.

Despite urgent hooting they had slowed to a walking pace, as the sea of pedestrians crushed in around them. The nearby mosque was doing brisk business; no doubt telling the population that Allah was with the Revolution. Fraser nosed the vehicle on as fast as he dared. Heads turned in curiosity but no one attempted to allow them passage.

"Road-block, boss," Brummie warned. "Just ahead. Police."

"There aren't supposed to be any police road-blocks."

"Perhaps they're sellin' tickets for their ball?"

"Or using the chaos as a chance to screw the locals."

"More like," Brummie agreed.

"That we can do without. Can we get round it? Up a side-alley?"

"Sorry, boss. Too late. We've just passed it."

At last the crowd thinned across the dusty road between rows of stalls and the corrugated-iron compound beside the brick police-post. A tall blue uniformed Guinean stood beside the small *Police STOP* notice in the centre of the tarmac strip. Half-a-dozen vehicles were pulled over to one side. Fearsome debates were in progress between protesting drivers and implacable gendarmes.

The policeman flagged them down with his MAT sub-machine gun.

"Here we go," Brummie muttered.

Fraser leaned out of his window and smiled. "Morning, officer. How are you?"

The man was unimpressed. He stepped back and glanced along the side of the vehicle, then back in at the two occupants. "What are you?"

"Ambulance." Fraser kept the smile going. "We're doctors. We have to get to a sick patient. We must go now."

The policeman sniffed and peered over Fraser's shoulder into the back. "You got medicine? Drugs?"

"No. We carry patients. No drugs. Just transport."

The blackman's eyes fixed on his. "You think I'm fool?

338

All doctors carry drugs." He indicated the windscreen. "Where's your licence?"

God knows, Fraser thought. He knew for a fact that they were supposed to have been issued to all owners by January 1st. It was now nearly February and he knew that they still hadn't been printed, let alone distributed. This character either didn't know, or didn't want to. "I'm just the doctor. Ask the hospital."

"It is driver's responsibility. You think because you're a whiteman, you can ignore the rules of our country?"

"No, no. I'm sorry. I shall speak to the hospital as soon as I get back. I'll ask them. No problem." He tried to make light of it.

"This is not good enough." The policeman wiped his nose on the back of his hand, thought for a moment, then stooped forward. "You give me money for my trouble."

Fraser raised his hands, palms out. "Sorry, no money." It was true. "Brummie?"

The NCO shook his head. "Left in a rush."

"You give me cigarette."

"I give you fuckin' thick ear," Brummie growled under his breath. "What you give me?"

The policeman was not amused. "You pull over. I keep you here. All day if I want, you see."

Suddenly a commotion broke out at the roadside. A lorry-driver standing by his cab yelled at a gendarme. In return for his insolence, the officer prodded him vigorously in the chest with his forefinger. More shouts. Sunlight glinted on a blade in the driver's hand. Before he could raise his rifle, the gendarme squealed and staggered backwards. A thick red goo oozed from the front of his tunic.

A roar of approval and laughter went up from the gathering of onlookers. The policeman left the Dormobile and moved towards the scene, his MAT levelled; other officers joined him.

Someone in the crowd yelled in Mandinka: "Long live the Jato! Kill Jammeh's police!"

A shot cracked through the air, clear above the hubbub. The lorry driver clutched his face and pitched forward, dead.

Bankama detonated in a ripple of explosions. As though from nowhere, armed guerrillas wearing yellow bandanas appeared. The gendarmes took flight, backing off rapidly to the sanctuary of the police-post, dragging their luckless colleagues behind them. Another shot reverberated through the air. The policeman who had held up the Dormobile collapsed like a rag doll. The others dropped the dead man and ran, firing indiscriminately into the heaving crowd which was closing in. They looked mean and ugly. Cheers and jeers, punctuated by screams of terror, filled the dusty air.

"Christ, boss, let's get out of here!"

The Dormobile was jammed up with a lorry in front of it and a taxi that had nosed up to its rear bumper. Fraser selected reverse and stamped on the accelerator. The big tyres bit the tarmac and threw the vehicle backwards. The rear doors buckled and glass shattered over the interior as the van crunched into the taxi's bonnet. Fraser kept his foot down. The stink of burning rubber and burnt petrol drifted into the cabin as the Dormobile ploughed backward, grinding resistance aside.

The air was alive with ricocheting bullets as a full-blooded firefight broke out between Jatos and policemen.

Suddenly the windscreen shattered, blotting out the view, like an instant hoar frost. Fraser punched his fist through the glass crystals, ripping clusters of them away with bleeding hands. Changing gear, he accelerated forward, hooting loudly as he swung onto the opposite side of the road to get clear.

Yelling Jatos with angry faces leapt in his path, screaming obscenities. He drove on. An axe thudded into the soft metal of the door, buckling it, and bounced off.

Fraser swerved to avoid a child.

"Watch it!" Brummie yelled.

A brightly-coloured minibus 'bush taxi' was coming the other way, turning into the main street from the up-country highway.

Fraser spun the wheel and the vehicle careered back to its own side of the road, just clipping the snout of the 'bush taxi'.

Simultaneously, both vehicles were caught in a murderous cross-fire. The two SASmen heard the hungry shells chew into the bodywork, and felt the sickening lurch as the tyres blew. The bodypan of the Dormobile went down like a lift in a shaft. It tilted over, the left-hand side hit the road, bounced and the entire vehicle slewed across the road in an arc. It came to rest in a drifting spume of red dust.

"I'm trapped!" Fraser gasped. The steering wheel had jammed him in the stomach, coming up under the ribcage and pinning him against his seat.

Using both hands, Brummie wrenched the wheel free, twisting it aside with a savage, urgent strength.

"No bones broke?" he hissed.

Fraser gasped and shook his head. Trembling, he hauled himself across the tilted cabin and out of his window. Painfully, he clambered over the buckled door and dropped down beside the underside of the vehicle. A wheel still spun freely, like a roulette game. Thirteen red, unlucky for some.

Brummie Turner dropped down beside him, carrying his sports bag.

"You forgot somethin', boss."

Fraser took the Hockler and cocked it. "Thanks. I'm slipping."

"You all right?"

"Dazed and a bit bruised, that's all. It's nothing."

Still crouching, they surveyed the scene. The crowds had vanished for cover in the maze of ghettos and market stalls. A steady rain of fire zipped back and forth across the road. The Jatos were giving the police-post a hard time.

Thirty yards away the 'bush taxi' had buried its nose into a vegetable stall. Anxious faces peered out of the windows. One of them was white, bearded.

"Isn't that Ian Hammond?" Fraser asked.

Brummie glanced across, but wasn't interested. "This is no time for fuckin' playing Spot The Face."

A bullet twanged into the suspension of the Dormobile above their heads and bounced off the underparts like a pinball before it spent itself.

"This is bloody dangerous, boss. And if that petrol tank goes . . ."

"Okay."

"Where to?"

Fraser glanced across to the nearest side alley. "We'll have to 'tab' it." Army slang for walking; *Tactically Avoiding Bullets*. "Shanks's pony down the back way. Away from the main street. It can't be more than five miles."

Brummie said: "A piece of piss." He wasn't smiling.

They heard the noise of the gunfire five miles away at the Agricultural Research Station.

"I can't understand it," Mo said. She let the curtain drop back into place. "I was sure Johnny would do something. Even if he couldn't come himself, I thought he'd send someone."

Ralph Sinclair stretched out in his armchair. "He'll have a lot on his plate, Maureen. There are a lot of expats to look after. Perhaps he doesn't think we're in danger. It looks as if it's passed us by."

Mo smiled. "I see, Dad. That's why you're keeping the shotgun on your lap, is it?"

He chuckled. "Well, can't be too careful."

Insect didn't understand the joke, but she giggled nervously. She was seated on the settee with the baby on her lap, still feeling uncomfortable in such luxurious surroundings. Opposite her, Diamante was sitting in a classically demure pose. Her discomfort was in realising that her pink dress was far too short for the company of these respectable *toubabs*. And she could never be sure when Insect was looking at her with her crossed-eyes. It was very unnerving. She wished desperately that Broomie would come.

The knock on the door was gentle.

Mo and her father exchanged glances. Her eyebrows raised. "Perhaps that's Johnny." She turned to the window. "Sunday? Sunday!"

Sunday jumped from the seat where he had fallen asleep in the warm pool of sunlight.

"For goodness' sake, Sunday, you're supposed to be keeping watch! Can't I trust you for anything?"

Still groggy with sleep, he looked puzzled as he peered out. "There is no one here. I cannot see no one."

"Of course you can't see the door from here. That's why you're supposed to be watching who approaches."

She turned towards the hallway, tucking her T-shirt into the top of her jeans as she walked. Instinctively, she wanted to look her best.

Ralph Sinclair was on his feet. "Careful, Maureen, it might not be him."

She laughed brightly. "Well it's certainly not the dreaded Jatos knocking timidly like that . . ."

She reached the door, unslid the bolts and threw it wide.

Her mouth dropped in astonishment.

The towering, muscled bulk of Jato Pheko filled the doorway. Behind him, stood two khaki-clad rebels; they were armed and wore yellow bandanas.

"Kali?" A smile hovered uncertainly on her lips as she took in the sight. She had been used to seeing him in Western clothes or the vets' overalls he used when helping her. The skin waistcoat and the broad, bared chest, blueblack and lustred with sweat whipped at her senses. He had changed almost beyond recognition. The head shaven in Islamic fashion.

"Are you going to ask me in?" He spoke quietly.

"I . . . I . . . Kali . . ." she hesitated. "I don't understand . . ." Her eyes flickered beyond him to the Jatos.

"Who is it?" Ralph Sinclair's voice came from the living room. She didn't hear it.

"Let me come in," Pheko said, "and I will explain."

She was drawn by his eyes. They burned into her subconscious, just how she remembered them. A tight feeling contracted in her chest like a small fist.

Her head inclined nervously towards the Jatos. "Are you with them?"

He smiled gently. "No. They are with me."

As she stepped back to let him in, he snapped brief orders to them in Mandinka. They nodded immediately; instant obedience.

"Who is it?" Sinclair repeated.

Mo stepped into the room. "It's Kali."

"Kali? Our Kali?" He was amazed; he hadn't heard from the boy; no letter to say he'd finished his studies in Moscow.

He certainly wasn't expecting the tall, well-built figure who followed his daughter into the room. The natural presence; the hint of arrogance. He seemed a completely different person from the shy, veterinary assistant he remembered. "Is it you, is it, Kali? By God you've changed . . ." Instinctively, he held out his hand.

The blackman didn't seem to notice it.

Hesitantly, Mo said: "Dad, I think Kali is with the Jatos." Her voice quavered slightly and she realised that she was trembling.

Sinclair's mouth dropped open. It was impossible. But maybe not. That would explain the man's strange dress, his transformation. Suddenly taken with panic, Sinclair backed towards his chair where the Holland & Holland lay across the arms.

"Please don't, Mr Sinclair!" Pheko had raised his voice only slightly, but it carried unmistakable authority and menace.

Sinclair paused, looking at the dark anger in the other's eyes.

"There are two of my Jatos on the door, and a dozen more around your compound. All armed. If anything happens to me, they will kill you."

"I – I don't believe it." Sinclair was stunned. "What do you mean *your* Jatos?"

Not a trace of a smile touched Pheko's lips. "I am the man they call the Jato. Jato Pheko."

"You?" Sinclair half-snorted with disbelief. "The bloody Lion of Freedom. You're pulling my leg . . ."

"Dad," Mo warned. Somehow she knew it was true.

Pheko turned his head, sparing a mere glance for the dumbfounded expressions on the faces of Diamante and Insect, before his eyes narrowed like a cat's as he focused on Sunday. The boy was frozen, petrified, a sprinkling of sweat on his brow and upper lip. "Hallo, Sunday."

The boy couldn't speak. He tried to smile, but it looked crooked and sick.

"Tell them, boy," Pheko demanded. "If you value your life, tell them who I am. Confirm it."

Sunday nodded. "It is true, Mr Sinclair. This man is Jato."

344

Sinclair's thick eyebrows knitted together in a deep frown. "How the hell do you know, Sunday? Don't tell me you're one of them?"

"He *was*," Pheko answered. "But he thinks twice. That is why he trembles like a woman. He betrays me."

"Good God," Sinclair muttered. The world had gone mad.

Mo had regained some of her composure. "Why have you come here, Kali? We have never done anything to hurt you."

This time he did smile, and for the first time, the hard face seemed more familiar. "To assure you that you will not be harmed. There is much trouble, much fighting. My Jatos reach Bankama now. It will soon be over. However, I wish to assure you there will be no harm to you peoples. I will leave Jatos to guard you."

"We don't need your bloody guards, thank you!" Sinclair snapped.

Pheko's mouth twitched. Nowadays, he wasn't used to being spoken to in such tones. Then his features softened. "I think it is the best. It is a problem in such circumstances. There are bad elements. Deserters from Jammeh's Guards. And prisoners have been let free. Those people may wish to harm you."

"I see," Mo said.

Sinclair sank back into the arms of his chair. He felt like a punch-drunk boxer. After all he had done for the young Kali, helped and encouraged him, all of this now seemed like a personal insult.

He looked up. "Why all this, Kali? What in God's name made you do it? The upheaval and the financial ruin this will mean for your country. The lives that'll be lost. Innocent men, women and children. We've heard the gunfire. They must be out there dying already."

"Freedom has its price." Pheko's voice was cold, distant. "There is always a price."

"Didn't I teach you the value of life when you were here?" Sinclair persisted. "Didn't I tell you that every form of life is sacred, however lowly? Nothing is worth the slaughter you will make happen."

Pheko turned his head towards the window. The light

345

caught the side of his face, emphasising the strongly-moulded and determined line of his jaw. As he gazed into the compound, they knew that he was reliving the days of his youth spent there. So long ago, it seemed.

"I remember one day," he said, "when I was helping Miss Sinclair to prepare some apes for their return to the wild. Chimpanzees. They had been held in captivity since birth and now we help to get them back to the wilds. To teach them to survive."

"I remember," Mo said quietly. She found herself under the spell of his words. "There were three at the time. One became very sick."

"Yes, very sick. And you arranged with Jammeh's Government to have an expert come down from Dakar very quick. To fly in. And he gives his diagnosis. The chimpanzee has malaria."

"Yes." She gave a small smile. "He had injections and he was saved . . . In fact, he is still around up-country at Kunkunda Island. I see him sometimes."

Pheko didn't seem to hear her. His eyes were slits, as though trying to see some distant horizon. "And I understand about our children in Free Guinea who die of malaria every year. And I wonder for them, how many have doctors flown in from Dakar . . . ?" He turned then to Ralph Sinclair. "That is what you teach me about the preciousness of life!"

The room fell into a hushed and uncomfortable silence.

Sinclair didn't trust himself to speak for a moment. What could he say? Kali would never understand.

At last, he made his decision. "You have told us why you've come, Kali. To promise us protection. We'd rather not have it, but we seem to have little choice. Nevertheless, I must thank you for your consideration. But I think we probably have nothing else to say to each other. It is best, I think, that you go."

A fire seemed to glow like bright embers deep in Pheko's eyes. "You do, old man, do you? Still you give your orders to me like the old days. Always so superior. Always you know best. Treat the blackman like a naughty child and that is good. Firm but kind."

"You'd best go, Kali."

Pheko's eyes darted momentarily towards Mo. "I also came here for another reason."

And, as he spoke, Mo's heart fluttered and sank. She knew that the most sacred and precious secret of her life was about to be prised open to the world.

His eyes travelled across the room to the sofa where Insect sat looking bored with the half-caste child.

"I have also come to see my son."

Another stray round crashed into the pottery wares on the market stall above their heads. An avalanche of shattered pieces cascaded over them.

From their position, prone in the dust beneath the stall, they had an uncomfortable half-view of the withering crossfire. Before them, dozens of bodies lay sprawled in the road. Policemen, PGs and Guineans. Some wore the yellow of the Jatos. Some didn't. No one seemed to care.

Beside Ian Hammond, the black youth watched wide-eyed with his hands over his ears. It was just his luck, the Scotsman mused, that he should have been thrown together with the one 'bush-taxi' passenger he had wanted to avoid. Although, strangely, the Guinean had not recognised him – or pretended not to.

Hammond made a decision. He nudged the youth. "Listen, lad, Ah know who y'are! An' y' know me. Ah dunna know y'game, but if we dunna get oota here soon, we're no gonna get out atall!"

Dawda looked up, unsure. "You are with the Jatos?"

"*Me*, laddie, no bleddy way!" Crazily, Hammond found himself laughing. "Ye're th' only Jato around here."

"No more."

Hammond didn't follow. "You were there when they killed Fofana?"

Dawda looked awkward. "Yes. That is why I leave. Now I am no Jato."

"We gotta get away from here," Hammond repeated aloud. But he was blessed if he knew where to. It was still a good fifteen miles to Sakoto where he might find the British soldiers. And that was assuming he was able to cross the Kebba Bridge.

Dawda could have been reading his thoughts. "My brother is near here. He has a house. He is a good man, and he will look after us. No problem."

Hammond nodded towards a MAT sub-machine gun that had been dropped in the road by a dead PG. "You can handle a gun, lad, can't ye?"

Dawda shook his head vehemently. "No, man, never again! I do not want to kill my brothers an' my sisters. I have seen enough of this. All these people shooting, they are all fucked-up. This thing is bad."

"Okay, okay," Hammond retorted, "Ah get the message. Well, let's jest get the hell out."

Once into the back streets of the ghettos, Hammond felt safer. There was a strangely unreal quality about the place, as they rushed through the dusty, sun-baked maze. Turn after endless turn, Dawda threaded his way expertly through the back-doubles, where mostly women and children stood gossiping in groups. Probably their menfolk were on the main streets, watching the revolution unfold. Some, no doubt, were participating.

The Guinean set a devastating pace that left Hammond panting like a pig as they reached a gap in a compound wall between two corrugated-iron sheds. Chickens shrieked and fluttered as they entered the yard. A blackened pot simmered on charcoal embers and, beside it, a skinny naked child stared up and picked its nose in wonder at the sight of the whiteman. There were flies everywhere and the cloying stench of cooking and sewerage hung in the hot air in an excruciating blend of smells.

A plaintive wailing came from the first open doorway in the yard. Dawda ducked inside and Hammond hesitated before peering in after him. The room was dark and hot, the tin walls daubed white and the floor just dust on which a mattress had been strewn. A gross Guinean woman sat in a vast and colourful robe. Her turbanned head was in her hands and she sobbed hysterically.

She was pleased to see Dawda, and threw her arms

around him as though he was a long-lost son. For a few moments, she gabbled in Mandinka, punctuating her story with bursts of tears and much waving of arms. Then she broke down again. She was inconsolable.

Dawda stepped back into the yard; he looked deeply troubled.

"What is it?" Hammond asked.

"My father has been killed in fighting."

"Your father. I thought he was the alkali at Massang?"

"Yes. This man is an uncle. He is my father, too."

"Ah see, he was like a father to ye?"

Dawda nodded absently. "Now, my brother goes to avenge him. My mother weeps that he will die, too."

"Your aunt."

The Guinean didn't hear. "She wants that I find him and bring him back."

Hammond scratched his beard. This was crazy. "Listen, Dawda, he might get killed – but so might we lookin' fer him! It's no a safe place out there."

"You wait. I go."

The Scotsman shook his head in despair. "Listen, Ah'm comin' wi' ye. Ye're the only man who can get me outa this place!"

Together they set off back into the maze. They didn't have far to go before they found themselves at a main road junction where a firefight was in progress for its control. Crowds of men stood around, seemingly unaware of the exchange of live ammunition all around. Out in the centre of the road, an ambulance had pulled up, its tail doors thrown wide. Three white-coated Guinean medics were struggling to get dead and wounded into the back. Around them, bullets were dancing in the dust.

Dawda's eyes widened. "That man! He is my brother!"

Before Hammond could restrain him, he had sprinted out into the road; the Scotsman felt reluctantly obliged to follow across to where a bearded Guinean in his mid-thirties lay sprawled behind the ambulance. The man was clutching at a bloody patch in his chest.

He reached up a hand and smiled into his brother's eyes. "It is good to see you, man. You see I am hurt."

"Hurt bad?" Dawda asked, taking the man's wrist in both hands.

The answer was a bubbling red froth at his mouth. Pain racked at his body and he fell back into the dust.

"You help me," Dawda called.

"No problem," Hammond found himself saying. They staggered the few feet to the ambulance with the man and heaved him in, squeezing his body into the untidy mass of dead and dying.

A flurry of shots broke from the far side of the street and bullets peppered the road around them.

Hammond grabbed a medic by the arm. "Where'ye takin' these people?"

"Hospital. Sakoto."

"Can we come, too?"

"Sure, man, if you can get in. We need help." Another volley sang overhead. "Just let's go *now*!"

Hammond and Dawda scrambled on top of the groaning bodies, trying to close the doors. The Scotsman slammed them twice. They wouldn't lock. Someone's limp hand was trapped beneath the hinge. He hooked it in with his foot. The lock caught.

With a groan, the ambulance edged forward with its heavy load. Inside the sheet metal hull, it was stifling, with the stench of death and sweat. To his horror, Dawda found himself lying on top of a bloated corpse, the gasses already swelling the body after hours in the sun. He wanted to vomit.

It was then that the stray round hit the ambulance.

With a crackle of splintering glass, it entered the rear window, bounced off the door support strut and slipped into Hammond's temple as easily as a knife through butter.

Immediately, the pain hit him and the sight in his right eye was extinguished. He gasped for air, clutching at Dawda, who looked on in horrified disbelief. The Scotsman knew instinctively that his life expectancy could be counted in minutes. Perhaps only seconds.

He tried with great effort to overcome the excruciating pain that numbed his mind, in order to give Dawda a message. He attempted to emphasise how important it was that it must be taken to the Britisher known as 'The Captain'. That the message was vital. Slowly, agonisingly slowly, as the blood seeped from his eye socket, he tried to concentrate on each word of the message.

Whether or not Dawda understood, he never knew. He died as the ambulance lurched to a halt outside Sakoto Main Hospital.

For his part, Dawda staggered out into the sunlight, gasping for breath and with raging tears streaming down his face. They just poured out of him until he thought they would never stop.

His beloved brother was dead and he felt he had let him down. And the strange Scotsman, too, had been shot right in front of his eyes. Splattering his face with white bone splinters glued to flecks of blood. During that day they had become friends, brothers almost.

Blindly, Dawda wandered away towards the vast urban slums of Sakoto. There were few signs of fighting here, but everyone was expecting it. Everyone was out on the streets. That was why there was no one in his friend's compound when he got there.

It didn't matter. His friend wouldn't mind. There was a standpipe outside the compound which supplied the street's water. He pushed aside a dog that had come to drink and put his head under the tap.

He scooped a handful of water and drank it thirstily, clearing the bitter taste from his mouth.

But, as he stood, the stink of death was still in his nostrils. Inside his head. And he knew it would never go. Again the tears began to roll.

He stumbled into his friend's room. There was a small cupboard where he knew the drink was kept. There had been many parties there. Today, there were three bottles; there must have been some looting going on. It was Scotch, but Dawda scarcely noticed.

He threw himself down on his friend's mattress, yanked the top from the bottle and filled his mouth with the stuff.

An hour later, the bottle lay empty on the floor. Only

then the smell of death left his head. To be replaced by blessed oblivion.

The Jato guard made himself comfortable under the drooping branches of an ironwood tree, enjoying the delicious shade offered by its pale grey-green foliage. There was precious little other shade around the perimeter fence of the Agricultural Research Station as a swathe of vegetation had been cut down as a fire-break.

In the distance, he could hear the faint pop of the rifle-fire. The battle of Bankama was still raging but, in truth, he did not envy his fellow rebels; he preferred it under the tree during the midday heat. Cool. Safe.

As his lids began to droop the Jato suddenly felt the iron jaws of a man's forearm and biceps snap tight around his neck. He tried to scream but the hard flesh crushed in his lips and his larynx. Then he felt the lancing pain just below his ribs. A red-hot poker. It burned inward and upward, into the very centre of his being.

By the time the black blade of the combat knife described a hard, vicious circle around his heart, severing the arteries, he was already unconscious. So, when death came a split second later, he knew nothing about it.

The blade had jammed with suction and it took a moment for Johnny Fraser to work it free.

Brummie Turner joined him. "Okay, boss?"

"Yes." The SAS officer wiped the sticky mess on the dead Jato's shirt and resheathed the knife. The retaining spring-clip gave a reassuring click. "And you?"

"He's sleeping like a babe, boss." In fact, he'd nearly botched it, but there was no point in going into that now. He just made a mental note never to make the same mistake again.

"These two should be enough," Fraser decided. Before them, was a thirty-foot fire-break of red dust. Then an eight-foot wire link fence. Beyond that was a hundred yards of neatly-cultivated onion and lettuce beds which ran almost up to the rear of the Sinclairs' bungalow.

Brummie nodded towards the wire. "Under or over?"

"Got the cutters? Then we'll go through. Less of a target."

There were two Jatos just outside the bungalow, but both were making the best of the shaded verandah at the front.

Quickly, Fraser snaked his way across the red earth tract, head and buttocks low, until he reached a spot where a creeper fanned out across the wire. Its foliage would give him a little cover. Poking the snout of the Hockler through the chain-link fence, he beckoned Brummie.

Seconds later, the NCO was by his side, prostrate, as he worked the blunt jaws of the wire-cutters at the strands of the fence. They gave easily with a slight rasp.

Brummie changed position to give Fraser cover while he ducked through the aperture and began the slow and exposed crawl through the test-beds.

At last Fraser's back was pressed against the cool concrete of the bungalow wall beside an open window. The murmur of voices drifted out. A Guinean was talking softly, too softly to distinguish the words. Then he heard Ralph Sinclair. He sound uncharacteristically angry. No sound of Mo.

It was a further nerve-fraying five minutes before Brummie Turner joined him, and they were able to gain access to the bungalow through a gauze-covered pantry window. Once inside, the sound of voices was much clearer . . .

Ten minutes later, the kitchen door suddenly burst open into the living-room. The hinges shrieked in protest as the timber crashed against the wall, dislodging lumps of plaster.

All heads turned as Johnny Fraser side-stepped briskly into the room, his back against the other wall. Behind him in the doorway, Brummie Turner knelt in readiness to give a solid arc of covering fire.

"FREEZE!" Fraser yelled, the sudden confrontation of half-a-dozen mixed black and white faces momentarily confusing.

The door swung to a standstill then, without warning, the upper hinge gave, and the structure lurched of its own volition, hanging drunkenly.

It took a split second of disbelief before Fraser realised he was actually face-to-face with Jato. Kali Pheko himself. It was surprise enough to find him there at all. What completely threw him was that the large muscled guerrilla was clutching a half-caste baby in his thick forearms. Insect's child.

Immediately, the layout of the room and everyone's position in it registered in Fraser's mind; years of training had made his mental process in evaluating a hostile situation work with mind-blowing precision. An instant mental camera: Kali Pheko with child, standing before sofa. Insect and Diamante seated. Sunday standing by window. Mo and Ralph Sinclair standing together to his left.

Mo gasped. "Thank God, Johnny. I don't believe it."

"If you shoot," Pheko hissed, "I could break the baby's neck!"

He moved his sinewy forearm to cover the baby's face.

"Shoot anyway, Johnny," Ralph Sinclair snarled. "It's his bloody child!"

The words jarred in Fraser's mind. His finger hesitated on the trigger.

"For God's sake, don't risk it, Johnny!" Mo screamed. "It's my baby, too!"

"I warn you, Captain!" Kali Pheko growled, backing away. "Stop and think! This place is surrounded by my men. People will get hurt! Let's talk."

The muzzle of Fraser's gun lowered a fraction. "Put the child down, Kali," he said softly. "Then we can talk all you want."

Mo rushed across the room.

"Careful!" Fraser warned.

She snatched the baby away from Pheko's grip and snuggled it protectively to her breast.

The guerrilla leader looked down pleadingly at Mo. "Believe me, I would not have hurt him. Not for anything!"

But she turned brusquely with her back to him, nursing the child consolingly in her arms as she went to her father's side. As she did so, Diamante recovered from her state of paralysed shock and rushed over to Brummie.

"Broomie! You come! You come!"

The NCO steered her to one side to keep his arc of

fire clear. He looked embarrassed. "Later, love, just stand back, eh?"

"Put your hands on your head, Kali!" Fraser ordered.

Pheko seemed amused. "I am not armed, oh mighty Captain," he sneered.

"I said hands on head!"

Sluggishly, Pheko obeyed.

"Turn. Slowly."

The big man swivelled round and waited as Fraser approached cautiously and checked him out. He was as good as his word, clean.

"Okay," Fraser snapped, "you can bring your hands down. Slowly! And turn around." He flicked a glance towards Brummie. "Keep friend Kali covered all the time. If he as much as breathes too fast, I want him dropped dead."

"It'll be a pleasure, boss."

Fraser said: "Right, Kali, now before you say your two penny-worth, I want to know what's happened to Lionel Witcher and Rod Bullock?"

A sly smile crossed his face. "They are all right, man."

"You're an arrogant bastard," Brummie grated.

"They are both alive and well. That, I promise you."

"Where?"

"With my rear echelons."

"Who the fuck do you think you are?" Brummie snorted. "The soddin' Duke of Wellington?"

"They are under guard at Mansakunda. And I will say they have more understanding of Free Guinea than you two ever will!" He spat contemptuously on the floor.

"Is that all you wanted to say?" Fraser asked sarcastically. "If it is, you needn't have bothered."

The sly smile returned. "You don't even know your own men, Captain. No, I want you to go to Jammeh and tell him to withdraw his PGs and his police."

"Don't talk wet!"

Pheko spoke slowly, that burning look returning to his eyes. "If you kill me, or take me, how long do you think my men will keep your friends alive in Mansakunda? Dear Mr Bullock and Corporal Witcher. Not long, I fear. Besides, as I say, my Jatos surround this place. Even if you use me as hostage, you cannot trust on them not to shoot. *I* shall not tell them." He glanced around the room. "I suspect one or more will not survive if you try to get them back to Sakoto with me."

"Right smart-arse, aren't we?" Brummie jeered.

"He's got a point," Ralph Sinclair added.

"So," Pheko said smugly, "why do you not stop pointing that gun at me and listen. This is not one man's revolution any more, Captain. It is the nation. My commandos, the mullahs, the peoples. I am just a figurehead. You may kill me but, if you do, I will just be a martyr."

The room was still. "Got it all worked out, Kali, haven't you?" Fraser said, his green-grey eyes frosted with anger and frustration.

The Jato shrugged. "It is how things are. People die out there. My peoples. They die, not because of me. They die because Jammeh is finished but will not recognise it. They die because his PGs still fight."

"That's rich!"

"It is also true, *toubab* soldier," Pheko replied evenly. "Take this message to Jammeh. Tell him to withdraw his soldiers to their barracks, that innocent lives will be spared. Tell him he shall be allowed to leave the country without hindrance. That is all. It is a simple enough request. Do this thing and I will give you and these people here safe escort back to Sakoto."

Fraser exchanged glances with Brummie. The dour NCO shrugged. It didn't seem that they had too many options. For once, holding lethal items of hardware didn't make the slightest bit of difference.

Ralph Sinclair saw it, too, and he was seething with frustration. "And what about my daughter's child?"

Pheko raised his eyebrows and smiled. He knew it hurt the old man. "*Our* child. That is a problem. Does he go with you and be a *toubab*? Or does he come with me and become a snivelling Free Guinean? Maybe he knows nothing but poverty and malnutrition with a life expectancy of maybe forty?"

Mo had been trying to avoid Fraser's eyes, but at last they met. She trembled and two tears detached themselves, rolling down her freckled cheeks.

The Scotsman's eyes were deep, fathomless, as they bored into hers, seeking the truth, some explanation.

How, though, could she tell him? Tell the SAS officer that he had awakened a deep emotional and physical need in her when, those years before, they had made love on the tranquil banks of the Kebba River outside Massang. Would he understand how desperate she had been after he had returned so suddenly to Hereford? Back to a life of high adventure in which she played no part.

Trying to escape her loneliness, she had busied herself in her work. She had been helped by the quiet and gentle Kali who was maturing into a handsome young man. His loyalty was never questioned and they had slowly grown to like each other during those lonely weeks on Kunkunda Island.

She grew to rely on him. His cheerfulness in adversity and his natural sense of humour. To trust his strength and his natural skills at hunting and fishing. At keeping them both alive.

Mo Sinclair had always lived and worked alongside black Guineans. Her strict and orderly *toubab* upbringing had never really allowed her to think of the natives as true equals. In the family, they would laugh at the different characters and their moods; in much the same way as they did at chimpanzees and other animals in their care.

Only gradually did she become aware of Kali as a man in his own right. With feelings and emotions. Ambition.

Exactly when she had fallen in love with him, she didn't remember. It must have been happening for some time. But she would never forget the day when she had fallen from the island landing-stage into the swift current of the Kebba. Her shouts for help had brought Kali running from his tent. As strong and powerful and naked as a black bull.

He had plunged into the swirling water without a second's hesitation and caught her in his arms as though she was a mere doll. He had never been taught life-saving, but he managed it effortlessly and she recalled gasping for her life, safely cradled in his left arm, as he struck out easily with his right.

And then sitting, trembling in his arms on the bank as the hot sun dried them. And the smell of him in her nostrils.

The smoothly-muscled black velvet skin against hers. His hardness pressing into her. Natural spontaneous desire. And his smiling purple lips around an irresistible smile. He was so pleased to have her back alive.

Their lovemaking had nearly torn her apart. It had fulfilled her like nothing she had known before. Not even with Johnny Fraser.

But looking across the room at the Scotsman now, her eyes swimming in tears, she knew she had been right. Right to have avoided him while she could. She could see the hurt in his eyes. He would never be able to understand. Never accept that, however much she regretted it, there were two men in her life. She loved them both and always would.

Her voice was a whisper. "It's true, Johnny. Please don't ask any more. You'll be gone from here soon. It won't matter then."

Mo glanced across at Pheko. He was looking at her strangely. That old look of youthful humour and desire was gone. He had changed beyond recognition. Hard. There was almost hate in his eyes, she thought.

He said: "I am sure my son will be proud to grow up with a mother who gave him to a retarded girl and pretended he was hers. Because she was *ashamed* of having loved a black-man!"

"Leave it out!" Fraser shouted irritably. He was confused and bewildered by events. It was like some horrendous personal nightmare.

Mo shook her head. "No, Johnny, I am afraid Kali is right. I didn't even tell my own father. I went away to Kunkunda for six months." She looked up at Ralph Sinclair and pulled a tight smile. "Sorry, Dad, really."

Sinclair nodded gravely. His eyes were moist.

Slowly, Mo stepped forward and handed the small bundle over to Insect who had been looking on bemused. Now she beamed with happiness.

"I'm sure," Mo said, "Insect will be happy to go with you and look after your son."

The baby began to cry.

14

"You mean you actually had him in your gunsights?" Sir Nigel de Burgh blustered.

Captain Johnny Fraser was seated in the elegant drawing-room of the High Commissioner's private residence. The white-coated houseboy had just delivered a silver tray of nightcaps. It was two in the morning.

Standing by the mock-Georgian fireplace, US Ambassador Eddie Brunswick sipped at a bourbon-on-the-rocks. "A mite careless, I must say. I'd give my eye-teeth to have that bastard in custody."

"It wasn't like that," Fraser explained again, wearily. "We had little realistic chance of getting back to Sakoto with everyone and no transport. Using Pheko as a hostage would have been a double-edged sword. It would cut both ways and would have probably ended up with us all dead. Including the Sinclairs."

Sir Nigel sniffed sarcastically at his sherry. "So what was the message Pheko gave you?"

"For Jammeh to withdraw his troops and leave the country. A guaranteed safe passage."

At the fireplace, Brunswick fiddled with his bow-tie. "A bit academic, now, I'd say."

Fraser frowned. "How d'you mean?"

"Of course, you wouldn't know," Sir Nigel said lightly. "It happened whilst you were gallivanting off to the Sinclairs."

"What, for God's sake?"

"Jammeh's gone."

Fraser felt as though he'd been hit between the eyes by an ungloved heavyweight. "What do you mean gone?"

"He flew out of Jakoto earlier this evening. As soon as

it was dark." It was Brunswick who answered. "I guess you might even have passed each other on the road. Lady Precious was with him."

"He's resigned?" Incredulous.

"We'll make an announcement in the morning," Sir Nigel added.

"Where's he gone?"

"London first," the High Commissioner replied. "But then probably on to the States."

Fraser jumped to his feet and glared at Brunswick.

"So you've managed to wheedle your own sodding way at last, have you?"

"Fraser!" Sir Nigel reprimanded. "That is no way to address the Ambassador."

Brunswick waved the verbal assault aside. "One of those things, Major. But it isn't all quite worked out yet. We still can't locate Colonel Kwofie."

Angrily, Fraser snatched a cigar from his pocket; he needed something to calm his fury. "So who's running the bloody country? You two?"

The US Ambassador was unmoved. "Until Kwofie can be found, the Minister of Finance has agreed to be caretaker President." A soft chuckle. "We have enough against him to make sure he relinquishes his temporary title without protest as soon as we find Kwofie. Oh, and, by the way, your services as Special Military Adjutant are no longer required by the Free Guinea Government. Jammeh's last act before he left, you understand."

Fraser lit his cigar and blew a long steady stream into the centre of the room. "All very neat, gentlemen, but it doesn't stop the fighting, does it? I've seen absolute carnage out there in Bankama today. So what about those British troops I requested when I *was* Military Adjutant?"

"Ah, Major, your request, I'm afraid, was turned down by Whitehall," Sir Nigel answered casually. The relish as he took another sip of sherry was unmistakable.

Eddie Brunswick downed his bourbon and wiped his lips with the back of his hand. "The 82nd US Airborne is dropping on Jakoto Airport at first light this morning. Direct flight from Stateside."

"Jesus Christ!" Fraser exploded. "This is unbelievable! You're joking!" But he knew they weren't. He spun on the High Commissioner. "You'll get the bloody Congressional Medal of Honour for this, Sir Nigel, no danger."

The diplomat was unperturbed; he was even enjoying it. "Sorry, Fraser, the simple fact is we can't be seen to invade our old colonies – much as the Guineans may love us and all that. The thing is HMG doesn't *want* to get involved in Africa. We're lucky to be out of the Rhodesia – sorry – Zimbabwe mess at last. We don't want to start again. The US, on the other hand, are keen to stop the spread of Communism, even if it is dressed up like the Jato's Islamic Fundamentalism, or whatever they call it. They consider Free Guinea of vital strategic interest."

In the corner, a white telephone rang.

"Excuse me, gentlemen." Sir Nigel eased himself out of his chair and crossed the room to take the call. For a full minute, he listened, his expression turning to one of grim disapproval. Dark patches were spreading on his cheek.

He put his hand over the mouthpiece. "It's your head-quarters at The Oceanic, Fraser. They want to speak with you. Apparently, Jakoto Airport is swarming with Jatos."

Fraser tossed his cigar into the fireplace as he crossed the deep pile carpet. "Ambassador, when is the 82nd due to drop on Jakoto?"

Eddie Brunswick glanced at his watch. "In three hours. At first light."

The sub-machine gun barred his way.

"No!" The PG was adamant. He looked nervous. "No one goes through! You must understand this."

Dawda was desperate. Mostly he cursed himself for getting drunk and falling into a sleep of the dead for so many hours. Then, when he finally staggered off with a throbbing head to deliver the message from Ian Hammond, he cursed the fact that Captain Fraser was not at The Oceanic Hotel. By chance, he overheard that the British soldiers had gone to Jakoto Airport where Jatos were involved in a big fight with Jammeh's forces.

But now, as he stood with the crowd in the dim pre-dawn

light by the perimeter-gate of Jakoto, he found himself cursing again.

"This is of much importance," he pleaded again. "I have very important message for 'The Captain'!"

"Are you a soldier?"

"No."

"Then you don't come. Only soldiers. You could be Jato. Or a mercenary. No one passes." The gun came up again.

Reluctantly, Dawda stepped back to be absorbed into the crowd which had grown in expectation as soon as the word had gone round that the British soldiers had gathered near the scene of the big battle. Standing on tip-toe, Dawda could just determine the silhouette of the Land Rovers and the shadowy figures standing around them.

Acting-Major Johnny Fraser was running over the last few details of the plan with seven SASmen and a PG officer who commanded a company of loyal guards.

"So the PGs will man a sweep of the airfield using our vehicles in ten minutes. The objective is to use firepower to get the Jatos running for cover. To keep the main airfield clear for the drop. The rebels are poorly armed, most of them just followers, so I don't expect much resistance. My bet is they'll just scoot. If they don't, you must obviously concentrate on any groups that pose a major threat to the drop. Even badly-trained rebels could cause havoc on a drop zone."

The PG officer nodded solemnly; he seemed competent enough.

"Just one thing," Fraser added, "when the Yanks land, you pull back fast. They'll be nervous and confused when they first hit the deck, especially if anyone is shooting at them. They'll fire first and ask questions later. I don't want any unnecessary PG casualties. So once they've landed, pull back and let the Yanks get stuck in. They're seasoned and experienced men."

Fraser turned to the SASmen. "Our task will be to re-take the control tower. That's where the main resistance is. They've got heavy stuff up there. Mortars and machine-guns. Stuff that can reach most parts of the airfield. And they've got a bird's-eye view. So we've *got* to take it out. Any questions on the battle-plan?"

In the darkness, heads shook.

Fraser turned to the figures of Sir Nigel de Burgh and Ambassador Eddie Brunswick, both huddled in overcoats against the chill air.

"Are you gentlemen sure you won't or can't abort the drop?"

Brunswick's squeaky voice came from the smaller of the two bundled figures. "My Government says we go, Fraser. If your boys can keep your promise to clear the control-tower, it's go."

"I said we would *try*," the SAS officer reminded tartly. "Another twenty-four hours' preparation and the time to get more of my men together would give us a better chance."

"In twenty-four hours," Brunswick retorted, "the Jatos will have total control."

"Get on with it, Fraser, there's a good chap," Sir Nigel added. He sounded uneasy.

Suddenly a roar of cheering went up from the crowd that had gathered near the perimeter. Excited shouts and whistles added to the commotion.

"See what's going on, will you, Brummie?" Fraser ordered. "I don't want any trouble now."

The NCO sprinted across the tarmac, the promise of action injecting him with new vigour. Minutes later, he returned, breathless.

"Turn up for the book, gentlemen. The Jato himself has turned up. Thinks he's Big Chief Sitting Bull. He wants to pow-wow. Maybe smoke pipe of peace."

"What? Kali Pheko here?" Sir Nigel demanded.

Brummie grinned mischievously. "I know what you're thinking, sir. Forget it. He's got two armed Jatos with him. I said yes. I thought you'd like to talk."

"Good man," Fraser congratulated.

Sir Nigel began rambling. "I don't want this to prejudice things . . ."

His voice tailed off as a battered open-topped VW Safari broke through the distant line of spectators and drove steadily towards them. Yellow streamers trailed in its wake as it slowed and braked a few paces from them.

Two Jatos climbed out warily, keeping their Kalashnikovs pointing at the sky. White scraps of cloth hung limply from the barrels.

'The Jato' Kali Pheko stepped down after his men with all the regal poise of a newly-crowned monarch.

"Who is British Ambassador?"

"I'm the High Commissioner," Sir Nigel replied tartly, hiding his nervousness. "I suppose you're Pheko? Well, what do you want?"

"I hear that Jammeh goes."

"So?"

"I tell my men to leave this airfield. If you agree to me they will stay away. No more fighting."

"What's yer deal?" Brunswick asked. It sounded like a snarl.

"Jammeh is gone. Put your soldiers into barracks. My Jatos, they put down their guns. Then we have election."

"What?" Fraser couldn't believe his ears.

"No way," Brunswick chipped. "We have a new President to finish off the term until the next election."

Pheko shook his head vigorously. "The people will not take this. All ministers are Jammeh's ministers. They are worse than him."

"The man is not a minister," Sir Nigel explained, sounding like a father consoling an upset child. He would have called it diplomatic.

"Who?"

"Colonel Kwofie, the country's former Head of State Security."

A strange expression passed over Pheko's features. His brow furrowed deeply and his eyes darted from the High Commissioner to the US Ambassador to Fraser. And back. Then a light danced in his eyes, his lips opening in a curious smile. "You joke with me? You should not joke on this."

"I do not joke," Sir Nigel answered.

Pheko threw back his head and bellowed like the lion that gave him his name. Sir Nigel and Brunswick exchanged glances.

The rebel's mirth subsided. "Do you know what Colonel Kwofie is?" he demanded savagely.

"He's a . . . a . . ." Sir Nigel searched for the word.

"A JATO!" Pheko screamed. "He is a Jato! He has done his work for me! For ME-EE!"

The meaning, not the ferocity, with which the words were uttered jarred Fraser's heart like the bolt from a cross-bow. He gulped in surprise, opening and closing his mouth like a floundering fish.

Instantly, the events of the past months flooded into Fraser's mind. All the pieces started to fit. As Head of State Security, Kwofie had been in the perfect position to tarnish Jammeh's name in the minds of the population. And he had done it with a vengeance.

In his mind's eye, Fraser could see the mutilated bodies at Massang. And there were others, many others. All actions designed to drive the inhabitants of Free Guinea into the hands of the Jatos. The liberators.

Ambassador Eddie Brunswick began to look like a sick man. His choice for the new President had the same qualities that appealed to the enemy. A hard man, hard but malleable, if you were prepared to pay enough money into his private overseas bank account. And Brunswick knew full well it was not just the simple Guinean vet called Kali Pheko that Kwofie worked for. It was those beyond who pulled the puppet's strings in Libya. And, beyond that, in the minaret towers of the Kremlin.

"Oops!" Brummie Turner said.

Sir Nigel scowled.

"We're running out of time," Fraser reminded.

Eddie Brunswick had recovered slightly. "*If* what you say is true, Pheko, then we do not have much option. I guess you reckon you'll sweep the board with an election now . . ?"

It was a rhetorical question and Pheko knew it. He smiled smugly.

Fraser said: "Before there's any deal, Kali, I want Corporal Witcher and Rod Bullock delivered to the British High Commission. Unharmed."

A sarcastic smile crossed Pheko's lips. "I anticipate this.

They are beyond the perimeter, there. Their release will be my pledge of honour."

Brummie Turner stepped forward. "Pardon me, but what about your chums in the control-tower? Can you tell them to surrender themselves?"

"They are not Jatos," Pheko said.

"They call 'emselves Jatos."

"They are not Jatos," Pheko repeated. "They are deserters. Jammeh's Guards with a man called Major Badji. They cause much trouble. Kill many. They do not obey me."

"What's his game?" Fraser asked.

Pheko shrugged. "They are just bandits."

Fraser wasn't so sure. Bandits went in for looting and robbery during civil unrest. Apart from Jakoto's abysmal 'Duty Free' shop, there was nothing much the terminal and control-tower had to offer.

He glanced at his watch. "In that case, gentlemen, it's time to go."

Against the yellowing sky, the small terminal complex resembled a model building on a child's railway layout.

"Made of Lego," Johnny Fraser recalled Brummie's earlier apt description as he studied it through the binoculars.

No doubt it was the prefabricated laminate materials that gave it a fragile plastic look. That, and its toytown structure with four humped roof sections which looked, for all the world, like giant cardboard lavatory rolls cut down the middle, and glued on the top of the plastic walls. The cluster of feathery palm trees added to the effect of unreality.

The roof humps ran lengthwise from the front of the building where the plate-glass doors and windows to the entrance lobby now lay shattered on the steps after the previous night's fighting.

For the last time, Fraser ran his gaze along the line of the roof humps to the flat-roof administration block that adjoined the rear of the two-storey building. On top, was the unmistakable angled glass bowl of the control-tower.

It was that commanding position which had to be re-taken in the remaining minutes before the first American Starlifter appeared on the western horizon.

No movement had been detected from the tower for the past hour. However, Fraser couldn't rely on the rebels staying drowsy as the growing light gave them something to look at.

One thing he definitely did not want them to see was the bright red fire-engine that was now parked behind a screen of bushes, its proud Guinean crew resplendent in shiny black helmets and gold badges. Unfortunately, their immense pride extended to ringing the brass bell all the way from Sakoto, despite orders to the contrary.

The chief had been delighted to have his help enlisted by the British soldiers, but it had somewhat flustered his crew who had previously had little cause to use the turntable ladder in the low-level shanties of the capital.

Despite the chief's profuse assurances, Fraser remained unconvinced that they could back the vehicle up to the flat roof of the admin block with four SASmen perched on its raised half-ladder. But it was a worry he would just have to live with. In the same way, he would have to accept that it would be left to the PGs to put heavy covering fire into the base of the terminal building while his team made a surprise arrival on the roof.

Nevertheless, he had decided to 'mark' the PG commander with Mark Benjamin to ensure that the right orders were given at the right time. Or that some free-shooting PG didn't decide to change allegiances halfway through the proceedings. Even more important was that the over-excited PGs stopped firing when the rest of Benjamin's Four Team – comprising John Belcher, Gene Slenzak and 'Young Tom' Perrott – put in the second assault on the ground floor.

"Thirty seconds, boss," Brummie Turner warned. Despite the heavy smearing of camo cream, the pensive expression was all too obvious.

Fraser nodded, and joined the rest of the team clinging on the back of the fire-engine. He waved to the chief and the engine spluttered into life.

The sudden noise was drowned by a ragged report of gunfire from the line of PGs hidden beneath a hedge. As the curtain of blue gunsmoke drifted aside, the first phosphorous grenades from the launchers of Four Team's Land Rover arched high above the terminal building. Each wavered at the peak of its trajectory before spiralling untidily downward towards the flat roof of the administration block. They clattered onto the asphalt at split-second intervals. Hissing clouds of white smoke pumped skywards as the grenades breathed out the obnoxious contents of their small tin lungs.

The windows of the observation tower were already obscured from view as the fire-engine jolted backward. Anxiously, Fraser peered towards the on-rushing terminal that filled his vision as more phosphorous grenades found their mark and another barrage of rifle-fire poured from the PG support group. Raking bursts tore into masonry and laminate with devastating ease and blasted out windows from which Badji's men could be watching.

Fraser pulled on one of the oxygen-masks they had borrowed from the firemen and, judging his moment, he grabbed the ladder as the vehicle rocked to and fro across paths and flower gardens. Swiftly, he clambered to the uppermost rungs, and levelled the Hockler.

He felt absurdly like some aerial buccaneer on a boarding party.

There was no sign of life from the control-tower. The entire roof was swathed in rolling billows of burning white fog.

Clouds of the stuff reached out to engulf him. As his vision blurred through the perspex facemask, he became uncomfortably aware of the hot, clammy feel and smell of the rubber hood, and a sensation of blind isolation. The sound of gunfire receded to a mere crackle beyond the noise of his own laboured breathing. He felt claustrophobic and sweaty, cocooned from the strange white world outside.

Suddenly, the roof parapet loomed into view. The reversing momentum of the fire-engine didn't slow.

There was a bone-jolting crunch as the top of the ladder punched into the edge of the building, demolishing the parapet wall. The ladder vibrated like a tuning-fork as dust and debris cascaded over them.

Coiling his muscles, he sprang up the last rungs and launched himself into the white mist.

He took the parapet painfully on his outer thigh, half-rolling and half-bouncing over the wall. Hitting the asphalt in a prone position, he already had the Hockler up and pointed at the control-tower which protruded from the flat roof some thirty feet away. Segments of shattered window glass hung in their frames like ice stalactites, witness to the magnitude of the onslaught from the PGs on the ground.

A hint of a breeze had gathered over the open tract of Jakoto Airport and the smoke was now waning noticeably.

Brummie Turner arrived, landing inelegantly but without mishap.

As the sergeant swung up the Remington repeater shotgun from his shoulder and snapped open the skeleton butt, it occurred to Fraser how movies always gave the impression that military action was fast. In reality, everything seemed to move with excruciating slowness. Therefore, it seemed an age before Bill Mather bounded over the parapet and dropped down beside them, his Hockler already cocked.

"Kangers caught one," he announced matter-of-factly. "Nothing serious, it looked like a ricochet. Just a flesh wound in the thigh."

Fraser grunted. That was all he needed. The team often teased the laconic Aussie that he could never move fast without a woman in front of him, or an enemy gun up his arse. But in action he was very quick on his feet, particularly in the sort of close-quarter fighting they anticipated.

Not for the first time, Fraser cursed the speed with which he'd had to throw the operation together; most of his men were manning Tac HQ or other key strongholds around the capital.

Brummie nudged him, the eyes in the perspex oxygen-mask visor flickering westward. Through the misty aperture of his own grotesquely-snouted headdress, Fraser scanned the skyline. He sensed the slight tremble in the air before he saw them. Strung across the wash of opaque lemon sky like tiny black beads. It had to be the 82nd Airborne.

Immediately, Fraser unholstered the stubby-barrelled Very pistol from his side, cocked the hammer, and fired into the sky. The signal flare blasted upward, corkscrewing high above the terminal building, before it detonated in a glittering shower of green light.

It was the sign for Four Team to go in with the second assault on the ground floor and to let the 82nd Airborne know that the enemy on the landing strip was being engaged.

The three SASmen exchanged glances. The rubber-hooded faces nodded in unspoken agreement.

Fraser and Brummie Turner moved towards the control-tower at a running crouch. Behind them, Bill Mather's Hockler stammered out half a magazine, hosing the framework of the control-tower windows with a withering hail of 5.56mm high velocity rounds. The remaining glass teeth detached themselves, shattering on the roof like crushed ice.

It crunched underfoot as Fraser and Brummie made the last few feet to the tower, hunched below the window ledge.

They looked at each other and nodded. Brummie was on his feet, swinging the Remington over the sill into the confined space of the control room. A brief impression of chaos imprinted itself in the NCO's mind: glass and debris everywhere; upturned chairs; sprawled bodies, hands clasped desperately at searing throats.

As the Remington moved in a slow arc, it blasted three times, spreading its lethal seed with merciless ferocity.

Brummie ducked down onto one knee, so that Fraser could use him as a springboard. Up and over. Through the jagged rim of the window and into bedlam beyond. Bill Mather followed, pausing only to haul the sergeant after him.

Inside, Fraser was already moving cautiously across the obstacle-strewn floor. The place was full of bodies, several dead, others moaning or coughing. The SAS officer swallowed hard, and flicked the Hockler onto 'single'. Pressing the snout against the base of the skull of each living rebel, he fired one shot into the brain.

When he'd finished, he glanced up and found himself looking into Mather's pale, steady eyes. They said it all. Sorry, mate, I know how you feel.

But chances could not be taken. The last thing they needed was some injured Jato behind them, driven by the maniacal determination of a fanatic. No prisoners. It was a rule that had to be followed.

In the hot, moist confines of the oxygen-mask, Fraser felt suddenly nauseous.

"Boss, three o'clock!" Mather screamed in his ear.

Fraser was vaguely aware of the muzzle flash from a door which led to the rest of the building. But he saw nothing more as he hit the deck. He felt the slipstream of a bullet part his hair and a bright stinging soreness in his scalp.

He looked up as Brummie's Remington discharged, momentarily nailing the gunman starlike to the wall, like an animal pelt. Then, with a strangulated gurgling noise, the guerrilla slid to the floor.

Angrily, Fraser ripped off his oxygen-mask. The smoke still lingered but it wasn't too bad. Anyway, the soothing feel of air on his hot skin was more than compensation for the irritation in his throat. The others followed his example and felt happier for it.

Down below in the depths of the building, the snap of gunfire was reverberating loftily around the Departure Lounge. It sounded as though the ground assault was going well.

Fraser led the way down a short flight of steps to the first-floor corridor of the administration block. It ran to the right and left of them. And it was deserted.

"Where have all the cunts gone?" Mather hissed, hardly able to keep the disappointment from his voice.

"Scarpered," Brummie decided in disgust.

More echoing gunshot sounds came from the Departure Lounge below.

Fraser grinned. "And run straight into Four Team by the sound of things."

"Let's join 'em," Brummie enthused.

Fraser shook his head. "Not till we've cleared this floor. You take that side with Bill." He nodded to the left. "I'll take this end."

"Take it steady, boss," Mather warned. "You need pairs for this caper."

Fraser pulled a half-smile. With Kangers out of commission, there was no alternative.

He waited for a moment until the other two had begun their methodical search of the left-hand stretch. Brummie would position himself low outside each door with the Remington poised, while Mather pushed it open from the side.

After two rooms, Mather called up: "They've done a bunk, boss. Bullet holes everywhere and some blood. I reckon that broadside from the PGs unsettled 'em. Place is deserted."

Feeling happier, Fraser began his solo search of the right-hand corridor. Each careful inspection brought the same thankful results: empty. He shuffled cautiously through a sea of overturned furniture, papers, discarded palm-wine bottles and the brass spendings of the weaponry used. There were three corpses. One PG, and two guerrillas, dressed in a typical mix of uniform and woollen hats with the obligatory yellow ribbons.

Soon he neared the end of the corridor. The sounds of fresh fighting came from a nearby stairway that led down to the Departure Lounge. It spurred him on to the last unchecked room.

He eased his weight against the door, standing guardedly to one side – an invitation for some lurking guerrilla to make the first move and give away his position.

The hinge creaked. Nothing.

Something about the corpse propped against the wall beneath the window was strangely macabre. The PG had his eyes open and the same fearsome snarl of anger that he had been wearing the second he died. He still had a gun in each hand: one man's last stand against overwhelming Jato odds, like a hero from the Alamo, misplaced in time and history.

Fraser recognised the face; the youngster had been in one of the training cadres at Duntenda Barracks. He had handed over the 'top recruit' award himself.

The sudden vibration distracted him. It made the walls tremble and the windows shook free their remaining remnants of glass. The air welled with the awesome throb of powerful aero engines, the sound filling his ears.

He crossed to the window which overlooked the airfield.

It was a spectacular vista. In seconds, the sweeping panorama of empty sky and the deserted tract of runway and sandy grass was filled to brimming. As gigantic crucifix shadows flashed across the ground, the air was thick with blossoming parachutes. Everywhere, tiny black figures swung from their shrouds. The 82nd Airborne had arrived.

They had come in deadly earnest. After a cripplingly-long journey in the cavernous holds of the Starlifters that now thundered endlessly overhead. Straight onto the DZ with pin-point precision, combat-jumping into the unknown from a mere five hundred feet. They meant business.

Even to a hardened SASman, it was a stirring sight.

Without his being aware of it, he gave a grin of sympathy as hundreds of men hit the hard-baked earth. The mad scramble to unharness and find their gear before some son-of-a-bitch somewhere tried to blow away their young lives.

Fraser felt his spirits soar. Much as he despised the cynical political manipulations of Ambassador Brunswick, and the kowtowing compliance of Sir Nigel de Burgh, he was relieved to see the reinforcements he had requested so often. At least now, whether the Jatos fought on or not, they wouldn't win control of Sakoto by military means. The mass slaughter of innocent Free Guineans would be over.

Perhaps, he wondered, he should have given more credit to the diplomats. It was he who was naïve, and they who were the realists . . .

A slight movement to his left made Fraser turn. He brought up the Hockler and swung it round, his heart racing.

He breathed again. He had not seen the wounded Jato sprawled behind the overturned desk. The man began to whimper, curled in a tight ball and clutching his bloodied head.

Cursing his own carelessness, Fraser heaved aside the desk and squatted down. The Jato wasn't going to harm anyone. As he gently prised away the fingers, he could see the white brain matter where the skull bone had been chipped away. It was the size of a ten-pence piece.

Fraser couldn't bring himself to finish the man off. It had

been bad enough upstairs. But now the Americans had arrived, it was all over bar the shouting.

Laying the Hockler by his side, he pulled out a field-dressing pad from a pouch on his belt-order and tore open the sealed cloth wrapper. As he placed it on the wound, the man looked up at him with wide, pleading eyes. Fraser grinned reassuringly, and plucked a morphine syrette from the chain around his neck.

He had just given the man a 30mg shot, when he heard the running footsteps.

Someone was coming up the stairs from the Departure Lounge at a pace, his laboured breathing quite distinct.

Caught off-balance, Fraser dropped the empty syrette and reached for his Hockler. Frozen horror filled him as his glance met the fanatical gleam in the eyes of Major Badji who stood in the doorway.

Even as the SASman's fingers closed around the cool steel of the Hockler, he knew he had left it too late. His act of compassion was going to cost him dear.

An evil grin spread across Badji's face as he recognised Fraser. The splattering of blood on the Guinean's gnome-like black face added to his satanic appearance, as he pointed the MAT sub-machine gun.

With scarcely a grip on his weapon, Fraser flung himself backwards to avoid the welter of spitting lead. It hammered through the air, thudding into the PG corpse beneath the window, so that it jumped and jigged like an animated zombie.

Jagged splinters of glass lanced into Fraser's wrists as he put out his hands to break his backward fall. His torn tendons acted like unseen hands to wrestle the Hockler from his grasp.

He jerked his head around for a sight of Badji. The man stepped forward, eyes gleaming in triumph. Framed in the doorway above Fraser's prostrate figure, he seemed to grow in stature to the dimensions of a malevolent giant.

The muzzle of the MAT was like an evil black eye pointed at his head.

Fraser's heart seized. On reflex, his eyes closed to meet death at point-blank range.

The blast from the Remington shot-gun shook the room as the pressure-wave reverberated around the confined space.

Instantly Fraser's eyes opened, vaguely aware of Badji's body being hurled against the wall like a splattered insect. Slowly, the man's body slunk to the floor, trailing an ugly smear across the plaster. His mouth hung open in horror and surprise. One leg twitched violently. Then lay still.

It took a few seconds for Fraser to recognise Corporal Lionel Witcher. The mass of bubbly beard to match the wild fair hair threw him momentarily. So did the T-shirt and jeans.

Witcher prodded the plastic-rimmed glasses more firmly onto the bridge of his nose and rested the Remington on his shoulder.

He looked down at the disfigured body of Badji.

"The butcher of Massang is dead," he announced dramatically.

"Badji?"

"And he killed Fofana."

Still stunned, Fraser hobbled to his feet. "That was some entrance. Impressive."

Witcher pulled a half-smile. He looked older than when Fraser had last seen him at the Jato camp. "When I saw Kangers Webster hit, I thought you might be short-handed."

Relief forced a wide grin to Fraser's face. "I was!" He stared down at the man who had almost been his executioner. "Wait a minute, Badji was Kwofie's man. Fofana was working for the Jatos and so was Kwofie. So why should Kwofie want to have him killed?"

"That's what Kali Pheko wants to know, too. Kwofie was his right-hand man. His link with power in Sakoto. Yet it appears Kwofie ordered the murder of Fofana, the breakout at Central Prison and now this . . . taking the Airport."

"All against Kali's orders?"

"Mostly. Kali's no saint. He didn't mind putting press-ure on villages. But not massacres, it's not his way. Colonel Kwofie's been running his own campaign. I'm not so sure he's doing it purely for Kali's cause."

"Meaning?"

Witcher shrugged. "I'm not sure. Kali isn't either."

Fraser frowned. "You make Pheko sound like a friend."

"He is – now."

"I beg your pardon?" Fraser was bemused.

"I've turned him."

"Turned him?"

Witcher felt weary. The last weeks of captivity had drained him, and he wasn't sure how his commander was going to take his news. "It's my job, boss, remember. Psych-ops. Psychological warfare. I went back *deliberately*. After our escape from the Jato camp."

"You *went* back?" Fraser was aware he was sounding like a parrot.

"It was the only way. With you and Brummie around, there was no way I could get through to him. I tried to get Rod Bullock clear, but they picked him up later. As it turned out, it was a good move. He was a lot of help. Under protest. But still a lot of help."

Johnny Fraser could not believe his ears. "Help in what, for God's sake, Lionel?"

"Help in putting together a new political and redevelopment plan for Kali Pheko to implement," Witcher answered wearily. "Building a new capital, revitalising irrigation, new cash crops, new housing. Rod Bullock's got the organisation to get it done, but never the financial resources. They've always been controlled by ministers who prefer to spend it empire-building. And then the battleplan . . . ."

"Jesus!" Fraser snapped. "You've helped organise the bloody revolution?"

Witcher smiled thinly. "Just the final stages. I didn't want unnecessary casualties. Mind you, Badji's men rather put paid to that."

Fraser was shell-shocked. "Are you out of your bloody mind, Corporal?! Since when is it your place to start organising rebellions for our enemies?!" he demanded, his words booming in the small office.

Lionel Witcher's cheeks darkened. "Why the fuck do you think Kali offered to trade a ceasefire for an election, boss? Eh? That's not the normal thinking of a bloody fanatic, is it?

I told you, I've *turned* him. I've convinced the bastard that he can do everything without the Russians. *Without* their money, and *without* their arms! He can still have his Muslim revolution. But he's on our fuckin' side now. *Ours!*" His words hung in the air and Fraser could feel the rage in them.

Softly, Fraser asked: "Ours, Lionel?"

Lionel's shoulders dropped. It was unlike either man to lose his temper. "I've promised Kali aid. A lot of it. From Britain."

"You've what . . ?" Fraser couldn't help himself. He laughed. The humour of it all suddenly struck him and he laughed like a drain.

"You'll *have* to persuade Sir Nigel, boss," Witcher added, deadly seriously. "But Kali's got a winning programme. Rod Bullock and I put it together. The money won't get into the hands of individual ministers. It'll get to the poor sods who need it. Wells, clinics, schools . . ."

Fraser managed to stem his laughter. "I know, Lionel. I heard his broadcasts. I thought they were a bit unusual. I suppose you wrote them, too?"

"Well, influenced . . ."

"Good God, it's Psychlops!"

Brummie Turner and Bill Mather arrived at the door.

"How are you, old son?" Mather beamed. Then he saw the body of Badji, awash in a pool of fresh blood. "What happened?"

Fraser said: "Didn't you hear it?"

Brummie shook his head. "No, boss. There was such a din coming from downstairs. Looks like Four Team's cleared out the Departure Lounge."

Johnny Fraser smiled. "Let's go and meet our American cousins."

"Hey, man, there's a lotta hairy shit flyin' 'round here," the fresh-faced US lieutenant decided and ducked behind the wall of the Customs yard.

The angry chatter of a machine-gun broke from a well-protected alcove on the far side and began chewing its way into the brickwork.

Johnny Fraser's SAS team had been nearly caught in the crossfire as they came out of the terminal to meet the leading contingent of tough young paras.

Now they were all pinned down by the last pocket of resistance from Badji's men, whilst the lieutenant snapped a series of quick orders to his radio-man. "An' tell 'em to get that M47 up here before this motherfucker takes my scalp off. He's holdin' up the whole goddam' 82nd."

Behind them, the advancing airborne troops were forced into an undignified crawl as the heavy machine-gun raked the airfield. The huddled group was joined by the PG commander who threw himself down behind the wall. He looked flushed and angry as he shook hands with the American lieutenant.

"Hallo, how are you?" he asked formally.

"Sore knees and an aching back," the American returned sourly. "Can't stand up till we kill this sonofabitch."

The PG officer agreed. "We kill the others. But that man is a good man. A good position. He has powerful ju-ju." Seeing the American's puzzlement, the Guinean explained seriously: "Ju-ju makes bullets turn to water."

A para sergeant arrived with the portable M47 Dragon missilelauncher. The lieutenant pointed at the smoke-enshrouded target.

"I wonder what'll happen when we fire this?" the para sneered.

Bill Mather gave an evil grin. "I expect he'll drown."

The anti-tank warhead blasted from its breech in a powerful backblast of smoke and flame into the target like an express train, exploding on impact, dead centre of the enemy emplacement.

With satisfaction, the US sergeant lowered the launcher from his shoulder. The machine-gun was silent.

"CAPTAIN! CAPTAIN!"

Fraser turned round. "Good God, isn't that Dawda? He'll get himself shot at, running like that."

Although the nearest paratroopers watched the racing Guinean warily, they made no attempt to shoot.

"Captain!" Dawda gasped. "I have a message! Of most importance. You listen to me, man!"

Fraser put a friendly arm around his shoulder. "Calm down. Tell me what it is? Slowly."

Dawda glanced around at the hundreds of advancing troops, bewildered by such military might. "It is a message from the man called Hammond."

Fraser was surprised. "Yes, I know him."

"This man Hammond, he is dead. He tells me to find you. He knows where Colonel Kwofie is and says you must do something."

The Scotsman's eyes narrowed. "Where is he?"

"In Sakoto. He is in hiding."

"In the ghettos?"

"No. On a ship. A Russian ship. She is filled with motor cars."

Brummie Turner began to take an interest; port security came under his jurisdiction. "There are no Russian ships in port, lad."

"What about cargoes of cars?" Fraser asked.

"Just one. It's come from Liberia."

Lionel Witcher interrupted. "That would take it past Conakry. Soviet-influenced." He turned to Fraser. "Remember what occurred in The Gambia during their coup? There just *happened* to be a ship full of Russian cars in port. Petrol tanks full, ignition keys in and boots full of Kalashnikovs . . ."

"Jesus," Fraser breathed. Suddenly it became clear. Why Colonel Kwofie had done a vanishing act at the eleventh hour when the Jatos' victory appeared to be at hand.

Whilst he and the Presidential Guard were on the mainland thinking that, whatever happened, Sakoto was safely in their hands, on the other side of Kebba Bridge, Kwofie was already in the capital. Just waiting for his moment. State House, the Government departments, Parliament, the PG barracks, the main radio station, the treasury, the banks and one-quarter of the country's population – all within fifteen minutes' drive from the docks.

"How many men is Kwofie supposed to have with him?" Brummie asked, fully aware of the seriousness of the news.

Fraser shrugged. "It's guesswork, but there's at least a hundred PGs unaccounted for."

The NCO shook his head in despair. "If they arm the people of Sakoto, it'll take more than a battalion of Yank paras to put down the fuckin' riot. And there'll be more than a bloodbath when they try."

Fraser's frustration was replaced by anger. "That creep Kali's been taking us for a bloody ride. Let us think we've got the situation contained, whilst his men calmly snatch Sakoto from under our noses." He turned to Brummie. "Put Kali Pheko under arrest and tell him our deal's off . . ."

"Hey, boss." It was Witcher.

"What? Don't tell me this was part of your brilliant masterplan, too, Lionel? I don't want to know!"

The corporal restrained Fraser's arm as he went to move away. "Listen, boss. I'm *sure* Kali doesn't know about this. But I think I know who does."

Fraser was at the end of his tether. "Stop talking in riddles, Lionel. Who, for Chrissakes?"

Rubashëv was seething.

The din in the cavernous hold of the Liberian-registered freighter was deafening. The roar, as dozens of Lada cars choked, spluttered and revved into life, was like being trapped in a subterranean grotto with an entire colony of blood-crazed lions.

Appropriate really, he told himself bitterly. Jatos. A hundred bloody revolutionary Jatos, armed to the teeth, eager to kill or be killed, fully motorised. And totally impotent.

The entire operation had ground to a halt because half the men who had sworn they could drive, couldn't. It was as simple as that. The roll-off ramp had been lowered onto the slipway and the first two drivers had collided. They'd rehearsed all the theory a dozen times. Left lane first, then right. Left lane first, then right.

The words even now stayed in his mind like a needle stuck in a record groove. So why couldn't *they* remember?

Well, this was Africa, and they hadn't. And, when the forward momentum of the lead cars had stopped abruptly, half the following cars hadn't. They had shunted into each other, couldn't find the brakes, or reversed into the vehicles behind.

The chaos could not be imagined, but then it didn't need to be. It was all in front of Rubashëv, for him to see.

That had been half-an-hour ago and, gradually, they were sorting out the mess. He had sent out men to bring back taxi-drivers and others who really *could* drive from Sakoto, at gunpoint. So it wouldn't be long now.

But time was everything. Absolutely vital. Especially now that the US paratroopers had arrived at Jakoto Airport, twenty miles the other side of Kebba Bridge.

Rubashëv glanced at his watch. 0700 hours. Already the sun was well and truly up.

He turned to the tall, elegant black soldier beside him. "Well, Colonel Kwofie, where are these taxi-drivers?"

There was a supercilious smirk on the arrogant face that the Czech would have loved to wipe off with the barrel of his Makarov pistol. "They come. Today is Friday. Many are at the mosques, praying to Allah. So they are not easy to find."

The Czech grunted. "It's Allah's revolution, comrade, so perhaps he'll give them a divine message to come here. We must get our spearhead element to Kebba Bridge and take it before the Americans cross into Sakoto."

Kwofie was unperturbed. "They do not know we are here, so the Yankees will have no need to rush."

"A military expert, are we?" Rubashëv snarled in disgust.

Again the smirk. "I trained at Sandhurst."

Rubashëv bit his tongue. There was no point in antagonising the new President of Free Guinea.

After all, he was supposed to be the master of manipulation; to understand the psyche and make-up of African leaders, existing and potential. That was a joke!

The rusted hull was now a bell vibrating under the thrum of engines. In the confines of the steel cavern, the petrol fumes and exhaust were creating a rippling vapour haze. The stink was getting to him.

He was about to announce that he was going topside for a breath of air. But the thought froze in his brain. Through the open jaws of the ship's hull, he saw a flash of colour cross the sunlit square of slipway outside.

His heart stopped. There was no mistaking that crazy colour scheme on the vehicle. Painting-by-numbers. A complex camouflage pattern that changed for snow, mud or desert sand, which had been dreamed up by some idiot in the Pentagon. And the poor old American trooper, with more important things on his mind, invariably got it wrong.

The first cracks of riflefire crashed around the metal hull like cymbals.

Yells of alarm added to the bedlam. "Americans! Americans!"

Already paras were moving up the steel ramp. Cloth-covered helmets bobbed as they ducked and weaved. Inexorably, they came on.

Rubashëv nudged Colonel Kwofie hard in the ribs. "Come on, we go. Quickly!" He pointed at the steel vertical ladder beside them which led up to the lofty upper gantry.

But the President designate of Free Guinea had suddenly decided that he wanted to be a martyr.

"You go, brother. I will fight this American scum!" he snarled.

Almost before his Adam's apple finished bobbing, the black snout of Rubashëv's Makarov pistol was pushed up against it. Kwofie gulped.

"Up!" the Czech hissed.

Trembling, the Colonel obeyed and began fumbling up the polished rungs of the ladder. Clearly, he didn't have a head for heights.

They had a panoramic view of the fighting below. It had become fearsome. It was noisy and dangerous, with the Americans forcing themselves relentlessly on, working down the lines of parked Ladas.

After the stifling smoke and fumes of the hold, the rush of sea air was nectar. It snapped at their senses, as Rubashëv opened the hatch to the upper deck. The Czech knew that there was a small motor boat tied to the gangway pontoon on the port side. As usual, he had left nothing to chance. An hour by sea and they would reach landfall in a neighbouring state. He had spent too much time cultivating Kwofie to lose him now . . .

But, even before he had time to look over the ship's rails,

he detected the gentle burble of the throttled-back outboards. It only needed a glance to confirm his worst fears. A giant black Gemini assault dinghy was tied alongside his motor boat. Four troopers were moving fast up the gangway steps to the deck.

He swore. They were British. In baggy jungle-green denims. Hatless and scruffy. Of course! He knew this SAS squad had been drawn from one of the Regiment's Boat Troops. He should have expected it.

Pushing Kwofie before him, he started towards the stern. He had no fixed idea in mind. He just wanted to get as far away as he could from the Britishers. There was still time.

But, as they neared the after end, huffing and blowing as they pounded along the deckboards, the two men drew to a sudden stop.

Ahead of them, two more SAS soldiers were swinging over the rail. The tattered state of their battle fatigues and the powder-smudged faces suggested they had already been in a firefight that morning.

Rubashëv cursed. They must have climbed up the anchor chain from another dinghy. Or up a hawser from the quay. Either way, it suggested they were as tough as they looked.

The Czech turned. Behind him, he could see the four SAS men from the Gemini now closing up behind him.

"Die, *toubab!*" Kwofie suddenly yelled. A revolver had magically appeared in his hands.

"Shoot, you bastard!" goaded one of the British soldiers by the stern. "Go on, and I'll blow your fuckin' head off!"

Angrily, Rubashëv snatched the revolver from Kwofie's grasp and tossed it over the side in one quick movement.

"Bloody fool," he sneered. Kwofie smarted.

"That's a shame," said the approaching SASman. Rubashëv recognised the tall sunburned officer they called 'The Captain' from their encounter at the Jato camp. His dark hair was longer now, curling at the ends, and matted. "I just want the slightest excuse and you two are shark food."

The Scotsman spoke quietly, but the threat was unmistakable; there was no humour in the sunken green-grey eyes.

Rubashëv slowly proffered his Makarov, butt-first.

Keeping the Hockler sub-machine gun pointing at the Czech's navel, Fraser reached out and took it, passing it back to Lionel Witcher who stood behind him.

"Visited any good Jato camps lately, Rubashëv?" Fraser hissed, roughly pushing the man up against the superstructure wall. "Palms flat, legs open!"

His foot jammed between the man's ankles and kicked them apart. Brummie Turner and Bill Mather stepped in to frisk the prisoners carefully while the other two SASmen kept them covered.

Rubashëv was mumbling: ". . . I don't know what you talk about, this is all a mistake . . ."

"And you made it," Fraser retorted. "I'll remind you that the last time we met, you were asking Kali Pheko to put a bullet in my head."

"They're clean," Mather reported, throwing aside a collection of ammunition pouches and a combat knife from Kwofie.

"Turn round," Fraser ordered. Kwofie looked frightened as he obeyed, his knees visibly trembling; Rubashëv's face was a mask.

The Czech's cool got to Fraser. He'd caused so much trouble, directly and indirectly responsible for the loss of so many innocent lives. One of them had nearly been his.

"Remember the camp?" Fraser persisted. "You wanted me and my friends dead."

A hint of a smile crossed Rubashëv's lips. "There are so many faces."

Fraser's smile became fixed. "But I'd like you to remember this one." His knee came up with the force of a steamhammer. He felt the bone of his kneecap crunch into the Czech's testicles, causing the man to gasp with a force that nearly blew his teeth out. A long, low groan escaped the doubled figure.

"Steady, boss," Witcher said.

Fraser stepped back. "The trouble is, Lionel, it's always the same. Bastards like this spend their careers stirring the shit and getting some other poor sod to take it in the face when it hits the fan. Where're you from, Rubashëv? Is it KGB or maybe GRU?"

There was a wariness in the man's eyes now. A new respect. That was better. "I am Czech. I work for the trade union movement."

"Flying bushpigs," Mather observed.

Fraser turned towards Colonel Kwofie. His ebony face was drenched in the sweat of fear, his eyes wide as the SAS officer peered into them. "And you, you murdering bastard. Words fail me when it comes to you. But then words hardly apply, because your sort are a fuckin' sub-species. I was there after Massang . . ." His voice had risen as the anger filled him.

A restraining hand rested on his shoulder. Bill Mather said: "Major Harper's coming, boss. We'd all love to, but let's not do anything foolhardy. No doubt President Pheko will have plans for him."

"They'd be too good," Fraser grated.

"I'll take Kwofie down, boss," Mather offered. "I think the fireworks are over. Get the bastard safely under lock-and-key."

Fraser nodded. "A good idea. Before I stick my knife in him."

As the veteran corporal led Kwofie towards the hatch, Fraser turned. The stocky Welsh Intelligence Officer was having trouble getting his short legs over the ship's rail without straddling it with his groin. Mastering his dignity, he came forward. He looked pleased enough.

"Must be easier ways to board a ship!" he chirped. He paused and focused his attention on Rubashëv. "Ah, what have we here, boyo?"

"The Czech. Friend and mentor of Colonel Kwofie and Kali Pheko, Bill. Not to mention 'Commercial Boris'. Reckons he's in industrial relations."

Harper's florid face positively bloomed. "Hello, Igor, how are you?"

"I do not know you."

The IO grinned. "Ah, but I know you. From photographs and our files. Photographic memory, you see. Never forget a face."

Fraser smiled. "Tell me more, Bill."

"Meet Major Igor Dovzhenko of the GRU. It is still

Major, is it? Mind you, after this little fiasco, I doubt if you'll be welcome in the Officers' Mess for much longer."

"I do not know what you talk about."

Harper ignored the denial. "If you'd stuck with Kali Pheko, Igor, you might have got away with it."

Fraser was perplexed. "I still don't follow all this."

Harper didn't shift his eyes from the Russian; he was enjoying this. It was rare that he came face-to-face with his adversaries in the secret war. "It's simple, Johnny – if you've a twisted mind, that is. Igor here wanted a Soviet-style grass-roots revolution. One that would last. Islamic Fundamentalism and the like is great for starters. Kali Pheko the Jato was ideal. But who wants an idealist like that in control once the objective is won? As soon as the fighting was over, at the eleventh hour, it was planned for Kwofie here to snatch the Presidency. Am I right or am I right?"

Igor Dovzhenko said nothing.

"That, no doubt," Harper added, "would have meant the speedy assassination of Kali Pheko. They'd already ditched Fofana, the other do-gooding socialist, as soon as his useful life was up. No doubt the 'Islamic Revolution' would continue, but run under Kwofie's iron fist and Soviet guidance."

Fraser shook his head in disbelief. "Kwofie seems to have qualities of leadership everyone wants. The Americans wanted him for the same reasons, Bill. A hard, ruthless bastard . . ."

"And thoroughly corruptible, and therefore controllable," Harper finished off.

"It seems to me," Fraser said, "that while Kwofie's alive, there's always a chance he's going to end up running Free Guinea. One way or another."

"Where is he now? Did I see Mather taking him away?"

"Yes. He's been taken to a cell at the Police HQ. Let the new President deal with him."

Bill Harper glared at Dovzhenko. "That's what I'd like to do with this joker, too. But no doubt our lords and masters will just want him sent on his way with his tail between his legs."

"Oh, for the good old days," Brummie Turner murmured. He sounded as though he really meant it.

Instinctively, they turned as Mather appeared suddenly at the hatchway.

"You were quick," Fraser observed.

"Sorry, boss, there's been an accident."

"Kwofie?"

"We were going down the gantry ladder. I was above him. I accidentally trod on his fingers. He fell."

"Good God. How is he?"

"It was a long way down." Bill Mather's face was as impassive as his voice.

Epilogue

"I didn't know it was possible to love two men, Johnny. Not at the same time."

Mo Sinclair spoke in an earnest whisper, her small hands clutched around Fraser's fist on the table in the Airport lounge.

What could he say? The silence was brittle.

"I had to tell you before you went. I wanted you to know that all the things I said to you when you were here the first time, I meant them. I still do. I'll always love you, Johnny, always. It's just that, for a small time, Kali found a place in my heart, too. Do you understand?"

"I'm trying," he replied lamely.

"I know it was wrong. That's why I stopped writing. I was hurt and confused. If it hadn't been for the baby, you'd never have known. And I could have forgotten an unfortunate episode in my life . . ."

Fraser could feel the agony she was going through. He could see it in those sad, beautiful hazel eyes. But he couldn't help her. He couldn't reach her.

Perhaps he could, if he tried. But he knew that he didn't want to. Somewhere inside, something was dead.

"I have to go," he said.

"I'm sorry," a soft butterfly of a smile flickered around the freckled urchin face. "I shouldn't have kept you."

"That's all right." He stood up and hoisted the weighty belt-order over one shoulder.

"This time I'll write, Johnny, really I will. I promise."

He smiled down at her small frame and, in the corner of his eye, he caught a glimpse of John Belcher. He, too, was in jungle-denims, wrapped in a passionate goodbye embrace with the nurse from Mansakunda. Rumour had it that, soon, Sally Richards would be changing her name. Seeing the two of them together, he could believe it. And his heart ached.

"'Bye, Mo," he said hoarsely.

"Come back soon."

"Sure."

She reached up to kiss him and their lips touched. But she sensed that the warmth was gone. She drew back hesitantly.

"'Bye."

"'Bye." Half murmurs, half-truths. They both knew.

At the departure gate, Fraser found Lionel Witcher laughing with Brummie Turner and Bill Mather. They were all pleased to be going.

"Looks like the lads have brought all the white women of Free Guinea to see them off," Witcher observed. "I don't know when they found the time to fraternise."

Fraser glanced around the Lounge that seemed filled with soldiers and their personal equipment. It was a far happier sight than when he'd last seen it as a battleground against Badji's rebels.

Fraser said: "Let's get out to the Herc. Before this farewell party turns into an orgy. Talking of which, Brummie, I haven't seen Diamante."

The NCO shouldered his kit and they all began walking. "That's because I haven't told her we're leaving today. It was best. She'll be workin' now, I guess. I got her a respectable job. In the canteen of one of the Government departments. She's chuffed as anything. Hardly wants to know me now."

"Given up ideas of your buying her, eh?"

Brummie chuckled as they stepped out onto the apron. Out on the runway, the camouflaged RAF Hercules C130 sat waiting, its fat belly just kept clear of the ground by the giant wheels of the main undercarriage. The open rear ramp seemed to beckon. Home.

"I've tried to put the girl right, boss. I told her there was no future for us." He sniffed heavily. "Don't know what came over me, really. Some silly giddy kid. Just got through to me for a while. Stupid. Cast a bloody ju-ju on me, I reckon."

"They call it love."

"Bullshit."

Fraser squinted his eyes to focus on the bulk of the Hercules shimmering in the heat-haze, and the official Free Guinea farewell committee lined up alongside it.

It was strange to think that just four short weeks ago, they had been fighting for control of this very airfield.

So much had happened since, so quickly. The 82nd Airborne had been withdrawn within forty-eight hours and the caretaker President announced that it had all been a pre-planned deployment exercise. It had warranted hardly a paragraph in the international press. News of Jammeh's retirement due to ill health was widely publicised, together with the immediate plans for a General Election two weeks later. The BATT team was asked to command the remaining loyal PGs and gendarmes, and to supervise the event. It had been more like a victory carnival than a serious political battle.

The newly-elected President had insisted that the departure should not be a totally private affair as Hereford had wished. He wanted to be there. In person. To express his thanks for their assistance and as an outward token of his friendship, and a new era of understanding between Britain and Free Guinea.

You bloody hypocrite, President Kali Pheko. Your public show of concern is just to make sure you get the aid that was promised you while you had us by the short-and-curlies. Thanks to Lionel Witcher's private war.

The captain could see the VIP line-up clearly now, drawn up in the ample shadow of the Hercules' wing. Behind it, the Presidential Mercedes-Benz gleamed in the sunlight, whilst the grey-suited chauffeur expired gently inside it.

Beside the resplendent white-robed President Kali Pheko stood the Vice-President. Rod Bullock of *Direct Action*, looking ill-at-ease in a suit, was also there. And the British High Commissioner.

Not Sir Nigel de Burgh. Before the election, he had been

unexpectedly recalled. A new early retirement scheme, an additional pension, and the promise of more letters after his name. That was the rumour. Whether it was Whitehall's disapproval, a reward, or vindictiveness, Fraser had no way of knowing. He didn't really care.

The Americans had not been very happy about the outcome; perhaps pointedly, Ambassador Eddie Brunswick was not in the line-up. But Hereford seemed to think that the Foreign Office was cautiously optimistic. Only time would tell.

"Goodbye, Major. I understand it is Major now?"

"Yes, Mr President. Thank you. Goodbye."

The words were simple enough. No expression of gratitude. The bare minimum. Yet the shaking of hands seemed to take forever. Certainly long enough for Fraser to realise that the hand he shook was encrusted with gold rings.

He tried to look in Pheko's eyes, but the newly-acquired platinum-rimmed shades defeated him. His own reflection stared back at him.

Then, thankfully, it was over. Down the line. The Vice-President; the High Commissioner; Rod Bullock.

"Last in line, you notice, Johnny."

"Best place for you." Fraser grinned into the bearded, sun-blackened face. "I hope it works out."

"I'll try. Lionel and I had fun planning all the changes. I'll try all right to make it happen. But I doubt it."

"Yes?"

Bullock lowered his voice. "This *is* Africa, old man."

Fraser turned, wondering if President Pheko had heard. But he hadn't; he was shaking hands with Lionel Witcher. Even from where he stood, he could feel the warmth in their informal exchange. He felt unaccountably irritated.

They were talking in whispers, but their voices carried in the light wind that eddied across the airfield.

"You have the chance to make great changes, Mr President. You have your people with you."

"They say that every country gets the Government it deserves." Confident.

"Then, Mr President, just make sure they deserve you."

*

391

The Presidential limousine trailed a cloud of dust across the airfield as the Hercules transport lumbered awkwardly onto the tarmac runway strip.

At the terminal building, a young bewildered Guinean girl stared out into the sunlight, still panting after her run from the taxi.

Why hadn't he told her he was going? Why didn't he take her with him?

Two big tears of despair rolled down her cheeks.